"**I** can't do this. I—I don't want you . . . I don't want you near me," she said, stumbling over the lie.

He saw through her. "After last eve? I don't believe you." He reached out to her.

Raina flattened herself against the cool stone wall. "Stay away from me, please."

But Rutledge advanced. Two steps and his chest was nearly touching hers. "Why should I?" he questioned, his tone playful but the glimmer in his eyes too hungry to be harmless. He pressed a chaste kiss to her lips. "Why?"

"Oh, mercy," she breathed as he captured her earlobe between his teeth. "Please, don't . . ."

"Why, Raina?"

Why indeed? Because she should hate him? Because he was the most dangerous man she had ever encountered? Because she was so very afraid that if she surrendered her body to him, she might also surrender her heart?

Because she might be tempted to love him.

"Tell me why I shouldn't touch you. . . ."

LORD OF VENGEANCE

Tina St. John

FAWCETT GOLD MEDAL • NEW YORK

This book contains an excerpt from the forthcoming edition of *Lady of Valor* by Tina St. John. This excerpt has been set for this edition only and may not reflect the final content of the forthcoming edition.

A Fawcett Gold Medal Book
Published by The Ballantine Publishing Group
Copyright © 1999 by Tina Haack
Excerpt from *Lady of Valor* by Tina St. John copyright © 1999 by Tina Haack

All rights reserved under International and Pan-American Copyright Conventions. Published in the United States by The Ballantine Publishing Group, a division of Random House, Inc., New York, and simultaneously in Canada by Random House of Canada Limited, Toronto.

Fawcett is a registered trademark and Fawcett Gold Medal and the Fawcett colophon are trademarks of Random House, Inc.

www.randomhouse.com/BB/

Library of Congress Catalog Card Number: 99-90026

ISBN 0-449-00425-2

Manufactured in the United States of America

First Edition: June 1999

10 9 8 7 6 5 4 3 2 1

To John,
who walked every step of the journey with me
as if it were his own and never lost faith that I
could do this, though I often did.

You are
my husband, my hero, my heart . . .
forever.

Acknowledgments

I have been blessed with the friendship of many talented writers, but without the love and support (not to mention on-the-spot critiques) of Stacia Rudge Skoog and Patricia Rasey, I would still be just another dreamer.

Thanks must also go to Regina MacIntyre and my sister, Nicole Gandee, for reading the manuscript in its various early forms and offering encouragement and honest, thoughtful feedback.

I am grateful as well to my dad, for dinner-table vocabulary lessons and telling his children they had it in them to be whatever they wanted to be. And to my mom, for always being there to pick me up and dust me off when I stumbled along the way.

Prologue

The ground no longer rumbled with the thunder of horses' hooves and the clash of weapons. The air, still acrid with smoke from the smoldering ruins of the castle perched high on the motte and the sacked village at its base, was quiet. The damage was done; the enemy hadn't lingered. After all, it wasn't the castle he'd come to claim.

From across the trampled, body-littered field, a gentle breeze began to stir, drifting like a ghostly tendril over the carnage to where a boy lay, facedown and wounded. It ruffled his dark hair, coaxing him back to consciousness as it caressed his bruised and bloodied cheek.

"Mother?" he murmured, though he knew she was gone, slain before his very eyes just hours ago by Baron Luther d'Bussy, one of King Stephen's more ruthless warlords, when she refused to become his whore. Refused to share her bed with the man who had killed her husband three days past in a tournament gone awry.

Ten-year-old Gunnar Rutledge sobbed at the memory, gasping in a ragged breath and choking on the sweet, pungent scent of Wynbrooke's soil and the metallic taste of his own blood.

Just out of his grasp lay his father's signet ring, the token his mother had tearfully removed from her husband's stiff, dead finger as he'd lain in state. Despite the tremors of siege that had set the tiny chapel's stone walls quaking that morning, her voice had remained strong.

"Keep this always," she had said as she pressed the ring into his palm, "and remember your father's courage . . . his honor. When you are grown, wear it and make me proud."

But he hadn't made her proud. Instead, to his shame, he'd watched her die. Helpless and afraid, his arms twisted behind him by a large guard, he had pleaded with the baron to spare her. Withstood the man's drunken, taunting laughter. Weathered the physical blows.

And screamed in terror an instant later when d'Bussy's blade ended her life.

How he had managed to break free of his captor's iron grasp, Gunnar could not recall. His last memory had been of running. Running out of the castle, down the motte, and through the field as fast as he could with a knight on horseback close behind him. Legs pumping, lungs near to bursting, he headed for the stream, thinking he might be able to hide in the bramble that flanked it. The thought had scarcely formed when, over the pounding hoofbeats, he'd heard a sword rasp from its scabbard. Then, in an instant, his world, his life, had gone black.

Now, through the haze of pain enveloping his senses, Gunnar heard the squeak of a cart wheel and the murmur of voices. Men's voices. Two of them: one close, the other several paces behind. Footsteps halted near his head.

"Merrick, come!"

Gunnar knew the name of the man summoned, recognized the old healer's limp in the crunch of twigs and pine needles beneath his heavy gait as he approached, the familiar smell of herbs clinging to his clothes.

"Look ye what I found near this unfortunate thief."

Merrick clucked, his voice somber. " 'Tis the Rutledge signet ruby."

"Are ye certain?"

"Aye. Yestereve it rested on milord's lifeless hand in chapel. And lest you mean to keep it for yourself, my friend, think first on the price this lad paid for stealing—" Merrick suddenly sucked in his breath. "Jesu!" he exclaimed, falling to his knees. "This is no thief bleeding at our feet, man. Look closer! 'Tis young lord Gunnar!"

Heavy fingers inspected Gunnar's ravaged back, tore the sticky linen of his rent tunic away from his wounds. The old man swore an oath. " 'Tis by far the worst damage I've ever seen suffered on a child."

"Is he dead?"

"Nay, but soon enough, I reckon." Gunnar heard a rustle of fabric, then felt the rough wool of the old man's cloak cover him. "Half-dead or nay, I'll not leave him to rot out here like some hapless beast. If I cannot heal him, I can at least provide him comfort in his final hours. Come, help me lift him."

Limbs numb from loss of blood, Gunnar felt himself rise from the ground, heard the men's scuffling footsteps in the grass as they hefted him several paces from where he had lain. The sweet tang of moldy hay assailed his nostrils before he felt the crush of his own weight, and he was placed on his stomach atop a straw-lined litter. His rescuers hurriedly dragged him across the field toward the village.

Each rut they hit, every furrow, nearly jolted him senseless with pain, but his broken heart continued to beat. God help him, but he did not want to live. He had proven a coward; he deserved to die. Living would mean every day facing his guilt, his dishonor. He was too weak; he could not bear it. He prayed for deliverance from his suffering, from the anguish of his shame. His family was gone, his home destroyed. What reason had he to live? What purpose?

The answer came swiftly, softly at first, a dark whisper that curled around him, anchoring his soul to the earth with shadowy tethers. It called to him, beckoning him to hold on, entreating him to fight.

And as the healer carried him into his hut and went to work on his wounds, the whisper grew in strength and meaning until it filled his mind, his heart, his soul. It was a single word. A mantra. A vow.

Vengeance.

Chapter One

England, 1153

Baron d'Bussy's name was on the lips of well nigh everyone in England. For weeks past, criers had spread news of his grand tournament to the far reaches of the land, the scores of tents and pavilions now pitched on the wide plain outside Norworth Castle a testament to both his vanity and his thoroughness. Everywhere, pennons and colors flew, marking the independent warriors and those representing neighboring baronies and lords.

In the gathering twilight, men, women, and children—perhaps a hundred in all—wandered the wide avenue that ran through the center of the makeshift village. At the far end of the lane, two men, stripped down to their braies, fought bare-fisted to the gasps and cheers of a small circle of enthralled spectators. Boasting, swaggering knights were everywhere, many stumbling drunkenly toward their tents with a wench—some with two—under their arms. The more serious-minded competitors and dutiful squires tended destriers; others sat outside their tents polishing armor and inspecting weapons that would be well used on the morrow.

Amid this festival atmosphere, a distant flash of lightning went unnoticed.

It ripped across the darkening sky and reflected in a pair

5

of eyes staring not at the bustling valley but at the castle looming over it. Those emotionless eyes, deep and cool as the forest that obscured them, blinked once, then looked up to the dismal clouds.

Rain.

It began to fall almost immediately, pattering softly onto the canopy of leaves above, then swelling into a hard summer downpour that swept quickly toward the encampment. A grimace twisted the full lips that had until then been set in a determined line. Heavy rain meant a certain postponement of the morrow's tournament and worse, a delay of his promise.

Gunnar Rutledge cursed, his muttered oath swallowed up by a loud roll of thunder. Beneath him, his black destrier stirred in alarm, eyes wide and anxious. With a low murmur that sounded more like a warning than comfort, Gunnar quieted the beast, stroking its neck with a rough, unpracticed hand.

He had no use for fear, nor the experience to soothe it. Long ago he'd dispensed with his own fear, expelling it and any other emotion that might one day prove a weakness. He knew naught of celebration, did not indulge in dreams. His mind was fed on logic, his twenty-three-year-old body honed with hard work and countless battles until it now seemed more an extension of his armor and weaponry than it did flesh and bone. He had banished his feelings and exorcised his demons.

Save one.

And now that demon had invited him into his lair, offering an opportunity more perfect than Gunnar could possibly have conspired to arrange on his own. He wondered if the baron ever thought about the possibility that he had survived. Did he sit up there in that massive stone fortress and consider—even for a moment—that a reckoning was imminent? Had he ever tasted fear? Did he feel as damned as the boy he had left on that field thirteen years past?

Soon he would.

For according to the Holy Church, to slay a man in tourney was to condemn him to eternal damnation. Hence, melees were fought with ceremonial blades—dulled, though none-theless dangerous—and blunted lances.

Yet accidents happened.

Private scores were settled.

To avenge his mother, Gunnar would confront Luther d'Bussy. To avenge his father, he would triumph in the lists. The plan was simple enough. Best the baron, put the fear of God in his eyes. Make him plead for mercy.

And show him none.

The idea that he himself might not survive the day hadn't given Gunnar a moment's pause. He would keep his promise, no matter the price.

As the rain slanted down from heavy clouds, driving everyone to the shelter of their tents and turning the lists to mud, Gunnar wheeled his mount about and headed into the forest to make camp in solitude and search for patience enough to wait out the storm.

Bright morning sunlight filled the sky as Raina d'Bussy burst from Norworth's open gate astride a dappled gray mare and sped down the side of the motte. The fresh scent of the previous night's rains still clung to the air, but she scarcely noticed it. She rode at breakneck speed, the skirts of her bliaut rucked up over her knees and her un-bound hair billowing in a wild, sable curtain behind her. With a gleeful laugh she leaned forward over her mount's neck, urging it on faster and faster past the empty, bemired lists and across the marshy ground. Warm, muddy water splashed around her and kicked off the horse's hooves to dot her bare legs and splatter her face.

She rode at a hard gallop past the village of tents and up the gently sloping hill opposite Norworth Castle, toward the woods. Nearing the thick grove, she ventured a glance over her shoulder to judge her distance from the rider who fast approached from behind. His white stallion thundered up the hill, kicking tufts of ground loose under its heavy hooves. With an excited little shriek, Raina ducked into the shade of the tall trees.

She truly loved a race, and to the chagrin of her father and the young knight she competed with this day, she always played to win. Unladylike, to be sure, but having been raised by an indulgent father and without the benefit of a mother to correct her headstrong ways, Raina had developed her own set of rules. Giving less than all she had, be it suitable behavior or nay, was not among them.

A quick jerk of her reins brought her mount to a halt near the brook that marked the finish line of the race. Raina jumped to the ground as her challenger skidded to a stop beside her. She whirled to meet her lifelong friend with a wide, self-satisfied smile.

"Victory is mine, Nigel!" she crowed, nearly breathless with exhilaration from the run and the win.

Her grin faltered when she spied his expression. Somewhere along the way, the playfulness with which the two began their race had faded, and Nigel now glowered down his nose at her. His lips compressed into a tight, intolerant line in the center of his wheat-colored goatee. The sparse little beard he had tried for so long to grow had met with disappointing results, she thought, making him look like a pointy-chinned elf. A rather cross one at present.

"What a sight you are," Nigel chided with a slow shake of his head. He dismounted, then pulled off his gauntlets and draped them over his baldric. Pale blue eyes assessed her from head to toe. "You have ruined your gown."

Raina pushed a matted tangle of hair from her face and

looked down at her faded saffron-colored skirts, now spotted with water and mud. She shrugged. " 'Twas my oldest and a small sacrifice to the victor."

Nigel chuckled, taking her hands in his. "That's hardly the point," he admonished. "*Ladies* do not go about ruining their garments for the sake of a race. Besides, your competitiveness is . . . well, 'tis unseemly."

Frowning, Raina pulled her hand from his. In the past few months, Nigel had changed. He was now so gravely serious about everything. What had happened to the boy who used to encourage her antics, who cheered her on whatever she did? "You used to enjoy competing with me," she whispered, her observation sounding more like an accusation, even to her own ears.

"Aye, so I did," Nigel replied, "when we were children. You are no longer a child, Raina, but a grown woman. And I am a man. 'Tis time for our games to end." When Raina frowned sullenly, he moved closer, lifting her chin on the edge of his fist. "If 'tis surrender you crave, I give it. You have won your race, and I am vanquished . . . as ever when it comes to you, my lovely. Now, will you find it in your heart to mend my wounded pride? Afford me something to savor as I battle for your love in the lists come the morrow?"

He leaned in to kiss her.

"Nigel, don't." Raina pulled away, wrapping her arms about herself as she walked to the stream. His attempts of late to touch her were wearing thin her patience, but she tolerated him even as she rebuffed his advances, clinging to the idea that for nearly all her life, he had been her closest friend and confidant. She had noticed years before—and her father had issued stern warning—that Nigel had become a man, with a man's lusty designs, but it was painful to think that adulthood might spell the end of their friendship. "I don't understand. Why must it always come to this?"

Nigel strode up behind her. "Why must it always come to you casting me aside, you mean?" He exhaled sharply, a humorless, dejected sound. "Would that I knew, my lady love."

At his tender endearment, Raina squeezed her eyes shut, shaking her head. "Nigel, you must stop thinking of me like that. Please, for my sake *and* yours, cease regarding me as aught more than your lord's daughter . . . and your friend."

Nigel chuckled and the brittle sound chased a shiver up her spine. "I fear you ask too much," he said, and then she heard him breathe deeply of her hair, felt him sigh against her skin as his arms came about her waist. "How can I think of you in any other way than as the girl I would marry, the woman who would share my bed and bear my children?"

The very notion made her gasp with shock. She tried to move out of his embrace, but he only tightened his hold and pulled her closer. "God's wounds, but you are a be-witching temptation," he growled, and his lips found their way to her neck, where they lingered, laving her skin in a wet kiss.

Raina twisted in his arms, trying to escape his unbidden attentions. His verbal advances were one thing, but never had he taken such liberties! "Nigel, you are acting crazed. Let me go!"

He ignored her struggling and dragged his mouth slowly up her neck. "Will you have me beg you, Raina? Forsooth, I will, and find no shame in it. Tell me what I must do and I will do it." He pulled her tighter, his grip like iron bands about her arms.

"Nigel, you are hurting me! Please, release me."

"Never," he vowed. "I'll never release you. Let me love you, Raina. Let me make you mine . . . right here, right now. Let me have you, and your father will have naught to say about our marrying."

While that bewildering thought sank into her brain, Nigel's hand came up to cup her breast. Scandalized and enraged, Raina slapped him hard across the face. Nigel released her instantly, and his hand came up to touch the blooming redness on his cheek.

"Nigel, I—" She started to say she was sorry but couldn't find the words.

Without warning, Nigel seized her upper arms, savagely hauling her to him.

"Never strike me again, Raina," he warned through gritted teeth, "or I promise you, I will strike back and you'll never forget your place again."

His face was now very close to hers, breath heated with anger. In his eyes she saw a fierce, uncontrollable rage that shocked her, made her shrink away. A low, animal-like growl curled up from his throat before he slanted his lips over hers, pressing brutally, painfully against her teeth until she tasted blood.

She tried to wrench free, but he pulled her closer, his fingers biting into her arms as he forced his tongue into her mouth. She gagged at the unexpected invasion, revulsion instantly coiling her stomach into a knot. Nigel's grip was like iron, cold and unrelenting, and for the first time in her life, Raina feared him.

Was this what her father had meant when he warned that with a maturing of body came a corruption of thought? Was this the harm he alluded to when he said that for her own protection she was not to put herself alone in Nigel's company? Would that she had listened to him!

Nigel had her arms pinned at her sides as he reached behind her with one hand and began hurriedly gathering up her skirts. Panic clutched her heart with icy talons. Surely Nigel didn't mean to take her, willing or not!

Raina struggled, her frightened outcry muffled against his mouth. She was panting now, terrified and trapped in his bruising embrace. Nigel seemed to take her fearful response as encouragement and, groaning, pressed the hard ridge of his groin against her hip. At last his mouth left hers and she screamed, hoping someone would hear her, praying for deliverance.

A deep voice boomed in answer. "Unhand the woman or feel my blade between your shoulders."

Nigel's grip eased off immediately, and with a snarl, he freed her, whirling to face the source of the intrusion. Raina brushed her skirts down and from around Nigel's shoulder caught a glimpse of her rescuer.

A dark knight on a black charger held Nigel in a deadly looking glare, the threat in his eyes backed up by his large, gleaming broadsword, now leveled unwavering at Nigel's heart. A face that could have been carved of granite for all its harsh planes and angles remained impassive; the wide, square jaw set, the mouth an unforgiving yet shapely line.

This man did not appear a bright savior but rather a black specter, the devil himself. But as Raina stood wide-eyed and warily awed, Nigel charged forth with his usual blatant insolence.

"This is none of your concern," he barked, "and you know not whom you address."

"I am speaking to a knave who would force himself on an unwilling maid. Who you are is of little import, to my mind." The knight pressed his blade closer to Nigel.

With a brittle chuckle, Nigel held his hands in the air, palms up. This time when he spoke there was a hesitancy in his voice despite his bravado. "You have me at a disadvantage, sir. If you mean to dispute how I handle my affairs, I will gladly take the matter up with you, but as you can see, I am unarmed. The advantage you hold is unfair."

"As was yours with the woman."

"You would run me through, then, without courtesy of defense?"

"Nay," the knight replied. "I would have you leave the girl and go back whence you came." He nudged Nigel with his sword. *"Now."*

Nigel stumbled backward away from the blade, his voice rising to an incredulous pitch. "Who do you think you are? I'll have your damned head for this insolence!"

The knight seemed unconcerned. "Begone, little man." This time his jab was less gentle, and Nigel looked down to his chest where a small red stain had begun through his tunic.

With a hissing expulsion of breath, Nigel moved toward his horse, eyes narrowed as he climbed up into the saddle. But instead of taking up the reins, he reached down and drew his weapon. Raina gasped. All Nigel had to defend himself with was his shortsword; having been on a leisurely ride on protected lands, he was unprepared for battle. He brandished the stubby blade with a malicious grin, obviously pleased with himself despite the fact that it looked like a child's toy next to the knight's fine weapon. In the next instant Nigel charged toward the knight.

Raina watched through splayed fingers as the swords clashed against each other, sparking violently. The blades met again and again, the harsh grate of metal on metal joining Nigel's string of filthy curses. It seemed the confrontation had only just begun when, with an upward snap of his massive arm, the dark knight knocked Nigel's weapon from his grasp and sent it flying.

Nigel glanced at his empty hand. A look of outraged surprise came over him before his eyes narrowed on the knight. Then, with a bloodcurdling war cry, he lunged from his saddle. Raina shrieked for him to stay, but it was too late. Nigel flung himself at the knight, barreling into his broad chest. Both men toppled into the bushes.

The dark knight came to his feet first, yanking Nigel up with him by the front of his tunic. Nigel flailed and kicked and scratched, his technique sorely lacking the finesse and power of the other man's. While the knight struggled to capture Nigel's arms at his side, Nigel squirmed and thrashed about wildly. Somehow he managed to land the toe of his boot in the knight's shin.

Raina winced at the certain pain, but the knight uttered no response. He cocked his massive arm back and released it with the force of a January gale. An oath died on Nigel's lips as the knight's fist connected with his jaw. He spun on his heel, eyes rolled back in his head, then fell limply away like a stuffed cloth doll.

"Oh, mercy!" Raina gasped, dashing to Nigel's side. She fanned his face, her fingers hovering over the trickle of blood and the swelling bruise that had begun under his eye. He didn't respond, just lay there unmoving. "Oh, Nigel, you fool! Now you've gone and gotten yourself killed!"

"He's not dead," the knight drawled from behind her. "Though I cannot fathom why the thought would cause you such distress when it seemed clear the cur held little regard for your well-being."

Raina glanced up at the source of that dark, velvet voice. The knight had retrieved his sword from the bracken and now stood at her side, his broad shoulders and large torso blocking the sun as he resheathed the blade. A scowl that seemed born more of annoyance than concern wrinkled the center of his wide brow as he stared down at her. He was striking to be sure, a study in black, from his windswept, shoulder-length hair to his somber tunic, hose, and boots. From where he stood in shadow, even his eyes looked to be a potent midnight hue.

"Are you hurt?" he asked, and she realized he likely thought her dazed or simply dull-witted by the way she had been blinking up at him.

"Nay," she replied quickly, "though my pride is grievously wounded to admit I had to rely on the kindness of a stranger to save me from someone I consider a friend—more, at times a brother."

The knight held out his hand, indicating with a slight inclination of his head that she take it. "His intentions toward you just now were aught but brotherly," he said as he helped her to her feet.

Raina found the large, warm cradle of his palm against her fingertips such a keenly intriguing sensation, she nearly didn't hear what he had said. More intriguing were this man's eyes: a deep brown, so fathomless that upon first glance they seemed almost black. Unreadable as they were to her, their piercing stare seemed to penetrate her thoughts with ease. Feeling exposed, Raina pulled her hand away from his grasp, silently cursing the heat that now infused her cheeks.

The knight's scowl deepened, and he brushed past her to where Nigel lay. "How old are you, girl?" he asked as he hefted Nigel's dead weight up over his shoulder and draped him, prone, over the saddle of his white destrier.

"I-I'm ten and eight," she stammered, then added proudly, "we marked the day of my birth just last week."

She thought her newly advanced age made her sound mature and worldly. He, however, didn't look the least bit impressed, merely gave a grim nod that may as well have been a shrug. "Old enough to know better than to ride alone, particularly when the countryside is swarming with restless tourney competitors."

"I wasn't alone," she replied hotly, resenting the implication that he found her lacking good sense.

"*This* was your escort?" He hooked a thumb over his shoulder at Nigel's prostrate form, which from this angle provided a less than reassuring picture.

Raina bit her lip and the knight chuckled. "Like a lamb to the slaughter."

"What do you mean?"

"Men are wolves," he advised, taking up both mounts' reins as he walked toward her. "I would have thought a girl as comely as you might have learned that by now."

She felt fairly certain he hadn't meant to compliment her, but the effect of his appraisal was nonetheless pleasing. She masked her reaction with an upward tilt of her chin, but when he moved closer to her, she was helpless to contain the little tremor of excitement that shot through her veins and left her trembling in his shadow.

"Did your parents teach you naught of men and women? Or is it rather your practice to beguile men, then plead the innocent when they expect more than just a friendly kiss?"

Outraged, Raina drew in her breath and straightened her spine until it felt strained with the effort. "My mother is dead," she informed him tightly. "And aye, my father has taught me much. I should think he'd throttle me if he saw me alone in the company of a rogue like you."

"Rogue?" He looked duly offended . . . or perhaps surprised; she couldn't tell, and at the moment she didn't much care. " 'Tis rather haughty thinking for a bedraggled maid like yourself," he replied, his expression as wry as his tone of voice. "I should think your poor papa would be only too eager to push you into a knight's arms, rogue or nay."

She came within a hair's breadth of informing him that she was Lady Raina, daughter of Baron Luther d'Bussy of Norworth, and that her father would sooner see him flogged for his impudence than wed to his only heir. But she spoke the truth when she said her father had taught her much, and she had endured countless lectures about the dangers of her title, the hazards of being a wealthy baron's daughter in lawless times.

This bold knight thought her lacking sense; well, she would prove him wrong here and now. Let him believe her a peasant; better that than delivering herself into the arms of a potential ransomer. "I suppose, then, you would have me think you a prince among these wolves simply because you came to the service of a lowly maid."

One black brow lifted sardonically. "Admittedly, I am no prince, but do you reckon a wolf would rescue a lamb only to set her free?" He smiled lazily, revealing a row of straight white teeth, and for an instant Raina wondered if she was about to be devoured where she stood. Heart fluttering, knees trembling, she didn't dare move when he reached out and hooked a tangle of hair behind her ear. She might have swooned if not for the presence of her mare, grazing at her back. "Don't look so stricken," the knight said with a knowing wink. "I've come on business, not pleasure."

And then his large hands were at her waist, his grasp warm and strong, the line of each finger pressing through her bliaut and against her skin. Raina sought his shoulders for support as he lifted her off the ground and placed her on her mount as if she were no more cumbersome than a feather bolster.

He circled round then to Nigel's mount and, with a light smack to the stallion's rump, sent it off at a canter. Nigel began to stir with the jostling ride, his moans carrying back to where Raina sat, staring down at her dark deliverer, captivated by his gaze.

"Get thee gone, little lamb," he commanded in a low growl, "before this wolf rethinks his charitable mood."

Masking her startlement at his bold remark would have been impossible. She gasped, feeling the flood of heat fill her cheeks as she wheeled her mare away from him. With trembling hands, she gripped the reins tightly and started for the edge of the woods, very aware of the dark gaze fixed on her as she fell into place behind Nigel's destrier.

Logic screamed for her to flee, to send her mount into a gallop and count herself fortunate to have escaped the day with little more than rattled nerves and a skittering pulse. But, like Lot's wife, no warning would have been stern enough to keep her from venturing a glance back to what might have spelled her doom.

To him.

She pivoted in her saddle and found him watching her, the increasing distance between them seeming scant inches under the power of his gaze. Even as her mount forged on and the space between them grew, it seemed as if he were close enough to hear her racing heartbeat, to feel the shiver of excitement coursing through her. Close enough to touch her. Heaven help her, but at that moment, if he had beckoned her back, she might have gone.

Like a lamb to the slaughter.

His grim observation rippled through her memory, dousing her foolhardy, wayward thoughts and setting her body into action. With a swallowed shriek of fright, she forced her attention back to her mount. Heart pounding, breath hitching, she sped past Nigel, out of the woods and toward the keep as if the devil himself were at her heels.

Chapter Two

From his seat high in the tournament loges the next morn, Baron Luther d'Bussy was impossible to miss. Proud as a peacock and nearly as colorful in his expensive silk garb, he lorded over the tournament crowd and competitors with the regality of the king himself. More than a few passersby whispered behind their hands of the baron's audacity to sport on his balding pate a crown of braided gold. If people stared at his outward display of wealth, the baron feigned no modesty. He had spent his youth achieving the status he now enjoyed; to his way of thinking, he had every right to flaunt it.

"An impressive turnout, milord."

The baron grunted in acknowledgment and cast a brief, sidelong look at Nigel; then he turned away, taking a bite from a leg of mutton to discourage further conversation. For reasons he preferred to leave unexamined, Nigel's voice—and indeed the very thought of him—always had the ability to grate on the old man's nerves.

Evidently, Nigel had recently had the same effect on another man—one with less tolerance than the baron and a powerful right arm, judging from the sorry condition of the young man's face. His left eye was swollen shut and rimmed with a black-and-blue circle the size of a large fist, but Nigel's pride seemed no worse for wear. He stood beside the near-empty loges astride his destrier, taking in the gathering crowd of spectators and competitors.

When he spoke, an air of pomposity well beyond his rank or appearance filled his voice. "Pity King Stephen is occupied with affairs of state at present and unable to see Norworth's political weight so magnificently displayed, milord."

"Indeed," the baron murmured through a mouthful of food. He waved away a swarm of hungry gnats that had begun attacking his meal. If only he could as easily dismiss this greater nuisance in chain mail.

"Of course," Nigel continued, "a prudent politician might take the king's absence as an opportunity to gain support for his own. Particularly during this time of sovereign unrest."

Baron d'Bussy stopped chewing. He had long ago given up on posturing and conquest, and had intended the tourney be naught but sporting summer's entertainment. However, old habits died hard, and the politician in him found an irresistible measure of intrigue in Nigel's intimation of potential gain. Loath to encourage the young man's advice, however, he tried to appear merely conversational. "What make you of this *unrest*, lad?"

Nigel grinned, clearly satisfied with himself. "I'm certain I needn't tell you, milord, that Stephen's greater barons—many of whom I recognize here today—have been talking of securing England from France's rule upon the imminent death of our dearly loved king."

The baron harnessed a smug grin. Stephen was despised by many and revered only by the minority preferring his brand of lax rule. Loyal first to himself, Baron d'Bussy made sure to maintain ties in both camps. "Would this security not be accomplished when Stephen names Eustace heir to the throne?"

Nigel scoffed. "Stephen's son is a weak man with an

even less robust reputation as a leader. The Church has already refused to back him, and Stephen's allies grow fewer by the day. The barons will likely try to place one of their own as king long before they allow Eustace or Matilda's son, Henry, to destroy everything England has become. 'Tis merely supposition, but I reckon no one is eager to embrace the rigid order young Count Henry has pledged to enforce should he come to power."

The baron stroked his grizzled jowls, letting out a heavy sigh as he leaned back in his seat. Nigel was indeed abreast of political affairs. A notable feat for the bastard son of a peasant wench, but then, Nigel had never been one to ignore an opportunity to better himself. D'Bussy took a certain pride in the lad's ambitious nature and thus he smiled.

"Ah, you see, my lord, we think very much alike."

Nigel's comment, and his knowing grin, chased away any trace of the baron's admiration. He didn't care for his bold tone. He certainly did not appreciate the suggested comparison. "Mind your place, Nigel," the baron growled, "and guard your tongue. For what I am thinking is that you speak of treason and I'll have no part of it."

With that, he pitched his half-eaten shank of mutton to the ground to indicate the end of both his patience and the conversation. Returning his attention to the lists, the baron picked some meat from between his teeth, then wiped his hands on his voluminous robes. "Go," he ordered with a curt wave of dismissal when Nigel hesitated to take his leave. "Speak no more of this nonsense. Endeavor instead to find my daughter and send her along to join me for the start of the tourney."

The baron waited for a challenge from his insolent young knight, but Nigel said nothing. Jaw set, he wheeled his mount about and left the loges, riding negligently— and, the baron was certain, quite deliberately—through the freshly raked lists in the direction of the ale tent.

* * *

Gunnar stalked the gaily colored avenue astride his destrier, feeling like a ghost among this gaudy, churning throng of life. He felt none of the excitement, none of the apprehension he saw reflected in the eyes of the men around him. He scanned the dozens of faces, looking past the fresh, hungry expressions of the younger knights to the older men who had come to compete. Of those who met his stare, only a few held it for more than a heartbeat; then they, too, glanced away, letting him pass without taking issue.

He searched in vain for a pair of cold blue eyes that had haunted his dreams almost nightly; a round, pockmarked face and a scarlet, bulbous nose that bespoke too much drink. He would know that face anywhere, could still see the cocksure stance of a man with unchecked power, and the line of pebblelike, yellowed teeth bared in a malevolent smile.

But while the blue and gold of d'Bussy's standard fluttered from the lances of nearly every fourth knight in attendance, the baron himself was nowhere to be found. Perhaps he'd imbibed too much wine and had not yet risen from his bed, Gunnar thought. Nay, more likely the stout little rooster was being pampered in his castle, waiting until everyone had gathered so he could make a grand entrance onto the field.

Gunnar hoped to make his own entrance to the melee without fanfare, intent that d'Bussy have not even a hint of his presence until Gunnar had his blade poised at the devil's throat. To wit, his chain mail hung from his shoulders, polished but unadorned; his lance and shield bore no standard.

For all of the last seven years, he had served no one, save himself. Alone by choice this day as well, he had instructed the handful of mercenaries in his employ to remain behind at his keep. Only Alaric, his overeager young squire, knew Gunnar's true purpose for attending the tourney and the potential consequences should he, or should he not, accomplish his goal.

Loyal to a fault, the lad nearly had to be tied to a tree to keep him from tagging along. Alaric had insisted that his desire to accompany Gunnar had naught at all to do with the veritable feast of pink-cheeked lovely young maids sure to be in attendance at a tourney of this size. The memory of his squire's less than convincing denial solicited an amused grin from Gunnar. In its wake, his thoughts turned to the woman he had encountered in the woods last afternoon.

He wasn't in the habit of seducing innocent peasant girls. In truth, he wasn't in the habit of seducing anyone. Years before, he'd had his first taste of carnal pleasure, had sampled the bounty of a woman's body and the power that want of it could wield over a man.

He had recognized the danger then, and in the time since, he had managed to remain focused, purposely devoid of that particular distraction. Until yesterday. Something about that woman—that lamb—set his pulse thrumming and his blood pooling to the nether regions of his body. It had taken incredible strength of will to let her ride away, and even after she had, her memory and the heat it inspired lingered long into the night.

He had deliberately ignored the temptation to seek her out this morn, willfully reining in his gaze each time it strayed into the crowd to look for her begrimed but beautiful face or a supple feminine form hidden beneath a peasant's garb. Today of all days, he needed no distractions.

But then, over his shoulder, he heard her voice. He turned toward the sultry ripple of laughter and frowned.

There she stood, one of a group of four noblewomen. Her back was to him as she spoke, and though he could not hear what she said, her voice brimmed with excitement. She wore a silk bliaut, the color of the airy fabric a near match for the cloudless summer sky. A ringlet of violets crowned her head, her dark hair combed free of yesterday's tangles and hanging past her hips in a thick, glossy curtain.

She looked more queen than peasant today, and her friends seemed to be in agreement, watching her and listening with the rapt attention of bedazzled subjects.

Gunnar slowly guided his mount in her direction, telling himself the urge to be near her was more to confront her mild deception of the day before than to bask in her presence like the others. Though she all but whispered now, her voice became clearer to him as he approached.

"And then, without so much as blinking an eye—"

She drew her arm back, her hand curled into a small fist, then released it—a dainty imitation of the blow he'd dealt her attacker in the woods. Gunnar fought back a smile.

The other ladies gasped, bringing their hands to their mouths, their eyes no longer on her but on him.

She continued undaunted. "Granted, such a brutish resolution was shocking to witness, but Nigel well and good deserved it—"

"Lady Raina." A woman at her side gave a nervous tug of Raina's sleeve and pointed a trembling finger over her shoulder. Raina quit talking and spun around, her hazel-colored eyes narrowing the instant they lit on him.

"You!" she cried, and it sounded to Gunnar more a scolding than greeting.

No one, not even the boldest mercenary in his employ, had ever deigned to raise a voice to him. The idea that this slip of a woman did so now, with her hands on her hips and her pert chin tilted to a supreme height, amused him greatly. Intrigued him.

"Good morrow, Lady Raina." He leaned heavily on her

title, trying to cover his reaction to seeing her in this new light.

Yesterday, despite the mud and grime, she was attractive. Now, looking up at him, her face scrubbed clean and her cheeks pink from the sun and surprise, she was breathtaking. Her friends disappeared nearly without his notice.

"I see my lamb has traded her fleece for fine silk."

That proud chin climbed up a notch. "And you, my lord, may have hidden your black hide beneath steel links this morn, but I still see a wolf."

"Indeed?" He dismounted and came to stand before her. "I suppose, then, 'tis too much to hope that you might cheer me on to victory today as your personal champion."

She made a small noise in the back of her throat, surely intended as a denial, but he didn't miss the faint curve of her lips nor the blush that rose to her cheeks the instant before she tipped her face down to feign interest in the toe of her embroidered shoe. "I shall not be cheering anyone on," she said with a trace of disdain. "If I had a choice in the matter, I should rather not even watch the melee. Contrary to my father's fondness for the sport, I find tourneys but an excuse for violence and debauchery."

"Aye," Gunnar agreed with private reflection, "they do bring out the worst in men. Everyone seeking fortune or glory."

"And which have you come to seek, my lord?"

He nearly chuckled at her frankness. "In truth, I have use for neither. I've come in the name of honor."

"A lady's honor?"

"Aye," he acknowledged, taking far too much interest in the way her eyes dimmed at the mention of another lady. "I've come to right a wrong."

"My lord, you surprise me," she said with a light, teasing smile. "I hadn't taken you for the chivalrous sort. Tell me, is your lady here to see you defend her honor?"

Instantly, he thought of his mother and her efforts to teach courtesy and manners to a boy more interested in mock battles and raucous adventure. Chivalry and honor were two things she prized, two things he had never possessed and likely never would.

"She is dead," he fairly snapped, his curt response enough to wipe any trace of joviality from Raina's features, but he scarcely noticed her response. Caught up in his own contemplation, he muttered his thoughts aloud. "If all goes well, the villain responsible will pay in kind by day's end."

The peal of a trumpet punctuated his ominous statement and drew the attention of nearly everyone gathered. A shout went up from a group of knights in the ale tent, followed by a collective clanging of armor and stumbling of men toward their waiting mounts.

"Well," Raina said, looking over her shoulder toward the lists, " 'tis time for the tourney to commence."

"Aye," Gunnar acknowledged, scanning the crowd of competitors, impatience building in him with every heartbeat. "But I don't yet see the baron."

"He's there, in the stands."

Gunnar dragged his attention from the lists and followed her breezy gesture to the top of the loges, where a grizzled, paunchy old man sat beneath a striped canopy. Swathed in yards of bright silks that did naught to conceal his girth, the baron reclined like a sloven king, sipping from a tankard and fanning himself with his hand. As if he suddenly sensed their regard, his attention turned toward them and he leaned forward in his seat, squinting under the glare of the sun and righting his little crown when it slipped forward over his brow.

Gunnar's stomach clenched with a dawning realization. "He isn't dressed to compete. . . ."

"Compete?" Raina replied on a soft laugh. "Nay, of course not! 'Tis been years since he's competed himself."

Her voice was all but lost in the tumult whipping to a frenzy inside Gunnar. Rage, disappointment, helplessness, frustration—a swift torrent of emotion buffeted him at once, leaving him breathless and feeling as if the ground were opening up beneath him and sucking him down. He had waited all this time, come all this way . . . for nothing.

"Nay," Raina was saying, "the closest my father gets to the lists these days is to award the prizes to the victor."

Her father.

"Baron d'Bussy is"—he nearly had to shake himself to form the words without sputtering—"he is your father?"

"Aye, he is," she replied brightly; then she looked to his expression, and he could almost feel her shudder where she stood.

Gunnar fought hard to control his roiling, self-directed anger, summoning every ounce of control he possessed to keep his reaction bland, unaffected. What an idiot he'd been! What a fool! So taken with a becoming wench that he'd been oblivious to the baron's presence, and worse, chattering on with the villain's own daughter when he should have been plotting an alternative means of attack.

"Whatever is the matter?" she asked.

He breathed in deeply, feeling his nostrils flare with the effort, and slowly let the calming draught out. Shuttering his expression with the expertise gleaned from years of practice, he faced her. Smiled at her.

The wary frown that had pinched her brow faded quickly and melted into a hopeful-looking smile. "Do you know my father?"

"My lady," he said, "I should think there's not a man from here to the continent who does not know of your father or his reputation."

"Aye," she remarked, evidently pleased. "I reckon, indeed."

Clearly his light tone and affable mien had belied none

of the sarcasm he felt. Only he knew how his heart was pounding with hatred, his blood hot and coursing with rage for the demon of his past.

At that moment a young, towheaded page scurried to Raina's side. He halted at her elbow, and hands clasped before him, he cleared his throat. "B-begging pardon, m-my lady." The lad's stammer turned into a terrible stutter as his eyes darted nervously between Gunnar and her. He took a huge gulp of air and continued at little more than a whisper. "M-my lord has sent m-me hither to f-fetch you to his side for the start of the tourney."

"Thank you, Robert." She hunkered down to the page's level. "You are doing so much better," she whispered, combing her fingers through his overlong, white-blond bangs. "Walk back with me to the stands and I'll buy each of us a nice, sugary wafer. How does that sound?"

At the lad's enthusiastic nod, Raina giggled and rose, bringing him to her side in a sisterly hug. She looked to Gunnar, a warm smile still glowing in her eyes, and he felt the queerest pull in his gut. Caused by jealousy or longing, he knew not which, but he stamped the feeling down as quickly as it came.

She is d'Bussy's daughter, he reminded himself. Spawn of his enemy and he should feel nothing toward her.

"I must go," she said.

"Of course," he murmured. With the baron still glaring down from his seat, Gunnar took Raina's hand in his and brought it to his lips. He felt her tremble as he pressed a chaste kiss to her fingers, knowing from her quick intake of breath that her cheeks were flushed an innocent pink, but Gunnar's eyes remained fastened on her father's darkening expression.

Only when she drew her hand from his did he look from the baron's eyes and into his daughter's. " 'Tis been a pleasure, Lady Raina," he said, and wanted to kick himself because he spoke the truth in telling her so.

"My lord," she acceded with a polite nod. Then, blushing from her chin to her scalp, she pivoted on her heel and made to leave with young Robert gathered close to her side.

Gunnar watched her diaphanous skirts swirl about her legs, her gently flared hips swaying with each step she took. Suddenly she stopped, turned, and ran back to him.

She pressed something into his hand and placed a quick kiss to his cheek. "For luck," she whispered against his ear, and she was gone, running back to the page and leaving Gunnar standing beside his mount like a witless dolt.

Befuddled and utterly surprised, he uncurled his fist and stared into his open palm. A swatch of blue silk lay there like so much summer air, the edges of the fine fabric ruffling in the mild breeze, soft and delicate against his callused fingers.

Saints' blood, she had given him her favor!

He wanted to cast it away, along with the maddening feelings she had inspired in him after only two brief encounters. Instead, he brought the token to his face, breathing in her fragrance, recalling in its silky folds the pleasing softness of her lips as she kissed his cheek.

His sex roused with swift and potent desire, the likes of which he had never felt before. Desire for this lovely girl, bewitching woman, gentle lamb. His enemy's daughter.

How could so guileless a creature be born of d'Bussy's rancid blood? How could such apparent goodness come from such proven evil? He would likely never have the answer, for when the day was out and her father was dead at the end of Gunnar's sword, Raina would surely fear and despise him.

Resolving not to care, he shoved the scrap of silk into his gauntlet, then unfastened his helm from his saddle and

placed it over his head. The heavy, conical steel form settled into place, and he was no longer man but warrior. His
every muscle tensed for battle, Gunnar willed his heart to
equally stony composition. As he had done so oft in the
past, he systematically blocked out all feeling, all emotion, until all that remained was the cool logic of sword
and sinew.

He mounted his destrier and soberly took his place at
one side of the tournament field. If the baron meant to
award the victor alone, Gunnar would make certain he was
that man.

From the moment the trumpeter sounded the start of the
melee, Gunnar fought like a man possessed. He charged
forward relentlessly, taking advantage of the other competitors' fatigue and ignoring his own until the day grew
long and the field dwindled down to the remaining few.

At last only Gunnar and one other knight remained. The
latter, one of d'Bussy's men, was no match for Gunnar in
terms of size, but the grim set of the man's jaw beneath his
helm certainly attested to his determination. He charged
forward with a shrill war cry as Gunnar was leaning from
his mount to assist his last opponent to his feet.

Gunnar turned abruptly, wheeling his mount about and
placing his shield at the ready, having time enough only to
brace himself for the attack. The knight's lance met Gunnar's shield, knocking the wind from his lungs and making
him momentarily lose his balance. Gunnar's heart thudded
in his chest so loudly, he scarcely heard the collective gasp
from the spectators and the applause as he faltered in the
saddle.

He could not lose. He would not.

The knight wheeled his steed around and came upon
Gunnar again, lance poised to strike with perfect aim. With
a roar Gunnar charged forward, his lance leveled at his
opponent's heart. The earth rumbled as their great steeds

advanced on each other. Everything grew suddenly quiet as time itself seemed to slow. Gunnar kept his eyes trained on his opponent's shield and on the spot to hit that would surely toss him from his mount. His complete concentration transferred to that spot, he spurred his destrier forward.

In an instant Gunnar felt the familiar jolt and heard the sharp crack of a lance meeting its mark. Then, for the first time in his life, he felt his world tilt wildly . . . and realized he was falling from his saddle. He grasped at his destrier's mane, but his leather gauntlet prevented him from getting a firm grip on the beast, which was kicking and trying frantically to get away. Gunnar hit the ground hard, his breath leaving in a wheeze.

The stallion pawed the air, then ran to the side of the lists while Gunnar scrambled to his feet. Quickly drawing his sword, he stood ready as d'Bussy's man prepared to charge him. The knight jabbed his warhorse cruelly with his spurs, making the beast scream and rear before it barreled toward its target, snorting and huffing as clods of dirt sprayed in its wake. The white slash of a sneer showed under the knight's nasal as he leveled his lance. Gunnar knew without question this man meant to kill him and wondered for the briefest moment if this was how his father had felt in d'Bussy's tourney so long ago.

The thought scarcely had a chance to form before the horse and knight were upon him. At the last moment, Gunnar jumped out of the way of the snarling pair, swiping his sword at the destrier's hindquarters as it passed. The great steed shrieked and careened to the side, throwing its rider to the ground. The knight quickly gathered his wits, drawing his sword and charging Gunnar with a ferocious battle cry.

Sparks flew as steel met steel with an angry clang, then again and again, as each man swung his sword and met the other's strike. Gunnar's opponent soon began to tire, slashing wildly from side to side, hacking at the air in a blind

attempt to hit him. Sensing the man's fatigue, Gunnar re-
doubled his efforts, meeting his opponent's blade and holding it with his own. Each man pushed against the other, their
blades poised vertically between their noses. While keeping the knight's focus on his blade, Gunnar hooked his leg
around the man's calf and shoved with all his strength. He
hit the ground on his back, and Gunnar was on him in a trice,
his blade pressing into the knight's mail-clad chest. "Do
you yield?" he growled.

A tense moment passed, and he pressed the blade deeper.
"Do you yield?"

"Aye," the knight growled at last. "Aye, I yield."

Gunnar relaxed his hold and stepped away from the
man, leaving him to come to his feet on his own. The
knight rose and removed his helm, indicating his surrender and revealing his identity.

Raina's attacker from the day before clenched his teeth
and warned, "This is hardly the end of it."

Cheers went up from the crowd, but Gunnar's victory
was yet to be had. He remounted, steeling himself for the
final confrontation with the demon of his past. Hatred
raged in his veins as he approached the stands, his unflinching gaze fixed on the baron as he began his descent
from the loges, his daughter clinging to his arm.

Gunnar watched with dispassionate calm as the elderly
baron made his way down the center of the stands. He realized suddenly that Raina was not so much grasping her
father's arm to steady herself but to assist him as he carefully picked his way down the stands on hesitant, almost
feeble legs.

Gunnar felt a twinge of humiliation bleed through the
heavy shroud of rage and hatred he had cloaked himself in
for so long. This rotund, bowed creature was the demon
who had haunted his dreams for the past thirteen years?
But Gunnar refused to feel pity, refused to feel anything.

When the baron reached the bottom of the stands, he lifted a jeweled chalice in the air, encouraging the applause of the spectators. He turned to Gunnar, inclining his head to acknowledge his victory, then passed the chalice to Raina. She took the ornate cup and extended it for Gunnar to drink of it.

"Lauds!" the baron exclaimed, clapping his hands together in hearty applause. "Lauds to you, good sir! An excellent show of skill."

Gunnar accepted the goblet from Raina, nodding solemnly. Briefly distracted by the ruby- and sapphire-encrusted chalice, he wondered under what terms—at whose expense—d'Bussy had come to possess it.

"A lovely prize in itself," the baron said proudly. "A treasure befitting a king, no?"

Gunnar twisted the chalice between his fingers. " 'Tis worthless to my mind." Ignoring Raina's affronted gasp, he returned his attention to the baron and spoke loud enough for all to hear. "The boon I seek this day is much greater than this petty trinket."

The baron's mirth left his expression instantly. Gunnar met his stare, unflinching. Suddenly, the baron's brows rose high on his forehead, and a broad smile lit his features. He laughed aloud, a hearty guffaw, then turned to the sea of stunned faces behind him. "By the Rood! Here stands a man after my own heart!"

"That I am, d'Bussy," Gunnar muttered under his breath, "that I am."

He drained the chalice and tossed it negligently to the ground at his horse's feet. His right palm itched, resting on the hilt of his sword as d'Bussy's laughter echoed in his ears. His fingers curled around the leather grip of his sword, and he drew the blade from its scabbard, the metallic song bringing d'Bussy's attention slowly back to him.

The baron's mouth was still open and laughing before

realization dawned in his features and his mouth fell agape in surprise and shock. Time slowed to an exaggerated crawl as Gunnar swung his arm back, his eyes trained on d'Bussy's fleshy neck. But as his blade began its descending arc, he lost sight of his mark. A flash of sky-blue sendal whisked his mind back to a day he longed to put to rest. . . .

Surprise and fear had rendered Gunnar immobile when d'Bussy drew his sword, poised to kill. A blinding spark of sunlight kissed the blade as the baron raised it over his head. In the space of a heartbeat, the light was eclipsed. Gunnar cried out . . . but it was too late. His mother lunged forward, throwing herself between him and the falling sword. She screamed for d'Bussy to stay his hand.

And then she was silent.

Gunnar could still hear the blade as it bit into her slender neck, could still feel the startling warmth of the blood that splattered his face from the blow.

Could still taste the bitterness of loss . . .

A soft voice brought him back, stilling his hand in midair. Raina now stood in front of her father, arms spread wide to shield him, her neck in place of his. "Nay!" she cried, her eyes wide with terror. "Please, nay!"

Gunnar lowered his sword, unwilling and unable to strike the woman to get at his target. *Damn the wench!*

She stared at him in horror, shaking her head mutely, her fearful sobs having stolen her voice altogether. Gunnar's blade hovered with lethal steadiness at her throat.

"What the devil is the meaning of this?" d'Bussy railed, stumbling from behind her to face their attacker.

From the periphery of his vision, Gunnar saw several men closing in on him from the sides. He pressed the blade closer to Raina's neck, his glare conveying a lethal warning to the baron. D'Bussy raised his hands to still the advancing guards.

Heart pounding with unspent rage, Gunnar snarled,

"You may have escaped my sword this day, but mark you, d'Bussy, your crimes against me will not go unpunished." He then spoke to the crowd. "This ignoble bastard murdered my father out of greed and killed my mother before mine eyes when she refused to become his whore."

A deafening silence fell over the stands.

"Liar!" Raina cried.

"Who are you, knave?" the baron demanded, his rusty voice booming past his daughter's.

"No one of any consequence, or so you told me long ago."

The baron's brow furrowed in confusion.

"My face holds no recall for you, Baron? 'Tis been some years, I credit, nigh a lifetime. Mayhap you require a name to refresh your memory."

"I require only that you leave before I see you drawn and quartered," the baron growled, and Gunnar chuckled, for the beast he knew the man to be was now beginning to rouse.

"Perhaps," he said with malevolent calm, "you thought by wiping the name of Rutledge from this earth you might also remove it from your mind."

"Papa?" Raina interjected, her voice filled with confusion. "Papa, what is he talking about?"

Gunnar willed his gaze to remain on the baron's, watching with satisfaction as those rheumy blue eyes narrowed to lethal slits. "By all that is holy, you are mad! Insane!" the baron sputtered. "I have murdered no one, and I've never before laid eyes on you."

"Thirteen years have made you forgetful indeed, Baron," Gunnar drawled coolly. "Careless, too, to let your lovely daughter wander out among the wolves."

D'Bussy's face blanched and he moved his daughter farther behind him.

"Twice since just yesterday I've been close enough to

pluck her from your grasp," Gunnar continued, "but I've come for you alone. You cannot hide behind your daughter's skirts forever, old man. The moment you turn your back, you can be sure 'twill be my face you see, the steel of my blade you taste. Let this day serve as reminder and warning that I will return and vengeance will be mine."

With that he withdrew his blade and wheeled his charger about, leaving the lists in a cloud of dust with several of d'Bussy's men on his heels.

Stunned and trembling with fear, Raina collapsed into her father's arms and watched as the man who in the space of a day had been first her rescuer and was now her enemy thundered out of her life. She prayed she would never lay eyes on him again, but in her heart she knew he meant what he had said.

He would return. And heaven help all of them when he did.

Chapter Three

In the fortnight since the tournament, d'Bussy's numerous holdings had suffered nearly as many attacks in so many days. Village grain stores were burned, trade wagons were robbed, keeps were looted, and men had died. There was no question as to the identity of the raiders, for with each attack came the message that peace would be had only if the baron agreed to meet with their leader on the field of honor. Each request went unanswered.

The baron received the news of the nearly daily attacks with an uncustomary lack of emotion. When his men rallied, ready to meet the marauders on the field, d'Bussy gave orders to stay, refusing to leave Norworth. Refusing to fight back.

One by one his political supporters turned their backs on him, unwilling to help a man who would not help himself. His dreams of power were now laughable, absurd at best.

The most recent report of attack came from one of the baron's holdings just a league away from Norworth. D'Bussy sat mutely in his chair on the dais at the front of the emptied hall that served as his court between the daily meals. Nigel stood before him with the messenger from the neighboring castle.

"Milord, we must take a stand. These raids are growing more frequent, and with each passing day they draw closer to Norworth." When the baron did not respond, Nigel leaned in, his hand resting on the hilt of his sword. "You need but ask and your men will follow you to battle. Say the word and we can rid ourselves of this nuisance for good."

The baron said nothing, idly tugging an eyebrow, his unfocused gaze trained on the d'Bussy banner, which hung on the far wall of the great hall.

"Milord," Nigel implored, raking a hand through his hair in evident frustration, "each day we are losing valuable stores and money."

At last Nigel gained his attention. " 'Tis *my* money and *my* holdings. How I choose to handle the attacks is my own decision."

"Aye, milord," Nigel acquiesced with a respectful nod, "of course the decision is yours. I only wish to point out that—"

"I have heard enough," the baron announced, rising from his chair to descend the dais and thus ending the morning's report.

"Shall I ready the garrison, then, milord?"

"Nay," d'Bussy replied without turning to face his man.

"But milord! I warrant these raids will only increase if we do not act now. Will you wait until they come rapping on your door?"

At Nigel's bold tone, d'Bussy pivoted slowly and turned a narrowed gaze on him. A long moment passed in silence before the baron heaved a weary sigh. "Let the devil take what he will." He departed the hall with his guards close at his sides.

Raina knocked lightly on her father's solar door. When no answer came from within, she pressed her ear to the rough oak panel. "Papa? Are you in here?" This time she rapped harder, and the door creaked open enough for her to peer inside.

Her father sat slumped in his ornately carved, cushioned chair, staring out the open window. He did not turn when she entered; indeed, he hardly seemed aware of her presence at all. In his lap he held an object—a book. Her mother's Bible, she realized as she drew closer. The same book Raina herself used to pore over when she was feeling particularly lonely and missing her mother.

"I'm sorry if I have disturbed your reading, Papa, but when you didn't answer me—"

Her voice seemed to rouse him from his thoughts, and he looked up at her suddenly, his eyes sleep-weary and ringed with dark circles.

"Are you unwell, Papa? Since the tourney, you've been acting so strangely. You spend most of your days alone in here, and I know you are not sleeping as you should." She touched him tenderly on the shoulder. "I am worried about you."

Clumsily, he reached up and patted her hand, though if he heard her concern, his attention seemed focused elsewhere. With trembling fingers, he caressed the edge of a gilded, illuminated page in the book spread open in his lap. "How she loved this Bible. Beauclerc himself commissioned it for her when she was but a babe, can you imagine that? She was beautiful even then, my Margareth, beautiful enough to enamor the king on first glance."

"Aye, Papa," Raina answered softly, but in truth she could no longer recall her mother's features. Every portrait of her had been taken down—destroyed, according to castle rumor—soon after her death. Now as ever, her father spoke of his wife only when deep in contemplation or fraught with worry.

At the risk of upsetting him, Raina had learned long ago not to press for details of her mother, permitting her father his private reflection. But as a child she had been full of questions: What was her mother like? How did she enjoy passing her time? Did Raina resemble her, even a little bit?

Her father's answers, when they came, were doled out reluctantly, sparingly, as if his wife were a treasure too precious to share, even with his daughter. Raina had her own memories of her mother, though they were puzzling in contrast to her father's carefully measured accounts of a spirited woman who charmed kings and queens alike. The woman Raina remembered was a pitiful, sad creature. A fragile woman, given to bouts of deep despair, and a mere shadow of the bright angel her father must have known.

Often Raina wondered if her birth might have had something to do with her mother's decline, if perhaps in his vagueness, her father was trying to shield her from the truth. Blaming herself in part for the loss of such a cherished being, Raina had learned to accept her father's version, though her own troubling memories remained.

She pressed a kiss to his freckled pate. "I miss her, too. But at the moment, Papa, I am deeply concerned about you. I have been talking with Nigel—"

Her father stiffened instantly. "I told you to stay away from him," he snapped. "I don't want you speaking to him, letting him fill your head with lies!"

Raina stepped back, stunned and more than a bit confused at his outburst. "That we are under threat of attack is not a lie, Papa." He exhaled as if to regain his composure, then settled back in his chair while Raina continued. "The entire keep is abuzz with reports of these raiders. Nigel says 'tis only a matter of time before they set their sights on Norworth."

Her father shook his head soberly. "He won't come here," he said in a low, reflective voice. "He'll plunder my holdings and take what he feels he is due, and then he will leave. But he won't come here."

"He," Raina repeated. "You are speaking of the man from the tourney, aren't you? You are speaking of Rutledge."

Raina recalled well the name he'd given himself, recalled, too, her unsettling encounter with him in the woods and again at the tourney. Her head still rang with the baffling accusations he'd made against her father. Wild, incomprehensible charges of murder. From that moment on, she had turned the name Rutledge about in her mind, trying to place it among those of her father's numerous acquaintances, but it yielded no memory.

"Do you reckon these raids are some means of vengeance against you for the crimes he has accused you of? Perhaps you should talk to Rutledge, prove to him that you have done no harm to him or his kin—"

"I will prove nothing to the blackguard!" he shouted. "I see no point in deigning to refute a madman's allegations, and I will not hear his name upon your tongue ever again, do you hear me, daughter?"

"Of course, Papa. I'm sorry."

Looking at her now, his expression softened. He smoothed her hair as he used to when she was a little girl in need of comfort or consoling. "You needn't be frightened, child; I'll keep you safe. Put that damnable rogue out of your mind. Soon enough he will be out of our lives."

Raina nodded mutely, troubled to see the scarcely contained worry in her father's eyes.

"Now, be a good girl," he said, "and leave your father to some peace and quiet. I think I should enjoy a quick nap before we sup. Close the door on your way out if you would."

She left his side, crossing the room in silence to do as he bade her. Her father might crave privacy, but he would do no sleeping, of that she was certain. He was concerned, gravely concerned, and it seemed to have everything to do with Rutledge. Stepping into the corridor, Raina pulled the door closed behind her, her eyes trained on her father's slouched form as he steepled his fingers and resumed his pensive vigil at the window.

Supper that eve was a quiet affair, word having spread throughout the castle that the marauders loomed close by. Almost everyone ate in silence, and those who dared to speak did so in muffled whispers, for the baron gave orders that he did not want to hear talk of the raids in his hall. By all accounts it appeared the baron intended to ignore the issue, relying on hope and prayer that the danger would soon pass.

This idea did not bode well with the baron's men, least of all Nigel, who, having drained his cup of yet another serving of ale, was growing bolder by the minute.

"I tell you, the baron is losing his mind," he whispered mutinously to an older knight sitting beside him. The man smirked into his tankard. " 'Tis no laughing matter," Nigel said gravely. "The longer we wait to strike back at these thieves, the more we stand to lose. *All of us.*"

As intended, the comment drew the attention of several men at the table. They leaned in to listen as Nigel continued.

"I for one will not stand idly by and watch as everything I've worked to preserve—*everything we have worked to preserve*—is handed over to that rogue from the tourney."

Several knights nodded and grunted in agreement.

"Aye, I've a taste for thieves' blood," growled one man.

" 'Tis been a long while since my blade has seen battle. Far too long, I say," answered another.

"Then you agree," Nigel said. "We must take action, and soon."

"Aye, but what action can we take when our lord has said do nothing?" asked one of the men.

"Mayhap they can be reasoned with," offered someone

from the group. His hopeful comment met with collective snickering.

"I've heard there is but one thing alone that will appease these bastards," Nigel said quietly.

"Aye," agreed another man on a laugh, "half the countryside."

Nigel shook his head, smiling knowingly. "Nay, lads," he said. " 'Tis the baron himself they want." He took a long draught from his tankard, watching as the men absorbed the comment.

"The baron?"

"What mean you, Nigel?"

Nigel moved in and the others huddled low to hear his reply. "Prior to each raid, a messenger has come with word that were the baron to meet with the leader of these thieves, in battle, the attack would be called off." He paused, gauging the group, then said soberly, " 'Tis the baron they want . . . mayhap 'tis the baron they should get."

A knight about Nigel's age laughed out loud. "Oh, aye! A brilliant plan. We can't bloody well throw Baron d'Bussy to the wolves now, can we?"

The men turned expectantly to Nigel, who remained silent as he lounged back in his seat, the look in his eyes chilling in its blankness.

"Christ Almighty," hissed the knight beside him in disbelief. "There's only one man here who's lost his mind, and I warrant 'tis not the baron."

The other men exchanged looks of discomfort at the treacherous turn the conversation had taken before Nigel broke the awkwardness with a broad, mirthful smile and waved for a page to bring more ale. "My, but you are suspicious tonight, Evard." He slapped his hand firmly on the older man's shoulder. "Your hasty assessment of my loyalty wounds me to my core, old friend."

Evard's face slowly relaxed, and he chuckled at Nigel's quip.

After the page made his way around the table filling each cup, Nigel raised his tankard in the older knight's direction. "I drink to your health, my good friend, for your ghastly pallor troubles me much."

Nigel had just put the cup to his lips when a woman's shriek sounded from the gallery above the hall. All heads turned upward.

"Fire!" she screamed, pointing wildly over her shoulder toward the chambers. "The village is afire!"

The hall erupted in angry war cries as the baron's retinue scrambled to their feet, toppling benches as each man readied for a long-anticipated confrontation with the raiders.

Beside Raina on the dais, her father rose from his chair, his expressionless face ashen. Within moments, Nigel was standing before them, smiling with the devil's own triumph. "Will you give the order now, milord? Before the bastard makes further mockery of your rule?"

"Aye," the baron consented tersely. "Assemble the men. Assemble them all!"

With a jubilant call to gather arms, Nigel dashed from the hall, followed by a good number of the baron's men.

"And ready my mount," the baron called after him. "This battle I shall fight myself."

Raina placed her hand on her father's arm. "Papa, please, don't go. Let Nigel and your men meet these raiders. They are younger, more suited to fighting than you. Please, I cannot bear the thought of your meeting with harm."

"Nor can I bear the thought of any ill befalling you— the very reason I intend to see this bedevilment ended tonight. Don't fret, child. You'll be safe enough here in the keep with my guards."

Raina could manage only the weakest smile as he placed

a kiss on the back of her hand. Then, with a swirl of his mantle, the baron stepped off the dais and crossed the hall to the bustling courtyard where his men awaited their lord.

Raina's chest soon resonated with the clatter of horses' hooves as her father and his army crossed the drawbridge that separated Norworth Castle from the village at the base of the great motte. She chewed at her lip as the cries of the men grew increasingly distant. Unable to stand not knowing what lay beyond the protection of her home, she hurried to the keep stairwell. From the chambers abovestairs, the height of Norworth's tower would give her the best view of the village and the fate of her father and his men.

From his vantage point on a hill just a furlong west of Norworth Castle, Gunnar watched as more than two score men thundered out of the curtain wall and down the hill to the burning village below. They called a battle cry, brandishing their weapons, some carrying pitch torches to light the way. From the number of departing soldiers, Gunnar adjudged the baron had dispersed most, if not all, of his garrison to combat the raid.

He smiled.

While he would have battled the entire retinue to get to d'Bussy, he was no fool. It would be a much easier task if the baron's defenses were weakened.

He had not expected d'Bussy to allow his holdings to be pillaged for so long without retribution, but now that he knew the extent of the baron's cowardice, he intended to use it to his advantage. The diversion had worked, and now it was simply a matter of breaching the castle and locating the baron.

He would likely find the yellow swine cowering in his bed, and it was the first place he intended to look. With the anticipation of what would soon come to fruition, Gunnar spurred his mount and made his way to the postern gate of

Norworth Castle, where two of his men should have already secured the door and would be awaiting his arrival.

With a lighted taper in hand, Raina entered her father's chamber, padding across the dark room to the shuttered window. Frustrated after trying to peer from the small window in her bedchamber, she had decided to come here, to the window that afforded the best view of the village. As she drew back the wooden shutters, her breath caught in her throat.

The orange glow of fires stood out starkly against the darkness of the night sky. Black smoke rose in great billowing clouds to fill the air with the stench of burning grain and thatch. Even from her perch at the window, a fair distance from the village, the sounds of distressed villagers and knights shouting orders carried on the wind to reach her ears with horrific clarity. Closing her eyes, she prayed in silence for a peaceful end to the terror that now gripped them all.

Footsteps approaching from the far end of the corridor interrupted her private intonation.

As the chamber door opened, a gust of air breathed in from the open window, snuffing her candle and throwing the room into darkness. Pivoting on the ledge, Raina gazed at the large and menacing silhouette of a man that now filled the width of the doorway.

At the sight of him, the hairs on her arms and the nape of her neck rose, her body sensing the danger before her mind had the chance. She didn't dare speak, instead prayed the darkness had concealed her before he happened to spy her in the window. Clinging to that salvation, Raina abandoned her candle and rose very slowly, inching her way toward the shadowy corner.

The man took one wary step into the room, then froze. Raina sensed him scanning the darkness, and she held her breath, though she feared he could easily hear the wild thrumming of her heart. A throaty chuckle broke the silence, and the chamber door gently closed. The deep whisper that followed sent a tremor down her spine. "So we meet again, little lamb."

Dear God, it was *him*!

As he stepped farther into the chamber, Raina moved along the wall toward the door, her hands feeling their way over the cold stone as her eyes remained rooted on his menacing silhouette.

He stood in the center of the room now, his imposing figure softly illuminated in the column of dim orange light that shone through the window. He was dressed for battle in a chain mail hauberk, his great sword belted at his side. He wore no helm this night, his head concealed beneath the hood of a dark mantle. He turned in her direction, and though she could not see his features, Raina still felt the heat of his predatory glare.

There would be no escaping him, but still she had to try.

Taking a deep breath, she lunged for the door. Her hands searched out and easily found the cold iron latch. Terror fluttered into her throat as she curled her fingers around the metal ring to yank the heavy panel open. She might have screamed, but her voice was choked off as she was flung back into the room.

Stumbling forward, her hands out before her, she fully expected to hit the floor but instead collided with the side of her father's bed. The impact brought her facedown onto the mattress. She clawed at the ermine coverlet, struggling to move herself from Rutledge's reach.

"Where do you think to go, my lamb?" He seized her by the ankles and pulled her easily toward him with a low chuckle. Raina's heart pounded fearfully in her bosom as she felt herself sliding back into his clutches, she as powerless as the tide against the pull of the moon.

But she wasn't entirely defenseless, and she refused to give up without a fight. As he dragged her closer, Raina managed to turn in his grasp, flailing her hands wildly in the dark as she tried to fend him off. In her frantic struggle, she managed to dislodge his hood and felt his cheek beneath her hand. Instantly curling her fingers against the warm flesh, she raked her nails down his face.

"Saints' blood!" he spat, then yanked her to the floor with a mighty tug.

Raina huddled in the rushes, panting with fright, instinctively covering her face to ward off what was certain to be a violent retaliation. He gripped her wrists and she cried out as he hoisted her to her feet to meet his rage face-to-face. "Behave prudently and no harm will come to you," he rasped in a clipped tone. " 'Tis your father's blood I seek, not yours. Now, where is he?"

She refused to answer.

"Tell me!"

"I should rather die than let you near him!" she vowed, the bravery of her reply belied by her tremulous whisper.

"Do not be a fool," Rutledge returned, drawing a misericord from its sheath on his belt. "While I've no particular wish to spill your blood, do not think I am averse to doing so should circumstances demand it."

The blade's tip bit into her side as if to emphasize his meaning. She would likely die this night but vowed her death would not be in vain. She had to do whatever she must to keep Rutledge from her father. She had to alert the castle guards that Rutledge was within the fortress, spare her beloved father, no matter her fate.

Her only hope was to yell loud enough that the guards belowstairs would hear her. She opened her mouth, intent on screaming with all the strength of breath she could summon. She was vaguely aware of sound escaping her lips before Rutledge's hand gripped the back of her neck, pulling her hard against his chest as he covered her mouth with his, swallowing her scream in a crushing kiss. Raina's eyes flew wide open in response, her cry diminishing quickly into something akin to a whimper before he released her lips.

"Scream again," he warned, his eyes flashing in the dim moonlight, "and I'll silence you for good." He released her neck roughly, and she stumbled backward with the force. "Where is your accursed father?"

Her lips still burning from his harsh kiss, Raina was too dumbfounded to reply. When she didn't respond, Rutledge seized her shoulders and shook her. "Tell me, wench!"

"Never!"

"Damnation," Rutledge fumed, thrusting her away as he stalked to the window, all but forgetting her presence. Raina took the opportunity and bolted for the door. Frantically throwing it open, she stumbled into the corridor. But Rutledge came up from behind, wrapping one arm tightly about her waist as he clamped his hand over her mouth. "We will wait together for him," he whispered tightly. "And do not think to alert the guards, unless you crave death."

A man's voice carried up the stairwell from below. "Lady Raina?" A tense moment ticked by as Rutledge held her pinned and silent in the corridor. "Milady, are you unwell?"

Rutledge held a finger to his lips, his threat yet gleaming in his dark eyes.

Raina's heart sank when she heard the sound of men approaching on the spiral stair. Rutledge flew into action, dragging her in the opposite direction toward the narrow staircase leading to the postern gate. Her attempt to cry out a warning to the men was reduced to a strangled whimper by the massive hand clamped over her mouth.

She struggled against his iron hold on her. As he tightened his grip on her wrists, the hand on her mouth relaxed ever so slightly. Raina seized the opportunity to strike. Curling her lips back, she bit down on his hand, then screamed with all the breath she could force from her lungs.

Curses boomed from guards on the stairwell.

"Help me!" she called to them. Hearing their steps hasten, she pulled against Rutledge, who held fast to her left arm as he drew his sword from its scabbard.

Two of her father's men clambered to the top of the stairwell, the larger of them in the lead, sword drawn. His eyes flicked briefly to Raina as if to ascertain her condition. Would that he had kept his focus on her assailant instead, for in that instant, Rutledge heaved his blade with one hand and brought it down with a resounding clang.

"Nay!" Raina shrieked as Norworth's man dropped his blade, losing his balance at the top of the stair. He stumbled forward, bracing his hand against the step while the second man came up behind him, teeth bared, weapon raised. Rutledge deftly kicked the first man's sword out of his reach, then stepped on his hand, pinning him to the floor while he battled the second man over the knight's head.

Raina pulled against his hold on her arm, straining to reach the discarded weapon with her free hand. If only she could reach it! She knew she'd be no match for Rutledge, but she could prove a distraction, perhaps enough so that her father's men might have a chance to overtake him. She threw her weight into her sidelong lunge, wildly amazed that Rutledge was able to contend with both her struggles and the task at hand. Once more she jerked against his hold. Miraculously, he finally lost his grip on her wrist, and Raina fell to the floor.

The clash of swords rang behind her—once, twice— as Raina scrambled to the blade. Her hand closed around the leather grip, and she came to her feet, dragging the sword with her. She swung around to face Rutledge, the blade pointed downward, its sharp tip digging into the floor.

She gripped the hilt with both hands and hefted it up-ward, grunting with the effort. It scarcely lifted from the floor, then fell back with a clank. Mercy, it was so very heavy! She tried to lift it again with the same discouraging result.

The knight whom Rutledge had pinned at the stairs hissed for Raina's attention, his free hand reaching out to catch his blade. She glanced to the sword and back to him. He nodded impatiently. In a flash of wild hope, Raina crouched and shoved the blade across the floor toward him. It did not go as far as she had hoped, coming to rest halfway between them. The knight strained to reach his blade, wincing, his arm stretched long. It was no use; mere inches separated his fingers from the hilt, but it might as well have been a league. He grunted an oath, trying again to reach it.

At that moment Rutledge overpowered the second man, who stumbled backward, his sword sparking on the stone wall of the stairwell. Rutledge released the first knight's hand an instant before he planted his foot in the man's chest and kicked, launching him up and into the knight be-hind him. In a jumble of flailing arms and legs, both knights toppled down the stairs and out of sight.

Raina stood trembling, staring at Rutledge in mute terror.

He wasted not a moment, seizing her forearm. "I reckon there is one way to bring your father to me," he said, and dragged her behind him toward the postern stairwell.

All too soon they reached the secret gate at the back of Norworth's tower wall. Two armed knights waited beyond the door, turning expectantly as she and Rutledge exited the castle. Even in the darkness she could see their expres-sions register confusion at her presence. Rutledge offered no explanation.

"Bind her hands and feet," he ordered, pushing her

toward the larger of the two as he strode toward a great black destrier.

"Nay!" Raina cried as one man seized her hands and the other pulled a length of linen from his saddle pack. "Please do not," she pleaded, knowing her chances of escape were greatly hindered if she was bound. "I'll do whatever you say," she lied.

Rutledge mounted his steed and approached her, stopping near enough that she could feel the horse's heated breath. "Do you think me a fool, Lady Raina?" Rutledge asked, a glimmer of wry humor in his eyes.

Her refusal to answer seemed to further his amusement.

"I assure you, I am no more fool than yourself. And I trust you will understand why I must insist you be bound for what is sure to be a long and trying journey."

The large knight crouched to grip her legs as the other man wound another length of fabric round her ankles. Raina glared up at Rutledge, hoping the darkness did little to conceal her contempt. "Nay, you are no fool," she ground out. "You are a spineless, loathsome—"

"Bind the wench's mouth as well," he barked, his clipped tone filled with irritation.

His men hastily complied, and in moments Raina was sufficiently bound and gagged. She scarcely had time to wonder which of the three men would be her traveling companion when Rutledge reached down to lift her under the arms. She cursed him through her gag as he hoisted her onto his mount to ride before him.

Then he spurred the great black steed, and within moments Norworth Castle and the smoldering village at its base were little more than a faint light on an increasingly distant horizon.

Chapter Four

The angered roar that shook Norworth Castle nary an hour later was enough to raise the hair on the necks of man and beast alike. Women gathered up their children and hied to their chambers as the baron received word of his daughter's capture. Even the castle hounds made hasty retreats to the corners of the hall. The castellan, the man whose responsibility it was to guard the keep and its folk while the baron was away, had dispensed of his dreadful news and now stood before his liege lord wringing his hands as surely as the baron would soon be wringing his neck.

But as shaken and enraged as he was, Luther d'Bussy knew this was a time for calm. A time for reason. He could punish the man for his negligence once Raina was safe, and he took some measure of comfort in the fact that he would. The crippling initial shock of her abduction had begun to ebb, and now he needed to act.

"Remove him from my sight," the baron commanded in a low growl. With a glance, he beckoned his man-at-arms to his side. "I want parties dispersed to each corner of the land. I care not how many men it takes, nor how much time. I want my daughter found, and I want her found at once!"

The man acknowledged his orders, then turned to leave the hall to carry them out, passing Nigel in the arched entranceway. Nigel strode the length of the great room with haste and purpose, his blackened helm tucked under his arm. Soot and grime marked his face and hair, the acrid tang of smoke clung to his clothes, all evidence of the destruction Rutledge's men had wreaked on the village.

"The fires have been contained, milord," he said upon arriving at the dais. "I've set the villeins to salvaging what they can of the fields, but I fear we have lost a great deal of this winter's stores. Most of the huts will need to be rebuilt entirely, and I can only guess at the cost of—"

Baron d'Bussy silenced him with a wave of his hand. "Enough. I'll not be bothered with an accounting of such petty losses."

Nigel scowled. "Petty losses, my lord? Forgive me for saying so, but what this rogue has cost us is far from petty—"

"He's taken Raina."

Nigel's helm hit the floor, punctuating a sharp oath. "Nay! Damn it, nay!" He raked a hand through his hair and began to pace, agitated and nearly spitting with rage. "If the bastard so much as touches her, God help me, I'll tear him apart with my bare hands!"

When Nigel turned back to the dais, the baron saw the same rage he himself felt glittering in the young man's eyes.

"Why?" Nigel cried. "Why did we not see this coming? Where is the bloody castellan? I'll have his head!"

Feeling an odd sense of kinship with Nigel in this time of futility and helplessness, Baron d'Bussy rose from his chair and stepped down to place a hand on the knight's shoulder. "I've ordered a search in every direction, lad. We'll find her."

Nigel's hand was cold when he reached across his chest to grip the baron's arm. The two men's gazes met and locked. "I will find her, my lord. And this I promise you, as a man who treasures Raina nigh as much as yourself: I will see Rutledge dead for what he has done . . . to both of us."

With that, Nigel bent to retrieve his helm and departed the hall in a flourish.

"Godspeed, lad," the baron whispered as Nigel's hasty footsteps ticked down the corridor.

Perhaps he hadn't given Nigel enough credit in the past, the baron reasoned, watching him go. His concern for Raina's safe return was heartfelt, of that he was certain. In truth, Nigel's devotion to her well-being and happiness had been evident from the time they were children. Though it disturbed the old baron to think where that devotion might eventually lead—and he had told Nigel as much—the baron had to admit the young man had upheld his vow to keep a respectable distance. Now the baron could only pray that Nigel's ardent devotion would lead him to Raina before she suffered any further harm at Rutledge's hands.

Taking an abandoned flagon of wine from a trestle table, the baron retreated to the solitude of his solar. He had taken so much for granted and had never anticipated losing even a bit of what he enjoyed. Standing at the window in his private chambers, he scanned what remained of Norworth Village. Black smoke curled up from the thatched roofs of several huts and outbuildings while loosed chickens darted from the paths of working villagers. Many sheep and cows lay dead in the trampled fields while the remaining animals milled about uncontained.

Absently, the baron lifted his hand and brought the flagon to his lips. There he hesitated, smelling in the wine's heady bouquet a lifetime of anger and emptiness. Drink had taken so much of his youth, did he dare permit it to enter his life anew?

The pain of what he had forsaken bloomed before him so vividly, he nearly let the bottle fall from his grasp. But it was the numbing promise of inebriation that coaxed him past the old memories, and he tipped the flagon up and drank of it, heedless of the trickle that ran from his mouth to stain his fine silk tunic.

After so many years of abstinence, the wine seared his throat, burning a vaporous trail to his gut and providing a welcome—albeit, brief—distraction from the pain clutching his heart, nay, his very soul. The bitter heat brought on a spasm of coughing, but it soon ebbed, easing into a comfortable, warm mellowness the old baron had nearly forgotten existed.

How easy it would be, he mused, to douse his guilt in wine. How tempting the notion to drown in a drunken haze and escape his fear and guilt, if only for a few short hours. Another sip and he knew he would be powerless to stop himself from emptying the flagon entirely. Another taste and he would be lost again, perhaps for good. But what of it?

He had nothing left to lose. The baron caressed the flagon almost reverently, then chuckled aloud.

It was true; with Raina gone, nothing mattered. He had protected her from hurt and harm all these years, cherishing her, the only good to come from his wretched life. He had managed to bury the stain of his past misdeeds, keeping himself sober out of love for her. Out of fear of losing her, were she ever to discover the man her father truly was. And now she was gone.

Morosely, Luther d'Bussy stared into the flagon. He brought it to his mouth once more and drained it. He dragged his forearm across his mouth, coughing and wheezing in the wine's potent wake.

Bitter tears filled his eyes, burning like fire as the ache swelled in his chest and a gnawing guilt chewed at his heart. A rumble began in his belly and crept slowly up from within him to fill first his head, then the entire keep, with the anguished howl of a man who had lost everything.

* * *

A wolf bayed somewhere in the distance as Rutledge's mount plunged into a forest thicket with the other two riders at its heels. Raina felt each thundering fall of the beast's hooves, each stride jarring her to the bone so hard, she feared she would be thrown from the saddle. But every wild jolt was countered by Rutledge's firm hold about her waist, his thick muscled arm securing her to the wall of his chest.

Raina cursed herself for falling into his hands so easily. She should have died before she let him take her this way. The fact that he hadn't killed her only enraged her further, for that could only mean he intended to use her in some way to get to her father. She thought of her poor father, beside himself with grief at her being taken, knowing he would do anything to ensure her safe return.

That thought should bring her comfort, but it did not. Rutledge was likely counting on her father's devotion and would use it to his advantage. Despite her efforts to banish the thought from her mind, her imagination conjured all manner of examples, each one more horrific than the next.

She should be brave. She should wrench herself from Rutledge's iron grasp, no matter the outcome. Aye, in light of the outcome. The thundering steeds would surely trample her in the space of a heartbeat. If she were dead, Rutledge would have no bargaining strength, and her father might yet be spared.

She closed her eyes and concentrated on the relentless beating of the horses' hooves until it was all she could hear. The thrumming rhythm soon filled her ears and beckoned her to come. Holding her breath and praying for a quick end, Raina prepared herself to lunge from the saddle.

At that moment Rutledge pulled back on the reins, tightening his hold on her and slowing his mount to a trot as they passed beneath a canopy of branches and into a small clearing. The familiar jangle of armor and the impatient shuffling of horses drew Raina's attention.

A group of at least a dozen haggard men awaited, mounted and armed for battle. Most eyed her with mild interest; one man muttered something about "spoils of war" to the chortling appreciation of his companions. Rutledge's arm flexed against her stomach, but he wasted no time with greetings or explanations, instead barking out orders for some of the men to ride ahead while others were instructed to remain on watch for the baron's men.

Within moments they were off again, crashing through the bracken and over the dark countryside at an even greater pace than before.

Raina had no idea how long they had been riding, nor in what direction. Though she was exhausted, both physically and emotionally, she kept herself alert should the opportunity to escape present itself. She divided her waning concentration between fearing for her life and the practical yet impossible task of committing the dark landscape to memory as it sped by.

The moon mocked her, peering through the treetops as a great silvery orb, throwing light and shadow in every direction, creating form where none existed and masking what remained. Trees and hills, rocks and glades, blurred into amorphous nothingness with each stride of Rutledge's steed. The frantic beating of Raina's heart soon became lost amid thundering hooves and night sounds. Twigs snapped beneath them; branches reached out of the darkness with spindly fingers to tear at her gown and catch her hair as they passed. Naked fear and the chill of the night air raised gooseflesh on her skin.

Suddenly, with a lurching forward keen, Rutledge's mount bounded over the edge of a ravine. For the space of a heartbeat the air around them seemed to still, save for the unmistakable rush of water somewhere nearby. Raina hadn't realized they'd left the ground until the beast came down with a bone-jarring thud that crushed the wind from her lungs and dislodged one of her slippers on impact.

She felt Rutledge's powerful thighs grip the destrier as he urged it on along a mucky riverbed. All the while his heart thundered at her back, his breath coming fast and hot against her ear. He seemed to take the pounding in stride, while Raina could only pray for it to end before she was jostled to her death.

Though she imagined his backside must ache as sorely as hers, it wasn't until some time later, when the rosy hues of dawn began to seep through the pines, that Rutledge eased up on his mount. He reined in, slowing the snorting beast to a trot. Frothy sweat coated the destrier's neck and shoulders; its sides heaved with labored breaths. The saddle creaked as Rutledge leaned into her back and dismounted, then pulled her into his arms and set her on the ground.

Having been off her feet for so long, Raina could now scarcely feel them beneath her. At once her calves began to tingle in the most peculiar way, and her knees started to buckle. To her dismay and outrage, Rutledge reached out to steady her, his large hands circling her upper arms as if they were no more than slender twigs.

Then he released her and drew a small blade from his baldric.

Raina's shriek was only a muffled grunt behind her gag as she jumped backward and fell on her rump. Her skirt breezed up over her knees when she landed, but she did naught to cover her bare legs, her mind preoccupied with the weapon Rutledge brandished at her.

He glanced at the dagger in his hand, then chuckled. "Think you I would drag you all this way only to slit your throat here in this glade?" His expression grew serious.

"Come hither, girl." He held his hand out to her, palm up. "We haven't got all day, milady. Do you wish to be free of your bindings or nay?"

Tentatively, and half expecting him to lob off her hands at the wrists, Raina reached out to him, turning her face away lest she witness their loss. With a deft upward flick of his blade, Rutledge sliced through the linen ties, and they fell limp to the forest floor. Blood immediately raced to her hands, creating a dull throb of pain.

"As long as you obey me," he said, hunkering down to crouch at her feet, "you have no need to fear me."

His promise more resembled a warning, she thought, delivered as it was with his eyes narrowed and the knife pointed toward her face.

Raina's wary gaze followed the blade as one strong hand circled her ankle and he cut the bindings loose. Though the ties had fallen away, his grasp about her leg lingered, remarkably warm and unsettling, until he glanced up and found her staring at him, wide-eyed. Seemingly unable to mask his distaste for her, he released her ankle with a black scowl, then tossed her skirt over her knees in what appeared a hasty effort to hide her legs from his view.

He stood, holding his hand out to her with a look of impatience in his eyes. Raina accepted and he helped her to her feet, holding her close for the moment it took until her balance was righted. Her hands could barely close about his forearms, and when her eyes met his, she saw in them a wicked gleam—like that of a hungry wolf. At once she backed out of his strange embrace, balling her fists in her skirts and wondering how far she could get on foot.

"Do not think to flee, milady," he said as if able to read her thoughts. "You'll not get far before I catch you, and should I not, there are many others lurking in these woods who would prove to be far more worrisome to your well-being."

With that, he moved forward, reaching around her head

to cut away the linen gag. Before she knew what was happening, her face was in his chest and her nose filled with his scent. An arousing muskiness mingled with the tang of his chain mail and the faint smell of leather, creating an indelible stamp in her mind that would forever be him.

Raina stretched her jaw, rubbing at her chafed, raw lips as Rutledge sheathed his dagger. "W-where are you taking me?" she croaked on a dry throat.

" 'Tis none of your concern where. You have my word: No harm will come to you as long as you obey me."

"Your noblesse astounds," she seethed, "as does your arrogance if you truly expect me to heed your commands."

"Is that so? If I had the time, my lady, I should very much like to prove the substance behind my arrogance. As it is, I have other, more pressing matters to attend."

Without another word he reached out and grabbed her by the wrist, meaning to haul her after him, but Raina dug her heels into the ground, pulling against his grip.

Rutledge turned to look at her, obvious disbelief flashing across his features. He smiled wryly and gave her arm a yank. She skidded forward a pace but held her ground, lifting her chin.

"Stubborn chit," he grumbled as he moved toward her, catching her under the arms and heaving her over his shoulder like a sack of grain. The hoots and applause of Rutledge's men sounded the moment her feet left the ground.

"Show 'er who's in charge!" one man hollered.

"Seems the wench needs a taste o' yer blade, milord!"

Raina screamed her protest, kicking and pummeling his back with her fists, but if he felt her blows, he ignored them. He stalked away from the crowd of cheering men to deposit her on a cushiony seat of moss at the base of a large oak. Grinning down at her, he made to unfasten his mantle.

"W-what are you doing?" she gasped.

"You needn't fret, milady, I've no intention of ravishing you just now. We've stopped only to rest the horses." He dropped the cloak in her lap. "Sleep if you wish. We've still a long leg of our journey left, and you look exhausted already."

Raina kicked the woolen warmth away from her, preferring to freeze to death before she accepted any token of his consideration. Besides, his offering of comfort was likely just an ill-concealed attempt to put her off guard, to dispose of her, if only for a short time, so he could discuss his plans without her notice. Nay, she refused to so much as entertain the idea of sleep, no matter how tempting it might be. Never would she turn her back or close her eyes while in his treacherous presence. She trusted her glare to communicate her feelings about the notion.

Rutledge shrugged. "Suit yourself," he muttered, stalking away from her to tether his mount to a tree next to the other horses.

"Despicable brute!" Raina called after him. "You are dead! Do you hear me? When my father catches up with you—and mark me, he will!—you are dead!"

Amused laughter rumbled from his retreating form, and she thought she heard him say he was already dead.

Chapter Five

Nigel led his band of half a dozen men through the woods surrounding Norworth and onward, following only his instincts. He rode like a man possessed, ignoring the shrieks of his destrier as he jabbed his pick-spurs into its sides, ignoring the pleas of his men to ease off that they might conserve their mounts' stamina.

All Nigel could hear was his future fluttering away on Rutledge's heels. What filled his ears were the sounds of his mother cackling as she told him he would never amount to anything. That he was a bastard born and a bastard would he die. Nigel had refused to accept it then, and he refused to accept it now.

Raina was his best hope of gaining lands and the title he so deserved. That thought alone gave him strength, urged him on throughout the night and into the next morn, when he was given a small reward for his troubles.

They had stopped at a stream to water the horses and gather a few hours' rest when one of the men came bounding out of the bracken, shouting with alarm. He held his sagging chausses with one hand, clutching an object in the other and waving it over his head.

"Ho, Hubert!" called a knight standing beside Nigel. "What have you got there, a wee snake?"

Nigel's eyes narrowed, his focus narrowing on Hubert. "Nay, fool, not a snake," he snapped, recognizing Raina's slipper wagging in the knight's pudgy hand. Several angry strides and Nigel was at his side, snatching the slipper from the beaming knight with an impatient snarl.

"Ready the horses!" he barked, clutching the slipper to his chest, nearly giddy with relief.

It was clearly a sign, a confirmation that he had been guided here for a reason. God, it seemed, was smiling upon him for once in his life. He was on the right path, and Rutledge couldn't be far.

As his men hastily mounted, Nigel pictured his glory at bringing the fair flower of Raina back to Norworth, with Rutledge's head on a pike. Averse as he was to taking another man's leavings, Nigel would make exception when those leavings carried with them the promise of a dowry as generous as Raina's. With her safe delivery home, the baron would surely grant Nigel whatever he asked.

How ironic, Nigel thought, that in capturing Raina, Rutledge had given him an opportunity he would never have gained through his own machinations. Nigel did not even attempt to contain the broad grin inspired by that notion. He had waited far too long to let all of that simply slip through his fingers.

He crushed the slipper in his fist, then cast it into the mud before dashing to his mount and calling for his men to follow as he sped along the riverside.

Raina sighed heavily and drew her knees up to her chest, clasping her arms around them. They had been sitting in the glade for more than a couple hours, based on the position of the climbing sun, now nearly midsky. She calculated that she had been awake for an entire day, and her patience was waning with each passing moment.

Rutledge's men had nodded off long ago, snoring and making other more disgusting noises before settling into heavy slumber. He, on the contrary, remained awake and as alert as a spring falcon. His ears caught every snap of every twig; each rustle of the smallest forest creature quickly captured the attention of his keen eye. Nothing, it seemed, would escape his notice.

Raina attempted to study him from the relative safety of her position beneath the tree, but each time she dared to cast him a sidelong glance, she met with his steely gaze. After the third time, she decided it best to avoid the temptation and focus her attention elsewhere.

Though the air was warming with the day's progression, the ground of the forest floor was damp and cool beneath her derriere and her bare foot. Raina's gaze slid ruefully to her remaining slipper. Blood from the Norworth guards who had fought to protect her spattered the pale wool felt, a bitter reminder of Rutledge's evil doings.

She shot an angry scowl in his direction, only to find him still watching her intently over the rim of his cup. His gaze dropped to her bare foot, and suddenly feeling exposed, she tucked it under her skirts. "Is it entirely necessary for you to stare at me in such broody silence?"

"I merely wonder if you considered the consequences of your actions."

She balked at his attempt to toss blame in her direction. "I'm sure I have no idea what you speak of, sirrah."

"Truly? Then tell me why you hid your foot just now. Did you think I'd not notice the absence of your slipper?"

Raina frowned, unsure of his meaning.

" 'Twas a clever idea, I'll grant you, but you'd do well to pray your clue goes unnoticed."

"My clue?" She let out an exasperated sigh. "You are mad." When he scoffed, Raina leaned over her knees and hissed, "My slipper is missing through no scheme of mine. It fell off when you nearly killed us diving into a ravine."

He chuckled. "You play the role of innocent fairly well,

my lady. Your father no doubt would applaud your performance, for 'tis clear the fruit indeed falls close to the tree."

She ignored his slight, refusing to let him goad her. "You profess to know a great deal about my father."

"Aye, I know more of him it would seem than you do, based upon your foolhardy display of devotion at the tourney."

Raina bristled. "My father is a great man!"

"He is many things, but none of them great. And he who would slay an innocent woman is no man."

"You are a liar!"

"Am I?" His brows rose in challenge. "How can you be so certain, my lady?"

"My father is a good man. *You* are the knave, the rogue who would torture and slay a harmless old man."

Rutledge's gaze followed his thumb as he traced the rim of his cup. His voice, when he spoke, was soft, thoughtful. "Harmless old man, you say?"

"Aye!" Raina cried, desperate to appeal to any sense of reason that might lurk behind his dark eyes. "If only you would give him a chance, talk to him, you would see that I speak the truth. Whatever crimes you believe him guilty of, I swear to you, my father is incapable. He is pious and tenderhearted." She ignored Rutledge's bark of sardonic laughter and vowed, "I would wager my life on his honor."

On hearing that, his gaze lifted and leveled on hers. At first she thought he might be considering her plea—she hoped he was—but the twist of his lips was cruel. "Wagering your life on him would make you the veriest fool, my lady. A dead one at that."

"He is all I have, damn you!" Raina blurted, feeling hot tears prick her eyes before they spilled over the rims and down her cheeks. "He's all that I have."

With a casual flick of his wrist, Rutledge cast the contents of his cup into the bushes and came to his feet. "Then I pity you, my lady."

Raina buried her face in her hands, refusing to cry in his presence, refusing to give him the satisfaction of seeing what he had reduced her to. She took deep, ragged breaths to calm herself, trembling as she swallowed past the lump in her throat and dammed her tears with sheer will alone.

A faint rumbling vibration that started beneath her bare foot provided a distraction, and she lifted her head, coming to attention at the same time Rutledge's sword rasped out of its scabbard. In the next instant, a rider called out, waking the other knights, who hurriedly jumped to their feet. Rutledge sheathed his weapon as his man rode into the clearing.

"Riders spotted less than a league south, milord," the man announced, his breath heavy from exertion.

"How many?"

"I marked seven, and they're riding hard. Following the river."

If Rutledge was concerned, his countenance did not betray him. His gaze slid to Raina, piercing her with its accusing iciness. "Is d'Bussy among them?" His unmistakably hopeful tone sent a shiver down her spine.

"Nay, no sign of the baron."

Raina did not even attempt to contain her sigh of relief. Her reaction did not escape Rutledge, though he but smirked, then looked away.

"There's no use trying to outrun them," he said to his men. "We're better to conceal ourselves here and let them simply pass through unaware. Then we'll head due north. 'Twill be a longer ride, but one I warrant they'll not be eager to take. I know of a place we can stay for the night."

"What do you plan to do about her?" one man asked as Raina slowly came to her feet, gripping the rough trunk of the oak to steady herself.

Rutledge moved before her in a decidedly protective stance. "She is mine to do with, Burc. Concern yourself with hiding the horses, why don't you?"

The knight glared at him but said nothing as he and another man untethered the mounts and led them deep into the forest. Their steps faded and Rutledge turned, coming to her side.

"I warned you once to follow my orders if you wish to avoid bloodshed. Now we shall see how well you listen." Taking her by the arm, he pulled her into the bushes with him. Then, with military precision, he dispatched his men to various locations at the periphery of the glade with instructions to hold their attack unless he gave the order to strike.

"And if they spy us, milord?" a knight armed with bow and arrow whispered.

"Kill them."

Rutledge's cool command sunk into Raina's brain as the search party's leader came into view. One glimpse of the close-cropped blond hair and her heart plummeted.

Nigel.

Chapter Six

Raina held her breath as Nigel rode straight into the center of the clearing, flanked by three armed men on either side of him. They scanned the surrounding area as they passed through, even glancing up into the treetops as if they might be set upon from above.

Nigel's white destrier bore the evidence of a ruthless ride. Foam oozed from its mouth as it tossed its head, coughing and working against the bit. Sweat glossed its neck and legs; drying blood from overzealous spurring stained an otherwise flawless coat. The other horses had fared only slightly better, all of them looking close to collapse, as did the men.

Raina wanted to call out to Nigel, to warn him of the trap, but Rutledge's threat echoed in her ears. If she made her presence known, Nigel and his men would be killed. Mentally she pleaded for them simply to ride through, and with haste.

At the horses' approach, a small rabbit darted from the bracken and across their path. Startled at the sudden movement, Raina drew in her breath, but the simultaneous nicker of a destrier masked the sound. At least she prayed it had.

Nigel cooed softly to his mount as he reined it in. A couple of the other men followed his lead, drawing up and circling round to Nigel's side.

"What is it?" one man mouthed.

Nigel shook his head once, holding up his hand for silence. He cocked his head to the side and listened for a long moment as his man peered about the glade with a puzzled expression. Then Nigel's blue eyes narrowed, and he looked to the very spot that concealed Raina and her captor.

Dear God, had he spied them?

Raina's gaze slid to Rutledge to gauge his reaction. He gripped her arm tighter, his eyes never leaving Nigel. Without a sound, the man beside Rutledge drew his bow taut, prepared to let fly on command.

A tense moment passed in deadly silence, save for the frantic, helpless beating of Raina's heart.

Nigel frowned, then slowly lowered his hand. "Mayhap 'twas nothing," he said, though Raina detected the wariness in his tone.

"Aye," his man agreed, glancing over his shoulder. "Likely but a trick of the ear, I warrant."

"Aye," Nigel conceded, his right hand coming to rest on the hilt of his sword, "a trick."

A bird twittered nervously, taking flight in a rustle of wings and disturbed leaves. Several moments passed before Nigel's expression relaxed. "Press on," he commanded with a curt wave of his hand. "We've got to reach them before dusk if we stand a chance of finding her at all."

The two knights urged their mounts forward, trotting to catch up with the other riders, who picked along the periphery of the clearing. With a final lingering glance about the glade, Nigel gathered up his reins, then clucked to his horse, directing it onward in an easy, albeit guarded, stride.

Soundlessly, Raina exhaled her pent-up breath, watching Nigel's back as he made his way past them toward the edge of the clearing. Relief washed over her in a gentle wave as

Rutledge's man slowly lowered his arrow. As he did so, his knee came down to rest on the forest floor.

And a twig snapped under his weight.

The brittle pop echoed in Raina's ears like a mighty clap of thunder, seeming to ricochet off the trees until the air filled with the sound. In that blurry instant, Nigel yanked the reins of his stallion, pulling the beast back on its hind legs. It neighed, pawing the air as Nigel's yell went out to his men to hold. Wheeling the horse around, he drew his sword.

A bowstring drew taut, then sang as an arrow flew from the bushes.

"Nay!" Raina cried, vaulting to her feet. "Nigel, 'tis a trap!"

No sooner had the words left her lips when the arrow struck its mark, lodging in Nigel's left shoulder. He screamed in agony and Raina winced, though she knew not if her pain was more from the sight of Nigel's suffering or the tight hold Rutledge now had about her upper arm.

With a firm tug, he cast her to the ground and drew his sword. "Stay there!" he commanded, lunging from the bushes and into the fray.

Raina scrambled to her knees as the clearing erupted in a vicious clash of men and horses. A blurry hail of arrows came from behind trees and between bushes, instantly dropping two of Nigel's knights. Then one of Rutledge's men fell to a Norworth sword, and another. Raina tried to find Nigel or Rutledge amid the carnage, but both were lost in the crowd of fighting.

A movement behind a tree drew her attention, and she knew instantly that Nigel was hiding there. Rutledge knew it, too, for at that very moment he headed toward the spot, his sword raised high.

Raina shivered at the foreboding figure he cut as he stalked forward, one fist wrapped about the hilt of his sword, the other clenched in a tight ball at his side. His focus seemed to be on Nigel, and Raina knew for certain he would slay him before her very eyes. Just as in a short time to come, he would slay her father as well.

It was all too horrible to bear!

She wasn't even aware that she had left her spot in the bushes until she was at Rutledge's side, clutching the bloodied arm of his tunic. He stopped, looking down at her with a complete absence of any emotion. "Please!" she cried, searching for mercy in those fathomless eyes. "I beg you . . . please, spare him."

Rutledge's stormy eyes held her gaze for the longest moment, searching, probing. Then his knuckles softly grazed the line of her jaw. "What price such blind devotion?" he whispered as if for her ears alone.

Stunned by the intimacy and the lingering danger in his touch, she pulled away from it. He smiled vaguely, then brushed past her to face Nigel, leaving Raina quaking where she stood. She kept her back to him, not daring to watch what might transpire.

"Come out, coward, and face me as a man," Rutledge's voice boomed from behind her.

"I am wounded," Nigel called back weakly.

"Saints' balls! Are all the men of Norworth born without spines?" Rutledge taunted. "If I wanted you dead, you would be. Show yourself, man. I would have you go and take a message to your lord."

"What message?" Nigel queried warily, the rustle of leaves announcing his movement from behind the tree.

"Tell him the Lady Raina has pledged me her life in exchange for his honor."

Raina's breath caught in her throat. The scheming blackguard! "You have twisted my words!" she cried, spinning on her heel and meeting with Nigel's disbelieving expression.

Rutledge regarded her over his shoulder. "Do you wish to rescind them, milady?"

Damn him, he was testing her, trying her loyalty and trust. Raina caught her lip between her teeth; then, with icy conviction she replied, "Nay. I stand by my word. Will you?"

A grin tugged at the corner of his mouth. "You have my word." Turning to Nigel, he announced, "Tell d'Bussy I am willing to put his daughter's vow to the test. Should he meet me in ten days' time, alone and without his army, I will release the girl unharmed. But should his honor prove false when we meet, or should he send guards to seek me in the meanwhile, Lady Raina will forfeit her life."

Nigel snarled, "Curse you, Rutledge! She's an innocent girl! I implore you, free her to my care, and I give you my word as a knight that the baron will meet you . . . on your terms."

Rutledge's chuckle was sharp and surely meant to insult. "I have no use for your word. My interest is in d'Bussy alone. If he fails to appear on the appointed day, I shall consider it a testament to his lack of honor and his daughter will pay."

"God rot your black soul if you so much as muss her hair—"

Rutledge laid his hand heavily on Nigel's wounded shoulder, drawing a pained hiss from him. "You're in no condition to make threats. We could settle our differences here, but I prefer a more sporting challenge. Rest assured, our time will come. Go now, and tell d'Bussy we will meet where it all began. He will know my meaning."

Nigel glanced at Raina, then back to Rutledge. "I'm not leaving without her."

"The lady has begged me spare your life, man, but I do so only because I can use you elsewise. Try my patience a moment longer and you force me to devise another means of conveying my message to your lord. Doubtless your corpse would prove an equally convincing statement."

Raina stepped forward and Rutledge stopped her with a glance. "Nigel, go!" she pleaded. "He will keep me no matter what you do." She leveled a scathing glower on Rutledge. "Without me, he knows he stands no chance of getting close enough to my father for his evil intent."

"Your lady is wise, Nigel. I suggest you heed her." He motioned to one of his knights. "Fetch these men a horse." The man nodded, then dashed to retrieve Nigel's white stallion. "Nay," Rutledge called to him, "not that one. A less spirited mount will suffice."

"Son of a—!" Nigel sputtered as the man brought forth one of the more sorry-looking beasts. "This nag will take twice as long to make the trip back to Norworth!"

"Then best you be on your way at once, for the both of you will be riding it."

"What nonsense is this?" Nigel demanded, color rising to his face.

"Merely a reassurance that you carry out my orders and not give in to the temptation to follow us. This way you should have just enough time to return to Norworth and get word to d'Bussy."

"Thieving bastard." Nigel's gaze slid from Rutledge to Raina and lingered as he regarded her for what she supposed could very well be the last time.

"Do not worry for my sake, Nigel," she said, trying to soothe his regretful expression. "Tell my father that I love him and I will see him soon."

Nigel seemed to look right through her, then said to Rutledge, "Mark my words, I will see that you pay for this . . . with your life."

"I have already," he remarked dryly.

In a matter of moments, Nigel and the other knight were mounted and on their way. Tears filled Raina's eyes as she watched Nigel depart. She sniffed, wiping at them angrily as leaves crunched behind her and she felt Rutledge draw near.

"Tears, my lady?" he queried softly. "Pray, tell me, not for him."

Raina glared up at him, anger thickening her voice. "Aye, for him! And all the others your evil has touched, you heartless knave!" To her outrage, her shoulders sagged under the weight of his level stare. She buried her face in her hands, weary with fatigue and feeling altogether helpless and alone.

It took a moment for her to realize that Rutledge's hand had been smoothing her hair, now coming to rest lightly on her shoulder. She looked up at him, horrified that she should have allowed him to touch her, to comfort her. She jerked her shoulder from under his palm. "Never lay your hands upon me again," she seethed, mustering all the venom she could. "I've no need for your brand of consolation."

"I reckon you'd rather let that coward Nigel comfort you; is that it?"

She crossed her arms over her chest. "I'd rather you killed me as soon as touch me."

"Well, then, I shall bear that in mind, my lady, should the urge strike again."

He started to walk away.

"Bear this in mind as well, scoundrel," she called after him. "The day you are dead shall be the happiest day of my life! I vow I shall shout with glee to hear the news."

Spinning on his heel, he stalked back to her in two long strides. "And what then, my lady? Please, do not deny me the whole of your wishful fantasy. Will you wed Nigel? Bear the rotten fruits of his loins?"

At that, her hand shot out to strike him, but he caught her firmly by the wrist.

"You defend him," he said quietly, "and yet he took little convincing to abandon you to your fate."

"It would seem you gave him little choice!"

"He had a choice . . . and he made it. Think on that when next you see him." He released her arm and with a gentle brush of his thumb flicked a tear from the tip of her nose. "Waste no more of these on Nigel—or your father—for neither is deserving."

Cursing herself for trembling under even his merest touch, she struggled to find her voice, holding fast to her anger. "How can you speak of worthiness? What honor can you claim?"

His brow creased. "None at the moment, my lady. As I told you at the tourney, 'tis honor I seek."

"Nay," she whispered. "You seek vengeance. You'll find no honor in that."

He seemed to consider her comment for a moment. "Perhaps not," he conceded, "but that I must find out for myself. So it would seem you are right. I have no honor. However, noble intentions aside, my lamb, had the tables been turned, *I* would never have left you in the hands of someone like me."

Raina's cheeks flamed as she looked up into his face, which at the moment seemed to reflect no mockery, no malice. It was an honest remark, and one that left her shaken, unsettled. Without another word he simply turned and strode away, leaving her to stare after him in shock.

He beckoned a man to his side with a crook of his finger. "See to this mount's wounds and tether it behind me for the ride north. Tell the others we leave at once." He turned back to Raina with a courtly sweep of his arm. "After you, my lady."

Chapter Seven

The woman had spirit; Gunnar had to credit her that. But she was also tired, and the hours she had now been with him had done their share to batter even her hardy constitution. He supposed it was fatigue more than willing surrender that made her tread after him in silence, obeying his order to remount with nothing but a withered glare in his direction.

He pulled her up onto his destrier and had her ride before him, securing his arm about her waist and holding her closer than needed as they rode out of the clearing and onward to what was to be their evening's shelter.

As the land stretched out before them and time dragged on toward dusk, Gunnar fought a desperate inner battle to ignore the closeness of his unexpected captive, concentrating instead on plotting his next move. To his consternation, however, the only move he could envision at the moment was bedding the woman who, with every stride of his mount, bounced innocently against his fast-tightening loins.

The airy silk of her bliaut ruffled in the wind, occasionally leaping out to brush his wrist and arm. Her braid had since fallen out completely, leaving her hair fragrant and billowing against him. Her narrow waist nestled against the crook of his elbow, and he was powerless to prevent the image of its delicate curve from forming in his mind.

She was a fascinating abundance of temptations, each one too fine for a man like him.

Spurring his mount, Gunnar angrily thrust the notion aside, telling himself it was the night wind and not her hair that smelled so deliciously of roses and honeysuckle, that the heat of anger and not the blood of a vixen warmed her skin, searing his hand.

When her body finally relaxed against him and her breathing deepened in weary sleep, curiosity won over duty. Like the thief he had been forced to become, Gunnar casually moved his arm from about her waist until it rode under the buoyant fullness of her breasts, stealing the opportunity she would surely never grant him. Then, breathing deeply of her scent, he closed his eyes against her softness, telling himself that the core of her appeal surely lay in the simple fact that he needed a woman.

Badly.

Wynbrooke lay cloaked in the inky blackness of midnight as they approached the ruined castle and nearly deserted village, but evidently the sight was still enough to make Raina's breath catch in her throat. Gunnar had felt her come awake sometime earlier, though she hadn't found cause to speak until now.

"Where are we?" she gasped, her thready voice filled with wariness.

He supposed it was an eerie, awesome sight on first glance—even in darkness—but it had been a long time since Wynbrooke had set his blood to ice.

At first he might have felt some trepidation, some dread upon looking at what remained of his home. He had, in fact, visited this place often to remind himself of why he was alive, his purpose on this earth. Countless times he'd come here and simply stared out from the shadows at the rubble and the desecration; a silent, contemplative observer, never approaching the keep, never making his presence known to the handful of people who remained in the village.

But for many years now, the sight of Wynbrooke did not shock him. It did not move him. Like the years of battle and staring death full in the face, this no longer had the power to disturb him.

And so, when Raina asked, "What is this place?" he answered her with complete lack of emotion: " 'Tis your father's doing."

He clucked to his horse and led his band of men forward, deliberately skirting the sleepy cluster of ramshackle, wattle-and-daub huts as he and the other men rode up the hill and through the open gate of the crumbling curtain wall.

Wynbrooke, being a modest keep, had just one bailey, a wide grassy courtyard where as a boy, Gunnar had chased chickens and later, young girls his age. A small stable flanked the far side of the bailey, Gunnar recalled; now all that marked its existence were a few charred timbers and blackened stone. The mews were gone; the great hall was nothing but rubble—everything sacked or burned. Only the tower keep remained standing. The place he had once called home was an abandoned and lonely pillar of thick gray stone.

Standing in the shadow of that grim monument, he felt Raina shiver in his arms and vaguely registered his men muttering under their breath about sleeping in a tomb. For an instant he felt a chill sweep over him. Night air, he reasoned, and dismounted without comment. He turned and gathered Raina into his arms, setting her on her feet before unfastening a rolled blanket from behind his saddle and handing it to her.

"Secure the horses in here for the night, then find yourselves a place to bed down," he ordered his men, taking Raina's hand and starting with her toward the keep.

"You can't mean for me to sleep in this ruin." Her voice was pleading as she shuffled behind him, scarcely able to keep up with his long strides.

"You'll be safe here." He reached for the iron latch on the door, only to realize that the great oak panel had been smashed off its hinges. The blackness that greeted him at the top of the stone stairs was merely a yawning portal to a dank and musty room.

A bat took flight as they crossed the threshold, flapping over their heads and out into the night. Another quickly followed. Raina's startled yelp echoed in the cavernous chamber, and she buried her face in Gunnar's arm until the tiny creature had passed.

"Come," Gunnar ordered softly and guided her farther inside, using a thin sliver of moonlight that shone in from a crevice to help him find the spiral stairs leading to the chambers above. He held Raina's hand tightly as they mounted the steep, circling steps, trying to batten down the queer tremor that began a steady rise in his chest with each advancing footfall.

Unbidden images sprang to life in his mind: the grating rasp of d'Bussy's sword, the wicked laughter, his mother's crumpled body, and the blood. Jesu, the blood. Grinding the heel of his palm into his brow did nothing to ease the pain throbbing there nor the guilt that chewed at his conscience.

"P-please," Raina whispered from behind him, "I don't wish to stay here."

His lips curved wryly and without humor in the dark. "The idea holds little appeal to me, either, my lady, but I reckon 'tis the safest place for us to stop and rest for a few hours."

They crested the stairwell and Gunnar stalked toward the first chamber, his footsteps heavy under his purposeful gait. A sheen of sweat beaded his upper lip and brow as he neared the entrance, dread clutching his heart almost as strongly as Raina now clung to his hand.

"Wait here," he said, and moved to stand before the threshold, clenching his fists at his sides and steeling himself against what he might find within.

The door was slightly ajar, ironically so, as if the last occupant had departed quietly, without disturbance. He reached out to place his palm against the iron-banded oak panel, cursing himself for the way his hand was shaking and at the same time thankful for the darkness that concealed it from Raina's view. With little pressure the door creaked open on its ancient leather hinges.

Gunnar's gaze swept the room in quick assessment, and he let out the breath that until now he hadn't realized he'd been holding.

A cool wash of moonlight filtered in through open shutters on the window of the far wall, and with it came a lazy night breeze. He breathed in shallowly, surprised to find the air carried no smells of death or fire, only the fragrant perfume of summer.

In the pale moon glow, Gunnar could see that the rough-hewn plank floor had been cleared of old rushes, all evidence of the destruction that had visited here thirteen years ago seemingly scrubbed clean. His father's armor coffin was gone; his mother's distaff and spindles too. The stone walls of the chamber, which had once been warmed with colorful tapestries and the Rutledge banner, were now barren. The brazier was emptied of its ashes and long unused, home now to an industrious spider that had laced the hollowed opening in the far wall with an intricate web. The large bed in which his parents had slept was the only furniture yet remaining in the room, though stripped of its bolsters and straw mattress, it was now little more than a dust-covered, wooden frame, too cumbersome to have been removed from the keep.

But the room did not seem looted. Someone who must have cared for his parents had removed all traces of d'Bussy's desecration. And Gunnar was fairly certain he knew who it had been.

Turning to regard Raina over his shoulder, he beckoned her forward with a curl of his hand. She stepped out of the darkness and to his side without argument, evidently preferring even his dubious companionship to being left on her own in the corridor. They entered the room together, Raina so close behind him, he could nearly feel the press of her breasts at his back, her breath coming rapid and shallow against his skin.

He heard her footsteps halt near the center of the room as he made his way to the open window and peered out over the courtyard below. The men had already started a fire and were gathered around it, drinking from their flasks and chewing on chunks of dark bread.

"Are you hungry?" he asked idly of Raina.

"Nay."

That quick, firm denial was betrayed by a tiny growl of her stomach. Gunnar turned from the window and started slowly toward her. She stood unmoving, staring at him expectantly, fearfully, and clutching the rolled-up blanket to her like a shield. Despite the balminess of the summer air, she was shivering.

Gunnar passed in front of her and drew his blade to clear away the cobwebs from the fireplace. "You can make your bed here, by the hearth," he directed. "Perhaps while I'm out I will find some kindling to make a fire."

"You're leaving me here? Alone?" This last word she fairly gasped, in what sounded to him like utter disbelief.

"Aye," he replied, sheathing his weapon. "But don't think you'll be able to slip away while I'm gone. I shall be sending one of my men along to watch this door in my absence."

She took a hesitant step toward him. "Where are you going?"

"I've a bit of business to take care of," he answered with deliberate vagueness, and moved for the door. All at once, he felt her capture his hand between hers. He froze, stopping dead in his tracks.

"Please." She clutched his fingers with desperate tightness. "Don't leave me here." She took a small breath, her voice naught but a whisper behind him. "I'm frightened."

That naked admission shocked him almost as thoroughly as the feel of their hands, so incongruously entwined together. Where was the hellion who had claimed she'd rather die as soon as look at him? What had happened to the virago who had put herself between her father and Gunnar's blade without so much as batting an eye?

He whirled on her, heated and ready to pose those very questions to her himself.

Looking into her close, upturned face was a mistake, he realized too late. Even in the darkness he could see her rosy lips, parted slightly and trembling, looking too damned soft for his peace of mind. Her eyes met his, wide and beseeching under the delicate wing of her brows. Inexplicably, he longed to trace his hand over the smoothness of her cheek, the graceful line of her throat. Longed to touch her hair, sift the silky tresses through his fingers, and feel her body pressed to him in a soothing embrace.

And for a moment he was tempted to stay.

But what he had to offer her wasn't comfort, and it had nothing to do with allaying her fears.

"God's wounds," he muttered, his anger directed more at himself than her. With gruff aggravation, he extracted his hand and scowled at her through the darkness. "Stay put and no harm will come to you."

With that, he pivoted on his heel and quit the room,

slamming the door behind him in his haste to be away
from her before he changed his mind about leaving.

Raina regretted her words the moment they left her lips,
and Rutledge's irritated response only furthered her humiliation. Why she thought his odious presence would be
a comfort to her, she didn't know. If she truly felt even half
the loathing for him she'd attested to in the woods, she
would have welcomed his absence. She certainly would
not be listening to his departing footsteps, nor positioning
herself in the window that she might watch as he crossed
the bailey to his group of men and called for one named
Cedric to post guard outside her door. Raina scowled,
staring after his retreating form as if to bore holes in his
broad, arrogant back as he mounted his destrier and rode
out of the bailey and into the night.

With him gone and nothing left at which to direct her
ire, Raina reluctantly returned her attention back to her
temporary sleeping quarters. Mercy, but it was a dark and
depressing cell, devoid of life and not much better than the
rest of this ruined and forgotten keep.

'Tis your father's doing.

Rutledge's words as they had arrived came back to her
like a splash of cold water: startling, confusing. Chilling.

She had no misconceptions that her father—like any
baron of his day—was at times forced to wage war and
seize fiefs in the name of his liege. But this keep had seen
more than war. This place, with its mass of destruction and
absence of life, had been more than conquered. It had been
obliterated. Why?

Weathering a chill that spread from her limbs to her
heart, Raina came away from the window and moved farther into the room, searching fruitlessly for something
with which to light a fire in the brazier. The room was suddenly too cold, too dark.

Raina hated the dark.

It made her think of her mother, made her relive endless days as a little girl spent outside her parents' bedchamber, listening as her mother wept, alone in that large cold room, door bolted, shutters closed, heavy curtains drawn around the bed, refusing food, refusing comfort. Refusing to admit anyone into her bouts of private despair, including her only child.

Darkness, to Raina, meant an early autumn day in her fifth year, when she had been trying on her mother's jewelry and heard her parents returning home early from a tourney. She'd scurried into the garderobe and closed the door, standing silently in the cool, dark compartment. She'd heard their voices, filled with anger and growing louder as they ascended the stairs to their chamber. She'd heard the door slam, heard the hatred in her mother's seething accusation: "I am no fool, Luther! I know what you've done! For pity's sake, he was an innocent man!"

Her father's voice was desperate, pleading. "Margareth, my love, don't you understand? If I am guilty of anything, 'tis only of loving you too dearly."

A clatter of pottery hitting the floor punctuated her mother's hitching sob. "Don't touch me! You're a monster, Luther! A black-hearted, jealous monster, and I despise you more now than I ever did!"

Raina could still hear the loud crack of a hand striking a cheek and the deafening silence that followed, though to this day, she wasn't sure who had delivered nor who had received the blow. That evening, after declining supper and retiring to her chamber with a pot of honeyed mead, her mother had taken ill.

By morning she was gone, and her father, enraged and distraught, rode out that very day with his army in tow.

The argument she had overheard never did make much

sense to Raina, and fearful to admit she had been eaves-
dropping, she'd never had the nerve to question her father
on what was clearly a painful, private matter.

And now she had to face the very real possibility that
she might lose him, too. Weary and full of dread, Raina
curled up in Rutledge's proffered blanket and gave in to
the impulse to cry. Sometime later, in the hours that passed
during his absence, she drifted off to sleep.

Seated at a trestle table inside a musty waddle-and-daub
hut, Gunnar drank from a cup of wine and stared into the
flames of a now glowing brazier positioned at the center of
the single-room living space. The warm, orange light illuminated the lined and aged face of the man sitting across
from him, infusing fiery color into the healer's long white
mane of hair and chest-length beard.

"I know this is not the first time you've been here,"
Merrick said, filling Gunnar's empty cup for the fourth or
fifth time in half as many hours.

"Oh?" Gunnar prompted mildly, the wine having mel-
lowed him into a comfortable lethargy that even this surprising admission could not rattle.

"Aye." Merrick nodded. "I saw you once in the woods
several years ago, and again, this past spring."

"You didn't approach me."

"Nay . . . I could see from the look in your eyes as you
stared up at the keep that you had no wish to be seen."
Merrick drained his cup, then let out a wheezy sigh. "And,
as well, I knew one day you'd come to me, when you'd
had time enough to work out your hatred and begin living
again."

Gunnar pursed his lips and looked deep into his cup,
preferring not to meet the old man's wizened gaze and
suddenly glad he hadn't divulged his real purpose for stopping at Wynbrooke for the night. Merrick, a God-fearing,

gentle man, hadn't understood Gunnar's unquenchable need for vengeance then; he certainly wouldn't understand it now.

"And," Merrick continued, pushing himself up from his seat to lumber across the room, "because I knew you'd return, I saved this for you."

As the old man reached for a simple pottery container and emptied an object into his palm, something inside Gunnar suddenly clenched tight as a bowstring. His chest felt constricted, heart thudding heavily beneath the crush of wary anticipation as Merrick returned to the table and began to unfold a small square of fabric.

"You had this near you when I found you that day," he said as he produced a thick band of gold that embraced in its center a bold, bloodred ruby.

Staring at his father's signet ring, Gunnar felt the color drain from his face. Palms sweating, he clenched his cup so tightly, it should have crumbled in his fist. Damnation, how many times had he cursed himself over that ring? First for having been given it by his mother, for her thinking him worthy, for entrusting it to his care ... and then for his losing it as a result of his failure. His cowardice.

"Take it, lad," Merrick prompted when Gunnar could only stare at it mutely. "I reckon I should have given it to you all those years ago, after you'd healed well enough and I sent you north to live with my brother at Penthurst." He shook his head slowly, frowning in pensive reflection. "But you were so full of anger then, so consumed with thoughts of revenge, I feared this ring might only add fat to the fire. I had hoped the rigors of farm life would give you a means of working out your rage, but nothing seemed enough to cool your hatred.

"My brother thought me crazed for sending you to live with him," Merrick continued. "A demon, he called you: black-hearted, drinking to excess, seeking out new fights before the bruises and scrapes from your last had healed. I waited to hear that you had died, certain you would meet your end in violence, but that news never came. Then, some seven years ago now I reckon, my brother sent word that you had left Penthurst, sobered up and simply walked away. 'Twas the last I heard of you until you came through these woods a few years past, and now here you are before me again. Seeing the man you are today makes me glad I kept this ring for you. Take it now, my lord. It belongs to you."

Gunnar wanted to pitch the ring across the room, forget he'd ever seen it. More than anything, he wanted to cast away the obligation that accepting the ring again as a man carried with it. Instead he took the precious memento from Merrick's outstretched hand and curled his fist around its weight.

I will avenge you, he silently vowed. *I* will *make you proud.*

"It shames me to admit it now," Merrick said, "but often I wondered if I had made a grave error in coming to your aid that day. If perhaps my brother was right, that you might have been better off . . ." He cleared his throat suddenly. "Bah! Foolish talk from a foolish old man, eh?"

He chuckled, but Gunnar knew there was more truth than jest to Merrick's statement. He had been a danger to everyone around him then. Perhaps he still was. But something *had* sobered him that year he left Penthurst, something that made him realize with sudden, potent clarity the folly of blind anger and unrestrained violence.

He had been drunk, brawling in a tavern with another man over some nameless, faceless woman he'd just met. In fact, the woman had little to do with Gunnar's desire to fight. Something in the way the man looked at him—the way he carried himself—reminded Gunnar of d'Bussy and left him with an instant, overwhelming urge to tear the knight to bits, with or without cause. The man had the poor judgment to wink at the whore on Gunnar's lap, and it was all the excuse Gunnar needed. He flew into action.

He was so caught up in his misplaced rage that he didn't hear the tavern fall into a hush a few moments later as a nobleman entered with his entourage. Nor did he hear the wager placed against him while this nobleman enjoyed his meal just a few paces from the brawl. It wasn't until the knight lay beneath him, bloodied and begging quarter, that Gunnar was able to still his punishing hands and quell his anger. He heard the jingle of a purse full of coins hitting a table, the scrape of a bench, the slam of the tavern door.

By then it was too late.

Someone clapped him on the shoulder and thrust a tankard at him. " 'ere, this one's on d'Bussy."

Gunnar spun around, certain he could not have heard right. "Wha—"

"Baron d'Bussy," the tavern keeper confirmed. "Said ye looked to 'im like a man with a death wish and 'e wagered against ye. Twelve deniers 'e lost to me. Wasn't any too 'appy to forfeit his coin, I can tell ye that—"

But Gunnar wasn't listening. He shoved the tankard away and ran to the door, throwing it open and dashing out into a driving midnight rain. He was too late. The hoof-beats of d'Bussy's riding party were distant, scarcely discernible amid the storm. His enemy had been within arm's reach and now he was gone. An opportunity missed, perhaps never to be realized again.

In that moment the rage-filled animal Gunnar had been was swiftly brought to heel. Now it was a distant memory, a beast kept under tight rein, for to be enraged meant to feel, and to feel meant to be weakened, to be vulnerable to error. And so Gunnar no longer felt anything. Emotional numbness was his master now.

At least that was what he repeated in his head, over and

over again, as his father's signet ring bit into the flesh of his clenched fist.

Merrick was staring at him when Gunnar finally looked up and met his gaze. His tone had turned reflective, sympathetic. "Losing your family, your home . . . it could not have been easy for you, particularly at so young an age."

It hadn't been. But Gunnar didn't want to think about that now. He didn't need a reminder of the weak, sniveling boy whom d'Bussy had met at Wynbrooke that day, or the fool who had let him slip through his fingers not once but twice: in the tavern and then again at the tourney. "The past is . . ."

He was about to say the past was over, but in truth, it was far from over. It wouldn't be until d'Bussy's life was over. "The past is the past," he amended briskly, then downed his cup of wine in one gulp and pushed away from the table, ready to take his leave.

Merrick sent him off with a large wedge of cheese and a loaf of bread for his journey come the morn. Seeing his father's ring had suddenly sobered Gunnar, so he accepted the old man's offer of a skin of wine without a moment's deliberation. It wasn't until he stood up that he realized that despite his mental lucidity, his body had had its fill of drink.

On uncustomarily wobbly legs, Gunnar bade his thanks and farewell to Merrick, then untethered his destrier. With a bundle of kindling wrapped in his mantle and strapped to his mount, his cache of viands tucked under his arm, and the ring safely hidden in a pouch fastened to his baldric, he rode back up the hill to the keep and his waiting captive.

Cedric was awake and came to his feet without a sound when Gunnar reached the top of the keep stairwell. Of the dozen men in his employ, Gunnar found Cedric to be among the most dutiful, never failing to carry out an order, where others—and one in particular, by the name of Burc—seemed to take exception to every command he issued when it did not directly serve their interests. Cedric was the only man with him at the moment in whom he would have entrusted Raina's custody.

"No trouble?" Gunnar asked.

"None, milord." The tall, kindly-faced knight lowered his voice to just above a whisper. "I heard her snufflin' soon after ye sent me up, but she's been quiet as a mouse fer hours now."

Dismissing his man, Gunnar opened the door and entered the chamber, closing the panel behind him and stepping inside with surprising stealth, given his current condition. Raina, curled up on his blanket like a babe, slept undisturbed as he crouched down before the brazier with his gathered kindling and watched her from the corner of his eye.

Her sleep had been restless; he could tell from the way her bliaut had twisted and worked its way up her legs, baring her pale, delicate ankles and the supple curve of one shapely calf. Her single, discarded slipper lay off to the side of her makeshift pallet, and Gunnar marveled that even her feet were lovely, slender and fine-boned like her hands, which were pressed together and tucked under her cheek.

Her serene expression made her look to him like an angel in repose. So lovely, so innocent. So unlike the demon who had sired her. He could almost see how a woman like this could gentle a man. How a proud, loving daughter like her could temper even a man as evil as d'Bussy.

D'Bussy.

Damnation, but his thoughts should be on the man, not his tempting daughter.

Scowling furiously, Gunnar lit the fire and sat back on

his haunches, jaw clenched as he stared into the rising flames.

He should have left the woman. Saints' blood, what was he thinking in capturing her? Granted, she was his best, most certain means of getting close to d'Bussy, but would that she had been a hag, a soured, mean-spirited wench, and not this . . . lamb. Would that she had been anything but this strong and beautiful woman who had intrigued him from the moment he first laid eyes on her. Bewitched him with a pure and simple kiss at the tourney. Tempted him now, even in sleep.

Gunnar cursed silently, raking an angry hand through his hair. He had to remember his mission, had to remain focused. Had to distance himself from her and remove his distractions, beginning with the one that had been vexing him from the moment he'd received it.

Unfastening the drawstring of the leather pouch tied to his baldric, Gunnar withdrew one of the two treasures secreted inside, one that had proved nearly as troubling to his peace of mind as the token Merrick had returned to him this eve. But whereas his father's ring was heavy and cool, this prize was whisper soft, light as a feather and the precise color of a pale blue summer sky.

Gunnar brought the swatch of silk to his face, tempted to feel it against his skin as he had done privately, guiltily, in the nights that followed the tournament. Before he had the chance to torture himself with the pleasure once more, he crushed the fabric in his fist and released it into the brazier, turning away as the flames caught its edges and quickly devoured it.

He placed the satchel of bread and cheese beside Raina, along with the wineskin, then took his place at the wall opposite her, propping his back against the stone and resting his elbows on his drawn-up knees. A weariness settled in his bones almost immediately, weighing down his shoulders and dragging his chin to his chest, beckoning him toward sleep.

The nightmare started the moment his eyes drifted closed.

Chapter Eight

Raina awoke to the soft hiss and snap of the fire, and the yeasty aroma of bread and smoked cheese wafting over from somewhere near her head. Drowsily, she opened her eyes to mere slits in the quiet, dimly illuminated chamber, watching as the blaze cast flickering shadows on the wall. A draft of air from the window across the room fanned her backside, the coolness racing up her legs a clear sign that her skirts, bunched up and twisted around her knees, no longer covered her from view.

Rest had not come easily, she recalled, and wondered how long she had been sleeping. How long Rutledge had been away and where he had gone. She knew he was in the room now, could feel his presence even before she heard the deep breathing of a man sound asleep.

She rolled over to face him and sat up quietly, her body stiff and achy but not too terribly kinked, thanks to Rutledge's blanket spread beneath her. He slept sitting up, his back pressed to the wall near the window, his thick forearms propped on his knees and his chin slumped into his chest. He hadn't made personal use of his mantle; it lay next to the hearth with a small bunch of kindling atop it. He must have started the fire, too, and left her the supply of food and a skin of wine.

How hospitable, she thought, for a kidnapper. Lord, she hated to accept any more of his kindnesses, scant as they were, but she *was* hungry. Dreadfully so. She cast a side-long glance at the bundle of food and clutched her growling midsection.

Just to quiet the noise, she reasoned, unwrapping the pack. She broke off a corner of the cheese and stuffed it into her mouth, chewing the chalky morsel as she tiptoed to the window and, pressing herself flat against the wall, peered over the ledge to where Rutledge's men had posted camp. Not a one moved, all of them snoring like some strange, nocturnal chorus.

An anxious quiver sent her heart racing.

Good heavens, she was nearly afraid to think it . . . nearly afraid to hope. With everyone asleep, she could escape! Thwart Rutledge's horrible trade by simply walking out the door and riding off on one of the horses. Back to Norworth, back home to her father.

Seizing the opportunity, she crossed the chamber on light feet and stopped at the door, reaching for the iron latch and ready to take her flight when Rutledge's voice rumbled from behind her.

"N-No . . ."

It was a groan more than an order for her to stay, but nevertheless, her hand stilled. Her feet stopped moving. The murmured entreaty came again, this time louder, more pained. Slowly, Raina glanced over her shoulder.

Rutledge's head had lolled onto his shoulder, his eyes closed, but his brow was pinched, his mouth alternately quirking and grimacing. He drew a sharp breath and his body jerked. This time his voice was an anguished whisper. "Please . . . oh, God, nooo . . ."

Catching her lip between her teeth, Raina turned away from him at once, squeezing her eyes closed and trying not to feel a bit of sympathy for him. If he suffered from night terrors, let him. They were likely born of his own cruelty and certainly no concern of hers. Her only concern should be getting as far as she could from this hateful, slumbering monster and back to the haven of her father's arms.

Steeling herself against the troubled sounds of Rutledge's thrashing, his distressed moaning, Raina curled her fingers around the cold metal ring on the door and opened it. Behind her, his breathing had become labored, panicky.

Go, her mind pleaded. *Go and forget him!*

A moan turned to a strange-sounding whimper, then: "Nay, Mother! Oh, God, nay! Mur-murderer . . . *d'Bussy.*"

Raina couldn't move. Dieu, she could scarcely breathe! She stood stock-still in the doorway of that chamber, heart thudding, stomach clenched in a tight ball. Mercy, but even in his dreams he accused her father of murder. It simply could not be true! But the pain, the terror in his voice were undeniable.

It was impossible simply to walk away from it.

Hesitantly, she pivoted on her heel, and when her eyes lit on him, she was powerless to stop the wave of sympathy from crashing over her. This behemoth of a man, this heartless warrior, now lay there crumpled against the wall, a sheen of sweat glistening on his brow, bested by a bad dream.

Abandoning her plan to escape and cursing herself as a fool for doing so, Raina stepped back into the chamber.

The images flew at Gunnar in rapid succession behind his closed eyelids: the rumble of siege; terrorized screams and thick, black smoke drifting up from the bailey and into the window of the chamber; heavy, booted footsteps coming to a halt outside the door, followed by an order to open it; his mother's arms around his shoulders in a protective embrace, her steady heartbeat at his back as she whispered soothingly that everything would be all right, that he should not be afraid.

God, but he was afraid! Gripped with terror and so very, very frightened. But still he moved out of her arms to pick up his father's heavy sword, trying to ignore the aching strain of the weapon in his small hands.

And then the chamber door burst open.

Garbed in chain mail and armed for war, Baron Luther d'Bussy stood at the threshold, smiling malevolently as he swiped back his mail coif, his red-rimmed eyes ablaze with murderous intent.

"My lady, you insult me," he drawled. "I come to offer my condolences for the loss of your husband, and you greet me with locked gates and barred doors." The baron pinned Gunnar with a chilling blue gaze. "Now, what am I to make of this?"

"Leave us be!" Gunnar cried. "As lord of Wynbrooke, I demand you go!"

Even now, in his sleep, he felt the rush of anger, the impotence of his threat. D'Bussy had merely smiled—then, and in the thousand nightmares since—hooking one side of his mantle around the shiny hilt of his broadsword. "You are no lord," he said. "You are a child, and a pitiful weak one at that. *I* am lord here. Your father was my vassal, and now that he is dead, you, your mother, *and* Wynbrooke are mine to do with as I please."

And the baron had issued a challenge: "You want to kill me, do you not, boy? Aye, you want to shred me to ribbons." He chuckled, spreading his arms wide. "Come, then, test your mettle."

As happened nearly every night since that fateful day, Gunnar met the challenge, each time hoping he would indeed run the tyrant through, bury his sword deep in the baron's rotund gut and watch as he fell to the floor in a quivering, bloody heap. But his dreams were never any more kind than reality had been: He charged d'Bussy, heard his mother cry out from behind him, felt the swipe of the baron's mail-covered arm and the sudden, surprising weightlessness of his father's weapon, then heard the humiliating clatter as it fell to the floor.

Within moments the baron's men had Gunnar restrained, captured in a guard's crushing embrace as the baron advanced and withdrew a small dagger.

"Not only are you weak, but stupid, too," he said on a sour cloud of spiced wine. "Mayhap a reminder of your foolishness is in order."

Bravely, his mother rushed forward to his defense. "Nay!" she cried. "Please, milord, do not harm my son!"

With a smile that said the interruption was merely a postponement of their confrontation, the baron turned away from Gunnar. "I did not come with intent to harm, Lady Eleanor. Quite the contrary. I've come to offer you a place in my home . . . as my wife. You see, my own dear Margareth departed her life just yestermorn, through a dreadful misfortune." The baron heaved a sigh. "Poisoned herself, the silly, hopeless creature."

Gunnar's mother gasped, bringing a hand to her mouth, but she couldn't hold back her broken sob. It was no secret that the two women shared a fondness for each other.

"You should take my coming here as a great compliment, Eleanor," the baron continued. "Despite my own sorrow, I am thinking of you, of your welfare."

She scoffed bitterly. "Would that you had thought of my welfare before you murdered my husband—"

"Murdered? Nay, Lady, 'twas your husband's error that killed him. Your blame should rest on him, not me. For a skilled warrior, he made a careless mistake."

"Do you forget, Baron? I was at the tourney. I saw with mine own eyes how my husband fell. He made no error, save trusting your sense of sport."

The baron's voice was thin, lethally soft. "Have a care that you do not make his same mistake, my lady. I am growing weary of our game and would have your answer now. Do you come with me willingly or nay?"

"Never."

"Have you any idea what I am offering you?" the baron questioned incredulously. "Any inkling of the privileges you would have as my wife?"

"They pale in comparison to their price," Eleanor had answered, and a guard cleared his throat, not quite masking his chortle.

"Your sharp tongue doesn't suit," the baron hissed. "However, 'tis a malady I'm certain can be corrected with time . . . and discipline."

Gunnar saw the defiant tilt of his mother's chin, heard himself moan in anticipation of what was to come.

Nay, Mother!

"As you corrected Margareth's maladies, Baron? I suspect she preferred an agonizing death to the life she endured under your heavy hand—"

"Bitch!" d'Bussy spat, recoiling his arm and striking Eleanor with his gauntleted fist so hard, she crumpled to the floor.

Oh, God, nay!

Gunnar bucked against the man who held him, and somehow broke free of his hold. He charged the baron, empty-handed but ready to tear him apart for hurting his mother. D'Bussy turned, drawing his sword from its scabbard.

Gunnar froze, his gaze transfixed on the arcing blade as the glint of polished steel split a ray of sunlight and blinded him. He sensed movement beside him, then felt the vague, fleeting caress of silk on his face. Time ceased as the blade fell in a smooth, sweeping motion. His mother's cry for mercy echoed in the small chamber . . . and fell forever silent.

Murderer!

The baron had laughed upon seeing Gunnar's mother lying at his feet in a pool of blood, the short bark of amusement and disbelief raising the hair on Gunnar's nape and jerking him into action. He should have lunged for the baron, should have fought with all the rage he felt, battled on to his death. Instead he ran, gave in to his fear and fled like a coward, leaving his mother there, alone.

D'Bussy.

He would make him pay . . . make him sorry . . . make him dead.

Aye, he thought.

Make him dead.

Gunnar heard his voice curl low and deep around that comforting idea, and he came awake at once, righting himself to a sitting position with his back against the wall. His eyes flew open and met with the troubled gaze of his captive, blinking at him from much too close a proximity for his liking.

"What are you staring at?" he growled.

"You were having a nightmare," she said softly, moving away from him as if she had just awakened a viper. "You—you said my father's name."

"What of it?" he replied with icy dispassion, but inwardly he cursed himself for falling asleep and letting her witness the effects of one of his frequent night terrors. It shamed and enraged him that he could not control his thoughts while he slept, plagued him to no end that d'Bussy came back to haunt him night after night in vivid detail, leaving him awash in sweat and sometimes out of his bed and thrashing on the floor by the time he roused. He ground the heel of his palm into his temple in an effort to chase away the headache blooming there. God only knew what he'd said or done during this episode. Damnation, and in front of *her*, no less.

"How you must hate him."

Gunnar scrutinized her, looking for a trace of mockery, any hint of amusement caused by seeing him at his most vulnerable, his weakest state. But the soft gaze looking back at him held no sarcasm, no malice.

"Aye," he answered at last. "I do."

She pressed her lips together, busying her hands with a loose thread on her gown. "I'm sorry," she whispered. "I'm sorry that you believe my father capable of such horrid acts . . . and I'm sorry it pains you so."

Something stabbed him in the chest, nearly driving the air from his lungs and leaving him dazed, startled. Shaken. All at once he realized that sharp-edged something was an emotion—feeling for another person that seemed so foreign to him, so rusty with disuse.

Affection.

He felt it looking at her now, seeing her sympathetic expression, hearing the queer sadness in her voice. And the very idea that he felt anything but disdain for d'Bussy's daughter enraged him to death.

"Damn it, I don't want your pity!" he barked, his clashing emotions making his voice sound all the more savage.

She frowned. "But I—"

"And I don't need your concern!"

With that, he came to his feet and grabbed his mantle from the floor, upsetting the kindling, which scattered at his feet. He could not stay here—with her—another moment. He needed to be home, where he was in control. Where he could lock her away and damned well forget about her until it came time to trade her for her father.

"We're leaving!" he commanded, stalking across the room when she stood up and blinked at him in confusion. "Gather up that blanket and the food and come with me. Now!"

She bolted into action, snatching up everything and

scurrying past him through the open door and into the corridor. "I despise you." She turned to face him at the top of
the stairs, her voice thick, her eyes glistening with unshed
tears. "I should have left—"

She stopped abruptly, catching her lip as if she'd just let
out a secret, and Gunnar suddenly realized that the chamber
door was wide open—as it had been when he'd awakened
from his nightmare. He scowled, puzzled and more than a
bit annoyed. God's wounds, she could have easily escaped
while he slept!

She could have gone . . . and yet she'd stayed. *At his side*.

"Aye. You should have, my lamb," he agreed softly,
wishing now with every fiber of his being that she had.

Rutledge had obviously tired of her presence and had
no wish to share his saddle with her. After gruffly directing his men to their mounts, he made Raina ride Nigel's
stallion, tethered to his own black steed. He spared her
neither a word nor a glance in the hours that stretched on
into dawn, acknowledging her only when she pled a moment's privacy to relieve herself.

With dark, hooded eyes, he watched as she lumbered
back out of the bracken, Cedric leading her by the elbow
as if she would actually consider fleeing on foot. She met
Rutledge's intense stare with one of her own, marching to
her mount and refusing Cedric's offer to assist her up into
the saddle.

She failed in her first attempt, her cumbersome skirts
and bare feet no great help in mounting the big destrier.
Of course Rutledge's unflagging observance of her didn't
help matters either. She tried again, stepping into the
stirrup and hefting herself up with a grunt of exertion.
Surely not the most graceful of acts, but grace must fall
second to pride, she reckoned and flung her leg over the
beast's broad back. Settling into the saddle, she shot Rut-

ledge a withering glare and hiked up her chin. He merely chuckled, turning about in his saddle to lead them forward once more.

Mercy, but she loathed the man, she really did! Staring at the back of his head for what seemed hours, Raina decided to amuse herself by counting his many flaws, beginning with the most irksome. First on the list was arrogance, and he had been gifted with an abundance of that. He was also stubborn and prideful, overbearing and broody, morosely serious and short on patience most of the time, and, lest she forget, possessed of a grossly inflated sense of his own appeal.

His raven hair was too long and wild, his features much too sharply hewn to be pleasant. He scarcely smiled despite the fact that his teeth were enviably white and straight, and even though he had provided her with meager amenities when they'd stopped for the night, she doubted he had a charitable bone or a pinch of kindness in his body.

His body.

Here she struggled to find fault, save that he looked strong enough to snap her in twain with his bare hands, big enough to crush a woman if he had cause to lie down upon her. An image of him, prone, atop her sprang to her mind, and with it came a sudden heat that crept into her cheeks and spread to points shamefully lower. *Stop thinking about his body,* she silently admonished herself, and went back to her list. Rude, bullying, arrogant—had she already used that one?—maddening, infuriating, despicable . . .

The sight of a small tower keep looming off in the distance cut short her musings and spared her the irritation of soon exhausting what she had thought to be an endless inventory of Rutledge's shortcomings.

At his signal the riding party broke into a canter, drawing closer to the keep. While the men other than Rutledge hooted their greetings to the handful of soldiers posted on the battlements, Raina quietly took in the sight of what looked to be her captor's lair. Morning had just begun to peek over the horizon, painting the sky in rosy pastel streaks and haloing the squared tower and its aged, crumbling curtain wall with a warm, welcoming glow. A fine mist blanketed the ground at the base of the castle's craggy hill, lending an ethereal quality to an otherwise modest abode, in need of repairs and tucked away in a quiet, forgotten corner of the north country.

The land surrounding the keep sprawled out before her in a breathtaking mix of yellow and white wildflowers, patches of pale indigo heather and lush, green grasses—everything kissed with dew and sparkling in the early morning light. This place was so different from the bustle and noise of Norworth. It was peaceful here, tranquil and undisturbed. Not at all what she might have expected of Rutledge's home.

Her prison, she amended quickly, tamping down any further fanciful notions before they had a chance to take root. This inviting land and its cozy-looking keep were naught but illusions, like Rutledge himself had proved to be. Acting first as her protector, then her champion, before his true, dark nature had been revealed at the tourney. If she were clever, she would be looking for means of escape, not romanticizing what was likely stolen property, confiscated through the rogue's misdeeds.

Before she had a chance to consider flight or any other method of escape, the group of them ascended the hill and rode through the yawning portcullis of the gatehouse, into the bailey. That the old iron grate was operable surprised her, but it was, and it rattled closed on their heels, the resounding thump of metal hitting earth irrefutable testimony that her hopes of escape now lay trapped on the other side.

While his riding companions walked their exhausted

horses to the stables, Rutledge hung back, letting them move on before he turned to Raina. " 'Tis not Norworth by any means," he said, "but I trust you'll not be too uncomfortable here."

Raina smiled weakly with surprise, thinking his observation sounded curiously like an apology. Before she could consider the notion any further, a lanky youth appeared from around the corner of the keep, his straight, coppery hair cropped at the shoulder and hooked behind his ears.

"Greetings, milord!" he shouted, racing forth enthusiastically to take Rutledge's reins as he dismounted. "Did you meet with success, milord? Spare no detail, I beg you! Is the blackguard baron dead at last? Did he squeal when you stuck him, like the swine he is?" The lad's questions came one after the other, his voice brimming with ardent— if not morbid—interest.

Raina gasped, appalled. "For mercy's sake! What barbarism have you taught this boy?"

As if he had just noticed her, the youth's green eyes lit on Raina, and a flush filled his freckled cheeks.

"Alaric," Rutledge said, "this is Lady Raina, the blackguard baron's daughter." He was trying to hold back a grin, but Raina could see the amusement in his eyes as he came toward her and pulled her from the saddle. "She will be in my charge for the next several days."

"D'Bussy's dau . . ." The youth's narrow face flamed a deeper red. "Begging pardon, milady," he said with a quick, respectful bow, then smiled shyly and took her mount's reins. "We've never had a guest at the keep."

Rutledge cleared his throat. "Whether or not the lady shall stay on as our guest remains to be seen, Alaric. Cease your gawking now and go water these horses before they perish of thirst."

Dipping his head and murmuring a hasty "Aye, milord,"

the boy exited to carry out the order. Halfway to the stables, he glanced back at Raina and nearly tripped in the process.

"My squire," Rutledge explained, nodding at the lad's retreating form. "His appreciation for female beauty is exceeded only by his fealty to me, so do not think to beguile him into your confidences."

"Beguile him?" Raina retorted, more angered by his implication than she was swayed by his compliment. She tread after him with little choice as he grasped her by the hand and headed toward the keep. "I was thinking no such thing," she insisted hotly, "and I'm growing quite weary of you and your ceaseless suspicions!"

From behind them someone let out a low, malicious-sounding chuckle. "The wench 'as a sharp tongue, lord. Too 'igh and mighty fer 'er own good, if ye ask me."

"I didn't ask you, Burc," Rutledge growled, turning and smoothly putting himself between Raina and the approaching man. This burly knight was the one she had caught leering at her several times during the ride from Norworth. He had seemed impervious to her glowering earlier, but now, under his lord's level glare, he flinched, unable to hold his gaze.

When Rutledge clasped Raina's hand tightly in his, ready to escort her into the keep, Burc's voice rose to a coarse, bitter challenge. "Ye promised us a good, bloody raid and all the plunder we could carry out of Norworth Castle. What we got was empty bellies, arses sore from days of riding . . . and *'er*." He inclined his head in Raina's direction, then as if an idea had suddenly struck him, he smiled—a discolored and decaying smirk bleeding through his unkempt beard. " 'Course, seeing 'ow she's all what we carried away, may'ap we all ought to take a piece of 'er!"

The other knights had come out of the stables just then and they chuckled, making jests of their own, though none matched the venom in Burc's suggestion. His face remained mirthless, his beady, porcine eyes trained on Raina.

"Touch her," Rutledge warned with icy calm, "and you die. Make no mistake, Burc. The same goes for any one of you men. As long as she is here, this woman belongs to me." His hard, stormy gaze flicked over his shoulder to Raina. "I protect what is mine."

With that, he pivoted on his heel and yanked her to his side, stalking across the bailey and up the short steps leading into the shelter of the cool, dark keep. He fairly dragged her past the great hall and up the stairwell, his grip on her unrelenting.

"I am *not* your property!" Raina fumed in a hot whisper, trying desperately not to stumble as she struggled to keep up with his long, purposeful strides.

He stormed down a narrow corridor and flung her into an open, empty chamber, slamming the door behind him with force enough to rattle her teeth. Two steps forward and he was standing before her, clutching her arms in his strong hands and nearly shaking. His voice, however, was calm and lethally soft, his issued order lacking any emotion whatsoever. "Never challenge me in front of them, never contradict what I say, do you understand?" At her mute nod, his scowl softened. "Men like those mercenaries belowstairs have no use for insolent females—particularly those of *noble* birth." His dark gaze held hers for a heartbeat, then slid away. "Neither do I."

He released her arms and eased off, his attention now focused on a battered pair of wooden shutters that hung askew on the chamber's only window. He walked past her and grabbed the iron latch holding them closed, gave it a yank, and made a surprised-sounding chuckle when it came off in his hand. "This place will likely come down around my ears one day," he muttered, tossing the rusty ring into the corner of the room before drawing open the shutters.

The fragrant summer breeze swept in and immediately masked the mustiness of the dank little chamber, which, Raina noted, was devoid of furnishings, save a ragged straw pallet and beside it a dented overturned chamber pot.

"You will stay here," he directed idly, "and rest assured, the lock bar on the door is fully functional. As I said before, my keep is humble when compared to your home, this chamber hardly fitting a lady of your status. However, we've had no past cause for concern. My squire told you true: We've never had a guest here." From over his shoulder he smiled wryly at her, lifting one wicked brow. "Willing or otherwise."

"Am I supposed to find that amusing, my lord?" she asked, peeling away the stiff moth-eaten blanket that covered her pallet and trying not to cringe at the thought of laying her head against the undoubtedly flea-ridden straw. She moved the chamber pot with her toe and cried out in fright when a beetle scurried out from underneath the battered vessel. With a hand to her breast to steady her fluttering heart, she caught her breath and fixed him with a steely glare. "Should I find humor in your imprisoning me in a cell unsuitable even for the lowliest castle hound?"

"Oh, nay, my lady," he replied. "And please, forgive my insensitivity. Mayhap you'd rather stay with me in my chamber? I would not require much of you by way of personal service, and I do have a large, comfortable bed—"

"Never," she vowed, sorry she had given him the chance to tease her. "I shall sleep quite contentedly with the fleas and the beetles and heaven knows what else lurks in this chamber. I daresay I'd prefer even vermin to your disagreeable presence."

One black brow rose in mocking challenge. "Truly?

Why, just last night you were begging me to stay with you. Is your memory so feeble that you've already forgotten?"

Curse him for bringing that up! Would that she could forget pleading with the insensitive brute not to leave her alone in that terrible skeleton of a keep. She needed no reminder of his impatient reaction to her fears, or her folly in not leaving him when she had the chance. "Have you not yet tired of harassing me? Surely you have more important matters to attend to than tormenting defenseless women."

His wry grin belied his urge to retort, but instead he simply said, "Indeed I do."

"Then I should thank you to leave and afford me some time alone. Surely 'tis not too much to ask."

"Time alone?" He chuckled richly and shook his head. "In my keep everyone has duties, including you, my lovely prisoner. As you seem less than enthusiastic about serving me in my chamber, I reckon I can match you with another role. Have you any skills?"

"Of course I do," she replied warily. "I can read and scribe, and embroider—"

"None of which would be of much use here, my lady; however, I'm certain Agnes can find work to keep you busy and out of trouble." He went to the door, opened it, and called for the woman.

Within moments she appeared, a squatty, rotund woman in what looked to be the latter part of her life. The creases between Agnes's graying brows seemed permanent, likely etched from a lifetime of hardships . . . or scowling, as she was doing now despite Raina's attempts to set her at ease with a weary smile.

"Agnes," he directed, "I am leaving you in charge of my prisoner's daily duties. See to it she does not venture from your sight."

"Aye, milord," the old crone cooed, "it'd be me pleasure to take 'er under me wing."

Chapter Nine

Gunnar watched, more than a little amused, as Raina marched past him and out the chamber door. Agnes would see that Raina put in a full day's work, regardless of the fact that most of the morning was already spent. Tonight his captive would entertain no thoughts of fleeing or fighting, to be sure. If he knew Agnes, by day's end Raina would want nothing more than to lay her pretty head upon a pillow and collapse until sunrise.

A twinge of conscience needled him when he considered her assigned quarters. She was right; the chamber was hardly fit for a beast, let alone a lady of gentle breeding. Neither was his bedchamber, for that matter, but he hadn't actually expected she would take him up on his offer to share it with him. He felt a strange mix of relief and disappointment that she had declined with such vehemence, however.

He didn't know why he found such enjoyment in stoking her ire. Perhaps it was that haughty thrust of her chin, the proud flip of her hair, or the tiny crinkle that formed between her brows when she was pensive or angry. Everything about her affected him in one manner or another, and it seemed he found something newly intriguing whenever he looked upon her. Which was often, he realized with no small amount of chagrin.

Whenever she was near, he found it next to impossible

to keep his eyes off her. But more maddening was the fact that he could not keep his mind off her even when she was away from him. Whereas his eyes could not drink in her every move and expression, it seemed his mind eagerly conjured her image, unbidden and unrelenting. God's wounds, but she was driving him to distraction!

He had to burn off some of his frustration. Needed a means to work out the kinks in his back—to say nothing of the tension mounting elsewhere. He'd been battling verbally with his tempting captive for days now; perhaps a spar of another form was in order, with someone more deserving of his wrath. He heard Burc's voice in the bailey, and with renewed purpose, he headed down the stairwell to organize a war game with his men.

As he passed the entryway to the great hall, he spied one of the three women housed at his keep, this one a young maid by the name of Dorcas, a sweet girl who had been turned out of her home after being defiled and slandered by a nobleman the winter past. The petite blonde looked up from where she stood, sweeping old rushes into the brazier, and hastened to Gunnar's side when he beckoned her forth.

"Have a fresh pallet brought up to the chamber next to mine," he instructed, "and have the hearth swept out and readied with kindling enough for the night. Candles, too, if you can find some." He thanked her and turned, starting for the bailey. "And Dorcas," he added over his shoulder, "if she should ask, tell her 'twas all your idea."

With an acquiescent nod and a harnessed smile, the maid hurried off to carry out his request.

A heap of tunics, hose, and braies filled the corner beside the large bed in Rutledge's chamber. Agnes stomped into the room and headed for the pile of clothes while Raina lingered at the threshold.

"Well, what are ye waitin' for?" Agnes shot over her shoulder. "These clothes won't get up an' wash themselves!"

Raina stepped inside, nervously peering about the room. So this is where he sleeps, she thought, running her hand over the unmade bed as she walked past it. And this is where he must entertain his women. Everything about the spartan decor had an imposing presence: from the bed, uncurtained and big enough to sleep an entire family, to the gaping black orifice of the fireplace that had been hollowed out of the thickness of the facing wall. An armor chest stood at the foot of the bed, and next to it, a stand for a tunic of chain mail. Everything bespoke war and violence. Much like the man himself, Raina thought with a frown.

A coarse tunic hit her in the face.

"Stop yer bloody dreamin' and 'elp me gather these up." Agnes seemed as short on patience as she was on breeding.

Raina went to the old woman's side. "I was not dreaming," she said as Agnes shoved a smelly pile of clothes at her. "Phew!" she gasped. "Perhaps these would be better disposed of than washed."

Agnes only scowled and added a pair of worn braies to the top of Raina's stack, now nestled under her chin. "Well, now, that's the last of it," she announced, brushing past Raina with a small wad of clothes tucked under her beefy arm. "Follow me," she ordered.

Agnes gave her no chance to argue, disappearing out the chamber door and down the corridor. Raina started off after her, catching the various articles of clothing that toppled off her enormous stack with each step she took. She trudged down the stairwell after the stout woman, determined not to lose a single scrap or to trip in the process. She'd show her—and Rutledge, too! She was not some spoiled princess, incapable of doing a good day's work.

She could manage this and whatever else they meted out to her.

Agnes led her past the hall and out of the keep into the courtyard, where the sounds of swords and men grew loud. Raina grimaced. Good Lord, the old bat would have to parade straight through their practice, wouldn't she? Never mind, she would not even pretend to notice. Holding her breath, Raina tucked her head down and feigned the utmost concentration in the effort of walking.

"Agnes, me beauty!" someone yelled from the direction of the practice yard. "Tell yer little helper I got somethin' fer her to wash!"

Agnes cackled. "Ah, Cedric, ye scarcely find use fer the wee thing. It can't be needin' a wash already!" Her retort met with appreciative laughter, but Cedric's raspy voice rang out above the rest.

"Ye best hie now, Aggie, lest I show ye a use fer it!"

Raina picked up her pace, resisting the urge to run. It wasn't until she plowed blindly into the side of an outbuilding that she realized Agnes had made a turn along the way and she no longer followed her. The surprise and impact of the collision knocked Raina flat on her rump, the stack of dirty clothes raining down on top of her. Anger infused her cheeks even before she heard the men's mocking laughter.

A strong hand circled her arm and hoisted her to her feet. "Are you all right?"

Raina yanked her arm from Rutledge's grasp. "I'm fine," she snapped, shoving a hank of hair away from her face.

"Here," he said, bending down to retrieve a bunch of clothes, "allow me." He held them out for her, looking a bit sheepish.

Raina snatched them from his outstretched hand. "I don't need your help. Leave me alone and let me finish my work." She crouched down and began gathering up the rest of the clothes as quickly as she could, eager to be out of his shadowy presence.

"I cannot recall the last time my clothes saw a good scrubbing."

Raina shot a glare in his direction. "To say naught of your swarthy hide."

He frowned and crossed his arms over his chest, puffing himself up like a rooster. "Have a care you don't use over-much soap. I find it makes the cloth stiff and uncomfortable to wear."

"I will bear it in mind." She made to brush past him, but he caught her by the arm.

"You forgot one." He held a pair of braies out on the tip of his finger and grinned. "Ah, I see your hands are full. Shall I place it on the top of the stack for you?" Raina merely fixed on him her most lethal glower. "Very well, then," he said, unfazed as he tucked the undergarment beneath her chin. "Enough dallying. Off you go now."

A large hand landed on her backside with a *thwack*.

"How dare you!" she gasped, whirling to face him.

He was smiling wickedly, clearly pleased with himself as he leaned in and whispered, "Tarry a moment longer and you might find I dare even more."

She didn't hesitate for even a heartbeat, practically flying from the courtyard and his rich laughter. She found the pond, where Agnes was already washing her small bunch of clothes. Raina threw hers to the bank with a huff. Learning from Agnes's example, she gathered up the hem of her skirt and tied it in a knot on both sides. Then, grabbing up a tunic from the top of the heap, she stomped down into the water beside the old crone.

"Ye ever done this before in yer life, girl?" Agnes asked without looking up from her work.

"Nay," Raina admitted.

Agnes let out an impatient-sounding sigh. "Well, 'ere."

She shoved a chunk of soap in Raina's direction. "Swipe this over the dirtier parts, then rub the cloth between yer fists, like this." She demonstrated with vigor and waited for Raina to do the same.

Raina took the soap and ground it into the fabric as if it were Rutledge's arrogant face.

"Ach!" Agnes cried, tearing the wedge from her fingers. "Don't ye use too much soap—"

"I know," Raina said, hearing Rutledge's instructions at the same time.

"After we finish 'ere, we'll 'ang everything out to dry," Agnes said as she wrung out her piece and left to get another.

Raina sighed heavily, then did the same, passing Agnes on her way back down the bank. The old woman flashed her a nearly toothless grin and began to whistle, clearly enjoying her superior role. The clanking of weapons in the bailey provided a strange accompaniment to Agnes's cheery tune, the sound amplifying and echoing off the crumbling curtain wall that hid the soldiers from view. Raina dropped the clean tunic on a patch of grass and bent to retrieve another to wash. It was then that the realization dawned on her.

If the curtain wall hid the bailey from her view, it also shielded her from Rutledge's watchful eye. Clutching the tunic to her breast, she peered cautiously at the wall walk. Only one guard stood sentry near the gate, and he looked to be preoccupied with the goings-on in the bailey. Raina's heart began to beat a hopeful tattoo in her breast.

She could escape!

Mother Mary, could it be this easy? Dare she hope simply to walk away in broad daylight? Rutledge was indeed a fool to think the idea would not cross her mind. Or did he rather think she'd not have the nerve? Perhaps he felt Agnes's presence was assurance enough. Raina cast a wary glance over her shoulder and grinned.

Agnes, so engrossed in her washing and her song, would

likely not miss her until she was deep into the woods. And with Agnes's stubby legs and burdensome girth, she would never be able to catch her even if she did set off in pursuit. Thank the saints, but it appeared she might yet be free!

Raina tossed the tunic to the ground and made to dash for the cover of the woods.

"Milady, I would not."

The adolescent male voice halted her in her tracks. Shoulders slumping in defeat, she turned to face Rutledge's squire. He looked at her almost apologetically from atop his grazing palfrey. Agnes's whistling had since stopped, and she now stood in the water up to her thighs, her hands on her hips and a murderous scowl on her face.

Raina's mind worked quickly to form a reasonable explanation for her behavior. "I—I was only seeking a moment of privacy, my lord." She smiled warmly on the blushing squire.

"Let 'er tell it to Lord Gunnar, lad," Agnes called from the pond. " 'E'll give 'er a moment of privacy, I warrant!"

The squire frowned pensively, pursing his lips. "Mayhap she's right," he said at last. "Milord sent me here to guard you. He should be made aware of your attempt to escape—"

"Escape?" Raina feigned surprise at his accusation. She stepped closer to him, lowering her voice to a suitably embarrassed whisper. "I assure you, my lord squire, I meant only to relieve myself. I beg you spare me—and indeed yourself—any further humiliation and do not make mention of this misunderstanding to your lord."

By this time Agnes had lumbered up the bank to where they stood, her skirt soaked and dripping water in a steady stream where it splashed on her wide, hamlike feet. "Ye'll get a terrific floggin' fer this, wench," she said with a malicious, eager little grin.

Raina looked pleadingly at the squire, whose own expression told her that Agnes was likely correct in her assumption.

"She says she sought only to relieve herself, Agnes," the squire said. "I see no need to alert milord of that." He had clearly attempted to sound manly and authoritative, which made it all the more endearing to Raina when his voice cracked.

"Is that so?" Agnes challenged. "Why, then, don't keep 'er waitin', Alaric! Go and see to it she does 'er business so she can get back to 'er work."

The squire looked from Agnes to Raina, then back to Agnes again. His mouth opened and closed, but it was Agnes who broke the silence.

"Oh, never ye mind," she huffed. "I'll take 'er meself! A glimpse of 'er bare backside'd likely render ye witless anyway." She seized Raina by the elbow as if to haul her bodily into the thicket.

"Nay, wait!" Raina cried, "I no longer feel the need to go."

Agnes snickered. "Can ye credit that, Alaric? Comin' up on 'er like ye did, ye must 'ave scared the urge right out of the poor thing."

Raina looked to the squire. "Please, I'd rather finish my work and be done with it." He bit his lip thoughtfully, then nodded his agreement.

"I still says she needs a taste of the lash," Agnes muttered, and stormed back down into the water, leaving Raina standing beside the squire's mount.

"Not a word to him?" Raina pleaded. The squire broke her gaze and looked down at his hands, seemingly unable to confirm what might amount to a betrayal of his lord's trust. Raina reached up and touched his hand lightly. "I won't forget your kindness, Alaric."

That said, she bent to retrieve another tunic from the pile and joined Agnes in the pond. Several times she ventured a curious look over her shoulder and found the squire watching her intently from his position at the crest of the bank. She smiled at him on one occasion, and his cheeks flamed nearly the color of his hair before he looked away.

For the remainder of the morning, Raina made a point of smiling at him often and attempting to engage him in conversation each time she made the trek back up from the water. Not only did his pleasant nature make the time pass more quickly, but it also took her mind away from her hands, which had begun to show their abuse after she had washed the first couple of tunics. She still had a mound of things to wash, and had deliberately put off touching Rutledge's braies to the last. She longed to take a rest, but Agnes told her their time for rest would come when their work was done.

At last she could take the standing no longer, and did indeed need to relieve herself. She went to Alaric with her request. He looked dubious.

"If you try to run—"

"I won't. You have my word. Besides, I'm far too weary to even consider the notion."

He frowned. "Very well, but I must insist that you remain close by."

"You may stand watch yourself or send Agnes after me." She wiped her forearm across her sweaty brow. " 'Tis a minor humiliation amid the rest, I assure you."

Alaric exhaled a heavy sigh. "I'll not beleaguer your delicate sensibilities any further, milady. As you have given me your word, I warrant a few moments of privacy could do no harm."

"Thank you," she whispered, and stepped through the brush.

Raina had to admire Alaric's chivalry and wondered how he managed to acquire it serving a lord as brash and bullying as his. Rutledge, the blackguard, likely would have taken great pleasure in degrading her further. She thanked the saints that he had sent his squire in his place this morn.

Finding a likely enough spot a few yards into the thicket, Raina lifted her skirts and hunkered down. She had no idea how tired her legs were until she tried to squat and nearly toppled over. She broke her fall, but in so doing, thrust her hands into a patch of nettles. An instant itchy rash bloomed on her palms and wrists, made all the worse by the raw condition of her skin.

She scratched at the fine, nearly invisible hairs now lodged in her skin and swore an oath under her breath as the white bumps began to rise. Nettles! Next to impossible to remove, they were even harder to endure. She wiped her hands in her skirts, moaning when the friction only worsened the itch.

Alaric's voice called out to her. "Milady? Are you ill?"

She couldn't answer. Her hands throbbed and she just wanted to be home, away from this place. Damn Rutledge! If not for his edict, her hands would not be raw, and she would not be picking nettles from them. He was fast becoming the very bane of her existence. Would that she could give him a taste of his own medicine. If only she could find a means of causing him even the smallest measure of the discomfort he was causing her. What joy she would find in his pain, what satisfaction!

"Milady, if you do not answer, you leave me no choice but to seek you out!" Alaric's panicky voice was soon joined by Agnes's grim prediction.

"I shudder to think what Lord Gunnar'll do if ye've let 'er get away, lad!"

Raina suddenly stopped scratching her palm and looked over her shoulder to the generous patch of nettles where the germ of an idea took root.

Discomfort he prescribed, then discomfort he would get.

An untamed smile grew wide on her face, and she nearly

burst out laughing with satisfaction as she quickly collected a good number of the leafy stems and concealed them within the folds of her skirts. By the time Alaric and Agnes had crashed through the bracken, Raina was standing up and brushing herself off, her expression serenely innocent.

"I said I'd be along in a moment," she declared as she sailed past them.

Chapter Ten

"I think I am in love."

The solemn statement hung in the air for an overlong moment before the knights gathered around the trestle table burst into laughter. Alaric looked up from his cup of ale and frowned.

"Again so soon, lad? Or dare we think you should love the same girl for more than one week at a time?"

" 'Tis not like that," he said, shaking his head. "This time I am certain." The men laughed harder; someone beside him patted his head as if he were a pup.

"Poor Alaric, his lance goes stiff an' he credits he's in love! Pray, someone teach him the difference!"

"Odette could teach him," one man supplied. "She's schooled her share of lovelorn virgins."

"Laugh all you like, you grizzled sots," Alaric charged. "You'll be choking on your gibes when you see that I am telling the truth."

Burc sliced his hand through the air to calm the laughter and lowered his voice to mocking seriousness. "Tell us, lad, who is the misfortunate wench this week?"

"She's no wench, you great bag of ill wind; she's a lady. The most beautiful lady I've ever laid eyes on."

Burc stroked his jaw. "Ah, and where is it ye spied this . . . woman of such legendary beauty?"

Alaric stared into his mug for a long moment; then,

casting a furtive glance over each shoulder, he leaned in and whispered, "She is here, in this keep . . . the lady, Raina."

Burc's face split into a wide grin, and he let out a guffaw. "Saints' blue bloody balls!" he barked. "That wench is no lady. Why, 'twouldn't surprise me in the least if she were not already Rutledge's whore."

Alaric drew his dagger and lunged across the table at the big knight. "Withdraw that comment, Burc, or feel my blade rent your gullet where you sit."

The other men stilled but Burc remained unaffected, even chuckling, despite Alaric's grave tone. "Bloody Christ! Methinks ye are in love, lad. Only a stricken fool would be so willing to toss his life away in the name of a wench's virtue."

Alaric moved closer. "Withdraw the comment, you fat ugly bastard!"

Gunnar entered the hall and immediately spied his squire atop the table, his blade at Burc's throat.

"What the devil is going on here?" he bellowed.

"Seems your squire fancies himself in love with your hostage," Burc supplied, casually sweeping Alaric's blade away from him with the back of his hand. "I was advising him of the folly of the notion."

"Indeed. Alaric, a word if you please." As Gunnar crossed the hall to the dais, Alaric resheathed his dagger and made to follow. Gunnar pulled aside an x-chair and motioned for Alaric to sit beside him on the dais. "I would hear your explanation of the foolery I just witnessed."

" 'Twas much as Burc said, milord. He made a comment about a lady that I could not allow to go unchallenged."

"My prisoner."

"Aye, milord, Lady Raina. He said she was a—that she

was your—" He flushed, his gaze dropping to his chewed-off fingernails. "I could not abide his maligning her."

"And that was how you chose to handle it?"

Alaric looked up at him in confusion. "Milord, have you yourself not said that no man has the right to disparage a lady's honor? That 'tis a man's duty to protect a lady and her reputation?"

Gunnar exhaled and ran a hand over his face in frustration. He should have known his words would come back on his squire's lips to haunt him. He looked into Alaric's expectant gaze. "I . . . might have said something to that effect at one time or another."

"Aye, that you have, milord. You may think I don't listen to your advice, but I do." Alaric sat up straighter on the stool and brought his fist to his chest. "I take it to heart."

"So it would seem," Gunnar mused.

"Besides," Alaric continued, "Burc is a pox on the arse of mankind. 'Twould have been a favor to us all if I had split him wide open."

"You would have likely gotten yourself killed, lad. Burc is a pox, I'll grant you that, but he is also one of my most skilled men, and I can ill afford to lose him now. He was likely needling you, merely trying to goad you into tangling with him."

"Would you not have done the same thing as I, milord?"

Gunnar chuckled despite himself, slapping Alaric heartily on the shoulder. "Aye, I warrant I would have at that. But tell me, what interest have you in my prisoner?"

His squire's cheeks flushed crimson. "I . . ." He straightened his shoulders, running a finger around the collar of his tunic. "I . . . I fear I love her, milord." He met Gunnar's gaze, the youth's expression very grave.

Gunnar quelled the urge to laugh in light of Alaric's solemnity. Truth be known, he understood firsthand how easily a man could desire a woman of Raina's beauty and wit, but here was a lad who threw his heart to any comely maid who happened to glance his way. Normally, Gunnar would look upon it as naught more than a passing fancy, but the boy's developing feelings—and a possible alliance—with his prisoner was another matter entirely. He could have none of it. "Alaric, as my squire and as one day a knight, it is your responsibility to put duty before all else. That woman abovestairs is your lord's prisoner, and as such, your feelings for her must not exceed my own. Do you understand?"

"Aye, milord."

"Good. As long as she is here, she is to be treated with caution. Never turn your back on her, and never give her your trust. Understood?"

"Aye, milord."

"Now go. Surely there are duties you have left unattended. Mayhap polishing my chain mail will afford you time to reflect on your folly this day."

"Aye, milord," Alaric murmured. "I beg forgiveness."

As Alaric left the hall, Gunnar's gaze traveled to the group of knights. The table had quieted, but he noted Burc yet eyed him over the rim of his cup. Something had passed between Alaric and the cur—something more than the boy realized, and Gunnar knew from Burc's expression that the matter was yet to be finished.

He was about to rise and find out what was brewing when a large-breasted serving wench approached him carrying two tankards of ale. She smiled at him, and he might have thought her pretty if not for her missing front tooth, lost in a tavern fistfight the night he took her in. Odette was a whore and made no bones about it, unless she felt she was being cheated. Then she took no quarter: the sleeves were rolled up, fists flew, and even the toughest men had been known to fall.

She was still young, and if not for her large frame and muscular limbs, it might have been difficult to imagine her in the role of aggressor. Especially now, as she tossed her head, playing the coquette as she sashayed toward the dais, flipping a strand of pale brown hair over her shoulder and better exposing the open neckline of her well-worn bliaut.

Gunnar chuckled at her latest attempt at seduction, for each was notoriously blatant and short-lived. It seldom took long before the real Odette, crass and foul-mouthed, came to the fore. Ever since her arrival some six months ago, she'd been after him, offering to repay him for his kindness in taking her in. He always refused her advances, even on those occasions when he found her naked and in his bed in the wee hours of the night.

He didn't seek repayment for sheltering a fellow misfit; in fact, his entire garrison—if he could truly call the small band of men such—was made up of refugees and other homeless wanderers. Much like him, he suspected they were all searching for a place to call home. Though this ramshackle ruin of a keep was far from anyone's ideal, it was the closest thing Gunnar'd had to a home in nearly all his life. In the short time he'd been here, he never felt ashamed of it, never gave it a thought at all, until *she* arrived.

There were a good number of things Gunnar hadn't given a thought to before the arrival of Raina d'Bussy in his life. Thoughts like honor and pride, softness and beauty. All things he'd denied himself for so long, things he wished he'd never been reminded of. He pounded his fist on the table in frustration and found Odette standing before him, frowning.

"Milord, ye look painful thirsty," she said, handing him one of the cups.

"That I am." Gunnar quickly took a long draught and

nearly spilled the ale down his chin as Odette seated her ample backside on his lap.

"If ye thirst for somethin' sweeter than honey," she whispered, her breath stinking of old ale, "ye know I'm willin' to provide ye that, too."

"I appreciate the offer, Odette," Gunnar replied as she downed the contents of her cup in one gulp, then slammed it down on the table and let out a loud belch. He winced at the hearty roar of laughter that followed painfully close to his ear.

The sounds of men laughing and cups banging on tables in the hall reached the kitchen, where Raina stood over a boiling cauldron of cabbage stew, stirring with one hand and wiping the steam and sweat from her brow with the other. If the cracked skin of her hands yet throbbed from the laundry or the nettles, she hadn't had time to notice, for Agnes had kept her busy from the moment they'd hung the clothes to dry. There had been rushes to gather and lay, vegetables to harvest, and game to clean for supper.

Raina could still hear the cock she had been sent to fetch, clucking and protesting as she carried it out by the feet and brought it to Agnes in the courtyard. Agnes had been waiting beside a tree stump, holding a small ax in one hand and grinning broadly. She indicated the stump with a nod of her head.

"Now, 'old still and keep yer fingers out the way, else ye lose 'em."

Queasy with the very idea, Raina stammered, "B-but I-I don't think I—"

It was over in a heartbeat: Agnes grabbed the bird, placed her foot on the rooster's head, and chopped it clean off. The headless body fell to the ground at her feet and flopped about like a fish washed ashore while Raina tried to dance out of its bloody path. Agnes meanwhile roared with laughter, doubling over and wheezing as she sputtered, "Oh, to see the look upon yer face!"

When the bird had at last stilled, Raina dropped to her knees amid the flurry of drifting feathers and retched. Thankfully, Agnes had found some shred of pity and had decided to retrieve and butcher the other two birds by herself.

All three were now roasted golden brown and waiting on platters to be served up to the men gathering in the hall. Venison from the night before would also be served, along with Raina's cabbage stew and fresh breads and cheese. She should have a ravenous appetite, but instead her stomach roiled at the thought of eating, the swirling stew boiling in the pot before her making her feel as if she were adrift on the ocean and sick to her stomach with it.

"Enough stirring," Agnes barked, snatching the spoon from Raina's hands and thrusting a bread trencher laden with food at her. "Take this out to Lord Gunnar, then come back and I'll give ye more."

One whole capon sat in the center, flanked by a veritable garden of vegetables and a large wedge of yellow cheese. "He's going to eat all of this?" Raina asked in disbelief.

"If 'e don't starve waitin' on ye to bring it!" Agnes shouted, wiping her hands on her filthy apron.

Raina scurried out of the kitchens and onto the courtyard path that led to the hall. A hound sleeping in the shade of the keep's wall roused as she made to pass him. As the dog eyed the trencher in her hands, his floppy ears perked up. He whimpered and licked his chops before beginning a sideways lob toward her.

"Stay where you are, you ugly beast."

Raina picked up her pace. She felt the hound at her heels the moment before he leapt for the trencher. She cuffed him with her elbow, but he leapt again, this time knocking the trencher out of her hands and onto the ground. She caught the cheese in one hand, but the vegetables scattered everywhere. The dog snapped up the chicken in midair, then plopped down and began gnawing at it.

"Fie! Give me that!" Setting the cheese aside, Raina lunged for the bird, trying to tear it from the hound's jaws. He growled and hung on to a leg, his brown eyes showing nigh the same determination Raina felt. She pulled harder. "Let . . . *go!*"

The leg broke off in the dog's mouth, and Raina clutched the rest of the bird to her chest, then picked up a turnip and pelted it at the dog's big head. He winced, slunking off into the shade with his meager prize.

Raina stood, wringing her hands in her skirts and scanning what remained of Rutledge's meal. The trencher was still in one piece, but everything else was now lying in the dirt. It seemed she had two options: return the ruined meal to the kitchens and face Agnes, who would surely launch into a tirade over her carelessness, or salvage what she could and continue on to the hall and serve it to Rutledge.

Deliberating over which would be the lesser of the two evils, she retrieved the trencher and placed the bird and the cheese on it, then began collecting the spilled vegetables. She picked up a turnip and blew it off. It didn't look terribly damaged; surely everything was still edible. Besides, she decided as she wiped off the rest of the items, with Rutledge's unsophisticated tastes, he'd likely never know the difference anyway. Restoring the trencher to some semblance of order, Raina dashed into the keep and entered the hall.

She spied Rutledge immediately, on the dais, lounging in his chair with a wench on his lap and a mug in his hand. He saluted Raina with a smug nod as she appeared from behind the screens, he seemingly unaffected by the strumpet now whispering in his ear. His raven hair was still damp from a recent washing, and he sported one of the tunics Raina had laundered that morning. She only prayed he'd worn a fresh pair of braies, too. His entire wardrobe—meager as it was—was now laced with itchy nettles. Smiling in anticipation, Raina headed toward him with his supper.

"I was beginning to wonder if I might never be served," he quipped. Then his gaze went to the mangled assembly on the trencher and he frowned. "What's this? Did you first sample my meal before bringing it out?"

His buxom lapdog giggled and whispered something in his ear before Raina could stammer a believable excuse for the sorry condition of his supper.

"Odette here thinks you could do with some fattening up," he said with a smirk.

Raina felt her ire go from a simmer to a full boil. "And I think Odette could do with better taste in men."

"Aay!" Odette squawked. "I won't 'ave 'er insultin' me!"

Rutledge grinned, his gaze fixed on Raina. "I believe the insult was directed at me." Odette was dispatched to the floor with little ceremony.

Raina watched as the woman swaggered off the dais and quickly draped herself over another man. "Your lapdog seems rather fickle, my lord."

"And if I did not know better," Rutledge drawled, leaning over the table, "I might think my captive seems rather jealous."

"Hardly," Raina scoffed, plunking the trencher down on the table and turning to quit the hall.

From behind her, Rutledge cleared his throat. "I've not yet granted you leave; where do you think to go?"

Pivoting on her heel, she fixed a scathing glare on him and gestured around her. "I'm certain there are others here who wish to eat. Agnes sent me with directions to return once you had your meal so I might assist her with the other trays."

"Agnes can manage without your assistance. You will stay and tend your lord."

She crossed her arms over her chest. "Is that not your squire's duty?"

"He is elsewise occupied. Tonight, 'tis your duty."

"I have brought you your meal; what more do you require? Must I now feed you as well?"

His brows quirked in interest. "An intriguing suggestion," he said, but then he winced, reaching over his shoulder to scratch feverishly at an unseen itch. "What the devil—" he grumbled, now plunging his hand into the unlaced neckline of his tunic and scratching as if to draw blood.

"Fleas, my lord?" Raina suggested, trying unsuccessfully to keep the glee from her voice.

He shot her a perturbed scowl, but his expression softened with a flash of momentary puzzlement. His hand still obscured within his tunic, he stopped scratching suddenly and his face darkened with dawning comprehension. Very slowly he withdrew his hand, and pinched between his forefinger and thumb was a wilted nettle leaf. Eyes narrowed, he held the little discovery up for Raina's consideration. "Now, how do you suppose this got in my tunic?"

She shrugged lamely, trying not to laugh at his discomfort. "Perhaps the fleas put it there?"

"Indeed." He let the leaf flutter to the floor at his feet. "Perhaps the smug little flea standing before me ought to come up here and scratch my back."

Raina gulped, unsure what alarmed her more: the thought of touching him or the idea that she would have to do so in front of the entire keep. "I don't think—"

"Mayhap next time you will," he interjected with a wry smile. "And it wasn't a suggestion, lamb. Come up here."

With hesitant feet, she climbed the two steps of the raised platform and stood, fists clenched, at Rutledge's side. He began eating his meal, seemingly more interested in the roasted chicken than in her or her discomfiture. No one in the hall appeared to take notice either, everyone talking and paying no mind to the dais.

"Go on," Rutledge directed her with a nod of his head.

Scandalized at the thought of placing her hands on any part of him, Raina reluctantly complied, taking her place behind him and unable to do more than stare at the wide expanse of his back and shoulders, unsure how to begin. She flexed her tired fingers, took a deep breath, and placed her hands lightly on his shoulders.

She thought he might have flinched, but she could not be sure, for the jolt she experienced upon feeling his tight muscles beneath her palms took the breath right out of her and left her heart fluttering in her throat. At first she couldn't move and just stood there with her hands resting on those thick, hard shoulders as he bent down to his trencher, eating and drinking and apparently oblivious of the maelstrom of new and fascinating sensations she was weathering at his back.

Never had she felt such power, such masculine strength. Even with her hands spread wide, she couldn't span the width of his shoulders. Over the rough linen of his tunic, she squeezed the thick muscles, testing their strength and marveling at the ridges and valleys that formed with his slightest move. He made a low, rumbling sound in the back of his throat as she scratched and kneaded his shoulders, exhaling a deep breath that seemed to release some of the tension she felt within him.

Oddly pleased with that idea, she let her thumbs trace the column of his neck, scarcely resisting the urge to plunge her fingers into his glossy, dark hair, which fell in waves about his ears and tickled the collar of his tunic. She noticed idly that he had abandoned his supper and now reclined quietly in his chair, his head dipped forward, arms spread wide, hands fisted and braced against the edge of the table while she continued her ministrations.

Before long, however, the tension seemed to creep back into his muscles, and she wondered if she had been doing something wrong, for his wide back now rose and fell with breathing that had become heavy, a certain tautness seeming to come over his entire being. "Don't stop," he rasped when her hands stilled at his shoulders. But she couldn't move, not even to remove her hands from him.

Something had changed; she could feel it in herself as surely as she felt it in him. From the moment she touched him, she was no longer a prisoner begrudgingly carrying out an order but a woman willingly caressing—and aye, desiring—a man. She could not deny it, and heaven help her, but he was surely aware as well, for when his large hands reached up and curled around her wrists, she could do naught but sigh, a ragged, wanton sound that he echoed with a low, rumbling moan.

With precious little effort, he pulled her against him, the back of his head pressing into her belly as he dragged her hands down, over his shoulders, inside his tunic. Of their own accord, her fingers splayed the firm, muscular disks of his chest, wading through the mat of soft hair, his nipples hard as pebbles against her palms. She squeezed her eyes closed, desperate to shut out the keen ripple of pleasure, the fervent lure of curiosity that made her yearn to venture lower, to the flat plane of his abdomen and—heaven help her—lower still.

"Oh, please, nay," she whispered, and made to pull away from him, but Rutledge caught her hands, pivoting in his chair to face her, his eyes hooded and darker than she had ever seen them, his full lips set in a grim line, his nostrils flaring with breath that came hot against her skin. "Please, release me," she gasped.

"Is that truly what you want, my lamb?" he asked, his

eyes smoldering with dangerous promise. She nodded and made a feeble attempt to extract her hands from his grasp. "Nay," he challenged, "I don't think you want me to release you at all. Your lips may deny me, but your eyes speak the truth. As do these delicate, gentle fingers."

He glanced down to where their hands were joined—and he stilled. The warmth and passion she had seen in his eyes just a moment before evaporated like dew under the blaze of the hot sun and his expression steeled. As did his grip on her hands. He scowled. "Where did you get that?"

Confused by this swift change in his demeanor and the sudden flatness of his voice, Raina looked to the new focus of his attention. The ring on the third finger of her right hand twinkled in the light of the hall, the dark ruby in its center alive with bloodred fire.

"Where did you get it?"

Raina jumped at the heavy boom of his voice. "M-my father gave it to me," she stammered quickly. " 'Tis a family heirloom."

"Take it off," he commanded.

She shook her head, refusing to part with the token she had cherished for so long, the ring her father had given her on her sixteenth birthday.

"I said, take it off."

Inwardly cursing him and his bullying ways, Raina pulled the beloved memento from her finger and shakily extended it to him in her palm. He snatched it up, holding the ring between his thumb and forefinger and staring at it with quiet intensity. "A family heirloom, you say?"

"Aye, my lord," she replied warily, not trusting the odd calm that had come over him.

Rutledge chuckled then, a bitter sound lacking any humor. "Doubtless your father neglected to tell you *whose* family." The ring disappeared into his fist. "Now get out of my hall and leave me alone."

Raina hesitated. "But my ring—"

Rutledge ignored her, snapping his fingers to beckon a guard to his side. "Take her up to her cell."

"My ring!" she croaked. "Give it back to me!"

But Rutledge paid her no mind. The burly guard clutched her elbow and gave it a tug, prepared to drag her off the dais if he must. She dug in her heels, pulling against the guard's hold and glaring at Rutledge's impassive countenance, nearly spitting with anger. "All your bluster about honor and righting wrongs is a lie!" she charged. "You've accused my father of stealing and murder and cruelty, but how are you any better? You are naught but a petty thief! A bullying coward! Piteous fraud!"

A pall of silence cloaked the hall as the guard led Raina, thrashing and raging, away from the gathering. No one said a word. All eyes turned expectantly to Gunnar, who to all appearances remained unmoved, looking completely unfazed as he drained the last of his ale and set the cup down on the table with a soft thud. Only he knew the torrent raging within him. Only he knew the constant battle he fought inside himself, the desperate conflict that left him torn between wanting Raina and wanting her gone.

She was right, of course. He was a thief. Everything he had acquired in this life had once belonged to someone else, from his sword and armor, won by tournament ransom, to the abandoned keep that sheltered him and the stores he had recently filled with goods taken from d'Bussy's holdings. Now he had stooped to stealing a man's daughter. An innocent maiden who, if he were half the beast he knew himself to be, stood to lose far more to him than just a cherished bit of jewelry.

To the charge of coward he pleaded guilty as well, though he reckoned no one, save the hellion abovestairs—and his own damning conscience—would dare to call him so now.

He'd spent more than a dozen years trying to expunge the shame of having fled his parents' murderer rather than fight him, punishing his body with hard physical labor and countless battles, disciplining his mind to thoughts of war and vengeance, and girding his heart against the weakness of feelings. He had earned a reputation for fearlessness and ferocity that few had risen to challenge—all in preparation for one man, one meeting. But until d'Bussy was no more, Gunnar suspected that inside, where it mattered, he was forever doomed to be that cowardly boy.

And a fraud? Aye, he was. A fraud of the worst degree, for he'd been trying to convince himself from the moment he laid eyes on d'Bussy's daughter that she did not affect him in some deep, primeval way. Jesu, but he could still feel her hands on him, her slender fingers exploring and caressing him, she unaware of what her innocent ministrations had done to him.

The idea that she'd found pleasure in touching him had surprised him infinitely, rendered him stiff and near senseless with want, burning to show her what real pleasure was. How he would survive more than a sennight in her presence without giving in to that desire, he knew not. But if he needed a reminder of why he could not have her, a warning to uphold his vow of vengeance, he had surely gotten it this eve.

Clutching the tiny ring so tightly in his fist that it bit into his palm, Gunnar filled his cup, steeling himself against the urge to chase up the stairs after Raina to claim her as his price, and vengeance be damned.

Chapter Eleven

Hours had passed since Raina had been taken away from the hall and locked in her chamber. A young maid named Dorcas brought a tray of food that now sat in the corner, half-eaten. Raina couldn't think about food; she could hardly appreciate the fresh pallet beneath her or the dying fire in the hearth—both, she suspected, courtesy of the kindhearted Dorcas.

Raina's thoughts were yet on Rutledge and his unpredictable moods, his maddening and frequent turns from man to beast. Whatever had occurred between them in the hall had left her trembling and bewildered, and his angry, cryptic response at spying her ring only furthered her confusion.

Curse him! Never had she been more unsure of herself or her own feelings. In a matter of days, Rutledge had managed to make her at once like him, hate him, respect him, fear him . . . and aye, desire him. But it could go no further than that, and he could never know what he made her feel; she could not allow it. It seemed clear that the only true way to escape her traitorous thoughts was to escape his keep. A hopeless goal if ever there was one, she thought, and burst into tears all over again.

Even though Rutledge saw no need to post a guard outside her door, the lock bar was set and she was trapped well and good within. She had already checked the height of the chamber window and ruled it out as a means of safe escape. All she could hope for was a miracle, a wish that God might take pity on her and send her a deliverer.

And then the answer came—a soft tapping on her door, so faint she nearly didn't hear it through her sobs. It came again, louder this time and followed by an adolescent voice she had now come to recognize.

"Milady, are you all right?"

Alaric's concerned whisper drifted into the semidarkness; the lock bar began to slide slowly out of its sleeve.

Raina sniffed and sat up on her pallet, wiping her tangled hair away from her eyes. As the metal grated softly on the other side of the door, her heart gave a little leap. He meant to come in! While her mind raced to form a plan, her body sprang into action. Snatching her empty chamber pot as a weapon, she flattened herself against the wall behind the door. She truly hated to hurt him, but hers was not the only life at stake, and she hoped he would understand.

The old leather hinges creaked as Alaric pushed the door open a crack. "Lady Raina?" he whispered as his head peered into the darkness. He moved farther into the room. "Please answer me, milady. Are you unwell?"

He likely heard her whispered plea for forgiveness, for he started to turn his head toward where she stood with the chamber pot raised high above her head, but he hadn't the chance to utter a sound before she brought it down on him with a resounding *bong*. Alaric crumpled to the floor in a heap of gangly arms and legs.

Working quickly, Raina cast the dented pot to the floor and pulled him into the chamber lest he be discovered before she had a chance to make her escape. She dragged the limp squire to her pallet and rested his head on her pillow, trying to provide for his comfort in some small way. He looked to be sleeping so blissfully that for an instant she feared she might have killed him. She hesitated, pressing her palm to his cheek. Thank the saints, it was warm. He moaned suddenly and she nearly jumped out of her skin, vaulting to her feet.

Raina slipped out into the corridor and closed the chamber door behind her, quietly sliding the lock bar into place. With her heart pounding wildly in her breast, she fled down the empty hallway and descended the spiraling stairwell, creeping along the corridor wall toward the entry of the hall. There she stilled, listening for activity from within the sleeping quarters of Rutledge's men. Save for some heavy snoring, blessedly, all was quiet.

She peeked around the edge, and a movement in the far corner caused her heart to trip, but it was just Odette, stealing away from her lover while he slept on his pallet. Lifting her skirts so she might run unencumbered, Raina dashed on, past the hall and down the corridor that led to the bailey and freedom. She crossed the small courtyard, dodging puddles from a recent rain with only the moon to guide her. She reached the interior of the curtain wall, sidling along it until she found the stairs leading up to the wall walk.

Three guards armed with crossbows stood at the farthest parapet, engrossed in friendly conversation. There was no possibility of getting past the gate on foot; her only hope was to jump from atop the wall and pray she landed safely on the other side. Raina chewed her bottom lip as she climbed the steep stone steps, moving quietly and slowly as she dared, so as not to attract the guards' attention.

When she reached the top and peered over the side, her heart plummeted. Mercy, it was so very high! Though the darkness all but swallowed up the ground below, she could still discern scattered rocks and a very steep motte. The danger of breaking bones upon landing below was only worsened by the thought of rolling down that hill. Hers was a risky venture, to say the least. She glanced nervously over her shoulder at the guards.

It was also her only hope.

Without making a sound, Raina climbed onto the ledge of the wall walk, and on her belly, clutching the rough stone of the embrasure, she carefully slid her legs over the side of the wall. The chill night air lifted her skirts, exposing her bare legs and making her question the wisdom of her hasty plan. If she landed carelessly, she would likely be torn to ribbons. An image of herself lifeless and lying broken on the rocks sprang unbidden to her mind. What a tragic, heroic way to leave her life, she thought with a sudden surge of melodrama. Her father would be devastated, of course, and so very proud to learn of her courage. But what of Rutledge? she wondered. He would be furious that he'd lost his pawn, but would his feelings go beyond that?

She had little time to ponder the question, for the stony facade she was clinging to started to crumble. A small piece broke loose from beneath her fingers, ricocheting down the sloping wall and landing below. From the area of the battlements she heard the shuffling of booted feet, the murmur of voices, and then one of the guards leaned over the edge. "The prisoner!" he called, spying her instantly. "Curse the wench, she's escaping!"

The other guards swore, and a whistle of alarm went up, followed by the rush of footsteps drawing closer.

Heaven help her, but there was no turning back now. Closing her eyes, Raina whispered a quick prayer, then let go of the wall.

Her skirts filled with air as her body rushed to the ground, and she landed with a bone-jarring thud. She bit her tongue as her teeth crashed together, and she stumbled backward onto her rump, momentarily dazed with the impact. Mother Mary, she did it . . . and she wasn't dead! Shaking off her disorientation, she scrambled to her feet as a guard's voice rang out above her.

"Halt!" he called, but Raina paid him no heed. Hiking

up her skirts, she stumbled more than ran down the side of the hill as the guard issued a warning: "Halt, or I'll drop you, wench!"

She ran faster, heart pounding, waiting to feel the archer's arrow pierce her body at any moment. Her fears were confirmed within an instant as an object whooshed past her at great speed, lodging in the earth with a solid thunk. Raina screamed so loud in response to the near miss, she didn't hear the deep and angry voice ordering the guards to cease firing at once.

Running on fear more than strength, she neared the bottom of the motte, her lungs and legs aching with exertion. Her bare feet throbbed, surely bleeding and raw from the jagged stones that littered the ground. She felt nigh to collapsing but urged herself on. She had to make it to the woods, had to find a place to hide if she had a prayer of getting away.

Gunnar flew from the castle astride his destrier. The witless woman had no idea how close she had just come to dying. Forgetting for the moment the foolishness of jumping from the curtain wall, what idiocy overcame her that she believed she could flee his guards? If he hadn't been alerted to her escape and come to the courtyard, she would surely be dead now. His heart still clenched at the thought of seeing his archer level his weapon at her. Thank God he'd gotten there when he did! His man's aim was always true and would have met its mark this time as well, had Gunnar not managed to knock the bowman off target.

Spying Raina's fleeing form near the bottom of the hill, Gunnar spurred his mount in her direction. Aye, thank God his guards had not killed her; at the moment he wanted that pleasure for himself.

She was heading for the forest with great haste, despite her apparent favoring of one leg. If she made it to the cover of the woods, it would be hard to find her in the darkness of the bracken, and God only knew what beasts she would rouse in her fumbling about. He swore an oath and his destrier bore down on her.

Raina likely heard its thundering approach, for she turned to venture a glance over her shoulder. She stumbled, falling to the ground on her hands and knees. Her hesitation afforded Gunnar the moment he needed to close in on her, and by the time she had risen to begin her flight anew, he had reached her side.

"Cease your foolish running, woman!" he warned as he circled around her and brought his snorting destrier to a halt. "You'll not outpace my mount, and if you try, he'll likely trample you beneath his hooves."

"I don't care!" She made to dash away again.

"Damnation!" he cursed, dismounting and rounding his horse to chase after her on foot. He lunged for her, grasping the fabric of her skirt, and she fell to the ground with an *oof*. She kicked and fought him, rolling onto her back and trying to scramble away, but he held her fast and climbed atop her, pinning her beneath him in the heather. She flailed and thrashed under his weight, cursing him through her choked pleas for him to let her go. "Let you go where, Raina? You're days from Norworth and unfamiliar with this terrain, so where did you plan to flee?"

"I don't know," she panted. "Anywhere, as long as I'm away from you!"

"Why? Have I been that cruel? Have I mistreated you so, you were willing to risk your life to be away from me? You might have gotten yourself killed any number of ways this eve!"

"What if I had? Then you'd have naught to use against my father, and your wicked trade would have been thwarted. And I would be free of your loathsome presence for good!"

"Ah, I see. You want me to believe this was more deliberate suicide mission than fool's escape, is that it? Evidently, because if you truly wished to get away from me, my lamb, you would have done so back at Wyn—" He stopped himself, just short of giving name to the shameful ruin. "—when you had your chance."

"Damn you, I wish I had!"

Her thrashing began anew. Gunnar captured her wrists in his hands and held her arms pinned over her head. She glared up at him, her breasts heaving, heart pounding at his chest. "You may indeed want to be away from me at any cost, but you're no martyr, Raina. Nay, I suspect your reason for running had less to do with saving your father than it did with saving yourself."

"From what?"

"From me."

She scoffed, but the sound was a dubious one, the denial too quick, and her voice much too soft when she said, "You don't frighten me."

"Nay?" he challenged, more than willing to test her. "Not even when I tell you that I've wanted you beneath me like this from the moment I first saw you?" Her eyes widened at his admission but she held his gaze. "Not even when you can feel how much I want you this very moment? What about when I touch you, Raina?" he whispered, tracing his finger down the inside of her arm. She shuddered under him, her indrawn breath a weak hiss as she turned her head away, a strangled cry curling up from her throat. "Why do you tremble, then, if not out of fear? Tell me, lamb—"

"Cease tormenting me!"

"Perhaps 'tis something darker than fear, something you haven't the experience yet to name."

"Stop it," she choked as his lips descended toward hers. "Oh, God . . . please, stop . . ."

Gunnar watched as her eyelids drifted closed and her sweet lips parted, her breath shallow and warm, fanning his chin. The struggle leaked out of her slowly, and he felt her, pliant and waiting for his kiss. He hesitated, savoring the wanton look on her face, his lips only a hair's breadth from claiming her mouth. Here was the truth: She wanted him, perhaps as much as he wanted her. And then he chuckled, deep and rich and rumbling, his laughter full of masculine pride and surprising even himself.

Her eyes flew open and she gave a yelp of supreme indignation as Gunnar's amusement deepened. She bucked beneath him. "Lord, how I hate you! I wish I'd never laid eyes on you!"

"That's it, Raina," he coaxed teasingly. "Curse me. Fight me. Despise me if you must, but don't try to deny that you want me, because I'll not believe you for a moment."

" 'Tis not true!"

"Aye, it is," he replied, somewhat annoyed that the idea should give him so much satisfaction. "And I doubt either one of us will have the strength enough to resist it much longer."

"You are raving mad, and easily the most arrogant beast I've ever met!"

"Indeed," he acceded, unable to do much more than smile down at her outraged expression.

"Let me up this instant, you despicable rogue," she cried, twisting and struggling beneath him.

"Give me your word you'll not attempt a foolhardy stunt like this escaping nonsense again and I may consider it."

" 'Twould be a lie if I did," she declared.

"Then I shall have to make certain you don't. Personally, through another, more reliable method."

Her brow furrowed. "What do you mean?"

Rather than answer her, Gunnar rose, scooping her up

into his arms and carrying her back to his waiting mount. Holding the reins in case she tried to abscond with his horse, he pushed her up into the saddle, then mounted behind her and made haste for the keep.

"W-what do you mean by more reliable methods?" Raina stammered when they reached the bailey and Rutledge dismounted, pulling her to the ground. "What do you plan to do with me?"

"What I should have done in the very beginning," he snarled, hauling her past the hall to the stairs. Taking two steps for every one of his, Raina stumbled after him, nearly tripping on the stairs more than once. He met each falter in her gait with a rough jerk of her arm, righting her steps and keeping her scrambling at his side.

Dear God, did he mean to beat her? If the blazing of his eyes were any indication, she'd likely not survive if he did. She had never seen a man so dangerous in his control. In truth she found his quiet rage far more frightening than had he lashed out with angry words and punishing hands. Strangely, some part of her sensed he would not beat her, but punishment in some form was imminent.

She had striven to wake the beast, and now that she had, she wasn't entirely sure what she would do with it. She attempted a bold front. "You can lock me in my chamber for a thousand days—ten thousand days—and I will never yield!"

"I have no intention of locking you in your chamber," he replied coolly.

When they reached the top of the stairs, he pushed her into his chamber and kicked the door shut. "Since you have proven once again that you cannot be trusted, I have decided you shall remain where I can watch you personally. *At all times*."

"Then—you mean, you've no intention of beating me for my actions?"

"Beating you?" The corners of his lips turned up and he chuckled lightly. "Nay, Raina, I'll not beat you. I expected as much from you, and indeed I warned Alaric to be watchful of your every move. 'Twas he who failed to meet my expectations . . . 'tis he who will pay."

Raina's heart lurched. "You don't mean to punish him for what I have done!"

" 'Tis exactly my meaning." He made to walk past her, casually adding, "There is always a price to be paid for disobedience. Surely your father must have taught you that."

"Please, do not do this!"

But he would not meet her gaze, his expression remaining hard and impenetrable as he walked to the door.

"Please," she cried after him, "I cannot bear to think that a child should suffer my punishment."

He hesitated, saying over his shoulder, "Then mayhap you will think twice before you defy me again." He pulled the door closed behind him.

Raina stood in the center of his chamber, staring at the heavy door. Left to nothing but her own remorse, she considered the grave turn her actions had taken. Her situation was growing more hopeless by the moment. What had begun as a means to acquiring freedom had resulted in even graver captivity.

The boy whom she had come to think of as a friend would be punished severely for her deceit. She had used him terribly, preying upon his obvious fancying of her, and now he would learn a bitter lesson about trust. Would that Rutledge had beat her, even to death, she'd have accepted her fate. But she had never given thought to what punishment Alaric might suffer in the end.

Whether intentional or not, Rutledge had also prescribed

a fitting punishment for her. Locked in his quarters, likely to become his whore at his bidding, she would suffer as well. For in her heart, she could not deny what he had said to her in the meadow. Her pulse did indeed race in his presence. Curiosity easily overcame any measure of decorum when her eyes chanced to spy him. And as for her body's reaction to the mere thought of him, that might very well be the worst of her troubles.

Gunnar stormed down the stairs and toward the hall in a rage, his mantle swirling behind him like a black tempest. He had a mind to strangle Alaric, squeeze into oblivion the reckless disobedience that had almost cost Raina her life at his archer's hand. Over and over again he saw the arrow aimed at her back as she fled, and like the longbow's string, the muscles in his gut drew taut with each vivid recollection. His heart yet thundered in his chest, the perspiration moistening his brow and upper lip a reminder of the fury that clutched his entire being to think what might have happened. God's wounds, but he knew not who was the greater fool, his stubbornly defiant captive or his naive squire.

In frustration, Gunnar slammed the heel of his fist against a wooden door beside the entryway of the hall. He barked out Alaric's name, his angry voice rising over the din of anxious activity within the hall. Conversations died immediately as the keep's inhabitants looked in quiet attention to their lord. Though the hour was late, the hall was now awake, likely due to curiosity over the night's excitement and in anticipation of what its consequences might be.

Gunnar strode the length of the room toward the raised platform of the dais where Alaric sat waiting for him, his face downcast, the purple knot on his forehead pronounced and seeming to grow larger by the moment. At his approach, the squire looked up but did not quake when he spied him, as the others in the hall did. Rather, he rose and squared his shoulders. The lad's pride took Gunnar aback, infuriating him all the more and making his voice boom with rage. "Have you any idea what your interference might have cost me?"

A hound whimpered in response and slunk out of the hall. Alaric remained unflinching, though he swallowed hard.

"Aye, milord," he murmured, his voice cracking. "Is—is Lady Raina all right?"

"She is not your concern!" Alaric murmured a quiet apology, tipping his head downward. Gunnar came to stand before him, toe to toe. "You willfully defied my orders to stay away from her."

"I'm sorry," Alaric mumbled, "I only meant to—"

Gunnar seized the squire's shoulders, fighting the urge to shake him senseless. "Never mind what you meant to do, boy! You disobeyed me and nearly got her killed!"

A small group had begun to gather around the dais—Agnes, Burc, and Odette among them—each taking their place amid the curious. Like vultures scenting the imminent spilling of blood, their ranks tightened. Nearly everyone in the keep closed in on lord and squire, their eyes glistening with morbid anticipation of the first blow.

But Gunnar refused to afford them the satisfaction. He released his hold on Alaric, thrusting the squire before him and pointing a finger toward the door. "To the stables, lad," he commanded grimly. As Alaric strode forward with quiet dignity, Gunnar fell in behind him.

Suddenly parched and in grave need of a drink to cool his head, Gunnar grabbed a flagon of wine from one of the tables on his way out of the hall. Several people shuffled at his heels as if yet meaning to witness the squire's punishment. Gunnar turned to face them, his angry scowl stopping the group in their tracks. "Get you to your pallets for the night," he snapped. "I've no need of an audience."

Without sparing them another thought, Gunnar resumed his march behind Alaric, seizing a torch from its sconce in the corridor as he quit the keep, then crossed the moonlit bailey to the low-slung building that served as shelter for the horses. Gunnar deliberately hung back, trying to distance himself from the young squire and the pain of the impending deed.

He breathed deeply of the night air and took a long draught from the flagon. Not surprisingly, neither held the strength to cleanse his overwhelming sense of dread and remorse. From the night four years past when Gunnar had rescued Alaric from what surely would have been a lethal flogging, the boy had been at his side, riding with him from one town to the next, foraging with him for every hard-won meal along the way. Trusting him. Of all the people who had drifted in and out of Gunnar's life, Alaric remained true. Constant. His closest . . .

Dare he call him friend?

The word had an unfamiliar taste to a man who trusted no one, who could ill afford any emotional attachments. Gunnar knew Alaric was fond of him—at least he had been. Be that fondness born of obligation or gratitude, Alaric had proven a devoted page and an eager squire, anxious to earn his own spurs one day. Though he had never made mention of it, Gunnar harbored a flickering hope that he might be the one to sponsor that dream. Someday.

Tonight, however, was no time for dreams. Tonight belonged to duty and honor, and the responsibility that came with both.

His squire had disobeyed direct orders and had done so in a public forum, leaving Gunnar no choice but to discipline him. His men would expect it of him, and so would Alaric.

Anxious now simply to be done with the deed, Gunnar threw open the stable door. The light from his torch flickered, dancing off the stalls and reflecting in the nervous eyes of the horses. Alaric had already taken his position at the far end of the stable, with his back to the door as he unfastened the ties of his tunic.

Gunnar stood in the oppressive silence of the outbuilding, averting his gaze to the rafters. "In all our days together, Alaric, you have never disobeyed me." He looked back to his squire. "Why now? What manner of explanation do you offer for your actions this eve?"

Alaric would not look at him, turning his head only slightly toward his shoulder. "No explanation would excuse what I did, milord," he admitted quietly. "I did not seek to disobey you, truly."

"Then why did you?"

The squire remained silent for a long moment, and Gunnar could scarcely hear his whispered reply. "I felt sorry for her. She was crying, milord, weeping pitifully."

Gunnar felt a twinge of guilt but dashed it away with a sardonic scoff. "A clever ploy, likely designed to lure you to her aid." He took a drink from the flagon and met with Alaric's ardent gaze.

"I think not, milord. She is a gentle lady, and even though she is a d'Bussy, her heart is pure. I know what her father did to you, I well understand your need to destroy him, but I could not bear to think that she might suffer at your hand."

"Ah, Christ," Gunnar muttered, and began to pace the stable. Did everyone think he was incapable of controlling his urges? Was he no more civilized to the world's eyes than a bloody beast? He could understand Raina's fear of him—damnation, he nigh scared even himself in her presence—but the fact that Alaric would doubt his honor burned Gunnar in a place deep inside. What had he become in the lad's eyes? But more to the point, why should it damned well matter what the boy thought of him? Gunnar came to a halt and rested his forehead against one of the supporting beams of the stable. "You don't understand," he began, but Alaric spoke over him.

" 'Tis the way of war, I know, but I would not have expected this of you—" The squire's voice dropped off suddenly. "I cannot deny my disappointment, milord."

Gunnar whipped around to stare at the lad in disbelief. "*You* are disappointed? *In me?*"

Alaric would not look at him. " 'Twas not my place to console her, and for that I apologize, but to hear her crying so . . . I was powerless to refuse."

"A weakness for which you should bear a lifelong reminder on your back, lad." The humor in Gunnar's voice made the threat sound more a chiding than anything else, and he grimaced. Clearing his throat, he began to pace anew. "Have I taught you nothing in these four years? A knight—hell, a man!—cannot allow himself to fall victim to his emotions, Alaric. 'Tis a painful lesson to learn, but learn it you must if you hope to survive."

"Aye, milord." A pensive look came over his features; then he gathered up the hem of his tunic and pulled it over his head. His shoulder blades poked against the pale skin of his narrow back as he tossed the tunic to the ground. Saints' blood, but Gunnar had nearly forgotten his reason for coming to the stables. Alaric, the lad so full of pride and honor, had not. He lowered himself to his knees in the straw and wrapped his hands about the beam before him.

With a frown, Gunnar set the torch in an iron brace bolted onto a supporting beam. Moving with steps made heavy from wine and regret, he retrieved the whip from where it hung nearby. A horse nickered at the disruption, stirring in its stall. Gunnar took his place several paces behind Alaric and slowly uncoiled the lash, his grip tightening and flexing as he stared at the pale canvas of Alaric's skin.

His pulse began to thunder in his temple. A sickening

feeling settled in his belly. Hoping to douse his indecision, Gunnar tipped the flagon to his lips and downed a good portion of the wine, welcoming the burn in his throat and wishing he could take the lad's place again as he had four summers past. God's wounds, but he hated like hell to have to do this! He had never raised a hand to anyone weaker than himself and had sworn he never would. Dragging his forearm across his mouth, he blinked away the remorse that pricked his eyes.

This was different. He had no choice; he had to make an example or risk losing control of all his men. "You understand," Gunnar said in a hoarse whisper. "I must . . ."

"Aye, milord, I know." Alaric's voice, though quiet, seemed stronger than Gunnar's own, and filled with resolve. "I'll not dishonor you . . . or myself . . . by begging for mercy." Gunnar heard the squire's breath catch in his throat before he exhaled a ragged, heavy sigh. "Whenever you are ready, milord."

Chapter Twelve

Raina's head lolled forward to her chest, and she jerked awake for what seemed the hundredth time. Sitting on a pallet with her back against the stone wall, she had been awaiting Rutledge's return to his chamber, hoping to hear that he had changed his mind about punishing Alaric, needing to hear that the boy was all right. But as the hours dragged on and the night began to wane gently into dawn, she realized she had been waiting in vain. Not only had Rutledge likely carried out his threat, but from the undisturbed condition of his bed, he had been at the woeful task all night. The merciless wretch!

She rose to her feet and peered out of the open window that overlooked the bailey. Neither man nor beast stirred in the courtyard below. Nothing bespoke the events that had transpired just a few hours before, nothing to indicate their consequences.

Settling herself on the thick ledge, she breathed deeply of the refreshing northern air. It smelled crisp and wild, and made her pulse quicken, so heady was the scent of freedom. Dawn loomed hesitantly on the horizon, the sun still too shy to peer over the edge of the farthest hill. The keep, and indeed the countryside, stood quiet. Raina could almost imagine she was home, at Norworth, sitting on her window ledge greeting the day as she'd done countless times before. How she wished she were home . . . away from this place.

Away from him.

Away from the feelings he aroused in her.

Her gaze slid to the large, empty bed, and she wondered what he would look like were he sleeping there. Would he sprawl across the width of it or rather sleep rigidly, with the same control and self-awareness he possessed when awake?

An image of him, naked and prone on the mattress, sprang to vivid life in her mind. A shiver skimmed over her, for heaven help her, she could so easily picture herself beneath him! And surely to think it was nigh to do it!

How could she desire this man—for desire it plainly was—how could she ignore all that he was, and indeed, all he was not? How could she feel anything but contempt for a beast like him? What manner of fool was she to crave his touch? Yet in light of all he had done . . . despite all he would do . . . she desired him.

Lord, but she should be praying for Alaric—and for her wicked soul—but here she was, wondering and fantasizing about Rutledge!

Booted footsteps sounded in the corridor beyond the chamber door, sparing her from venturing farther into such treacherous imaginings. They approached quietly, as if seeking to go unnoticed. Who would be sneaking about at this early hour when all were yet abed? She rose from the ledge and faced the door as it opened very slowly.

Rutledge slipped around the panel with the sure-footed stealth of a cat, closing the door without making a sound. He turned then and met Raina's surprised gaze. She crossed her arms over her chest and shot him an imperious glare, but all he did was grunt in response, casting her a disapproving sideways glance as he passed her.

She noted at once his disheveled appearance, the dark

circles beneath his eyes, his drawn and weary expression. He looked thoroughly exhausted, as if he had been awake all night. His worn linen tunic was rumpled, his hair wild and tousled about his face and shoulders. Evidently, his cruelty had kept him awake for a good part of the eve. "You look dreadful," she said with more bravery than she felt.

"A good match for my mood." He sat on the edge of the bed and began unfastening his cross-garters. Belatedly, he lifted his gaze and slowly took her in from head to toe. "You, contrarily, look well rested," he said with a smirk as he turned his attention back to what he was doing. "No worries to keep you awake, 'twould seem."

"I did *not* sleep well, if you must know." He scoffed and she had a notion to scold him. "I was awake most of the night, sick with worry over what cruelty you were imposing on that poor boy. Your nightlong absence from your chamber makes me wonder if you weren't at your torture all this time."

He raised a black brow in mock surprise. "Milady, I confess I hadn't thought you would take notice of my absence. I am flattered to think you would miss me."

Raina's cheeks warmed. "That is not what I meant, and well you know it. I take it now that you have tired of abusing your squire, you've come to torment me?"

He chuckled, shaking his head. "Nay, tempting as the prospect might be, I've come only to change my clothes." As an afterthought, he added, "To set your mind at ease, I was not beating Alaric all night. When I finished with him, I sought rest in the hall with my men."

Raina considered him dubiously, narrowing her eyes. "You smell as if you slept in the stables." To emphasize her point, she sniffed and wrinkled her nose.

Rutledge regarded her with the beginnings of a crooked smile. "Aye? Well, a gentleman would be loath to tell you, lamb, but you're no spring bouquet yourself."

Raina blushed, duly stung. She supposed she wasn't in the best of form, but she hadn't given it a thought until now. Her dress had been stained and torn before her failed escape. Now it was in a truly sorry state of disrepair, the hem frayed and black with dirt, the skirt streaked from numerous falls and general abuse. She had long given up on the sleeve ripped loose when she was taken, leaving her shoulder indecently bared; the other sleeve hung on by mere threads. As for her own odor, she supposed it hadn't improved any in the days past.

She scowled.

Curse Rutledge for making her feel ashamed for something he brought upon her! He was likely only trying to distract her from an uncomfortable topic. Well, she would not prove quite so obliging. "What have you done with poor Alaric?"

"Never you mind about him. I'll not have you attempting to further beguile the lad. Besides, I doubt we'll be seeing much of him today." Tossing one boot to the floor, he had the audacity to grin up at her smugly. "I reckon he's likely too sore to be sociable."

Raina's jaw went slack. "How can you make light of that child's suffering? What sort of monster are you?"

Rutledge's expression became grim. "I'm no more monster than the one you call Father."

"Aye, you are," she replied. "You're heartless."

"I never told you any different."

Raina stared at him long and hard as he went to work on his other boot, wanting to pummel him with her fists. Arrogant, bullying lout! She refused to think that her actions had anything to do with the severity of Alaric's punishment, consoling herself that it was simply Rutledge's way to pick on creatures unfortunate enough to be smaller and weaker than he. The same way he had chosen to pick on

her father, an old man who could bring no harm to anyone—
would never think to bring harm.

He called her father a monster and worse, but she was
surely looking at the monster now. This was simply the
way it was with him: the strong feeding off the weak, the
survival of the fittest and the meek be damned. His world
was one of war and conquering, buying what he could and
stealing what remained. She would not be party to his
predatory ways.

"Do you seek to bore holes in my skull with your stare,
lamb?"

"Would that I could," she vowed hotly, "but I reckon
'tis too hard for even an iron stake to penetrate."

He chuckled, determinedly unaffected by her barbs.

"How could you do it?"

"Milady?" he queried mildly, meeting her gaze.

"How could you beat that boy for showing compassion for
another person? How could you punish him so severely?"

A sardonic curve played at the corners of his mouth.
"And what know you of his punishment?"

"I need only know you to surmise what the boy might
have suffered."

"And do you?" He rose from the bed, his expression
questioning, searching. "Do you know me?" He moved
closer to her, but Raina held her ground, lifting her chin.

"More than I care to know, aye."

He reached out to toy with an errant lock of her hair,
twisting it between his fingers. "Then pray tell, lamb,
what do you know of me?"

Raina pulled the strand from his grasp and drew herself
up to her full height, refusing to wilt under his attempt to
unnerve her. "I know that you are the type of man who
bullies women and children and old men. The type of man
who takes pleasure in lording over those weaker than him."
She gave a flippant toss of her head, emboldened by the

sudden tension now visible in the set of his jaw. She pressed on, seeking to wound him. "In my mind that brands you a coward and unworthy of honor."

He seized her by the arms, bringing her near enough that she could feel his breath stir the fine wisps of hair at her forehead. "Then you must also see me as the type of man to take my pleasure where I will, do you not?" He looked long and hard into her eyes. . . . Then he scoffed. "God's truth, you make me wish I were."

He released her as if he wished he could thrust her from his very sight. Instead, he reached out and merely stroked her cheek with the back of his hand.

Raina flinched, more from the pure shock of feeling him touch her so softly than from the idea that he touched her at all. His hand lingered against her face, his fingers so hard and full of strength, yet gentle enough to wring a sigh from her lips. His mouth twitched nearly imperceptibly at her unwilling response; his gaze dropped to her parted lips.

He wanted to kiss her, that much she knew, and in that same instant Raina found herself wishing he would. She tried to conceal her longing, to quell it with the knowledge of what kissing him would mean. Betrayal. Not only to herself but to her father. Shame engulfed her, for she doubted even that could keep her foolish heart from wishing, from wanting.

He tipped her chin up on the edge of his fist and looked into her eyes, searching and surely, easily, finding her desire for him. The shadow of a smile softened his mouth as his head dipped down slowly, his eyes smoldering and heavy-lidded. Raina drew in her breath as he descended on her mouth, brushing his lips, so painfully soft, against hers.

It was his tenderness that so unnerved her, for she might have expected him to plunder her senses and her body as well, but here he was, testing, not taking, and it nearly made her weep. How could this steely warrior, who professed his lack of heart with such pride, be so tender?

The answer came swiftly.

Because he was skilled at bending people to his will. Those soulful eyes had stripped her of her secrets, and he knew them one and all. He sensed her weakness, and as sure as he was standing before her, coaxing her with tender kisses, he would use it against her.

Cursing her own naïveté, Raina shrank away until she felt the window ledge at her back. He looked puzzled, frowning at her sudden flight and questioning with his eyes her apparent change of heart.

"I can't do this," she whispered, surprised she had enough strength of will to form the denial in her head, let alone voice it to him. "I-I don't want you . . . I don't want you near me," she said, stumbling over the lie.

He saw through her even still. "After last eve? I don't believe you." He reached out to her.

Raina flattened herself against the cool stone wall. "Stay away from me, please."

But Rutledge advanced. Two steps and his chest was nearly touching hers. "Why should I?" he questioned, his tone playful but the glimmer in his eyes too hungry to be harmless.

Raina broke his gaze, turning her head to look askance. "Because, I—"

He caught her chin and brought her back to face him, pressing a chaste kiss to her lips. "Why?"

"B-because," she stammered, searching her brain for a reason and shocked that she could find none. At her hesitation, he dipped his face to her neck, nipping and teasing the soft skin below her ear. "Oh, mercy," she breathed as he captured her earlobe between his teeth. His breath came fast and hard in her ear, filled with want. She shuddered. "Please," she hissed, "don't . . ."

"Why, Raina?" His silky lips brushed against her skin, his deep voice reverberating in her ears, her heart—dear God, her soul!

Why, indeed? Because she should hate him? Because he was the most dangerous man she had ever encountered? Because she was so very afraid that if she surrendered her body to him, she might also surrender her heart?

She pressed her hands against his chest to push him away and felt his heartbeat, thudding beneath her fingertips as strong and sure as her own. Heaven help her, but she thrilled at the feel of his hard muscle under her palms. More than anything, she wanted to feel his hands on her as well.

The reasons why he should not were many, each one more treacherous than the next, but perhaps the most perilous of all was the one that whispered of the greatest pleasure.

Because she might be tempted to love him.

"Tell me why I shouldn't touch you." From the seductive tone of his voice, Raina knew he understood her indecision, her lack of mettle. A moment longer in his embrace and she would be lost. . . .

Her answer, though feeble, came blurting out in a rush. "Because you stink of wine and horseflesh!"

In truth, he didn't smell as bad as she would have him believe, but she felt wounding his pride a likely means as any of dissuading his attentions. He needn't know that she found him, and his wholly masculine scent, a troubling distraction and longed to be away from his vexing presence.

He appeared thoroughly taken aback and he laughed, though his brows crashed into an affronted scowl. Raina didn't dare flinch, maintaining her rigid stance and even squaring her shoulders. Rutledge's expression swiftly changed to one of defensive coolness, not quite masking his injured masculine vanity. He lifted his arm and sniffed at himself with what was certainly deliberate crudeness.

"Forgive me, *my lady*," he replied, with an almost convincingly apologetic tone, "but it seems you are right. And I have forgotten my breeding. What manner of rudeness not to offer my lovely *guest* a much needed bath?" That dazzling, ruthless grin was back in full force, and Raina knew she had ventured into deep waters.

It was her only warning. He swept her into his arms and headed for the chamber door, ignoring her demands that he put her down and undaunted by her efforts to squirm out of his hold. She was able to make opening the door a difficult task, but it only served to frustrate him and in the end delayed him but a moment.

"What are you doing?" Raina cried as he carried her swiftly through the corridor and down the stairwell. She cursed him—loudly—when he refused to answer her, and as he hustled past the hall, she cringed in outrage to see the numerous sleep-wrinkled faces blinking at her in disbelief.

In the next moment he was crossing the length of the bailey, headed for the portcullis. Was he turning her out of the keep? Had she irritated him so much that he no longer wished to be burdened with her? The idea should have elated her, but instead she found she was disappointed that he would give up so easily.

As they approached the iron gate, he called for the guards to open it. They shot perplexed looks at him but obliged without a word. Rutledge slipped out as soon as space enough permitted the both of them to clear the gate. Raina waited for him to set her on her feet and slam the gate behind her, but he kept walking.

"Where are you taking me?"

"You're going to take a bath, milady," he said, not even huffing from the trek. "And so am I. A very cold one. Mayhap it will shock some sense into me."

"I am not going to bathe with you!" she gasped, terrified at the prospect.

He didn't bother to reply, merely headed purposefully in the direction of the pond. At their approach a heron took flight from the reedy perimeter of the water. A hazy mist floated above the moist ground and at the fringes of the placid surface. Raina shivered just looking at it.

"I am not going to bathe in that icy water," she declared. "And most assuredly not with you!"

Rutledge kept walking, heading straight for the sloping embankment.

"Do you hear me?" If he did, he ignored her. "Unhand me at once!"

He tromped down the bank and into the pond, stopping when the water reached his knees. "Perhaps 'twill also cool my lady's hot head."

With that, he tossed her into the air.

Raina experienced but a moment of disbelief before she hit the water with a loud clap, rump first. Waves of cold, murky water splashed over her head as she descended like a stone below the surface. She gasped at the chill, drawing in a mouthful of water as she did. Her feet touched the velvety silt that blanketed the pond floor, and she vaulted up and out of the water, coughing and sputtering while she tried to wipe the hair from her eyes. Her composure somewhat restored, Raina summoned breath enough to hurl a flurry of curses at him that doubtless would have crossed her father's eyes to hear upon her lips.

Rutledge merely chuckled where he stood, several feet away.

"You—bastard!" she croaked, standing waist-high in the water, peeling slimy weeds from her gown and hair. Her skirts floated up in a wide circle around her, exposing her legs to the chill water. A queer tickling sensation at her knees drew her attention away from Rutledge for a moment.

Like little kisses, something pecked at first one knee, then the other. She felt a quick brush against her thigh and gave a little hop, peering into the water. A small fish darted out from under her billowing gown, followed by another. Raina screamed, jumping backward and shoving at her skirts, trying to keep them down about her legs.

Rutledge evidently found her struggles highly amusing, for he crossed his arms over his chest and laughed deeply. She didn't find the situation—or him—the least bit funny. Raking her arm over the pond's surface, she swiped a wave of water at him. "Detestable, overbearing boor!"

His laughter died abruptly as the splash soaked his head and shoulders. Satisfied, Raina turned to swim a safer distance from him, should he think to retaliate. When she spun about to gauge his reaction, her heart slammed into her ribs.

With his eyes trained on her, and water dripping from his hair and nose, Rutledge waded farther into the water.

He pulled off his tunic.

"Don't you dare think to bathe while I'm in here!" But Rutledge only grinned, then flung his discarded tunic to the shore without a backward glance. "Oh, sweet Mary," she whispered on an intake of breath.

What an awesome vision he was, striding toward her bare-chested. A dark mat of hair covered his chest but did little to conceal the sculpted power of his torso, the rigid planes of his abdomen. His skin had been kissed bronze by time in the sun, his arms thick with sinew, honed from years of battle and physical toil. Gaping at him as she was now, Raina could think of only one word to describe his ruggedly masculine appeal.

Magnificent.

A queer shiver wormed its way through her body and set her teeth to chattering. The water no longer felt cold but rather warm . . . alive . . . and she knew it had everything to do with the sight of him. "Come no further!" she pleaded, knowing he would ignore her.

When the water reached his waist, he unfastened the ties of his braies and bent to step out of them. He drew them out of the water, wadding them into a ball that he then pitched casually over his shoulder. The knowledge that he was now naked sent a tumultuous shiver down Raina's spine.

Good lord, what had she gotten herself into?

"Stay where you are!" He ignored her plea, ducking down to his shoulders in the water to swim slowly toward her.

Silently, stealthily, he drifted closer.

Raina took a step backward, then another. Still he advanced. A wickedly mischievous grin tugged at his lips the instant before he disappeared under the pond's rippling surface. Mercy, but he was coming for her! Raina shrieked, then turned to swim away from him, paddling and kicking frantically against the weight of her bliaut.

A moment later his warm hand closed about her ankle, halting her flight and easily pulling her back. She twisted and turned in his grasp, trying to writhe free. Her attempts were at best futile, and judging from the look on his face, served only to amuse him. "Let go!" she sputtered as her face dipped below the water.

He obliged but caught her by the waist and pulled her to him. He held her close, just looking at her, as their legs entwined beneath the water. Raina blinked at him, her heart fluttering into her throat, scandalized at the feel of his thigh between her knees. For a long, wondrous moment, they gazed at each other in silent appraisal. In his eyes Raina saw a man . . . not the soulless blackguard she so desperately needed to believe he was, but a living, breathing—and oh so dangerously arousing—man.

He curled his arm tighter about her waist, bringing her closer. The water, made warm from the heat generated between them, lapped sensuously about their shoulders. Raina squeezed her eyes closed as her breasts pressed against his bare skin. Even through the fabric of her gown she could feel the hard ridges and planes of his chest. He felt too good against her body, too enticing. Bracing her hands on his shoulders, she tried with feeble effort to push away.

"Tell me what you know about me now, Raina," he whispered, moving wickedly against her. "Do you know how much I want you?"

Aye, dear heaven above, she did know. She could feel the very evidence of his desire, his rigid shaft, pressing boldly against her hip. Inwardly she rejoiced at the knowledge that he wanted her, knowing it was shameful, cursing her fool heart for wishing for this. She abandoned the pretense of trying to flee his arms and felt his grip about her waist relax, though he still held her firmly against his body. A mewling sound curled up from her throat, seeming to please him, for he echoed it with a rumbling groan as he dipped to press his lips against her neck.

"Have you any idea what pleasure we could share? Say you want me, Raina," he coaxed, his voice nearly seducing the awful truth from her lips.

"Nay." Her voice was reduced to a desperate whisper as his hand splayed across her back, caressing her, his touch so warm and strong. Oh, sweet Mary, what desire she felt for this man! She closed her eyes against the feelings he so deftly churned within her, steeling her heart against wanting to love him. "I despise you," she murmured feebly.

"But still you let me touch you."

His voice stirred her very soul, its richness only adding to her heightened awareness of him and the effect he had on her body. Raina stood spellbound, caught in a liquid web of longing and helpless to deny him—to deny herself— the sweet, swelling ache. Some distant thread of sanity might have urged her to hold him off, but instead she clung to him, even pulled him closer still, thrilling to feel each bulge and crevice of his sculpted, powerful arms. She smoothed her hands up his arms to twine her fingers in his hair, so soft and silky, his nape warm and strong. This close his scent was maddening, at once musky and spicy. Infinitely male.

Beneath the water his fingers skated over her back and down to her buttocks. He made a pleasured sound in the back of his throat when she made no move to stop him. "You let me touch you, and you wish I would do more," he whispered huskily. "You wish I would do the things you haven't the nerve to imagine, let alone ask for."

His fingers skimmed down her thigh and under her knee, hooking her leg and bringing it up the length of his own, anchoring her around his hip. The crisp hairs on his thigh tickled her skin, so warm, nestled snug against the juncture of her thighs. The thrill was so shockingly intimate, Raina gasped, dizzy with this sensation that was so new to her, her breath swept nearly clean away.

"Please . . ." she whispered, "don't . . ." His hand cupped her bottom and she held her breath, feeling him caress her, gently, tentatively. She shuddered against his palm, biting her lip to keep from crying out as he explored her with such aching tenderness. "Don't do this. . . ."

"What is it you think I intend to do? Pray, tell me, lamb, for I myself am at a loss. Should I ravish you right here and now, claim you as my vengeance and put us both out of our misery? Or mayhap you think I should do the honorable thing, let you keep your virtue so you can later relinquish it to some spineless whelp like Nigel?"

Raina swallowed convulsively, unable to find her voice, unable to form words. She wanted to lash out at him for saying something so crude and shocking, but instead she remained, captive in his arms, watching as his eyes grew deep and smoky with the waging of some inner battle. Then his embrace loosened and fell away.

"Nay, Raina," he said, "I won't do this. When you and I come together, it will have nothing to do with virtue or vengeance. Ours will be a coupling of pleasure alone, and a time, I promise you, neither of us will likely ever forget."

He moved so their bodies no longer touched, leaving her cold and shivering in the water. "Go on." He dismissed her with a gentle jerk of his head.

Raina hesitated, unsure what to do. Part of her wanted to stay, wanted to know him in a way she'd never known a man before. Another part begged her to run and spare herself certain heartbreak.

Tentatively, she moved closer to him.

"Go!" he barked. "Before I no longer have a care for what you think of me!"

Raina bolted from the water at his outburst, half stumbling as the weeds and her heavy skirts tangled about her legs. Biting back her tears, she fled up the bank and toward the keep, never once looking back. What had she been thinking? She was nothing to him! His enemy's spawn, had he not called her that? How could she have let him touch her so intimately? She felt his hands on her even now, and curse her strumpet's soul, she clutched the memory of his touch to her heart, determined to cherish it always.

What madness did she suffer that she could so easily dismiss all his treacherous deeds for a moment of stolen pleasure? She had set out to scold him for his maltreatment of Alaric and instead had wound up letting him do things to her that no one had a right to do. It shocked her infinitely that the fact he had proven himself a liar and a bully—verily a cold-blooded murderer—meant nothing to her. In truth, she was eager to make excuses for him, to believe that beneath his steely demeanor he did in fact have a warm and beating heart. What a fool she was!

With her wet skirts draped over her arm, Raina slipped

through the open gate and dashed across the bailey. All she wanted was to be alone, to never have to look upon his face and see her shame reflected in his cool gaze! All she wanted was to be home, safe in her father's protective arms.

She fled past the henhouse and sent a handful of chickens scattering in all directions. They clucked and complained noisily, drowning out her hitching breath. When she reached the stable she stopped, ducking around the corner of the building and leaning her back against the cool exterior wall. Pressing the back of her hand to her mouth, she tried to compose herself enough to enter the keep and face the rest of the folk within. No one could know her shame. It was bad enough he knew; to be the laughingstock of everyone here would be her death.

She took a deep, cleansing breath and heard the stable door creak open. Alaric appeared at the corner of the building. His expression tightened when he spied her, and he hastened away toward the keep.

"Alaric!" Her own worries forgotten for the time being, she started after him, wanting to make her apologies and see for herself that he was all right. "Alaric, please, I must speak with you."

The boy cast a quick glance over his shoulder at her, then hurried his pace. Raina's heart sank to see the young man who once regarded her with affection now flee from her. It was surely understandable, she reasoned ruefully.

"Alaric, stop!" she called. "I demand that you stop and listen to me." At her direct order, the boy halted. He stood motionless, his back turned to her as she approached him.

"I am not to speak to you, my lady."

"Is that what he told you to say?"

Alaric nodded his head. "Milord has forbade it."

"Is that what you wish as well?"

Finally he turned to face her. "It matters not what I wish, milady. I am a squire in training to be a knight, and I have been given an order. I shall obey it." His brows were knit together determinedly, but his eyes looked upon her with the same softness they always had.

She smiled and touched his cheek with the back of her hand in a decidedly maternal gesture. "I am so sorry for what you have gone through because of me. Can you ever find it in your heart to forgive me?"

"There is naught to forgive, milady. You behaved exactly as Lord Gunnar said you would."

"Aye, but you must know, I had no idea that you would suffer for it." The youth looked at her blankly. "Were you hurt badly?"

"Nay, milady," he said, with a shake of his head. "Your aim was true, but thankfully, I've a hard skull and escaped with only a bump."

"Oh, mercy, your head!" she exclaimed, suddenly recalling the blow she dealt him. "I'm truly sorry about that, too. But I was speaking more of the punishment met at *his* hand."

"Milady?" Alaric regarded her with a look of confusion.

"It should have been me who received a beating, not you. I suspect it was some sense of twisted justice for him to punish you in my place."

"Oh, nay, you have it wrong, milady. Milord but lectured me."

"Lectured you with his fist or the end of a whip, no doubt."

"Nay, though had I known the hell I would pay"—he blushed—"begging pardon, milady, had I any idea how I'd feel this morn, I might have preferred a sound flogging."

Raina frowned in astonishment. This couldn't be! For all of Rutledge's boasting over the task to her, for all his apparent pride in his cruelty, he had done nothing? "You mean to tell me he did not beat you?"

Alaric shook his head. "Just a lecture." He gingerly

clutched both temples in his palms. "And one too many flagons of wine."

Raina's eyes narrowed. How dare he let her believe the worst about him! How dare he let her stew all night with worry over Alaric's well-being when he intended only to corrupt the boy with spirits and a tongue lashing! She didn't know which made her more furious, the fact that he let her call him all those terrible things, or the idea that she had actually believed them herself.

Raina scarcely acknowledged Alaric's departure; she heard his murmured "by your leave" but was too caught up in her consideration of his lord to reply.

So, not only did the blackguard mock her desire for him, but he also sought to build himself into a far greater menace in her eyes—and, it would seem, in the eyes of everyone else in the keep—than he actually was. She could hardly wait to let him know that she, for one, would not be fooled.

Chapter Thirteen

Raina was nearly excited to be summoned to prepare for the midday meal. The morning had passed quickly enough, despite the fact that she had spent it in the solar beside Agnes, mending various items that were almost beyond repair. The old crone had said nary a word to her, and Raina didn't dare open the door to conversation for fear she would learn that the entire keep had been made aware of her early morning sojourn to the pond with their lord.

Instead, she had minded her work in silence, then, upon Agnes's direction, followed her down to the kitchens to assist with dinner, the heartiest meal of the day. Two hares had been caught on the morning's hunt and had been added to a venison stew. Several cheeses and fresh breads rounded out the dinner, filling the kitchen with wonderfully mouthwatering smells.

With Agnes on her heels, Raina carried a large tray out to the hall. It seemed quieter than usual, the men more well behaved and orderly. No dogs assaulted her tray nor did they lurk under the tables. In fact, the hall looked positively respectable: The old, yellowed rushes had been swept clean away; no cups or forgotten food littered the floor. She wondered what had come over everyone, why the sudden semblance of order, and then she spied *him*.

Rutledge sat at his table on the dais, clean-shaven and dressed in a cream-colored tunic that sported only one patch. His dark hair curled at his collar and over one eye, making him look rakish and charming at the same time. She had felt him watching her from the moment she entered the room, and now that she dared look his way, he smiled. Her cheeks flamed in recollection of what that smile had gotten her into earlier.

Agnes took the last available seat at one of the trestle tables, leaving Raina standing conspicuously in the middle of the hall. She spun to her right, then to her left, praying someone would take pity on her and make room on their bench. No one moved; they all simply stared at her, some of them already stuffing bread into their mouths, others outright content to enjoy her discomfiture.

It was then she felt him rise from his chair. Without looking his way, she knew that Rutledge was now standing on the dais and waiting for her to turn his way. She did and saw that he was indicating a chair to his right. Raina glanced to the expectant faces surrounding her. They were all waiting for her to take her place beside him. They offered her no room among them because she didn't belong there. Her place was at their lord's side, as his prisoner.

Steeling herself against the sea of disregard engulfing her, Raina marched toward the dais. She'd be damned if she would let them think they had beaten her! She did not care what they thought—or, heaven help her, what they knew—about her circumstances. She would face this further humiliation with dignity. And if he thought to intimidate her, he would be sorely disappointed. She knew his game and she intended to make him aware that she would no longer play the victim.

With a flippant toss of her head, she ascended the dais and stood beside him, glaring murderously lest he think to utter one word about their encounter that morning.

"Please, sit," was all he said.

Raina frowned, warily seating herself beside him and

refusing to look at him as he took his own chair. The hall
was soon abuzz with eating and conversation, no one
paying much attention to the dais at all. She breathed an
inward sigh of relief that a confrontation had been avoided
and dared a sidelong glance toward Rutledge. He poured
a cup of ale from the decanter in front of him and passed it
to her.

"What is the meaning of this?" she asked guardedly.

He peered into the cup. " 'Tis ale," he declared. "Do
you thirst?"

Raina simply stared at him, her frown deepening. He
held the cup out for a moment longer, then shrugged and
drank from it himself. He picked up a dark loaf of bread
and broke it in half, tearing a bite from one piece as he set
the other in front of Raina. Reluctantly, she accepted it,
nibbling on the edge as he poked through the venison in the
trencher with his poniard. Knowing that as the lord's prisoner she would likely be left with whatever scraps he had
the generosity to spare, she gnawed her bread more fervently. She would starve before she'd accept his leavings.

Raina watched him from the corner of her eye as he
speared a succulent morsel on his blade and brought it before him, inspecting it. Then he turned to her. She glanced
at him in startled confusion as he held the offering out to
her. Ordinarily it would not be uncommon for a man and
woman to share a trencher, but the way he was doing it,
and the look in his eyes . . . it was unseemly. In front of the
entire hall, he intended to feed her from his poniard.

Like a lover.

He grinned wryly. "I am not entirely devoid of breeding."

Awkwardly, tentatively, Raina moved forward to take
the small chunk of meat in her mouth. She pulled away as
soon as her lips closed around it, feeling a drop of the tasty
brown juice dribble from the corner of her mouth. His attention fell to her lips and remained there as she quickly

and self-consciously swiped the juice away with her fingers. His mouth spread into a lazy smile, but his eyes were dark, his gaze unwavering as he regarded her for a long moment.

Raina chewed the tender bit of venison for what felt like an eternity, the small morsel seeming to expand to fill her entire mouth under Rutledge's pensive scrutiny. At last he turned his attention back to his meal, taking a bite for himself as Raina gulped down the mouthful of meat.

Raina shook her head when he presented her with another bite from his trencher. "Please," she whispered, looking about the hall at the men gathered there. "You are embarrassing me."

Rutledge scowled. "Embarrassing you, how?"

He moved the poniard closer to her lips, and Raina swatted his hand away. "They will think we are lovers."

"Let them," he answered with a shrug, then handed her the poniard. Reluctantly, she accepted it and took the chunk of meat in her mouth. Rutledge watched her intently, remarking, "'Twill be true soon enough, I reckon."

She glared at him, feeling her color rise to her scalp. Her fingers closed about the poniard, and she counted him a fool for giving her a weapon.

"If you act on that ill-conceived notion, lamb," he warned sweetly, "I'll have you over my knee in a trice with your pert little arse bared for all to see the penance of your folly."

"You don't mean that," Raina returned, though she set the poniard down just the same. "I suspect your bark is worse than your bite."

"Really?" he said, his brows rising in challenge. "Perhaps you should ask those assembled here this eve whether or not I mean what I say."

"I've no need to ask them," she replied smartly, very pleased with herself. "Inasmuch as I already have my proof."

He chuckled, eyeing her over the rim of his cup. "What proof?"

"I saw Alaric this morning on my way back from . . ." Her voice trailed off as he slowly lowered his cup, and she immediately regretted bringing up either uncomfortable topic.

Unbelievably, Rutledge's face blanched. "What did he tell you?" Raina watched the emotions play across his features, first surprise, for she surely had caught him off guard; then a certain anxiety drew his mouth into a scowl. He blinked and fury burned in his dark eyes. *"What did he tell you?"*

Raina gulped. "Th-that you lectured him . . . got him sick with wine—"

"Damnation!" he bellowed, slamming his fist on the table. When several heads turned his way—Alaric's included—Rutledge lowered his voice to a tight whisper. "That boy doesn't know when to keep his fool mouth shut!"

"Do not blame him. Even had he not told me, like as not, I would have seen the truth of it on your face. You didn't beat him," she confirmed, relieved when the ire blazing in his eyes began to dissipate slowly. "You let me think you did, but you didn't. And now you would have these people think you have taken me as your whore." She shook her head soberly. "I'll not be a party to your games, whatever your motives."

Rutledge moved so fast, she scarcely knew what hit her. In one swift motion he had unseated her and laid her across the table on her back, covering her with his body. The hall, which had become as silent as a tomb just a moment before, now erupted into hearty cheers and applause as Rutledge pressed into her. Cupping her breast in one hand and holding both her wrists above her head with the other, he kissed her like the crudest of scoundrels.

Scandalized to feel his hips between her thighs, Raina kicked and bucked beneath him, outraged that he would demean her in such a manner before his people. Her struggles only raised the din in the hall to a fever pitch as cups and knives were banged upon the tables in appreciation.

"Unhand me!" she cried.

"Breathe a word to anyone and you force me to prove you a liar . . . on both counts."

Raina felt pinned by his eyes even more so than his body. His simmering gaze told her without a doubt that he did indeed mean what he said. "Beast!" she spat. But he only grinned, then he kissed the tip of her nose and stood up, straightening his tunic as if he had not a care in the world.

Raina rose up on her elbows. "Repulsive churl!" She tried to land her heel in his groin, but he jumped nimbly out of the way, chuckling, so full of humor. So full of himself! "Despicable toad!" she screamed, seizing her half-eaten loaf of bread and hurtling it at his chest.

"To the yard, men!" Rutledge called, weathering her assault and her epithets with irritating nonchalance. He flashed a devilish grin at her. "Ere this wench tempts me further with her dulcet crooning."

In a noisy blur of waving swords and scuffling boots, the men cleared the hall, whooping and cheering as they followed their lord to the practice field for an afternoon of war play.

Raina stood, squaring her shoulders in preparation for facing Agnes, Odette, and Dorcas, who had begun gathering up the trays and cups. None of them said a word about what had occurred, neither did they glance her way. Finding herself fortunate not to have to withstand further denigration by these women, Raina busied herself with clearing the lord's table.

Her skirts full of items to be cleaned or doled out to the animals, Raina followed the others out of the hall and toward the kitchens. The bread trenchers, which would have been given to the villeins at Norworth, were separated into two piles, one to be used again at the evening's meal, the other to be fed to the dogs. There was no leftover food at this keep, just a few scraps of bread and cheese, which the women sifted through and ate themselves. The cups and flagons were dumped into a washbasin to be cleaned. Raina pitched her collection into the water one by one, punctuating each toss with a curse on Rutledge's various body parts, beginning with his inflated head. It felt good to vent her frustrations, and she welcomed the respite from his vexing company.

With a final, colorful oath directed toward his entrails, she threw the last item into the basin, then peered about the kitchen, anxious to find something else to do. She had all afternoon to exorcise her rage, and besides, Rutledge still had several body parts left to denounce.

Intent on inquiring of the women what she could assist with next, Raina whirled about to face them and her question died on her lips. "What is wrong?" she prompted, her brows drawing together in a befuddled frown. "Why are you all looking at me so queerly?"

Three female faces, each in a different stage of womanhood, looked upon her with soft, knowing eyes. Agnes smiled. They were all looking at her as if they wished to embrace her! As if they pitied her.

Raina felt herself flush all the way to her bare toes with impotent rage and embarrassment. She shook her head, wanting to deny their suspicions, to defend her virtue—even if it were by some miracle alone that it yet remained intact. She wanted to speak out, but Rutledge's warning echoed in her ears.

He would prove her a liar.

"Ye needn't be ashamed," Agnes soothed, patting her hand and leading her to a chair. "Ye've lost yer 'eart to a man who only wanted yer virtue. 'Tis a woman's folly—"

Raina drew her hand from between Agnes's. "Nay, you don't understand—" she began, but Odette interrupted her, her voice surprisingly contemplative, rational.

"There's nary a woman alive these days what 'asn't been bought, sold, or traded for somethin' a man wanted." Raina knew from her bitter expression that the woman spoke from experience. " 'Tis only yer body they want. I say, make use of what ye got . . . while ye got it."

Dorcas, the petite blonde who had been so kind to Raina since she had arrived, hushed Odette with a curt wave of her hand. "Lord Gunnar's really not all that bad." She gave Raina a wistful little smile. "Have patience with him, and mayhap you can convince him to keep you."

"I assure you," Raina interjected, "I have no intention of trying to win that man's affection. Nor do I want him to keep me!" The three women merely smiled indulgently and went back to their cleaning. " 'Tis the truth!" Raina insisted. Damn him and his bullying ways. She refused to be the butt of his jest a moment longer. "And further," she said, stamping her foot and balling her fists on her hips, "I am not his leman!"

This vehement declaration earned a bout of giggles from the two younger women. Odette snorted as she plucked a fatty chunk of venison from a sopping trencher and tossed it to a waiting hound. They didn't believe her!

"I'm not!" Raina cried, her face warming from humiliation.

"Come on now," Agnes said, hooking her arm through Raina's bent elbow. "There's no need for all of us to sit about in 'ere. We've plenty of work to keep us busy elsewhere."

Raina peered over her shoulder as Agnes led her from the kitchens. Odette stood, mimicking Raina's angered stance of a moment before. "I'm not his leman," she cried in a falsetto voice, stomping her foot. "I'm not!"

Dorcas threw a wet washrag at the older woman, and both burst out in peals of laughter.

The remains of a tallow candle flickered in a puddle of lard and burned out, drawing Raina's gaze up from her mending. She stretched her arms and her back, then tried to rub the tight kink from her neck. She had spent the entire afternoon sequestered in Rutledge's chamber, even refusing to take her evening meal in the hall. Blessedly, he had not insisted on her presence beside him, and had allowed a tray of food and a tankard of wine to be brought up to her.

Raina picked at the portion of cold, boiled fish, then settled on the bread, washing it down with a mouthful of strongly spiced wine. With the chill night air blowing in through the window and the sting of embarrassment still fresh in her mind, she found the warmth of her drink a welcome balm to both her body and her soul. Tipping the cup to her lips once more, she drank until she spied the bottom of the tankard.

Her father did not permit her to drink anything but honeyed mead and occasionally ale at Norworth, as he himself never imbibed wine. The devil's own nectar, he called it. Raina didn't find it altogether unpleasant, though it was fast making her eyelids heavy.

She yawned and her eyes drifted to the empty, oversize bed. Draped in fur blankets with a fluffy down-filled bolster, it looked so inviting, so much more comfortable than her straw pallets of the past few nights. Raina crept over to it and sat on the edge of the bed, testing the mattress, and decided there would be no harm in lying down, just for a moment. . . .

* * *

Gunnar's empty cup hit the table harder than he'd intended, the wine having dulled his senses to a blissful numbness. Though he prayed for it, the drink did little to dull his awareness of the enticing creature awaiting him in his chamber. The hour was late, the evening meal long since cleared away as Gunnar sat with his men, partaking of his dwindling store of wine.

He was not surprised, and more to the point, he was inwardly thankful that Raina had declined to eat in the hall. Loath to face her rightful outrage over his behavior in the pond and his crude display of the afternoon, neither was he sure he could endure another meal in such close company with his captive. His plan to act as if she were his lover had been hastily concocted when he spied her distress as she stood alone in the center of his hall. The need to protect her, to shield her from insult struck swiftly, urging him out of his chair and requiring her to sit beside him.

Rattled from their encounter in the pond, he had merely intended to share some of his discomfiture with Raina, and if his men thought the two of them were lovers, so be it. The idea would surely keep them at bay should any man fancy himself a candidate for her charms. But when she so unexpectedly blurted out that she had talked with Alaric and knew the lad had escaped punishment, it was all Gunnar could do to contain himself.

It wasn't bad enough his loose-tongued squire likely told her all he'd said in his drunken lecture. In truth, he could scarcely recall what he'd said himself, but what he could remember created a dull throb in his temple even now. He'd carped on most of the night about women and the way they wormed into a man's resolve, leaving him crazed with want and willing to promise anything he had for the chance to taste of their sweetness.

The worst of what he had said was clear enough to be

painful: He had admitted his attraction for Raina, and—curse the wine!—he thought certain he'd confessed that he thought she would make some lucky bastard an enviable wife.

Gunnar groaned just to think on it. If Alaric let *that* unfortunate admission slip when he spoke with Raina, he'd bloody well pull the little whelp's tongue out!

Damnation, but he needed another drink.

"Boy!" he barked, sitting up sharply and waving his cup to Rupert, his page. "Another flagon of wine!"

"Have a care, milord," one man said with a wink. "Much more drink and you risk disappointing your lady."

"Or passin' out down 'ere with us again when ye could be abovestairs!" someone else added.

Gunnar groaned. The last place he wanted to be was abovestairs in his bedchamber. His men thought he had already sampled Raina's pleasures and in fact had been singing praises to his virility most of the night, which made his decision to refrain from doing so that much harder to uphold. His only hope was either to outdrink or outlast these men, and he would gladly take whichever occurred first. "Another flagon, I say!" He clutched his head in his hands, frowning into his empty cup as the knights around him chuckled.

" 'Twould take a bloody barrel of wine to keep me from beddin' that beauty," one man announced to the delighted assent of the others.

Where the devil was that page?

"She's a proud one, that wench."

"Aye," agreed another. "What I'd give to be the one to tame her!"

"Tame her?" countered the first man. "Mores the like she'd have you slavering at her heels!" His remark earned hearty chuckles from the others.

Gunnar remained silent, scarcely aware of the conversation until someone said, "Why, if I hadn't more sense, I'd say milord is afeared of that wench!"

"Who said that?" he barked, his head snapping to attention.

A young knight gulped audibly. " 'Twas a jest, milord."

Gunnar might have found it humorous if it were not so close to the truth. He rose, ignoring the swimming haze clouding his vision and making his legs unstable. Rupert arrived at last with the requested flagon of wine, which Gunnar snatched roughly from his hands. He put the decanter to his lips and took a long draught, negligently letting the wine trickle down his chin and onto his tunic. He exhaled deeply as he brought the flagon down, dragging the back of his hand across his mouth as the knights stared up at him in wonder. "Now, if you'll pardon my haste, lads," he said with a wolfish grin, "I'll leave you to your jests. There's a wench abovestairs in need of my attentions."

With flagon in hand, Gunnar strode away from the table and out of the hall, leaving the goading laughter of the knights behind him. He started up the stairs and paused.

Jesu, *was* he afraid of Raina d'Bussy?

He thought of what he'd likely encounter upon entering his chamber, pictured her haughty expression, her impudent mouth and flippant tilt of her chin . . . the tempting softness of her curves.

Hell yes, he was afraid of her. But like any other fear he had learned to overcome, he had to face her. That was the only way he could rid himself of the bothersome feeling.

He took the rest of the stairs two at a time, then drew himself up to what he hoped was an intimidating height and opened the door to his chamber. The light from a torch in the corridor traced a glowing path through the dark chamber to his bed. The scowl he had prepared to greet her with faded the moment his eyes lit on her sleeping form.

Curled up on his bed like a babe, Raina slept quietly, her

breath coming in short puffs between her parted lips. Gunnar stared at her for a long moment, fighting the urge to cross the room and touch her, contenting himself simply to gaze upon the willful beauty in repose. She didn't look so fretful now. She looked like an angel fallen from heaven who'd landed softly, blessedly, in his bed.

Damnation. How was he ever to harden his heart to this gentle, slumbering lamb? What sort of monster would it take to look upon her with anything but tender affection, with pure and absolute reverence? To his chagrin, it seemed he was not made of that stuff.

Insane as it felt to admit it, particularly to himself, Raina d'Bussy's virtue was safer with him now than it would be in an abbey full of octogenarian monks. A fact that had nothing to do with wine or want but rather fear. Fear that she would not turn him away, fear that she would feel too good in his arms and too pleasurable in his bed. Fear also that if he claimed her, he'd be loath to let her go when the time came to meet with her father.

So for tonight he would content himself with sleeping beside her, and for the rest of their time together, he would think no more of making love to her. Praying the time would pass quickly, he stepped inside the chamber and, as gently as he could, closed the door.

Raina awoke, startled by the sound of the door shutting with a clunk. A heavy footstep scuffed in the rushes, dislodging something that rolled across the floor. She heard Rutledge curse under his breath and her eyes flew open, though she herself was far too alarmed to dare so much as breathe. But she didn't have to draw breath to know that he smelled of wine. Goodness, he might have even bathed in it.

The room was dark, without even so much as the benefit of embers from a dying fire, but she knew for certain she was yet in his bed. Heaven help her, what a dolt she'd been to climb onto it even for a moment! Now she was faced with either feigning sleep and hoping he was too drunk or too chivalrous to consider molesting her, or she could throw herself from the bed before he reached her and avoid the issue entirely.

From behind her, at the other side of the bed, came the sound of his footsteps, the soft thud and slosh of a wine flagon being set on the floor. A rustle of fabric preceded the jingle of a buckle as Rutledge removed his baldric and set his sword against the wall beside the bed. She rolled over to find him facing her, pulling his tunic over his head.

"What do you think you are doing?" she gasped.

His reply was casual and rather tired-sounding. "Removing my clothing so I might go to bed."

"I can very well see that!" She sat up and scowled at him. "Cease doing so this instant!"

"My lady?" He looked up from the task of removing his boots and frowned at her in what was certainly mock confusion.

Though she was fully clothed in her gown and chemise, Raina felt exposed, vulnerable. She gathered up the sheet to her bosom for an added measure of security. "If you have designs on crawling into this bed to ravish me while I sleep, you are mad!"

"Indeed, I would have to be," he answered wryly, then added, "but 'tis my bed, and if you think a few scraps of fabric would prevent me from ravishing you if I wanted to, then *you* are mad." He shot her a smug grin as she scrambled off the mattress.

"I shall be content to sleep on the floor," she declared, "with one eye open!"

"You needn't trouble yourself, lamb. I have no intention of doing aught but resting my bones. It makes no difference to me where you sleep, but I should hate to stumble over you in the middle of the night should I have need of the garderobe."

It had been days since her back had reclined on something softer than stone and a bit of straw. And the idea of him traipsing about in his bedchamber during the night while she slept on the floor was rather unsettling. Warily, she climbed back onto the mattress. "If I am to share your bed with you—to sleep!—I must insist that you keep your braies on at the very least."

He shook his head. "I have always slept without the hindrance of clothing, and I'll do so as well this eve. You should try not to fret over it so."

Try not to fret over it? Good Lord, she could scarcely think of anything else! "The bolster will remain between us as a barrier, then," she said, placing the feather pillow in the center of the large bed.

He shrugged with apparent disinterest. "As you wish."

Raina stared at him helplessly as he worked to untangle a difficult knot, watching those deft fingers, her heart climbing to her throat. The tie fell loose and the fabric went slack around his hips. "For mercy's sake!" she squeaked. "Must you—must you *bare yourself* right here, before me?"

He chuckled like the very devil himself and glanced up at her. "You needn't watch if you find the idea too shocking."

"Heathen!" With a scandalized huff she spun about, crossing her arms over her chest and angrily giving him her back. "Never have I met a more ill-mannered, uncivilized brute! Did you learn naught of honor or the decent treatment of other people in your training to be a knight?"

The bed ropes creaked as he seated himself on the mattress. "I was knighted without training at ten-and-five," he said evenly, "on the battlefield. My appointment had more to do with necessity than honor, and as for decent treatment of other people, well, I'll credit you, a man learns little of chivalry when he spends nearly every day of his life fighting and killing just to survive."

Raina scowled at the wall. She might have expected him to defend himself, to dispute her accusation or perhaps apologize for affronting her sensibility. She certainly did not expect him to reveal anything of his past. Nor did she expect the sharp, humorless chuckle that followed a moment later.

"Chivalry and honor," he grated from behind her, his voice full of sarcasm. "If I had not been fostered out as a page at nine years old to be schooled in those useless skills, I might have been at the tourney—might have been able to do something—when my father was slain in cold blood. Chivalry and honor were of no help to me when I was sent home to be at my mother's side as she mourned, nor did they serve any purpose when Wynbrooke was beset by fire and battering rams."

"Wynbrooke . . ." she said, realization suddenly dawning on her. She regarded him over her shoulder, turning warily and finding him leaned forward over his knees, his head braced in his hands. It was the posture of a man in pain, a man dealing with old memories, bitter and left too long out of the light. "You took me there, that first night."

"Aye, you saw the place—what remains of it—in all its humiliating splendor." He would not look at her, and for some reason his rigidness of both body and voice created a small but piercing ache in her breast. "Tell me, did you see any lessons in chivalry or honor in the rubble, my lady? Any basis for the decent treatment of other people in the cinders?"

"Nay," she admitted softly. "I did not . . . and I did not know—"

"Nay, like as not, you didn't," he echoed, turning to face her at last, his expression hard, emotionally shuttered. "So if I am less than gentle with you, if I trample your delicate sensibilities, my lady, forgive me. I'm too old and tired to embrace chivalry's edicts and likely too far gone for honor, but my word is true and you can trust me. I have no intention of ravishing you this eve or ever. Now, get in this bed and let me have some rest, will you?"

Raina moved tentatively, tucking her legs under the bedcovers and snuggling deep within. The bolster felt cool against her arm, the awkward silence stretching between them colder still. "You confuse me so," she said into the darkness. "I know not whether to hate you, or—"

Her voice caught in her throat unexpectedly. She felt such overwhelming sympathy for him, such a keen ache in her heart for what he must have suffered . . . what he had lost. But more than that, she felt something else for him. Something that traversed the chasm of pain and enmity between them, surpassing even the threat of his vengeance. It was understanding, and something stronger still. Something she felt almost certain had to be . . . love. "I wish I'd never met you," she whispered, then rolled away from him onto her side.

Gunnar felt the soft tremors ripple through the mattress as she wept quietly beside him. He quelled the urge to comfort her, trying to shut her out, to gird his heart and be the man he had just claimed to be.

Fear her? Aye, he did, more so now than ever. Because in that moment, that space between one hitching heartbeat to the next, he could envision himself holding her.

Loving her.

Losing her.

And so he lay beside her in the dark, willing his arms to stay at his sides while he remained awake, not daring to move until her body stilled and her breathing deepened, and then for several hours more, cursing fate and her father for throwing them together, and damning himself for caring.

Chapter Fourteen

Raina came fully awake as a shaft of sunlight caressed her cheek and warmed the length of her bare leg, which stuck out from beneath the coverlet. She knew she was in Gunnar's bed, would have known it even if she could not smell his scent all around her. She feigned a stretch to determine whether he still slept beside her and found only a cool expanse of bedding. She sat up then and peered about the room. He was gone.

A fresh tray of food sat perched at the end of the bed, and feeling famished, she reached for a wedge of cheese. On a table across the room, a basin of clove-scented water beckoned. Gunnar had obviously taken it upon himself to see that she was fed and comfortable, and further, that she could enjoy a bit of privacy as well. Raina washed and ate, thoroughly contented and trying in vain to suppress her feelings of gratitude.

Finished seeing to her personal needs, she had just gathered up her mending when Gunnar's voice in the bailey drew her attention, along with the sounds of men's laughter and the clash of swords, now familiar. This morning, however, it was not the usual chaotic clattering of a dozen weapons meeting in practice but rather the measured duet of two swords. Curious, she rose and went to the window.

The knights had gathered in a circle watching two men spar. There was no mistaking Gunnar's large frame. He wore no mail nor helm, as did his prudent opponent. Despite the suit of mail, she recognized the lanky build of his challenger at once—Alaric. She was about to call out to him, to wish the lad well in triumphing over his swaggering, cocksure lord when Gunnar stripped off his tunic.

Mother Mary, would she always be so affected by the sight of him? she wondered, spellbound, watching him move. With his raven hair wild about his shoulders and his strong arms effortlessly swinging the heavy blade over his head in a show of skill and form, he looked every bit the pagan warrior. His deep voice, calling out instructions to Alaric, resonated off the walls of the bailey as he parried and easily lunged out of the reach of the squire's blade.

His massive bronzed chest and shoulders glistened in the heat of the morning sun, well-defined muscles flexing and bunching with every twist of his slim waist, each thrust of his sword a deadly testimony to his agility and strength. Alaric was no match, and it soon became clear that Gunnar was not playing to win but to teach.

Raina's belly fluttered at the sight of him, bare-chested and gleaming with sweat. A warmth began to spread over her, and for the briefest moment, she imagined what it would be like to be trapped under all that power, to have him sweating and straining above her, rather than on the field. Guilt inflamed her cheeks, and she quickly blinked the ridiculous notion from her mind. The warmth that had settled in her belly could not so easily be dismissed, however, nor could she seem to tear herself away from the window and the action below.

Gunnar had finally agreed to spar with Alaric to assess the squire's skill with the sword. He was truly pleased to see that Alaric was progressing so well. Though his defensive skills were stronger than his offense, the boy was serious and eager to learn. His determination alone would prove to make him a promising opponent in the future.

"Aha!" Gunnar deftly avoided a jab to his right. "I see you have been paying attention to my lessons." Their blades clanked as he deflected the blow.

"Aye, milord," Alaric said, a bit breathlessly, as he regained his balance and parried Gunnar's thrust. "I am quite good, am I not?"

"You show promise." Gunnar smiled at the youth's overblown confidence, deliberately swiping Alaric's mail-covered arm with his sword. "Though you still have a great deal to learn," he said as the steel blade grated against the links of the youth's protective armor. When Alaric's attention flicked to his arm, Gunnar took advantage, his blade poised at the squire's now vulnerable chest. "Never assess your damage in the midst of battle, boy. 'Tis a sure way to die."

"Damnation," Alaric muttered in defeat. "Once again, milord? Please?"

"You are a glutton for punishment."

"I will do better this time, milord." Alaric removed his helm and wiped the sweat from his brow, his cheeks flushed with exertion. "I was merely warming up."

Gunnar laughed. "You can scarcely breathe as it is. Another bout and I wager you'll drop dead of exhaustion."

The knights around them laughed, egging on the light-hearted challenge. "Come now, milord. Give it a go. He'll not let up till he's flat on his arse!"

Alaric replaced his helm and squared his shoulders, his breath becoming more steady. "I won't give up."

"Very well," Gunnar relented with a smirk. He spread his feet and crouched, tossing his sword from hand to hand. "I find I am of a mind to teach you yet another lesson."

"What lesson is that, milord?" Alaric queried, adopting a readied battle stance.

"A lesson," Gunnar replied lightly, lunging forward to strike the first blow, "in humility." The gathered knights laughed, goading Alaric on.

The mock battle began anew as student and teacher took turns dealing and avoiding blows. Steel met steel in a rhythmic crash for several minutes before Alaric, once again huffing and puffing, retreated to his side of the small circle.

"Do you give up?" Gunnar grinned, backing off the youth for a moment. While Alaric coughed, unable to reply, Gunnar planted the tip of his sword in the ground and leaned casually on the hilt. "Do you yield, young Alaric?"

"Nay," the youth wheezed, bending over to catch his breath. He stood again and raised his weapon.

Gunnar readied his stance. "I must say, what you lack in sense, you more than make up for in fortitude."

Alaric charged his lord, who dashed out of his path at the last moment, sending the youth stumbling forward nearly to his knees. He regained his balance and turned to charge again. Gunnar bent to meet his attack when a flash of pale green sendal in the window of his chamber caught his eye.

Had she been watching him?

In the second it took to ponder the possibility, Alaric's blade bit into his bare arm.

"Christ!" Gunnar roared.

Alaric threw his sword to the ground, tearing off his helm and casting it aside. "Oh, God!" he cried. "Milord, I did not intend—*oh, God!*"

" 'Tis just a scratch," Gunnar grumbled, more upset at having been distracted by the thought of Raina's interest in him than at his squire having landed a blow. He clasped his hand over the wound and made his way into the keep to have it dressed. "Resume the practice," he barked to his men.

Alaric followed at his side, spewing nervous apologies

and curses at his own carelessness as the two men entered
the tower and ascended the stairs.

Raina heard footsteps on the stairwell, but when the
chamber door was thrown wide, she looked up from her
mending with a start. "Good heavens!" she gasped when
she spied the blood seeping between Gunnar's fingers.
She had stopped watching the men in the bailey and gone
back to her mending when it became evident that they
could continue sparring for the remainder of the afternoon. She had not been prepared to meet with this. Dropping her work and ignoring Gunnar's perturbed scowl, she
was at his side in an instant. "What happened?"

"We were training in the bailey," Alaric supplied, his
brows knit with worry. "I struck milord—though I swear
'twas not apurpose!"

Raina showed her reluctant patient to a faldstool beside
the hearth. "How bad is it?" Kneeling beside Gunnar, she
glanced up to see his dark gaze fixed on her as she worked
to loosen his grip on the wound.

" 'Tis a scratch, naught more," he growled, looking away
from her at last. "I swear, you both act as if you've never seen
a flesh wound." He removed his hand at Raina's insistent
prying. The cut was clean and clotting already, but it was
fairly deep and would likely need to be stitched to avoid fes-
tering and scarring.

Raina rose to retrieve her needle and thread and the cup
of wine that sat beside the bed. Returning to Gunnar, she
knelt beside him on the floor; then, gingerly lifting his
arm, she poured the contents of the cup over the cut. He
tensed in her hands but his face remained impassive. "I'm
sorry," she said, wiping away the blood and wine with a
cloth. "I fear it needs stitching." She waited for his refusal,
recalling that many of her father's knights often preferred
to suffer out their wounds, gladly accepting horrible scars

over the thought of stitches. Gunnar simply shrugged away her concern.

Gathering the wound closed as gently as she could, Raina poked the needle into the dark skin of Gunnar's arm, wincing in empathy. "Alaric's skills must be improving, to have landed such a blow on his teacher."

"Oh, n-nay, milady!" Alaric sputtered at her praise. " 'Twas through no great skill of mine, I trow, but rather that milord's attention—"

Gunnar shot his squire a silencing scowl. "The sun was in my eyes," he grumbled.

"Oh," Raina said, and went back to her stitching. When she spoke again, her tone was insightful, teasing. "You must be more careful in future, my lord. And Alaric, you'd do well to learn from this. My father always said that a knight can ill afford to lose his concentration on the battlefield."

"Nay, milady," Alaric mumbled.

"The both of you may cease your babbling now," Gunnar interrupted. "Boy, fetch me a cup of ale. I grow thirsty and powerful tired of your presence."

Alaric rose and hastened out the chamber. The door closed behind him, leaving Gunnar in uncomfortable seclusion with Raina. He watched her work on his wound, her touch so gentle, her every concentration on causing him no greater discomfort. If she only knew the greatest discomfort came from her nearness and the lightness of her touch. It took great control for him not to seize her tiny hand and place it where her touch would do his body the greatest good.

If she but looked at him now, he knew it would be impossible not to take her. If in those green-brown depths he saw a hint of surrender, he would surely be lost. He squeezed his eyes shut, praying she would finish quickly so he could get as far away from her as possible.

"Am I hurting you?"

He found Raina's face tilted up at him, her eyes boldly searching his. Fearing what she would find there, his gaze dropped to her mouth. That was a mistake. Her lips were moist and supple as her tongue darted out to wet them.

God, he wanted to taste of that mouth.

"Nay," he finally managed to croak, the word just as much a command to himself as it was answer to her innocent question. Aye, she was hurting him, he reckoned. The pain she caused was the sweetest kind, a longing unlike any he had ever felt in his life. A pain he was certain only her kiss could cure.

"I'm finished," she whispered, mercifully turning her attention back to his gashed arm. When she dipped her head to bite off the thread and her lips brushed his skin for the briefest moment, he nearly bolted off his seat.

She looked up at him, her eyes registering surprise. Then she smiled. "Did you think I would bite you?"

He wanted to shoot back a clever remark, but to his infinite bewilderment, his voice was nowhere to be found. Instead he could only look at her, wanting nothing more than for her to flee, yet willing her to stay this close.

Closer.

She started to move away, and seemingly of its own accord, his hand reached out to take her wrist. She hesitated, slowly lifting her head to face him, so close he felt her warm breath fan his skin. Her lips parted in silent protest, but the invitation was clear in her eyes, in the way her arm relaxed in his grasp.

Before he could stop himself he was leaning forward, pressing his lips to hers. Christ, their softness far surpassed his memory! A groan curled up from his throat, his loins tightened in response to her pliancy, and he pulled her to his chest, his kiss growing hungry with want to consume her the way she had been consuming his every

waking thought. When her hand came up to cradle his
nape and bring him closer, he pressed into her, fighting the
urge to take her where she sat. The kiss deepened, ren-
dering him near senseless with desire. He groaned and
shifted on the stool, trapping her between his thighs.

God's wounds, he wanted her so badly. . . .

A soft knock on the door went unanswered; then Alaric's
tremulous voice sliced through the delicate veil that shrouded
them from the rest of the world. "Milord? I bring your drink."

Raina broke free of the kiss first, her eyes downcast as
she hastily moved away from him to the far corner of the
room. Gunnar gazed at her for a long moment, his jaw
clenched, angered at the interruption and willing the boy
away. When Raina pressed a trembling hand to her mouth,
he knew the moment had passed. "Enter!" he barked, his
voice gruffer than he intended, roughened by passion un-
quelled. He shifted uncomfortably as Alaric opened the
door and walked in with the requested ale.

The silence in the room was palpable, and Gunnar knew
the boy would have to be a fool not to realize something
had happened. "Forgive the intrusion, milord," Alaric
mumbled as he set the cup down beside Gunnar and cast a
quick glance to the corner where Raina stood. "Is there
aught else you require?"

Gunnar dismissed him with a curt wave and a shake of
his head. When the door closed, he stood and examined
his arm. "You make a better seamstress than laundress,"
he said, offering a lame attempt at humor.

She did not reply. Nay, she would not even look at him.
He had taken liberties he had sworn not to, had plundered
her mouth and nearly forced himself on her despite his
pledge to keep his distance. Now he was trying to make
pleasant conversation, jests. She must despise him. "Ah,
what's the bloody use," he muttered, and turned to quit the
chamber.

It was then he heard her gasp behind him.

He knew without turning around what caused her revulsion. Knew because he got the same response from everyone who chanced to spy his back.

His scars.

He reached for the door, anxious to be away, not wanting to see the expression of horror on Raina's face.

"Gunnar," she called softly.

He couldn't recall her ever using his Christian name. The sound of it, so tender on her lips, sent a tremor through him that he felt as surely as a bolt to the heart. She wouldn't always speak his name with tenderness, he reasoned. The day would come, and soon, that she would spit it with the self-same hatred he once felt for Luther d'Bussy. He couldn't change what had happened, couldn't change who he was. And he wouldn't allow himself to think of what could be. He clenched his jaw, refusing to turn around.

"Gunnar, what happened to you?"

At that moment he wanted to hurt her, to drive her away with a word if he could and spare himself the memories . . . the hope.

"Tell me," she prodded gently, "who did this to you?"

"Your father," he replied bitterly. Then he opened the door and walked out without even so much as a backward glance.

Chapter Fifteen

If he sought to wound her, he had done so with expert aim. As if struck by a physical blow, Raina dropped to her knees in the center of Gunnar's chamber. Painful as it was, she supposed she needed a reminder of just what had brought her to this place, to his arms.

Her father . . . his supposed crimes.

Though she wanted desperately to deny Gunnar's claims, she knew now that he was not the sort of man to carelessly fling accusations. Whoever was responsible for the havoc wreaked on Gunnar's back, and indeed his soul, was the worst sort of monster. Heartless, unconscionable. She understood now why Gunnar hated with such vehemence, for she felt her own rage churn at just the thought of what he must have suffered. And to have lost his family . . . to be so alone.

But her father?

What Gunnar said simply could not be true. It could not! Acknowledging her father's involvement in something so heinous would mean admitting that her entire life had been founded on treachery and lies. It would mean that her father—the gentle, doting man who'd held her on his lap when she was a little girl, who'd kissed her childhood scrapes and soothed her tears all those nights when she wept for the loss of her mother—was, in fact, a stranger.

A deceitful impostor. And she could not credit that no matter how the doubt niggled her.

Besides, Gunnar was young at the time of the siege— what had he said it had been, some thirteen years past? Perhaps his child's view had clouded reason. Surely that had to be it! And though her father had been unwilling to discuss his involvement or even his awareness of the crime with her before, perhaps having had time to think on it, he could now explain.

If only she could convince Gunnar to give him the chance to be heard.

Gunnar avoided facing Raina for the remainder of the day, even going so far as to organize a hunt with Alaric and his men despite the persistent threat of rain, so that he might be away from the keep for a number of hours. Fool that he was, he thought time away would keep his mind from wandering to her, from the thought of her in his arms.

But he saw her face at every turn, felt her softness in the brush of summer air, smelled her essence in the waft of heather rolling off the hills. The sound of his name on her lips lingered in his mind, fiercely stirring his loins with the promise of hearing her say it again, her velvet voice husky with passion. She was under his skin and in his blood, and he could not deny it.

More than once he had not heard his men speaking to him, and they had to repeat themselves. More than once his arrow went awry, and he missed the opportunity to fell easy game. Gunnar's mind was elsewhere, as it had been for the past few days, and finally abandoning the hunt to his men, he reined in his destrier.

He reached into a small satchel he wore tied to his baldric and withdrew the ring he had taken from Raina that first eve at the keep. So delicate yet strong. Beautiful and true. Like her . . .

His mother.

Gunnar's every memory of his mother had her wearing this ring. Often she told him the story of how she had come to have it, and how much it meant to her. His father had given it to her as a token of his devotion before he left for war, a promise that he would carry her love with him every day, a vow that he would return to dedicate his life to loving her and their son. And he had, she would tell young Gunnar with a wistful smile.

What he wouldn't give to look upon her gentle face again!

He enveloped the ring in his fist, holding it and her precious memory close to his heart. Luther d'Bussy had stolen the ring from her lifeless hand that day and then had the temerity to offer it to his daughter. He had taken a symbol of goodness and honor and attached to it a legacy of treachery and deceit. Not that Raina could be held responsible for the deed; she wore the ring with the same pride Gunnar's mother had, clearly treasuring the ring for its meaning to her, rather than its value.

Gunnar had reacted harshly when he'd spied the ring again after so many years, taking it from Raina without explanation, without apology. In truth, he had scarcely been able to think, let alone speak, when he realized he had reclaimed it at last. For so long he had alternately cursed and cherished its rugged mate, the ring his mother had fashioned for her husband upon his return home. The ring she had given to Gunnar upon his father's death and the one Merrick had returned to him just a few days ago.

The ring Gunnar would never allow himself to wear, nor could he bear to, until he had avenged his parents' murders.

It was unfortunate that in so doing, Raina would lose a father she so clearly adored. It pained him to think of her feeling any measure of the anguish he felt at losing his family. She would hate him for it, and rightly so.

But how she felt about him could have no bearing on his actions. It might have influenced him to repair his hall and respect her virtue, but this was different. This was about collecting on a debt owed for too long, and he would not be swayed . . . least of all by his emotions. Still, she had a right to an explanation, an apology.

Thunder rumbled overhead, drawing Gunnar's attention to the fast-darkening sky. Through the canopy of trees, heavy drops of rain splattered his face as the clouds rolled in. Placing the ring back in his satchel with the other, Gunnar stood in his stirrups, narrowing his eyes to search the woods for his men. In the distance he heard Alaric's short whoop of victory, and he headed in that direction.

The men were combing the bushes with their swords, and none looked overly enthused.

"Ye missed 'im, lad," Cedric muttered.

"Nay!" Alaric protested. "Did you not hear it squeal?"

"The only squeal I 'eard came from yer lips," Burc grumbled, slicing the head off a blossoming weed. "At best, ye might 'ave clipped the boar's arse."

Gunnar rode up to the group and reined in. "You men can finish the hunt without me," he said. "I'm heading back to the keep."

"Aye," Wesley, his archer, agreed, securing his bow to his saddle. "The rains are coming, and I've no desire to soak my bones chasing after phantom boars."

"Nor do I," Burc replied.

The opinion drew quick support from the majority of the men, and they prepared to abandon the hunt.

"My mark was true," Alaric maintained, "and I'm not coming in without that boar." He looked to the crowd of knights. "Who is willing to wager I'm wrong? Surely there's one among you who isn't afraid of a few drops of rain?"

An insulted murmur traveled the group, and Gunnar had to grin, for if his squire's aim with bow and arrow fell short, the lad knew precisely where to strike with his wit.

Alaric drew himself up in his saddle and went for the kill. "God knows, most of your ugly arses could do with a bit of water."

"Is that so?" Cedric said, unwittingly taking up Alaric's challenge. "I, for one, would very much like to see the look on yer face when ye see that yer *boar* is naught but a bunny or, mores the like, a puny rat, skewered with your arrow."

Another man laughed along with Cedric, agreeing that he, too, would like to witness the lad's humiliation.

With a knowing smirk in Alaric's direction and a slight shake of his head, Gunnar wheeled his mount around and rode out of the woods with Burc and several other men at his heels.

The foul weather had moved in quickly, carrying with it an uncustomarily cool wind. Rain slanted in through the open window of Gunnar's chamber, wetting the ledge and the floor beneath it before Raina hastened to push the shutters closed. Shivering from the dampness in the air, she stood before the fireplace, warming her hands as the door creaked open.

Gunnar entered softly, his hair wet, his mantle spotted with rain. "Are you cold?" he asked as his gaze lit on her. At her faint nod, he removed the cloak and cast it to the bed, then retrieved a log from the pile beside the fireplace and placed it on the hearth.

Dark, rusty-colored blood stained his sleeve where the cut in his arm had bled through, but he did not favor it as some might have. He seemed to take every adversity in stride; no pain seemed significant enough to give him any pause. Raina wondered what it must be like to keep all that pain bottled up inside. "How fares your arm?" she inquired softly.

He turned then, glancing over his shoulder to face her, as if startled to hear her voice. He shrugged. " 'Tis well enough, thanks to your expert mending."

The room was dark, save the now blazing firelight, which danced in Gunnar's eyes as he stood beside her, his striking features cast in shadows that lent him a mythical quality. Strangely, in that moment Raina could see the boy that Gunnar may have been, his fathomless eyes seeming to reflect the void of living alone, living without love. She longed to place her palm against his cheek, to feel the rugged plane of his face, the crisp growth of whiskers peppering the jaw of the man whom that wounded boy had become.

He cleared his throat. "About this morning," he said, a remorseful scowl suddenly furrowing his brow, "I . . . I'm sorry."

Raina shook her head mutely. "There's no need to apologize."

"Aye, there is." He took her hand and led her to the bed.

Raina sat beside him, stunned at his gentle treatment of her, the way he traced his finger along the back of her hand so gingerly. She held her breath while he seemed to struggle in finding his.

He spoke at last, looking into her eyes. "I wish to apologize to you for many things, not the least of which being the way I have treated you since you've been here."

Raina didn't need an apology; she understood. But there was one thing she simply had to know. "Gunnar, those scars—"

He dismissed her concern with a wave of his hand. "They are unsightly and no doubt turned your stomach."

He chuckled, but it was a forced sound. "They are inconsequential."

"But you said my father was responsible. . . . Gunnar, you must be mistaken."

He stood sharply and paced away from her. When he spoke, his voice was cool and flat, like the edge of a blade. "There is no mistake. It may not have been at his hand, but 'twas by his command."

" 'Tis impossible for me to believe—"

"You call me a liar, then?"

"I don't doubt that you believe my father responsible. 'Tis just that the man who could have done what you say he's done has to be the worst sort of villain. Not at all like the man I call Father."

"That doesn't mean he is innocent of the crime."

"Perhaps not, but what if your memory is cloudy of that day? You said yourself 'tis been thirteen years. You could have only been a young boy then. Children's memories are often exaggerated—"

"What more do you require to convince you?"

"I don't need to be convinced," she said, "but mayhap if you were to tell me what happened . . . exactly . . . I could help you to make sense of it."

"It will never make sense," he snapped, scowling furiously at her. He exhaled deeply and fixed his attention back on the fire. "I no more wish to dredge up the details than you will want to hear them."

"Then perhaps if you had some proof—" she blurted.

Gunnar spun to face her, his expression screwed with affronted incredulity. "Proof? Proof that I was there and saw with mine own eyes how your father, Luther d'Bussy, sliced my mother nigh in two with his blade when she refused to become his whore? Proof that I was cut down by your father's man and left to die of my wounds?"

"Nay," Raina covered her ears with her hands, trying to block out the horrible details. "Nay, 'tis not true!"

"You want proof?" he roared. "Here!" He jerked a small satchel from his baldric and pitched it at her. "Here's your damned proof!"

Long after Gunnar had stormed out of the chamber, Raina stared at the leather pouch, afraid to touch it, afraid to know what she might find inside. Perhaps she didn't want proof after all. Perhaps she would be wise to simply leave it lying where it landed on the bed. But still, the question begged an answer.

Could her father truly have been capable of these crimes?

Praying the satchel was empty, Raina hooked her finger through the leather drawstring and pulled it close. It felt light, its weight no more cumbersome than the material it was made from. But as she dragged it over a lump in the mattress, something small and metallic jingled in the bag.

Gooseflesh swept over Raina's limbs, a portent of a storm.

With her heart in her throat, she loosened the drawstring and poured the contents of the satchel into her cupped palm. The ruby ring her father had given her—the one that had so enraged Gunnar when he saw it on her finger—tumbled into her hand. Behind it came another ring, this one larger, fashioned unmistakably for a man but in the same design as hers.

Nay, not hers, she amended.

For these were clearly rings shared between a man and a woman. Symbols of a union between two people who loved each other, shared their lives. And the fact that her father had come to possess one half of the pair could mean only one thing. He *had* been at Wynbrooke that day.

Gunnar had been right: The ring was a family heirloom. . . .

His.

Her father, who raised her to cherish the truth, to live honestly, had lied to her, offering the ring to her as a token of his affection when it was rather evidence of his malice, his perfidy. Raina had been able to suppress her doubts until this. Until she saw the rings. Now shame swept over her in a wave that shook her to her very soul.

If her father had lied about the ring . . . what more had he been keeping from her?

Oh, mercy, but she had to find Gunnar, to tell him she was sorry . . . for everything. He had come to apologize for treating her unkindly, and she had smote him with doubt and questioned his character. Desperate to make amends, she fled the chamber and raced down the stairwell.

"Gunnar!" she called, dashing toward the sound of voices in the hall. "Gunnar!"

A handful of men seated around a trestle table halted their game of dice and peered at her inquisitively.

"Have you seen my lord?" she asked, heedless of the raised eyebrows and looks of surprise the men exchanged among themselves. "I must find him," she pleaded. "Did he pass this way?"

" 'E did," rasped a male voice from behind her.

Raina spun around to find Burc assessing her with drink-glazed eyes as he approached. He stank of stale wine and sweat, making her cringe inwardly with revulsion.

"Where is he?" she asked.

The knight shrugged. " 'E left."

The sporting glimmer in Burc's eyes raised the hairs at the back of her neck. Clenching her fists at her sides, she made to walk past the knight. He moved into her path, cutting her short.

"I beg you step aside, sir," she said, squarely meeting his gaze.

Burc's eyebrows rose to an amused height on his greasy

forehead. "Ye beg me?" he returned with a wicked smile. "I might very much enjoy seein' that, wench."

Raina pursed her lips and took a hasty step to the left. Burc followed, chuckling and clearly enjoying his little game of cat and mouse.

"Leave 'er be, Burc," Raina heard one of the knights call from the hall.

"Step aside," she repeated.

Burc didn't budge.

Summoning all her strength and resolve, Raina shoved at his shoulder, unbalancing him. She quickly slipped past him as he rocked on one foot. She fled down the corridor toward the steps leading to the bailey, unsure precisely where she was going, knowing only that she wanted away from Burc. She did not get far.

His hand wound about her hair, pulling her sharply to a halt. She cried out in pain, but Burc wound his hand tighter and pulled her close, placing a thick finger to his lips. "Shh," he hissed, his sour breath fanning Raina's face.

"P-please," she stammered. "Let me go!"

Burc grinned and shook his head grimly. "I didn't 'ear a *by yer leave*," he taunted in a low growl.

Raina gulped, trying to pry his hand from her hair. "Please, by your leave, let me go."

Burc's finger traced her lip. "Tsk, tsk," he clucked. " 'Tis too late. Now I require a kiss to sweeten me mood."

Raina squeezed her eyes shut, squirming her face away from his descending lips. "Nay." She shook her head. "Nay!"

Burc snarled, peering over his shoulder as if concerned her protests would be overheard. With an angry yank he dragged her down the stairwell and out of the keep. Lightning lit the sky with the eerie semblance of day for the briefest moment, then vanished, plunging the bailey into

bleak darkness. Raina was instantly drenched by the furious storm, her cries for help all but lost in the wind and
driving rain.

Burc pulled her along by the hair, leaving her twisting
and stumbling behind him, her bare toes squishing into the
thick mud that puddled in the bailey. He rounded a corner
of the keep and tossed her against the wall. Trembling
from cold and fear, Raina wiped the soaked tangle of hair
from her face. Her teeth began to chatter.

"W-what are you doing?" she cried, clutching her arms
across her chest. Above the roar of the rain, she heard him
curse. She took a sideways step, praying he could see her
no better than she could make him out in the darkness. His
hand shot out, trapping her flight.

"All I asked of ye was a kiss," he muttered. "Now I'm
going to take what I really wanted."

Another bolt of lightning rippled across the sky, illuminating him for one terrifying heartbeat. He fumbled under
his tunic with his free hand, trying to rid himself of his
braies.

Panic swirled inside Raina. A wall of stone stood at her
back and at her side. Burc's arm was like granite against
her shoulder, trapping her in the corner. "Oh God," she
moaned, "please, do not!"

In that black moment of terror, Raina prayed fervently
for Gunnar to save her, voiced his name over and over
again in her head, willing him to hear her, willing him to
come from wherever he might be and help her. His name,
which began as a whispered prayer on her lips, rose to a
desperate cry but a moment before she heard Burc's grunt
of surprise.

An instant later the bulking knight was jerked off his
feet and hefted away from her. He landed with a groan in
the mud just a few paces from her toes.

* * *

Gunnar sensed Raina needed him even before he had heard her terrified voice call out his name. Abandoning his destrier's maintenance in the stable, he bolted into the storm and toward her voice. Rage and fear boiled to a thunderous roll in his ears as he saw Burc standing before her, pinning her to the wall.

Clutching the ignoble bastard by the shoulders, Gunnar pitched him over his head and tossed him into the mud. He leapt on the stunned man, straddling him and holding Burc's arms beneath his knees. Pummeling the knight's face with his fist, Gunnar found the sickening thud of bone on bone a small comfort to his rage. Burc's lip split under the abuse and bled, fueling Gunnar further. God help him, he'd kill the bastard if he so much as touched her!

His fist met Burc's face, again and again, until all Gunnar could hear was the frantic beating of his own heart, all he could taste was the acrid fear of what might have happened. Soon his blows received no further resistance from Burc, who lay limp beneath him, his face a bloody, pulpy mash.

At last Gunnar found the strength to still his hand. His breathing was belabored and ragged as he stared down at the man, his hair soaked and dripping into his eyes, his tunic plastered to his skin. He felt a burn in his arm and glanced down to see fresh blood seeping onto his tunic from his reopened wound. The rain had all but stopped now, pattering softly in the puddles that surrounded them.

Burc moaned beneath him, drawing his attention back to the knight's beaten face. Repulsed, Gunnar rose off him, wiping his brow with his forearm. He glanced over his shoulder to where Raina stood, and his heart nearly stopped beating.

She was trembling, staring at him in mute horror, a hand covering her mouth. Tears spilled down her cheeks. Her eyes were rooted on him, wide and fearful, and he realized her terror now was not for the cur who might have raped her but for *him*. He reached out to her, to comfort her. Her gaze flicked to his hand and she backed away, shaking her head fiercely.

"D-don't—don't touch me!" she gasped, nearly hysterical.

Gunnar looked away from her, his jaw clenching as he stared at his outstretched bloodied hand. He scowled, curling it into a fist as Burc pulled himself up on his hands and knees, coughing into the mud.

"Ye broke me bloody nose," he slurred, and spit what sounded like a tooth into a puddle.

Gunnar ignored him; in truth he scarcely heard him. His focus was on Raina, on allaying the fear he saw reflected in her eyes. He could tell simply by looking at her what she was thinking. He had lost control, and she had seen him for the beast he truly was. Now she feared him. In her eyes he would never rise above the animal she saw tonight, and his heart broke a little with the idea.

"Raina." He said her name like a plea, moving toward her cautiously, wanting only to feel her in his arms, needing to know that she was all right.

She shook her head mutely and drew in a deep, hitching breath. "I don't want you to touch me," she whispered, her voice growing stronger. "Please, just leave me alone!"

She dashed past him and into the keep, leaving him standing in the rain beside Burc. Gunnar's woeful gaze followed her, absently registering the looks of shock painted on the faces of the rest of the castlefolk, now gathered about the entrance to the keep. In the light of their torches, he could see that they, too, thought him a monster. All these years he had not allowed anyone to provoke the beast in him, and though he had battled beside these men on countless occasions, he had always exercised cool control. Inhuman, they had called him, and Gunnar wore the badge without regret. Getting personal required emotion, and emotion meant weakness.

Gunnar had no weaknesses . . . until now.

Until Raina.

Steeling himself against the notion, Gunnar turned to face Burc. He could kill him and be in the right, he reasoned. The man dared to lay claim to something that belonged to his lord, and Gunnar had every right to retribution. The thought of Burc laying his hands on Raina's fair skin nearly made Gunnar's blood boil. The image of her defiled by this swine made him burn to carve the bastard's heart out.

Nay, wanting to see Burc dead had little to do with fealty or mistrust. It had everything to do with Raina. Killing him, just though it may be, would be nothing if not personal.

"Get out," Gunnar said through gritted teeth.

Burc sniffed, wiping gingerly at his upper lip. "Ye'll pay fer this, ye bloody—"

"Get out! And never let me see your face again, or I promise you, I will see you dead."

Burc muttered under his breath, then lumbered through the open gate as the afternoon's hunting party galloped into the bailey. They shot puzzled looks at the bloodied, broken knight as they passed him, but said naught, riding into the courtyard with marked urgency.

Alaric rode in front of Wesley on the knight's destrier, looking pale and exhausted from what appeared a successful hunt after all. Strapped to the squire's palfrey was a large boar, trussed and bound. The party reined in at the center of the bailey, and all but Wesley and Alaric dismounted. The knights who had returned to the keep earlier with Gunnar gave whoops of congratulations as they tromped through the mud to crowd around the hunting party.

"By the Rood, the lad did it!" exclaimed one man, clapping his hand on his thigh.

"Aye," Wesley said, his tone strangely grim. He dismounted and pulled Alaric into his arms. "But he will likely lose his leg for it."

Murmurs of confusion and concern rumbled over the group as Gunnar waded through them to the fore. He spied the injury at once, the slicing gash of the boar's razor-sharp tusks. A chill passed through him. "Get him out of this rain," he ordered, trying to ignore the disquieting pall of the other men. At Wesley's hesitation, Gunnar swore an oath and gathered Alaric into his arms, then hastened for the keep. "Fetch Raina!" he called over his shoulder. "Tell her to bring her needle and thread!"

Gunnar carried Alaric into the hall, yelling for someone to clear a table for the boy. Agnes hustled into action, raking her arm over the surface of the nearest table and sending the cups and dice game toppling to the floor. Alaric moaned as Gunnar placed him on the table and knelt beside him. "I should never have let you stay out there," Gunnar whispered under his breath. "Damned stubborn little whelp."

Raina's worried voice on the stairwell brought Gunnar sharply to his feet. She was at his side a moment later, leaning over Alaric and wiping his wet face with her sleeve. She peered up at Gunnar accusingly. "What has happened to him?"

"A boar . . ." Gunnar murmured, shaking his head gravely. "He was injured on a hunt. Ah, damn. His leg looks bad. . . ."

Raina's attention focused wholly on the boy, leaving Gunnar standing helplessly behind her. She unwound the wrapping from Alaric's leg and gasped, placing a hand to her breast. Her breath left her in a deep sigh, but when she spoke, her voice was calm, deliberate, and completely in control. "Bring me clean cloths, Agnes, lots of them! And blankets." She looked to Dorcas. "I'll need plenty of wine to cleanse this wound." Both women scurried out of the hall to carry out her orders as Raina went back to work on Alaric.

"Can you help him?" Gunnar asked hopefully.

"In truth, I do not know. I have never seen a wound this grave."

Gunnar swallowed hard. "Wesley said he may lose the leg."

She discarded the soiled wrapping and wiped her hands on her gown. Without looking at him, she replied, "I only pray he lives."

The weight of that comment settled heavily in Gunnar's mind . . . and his heart. Alaric might die? Nay, impossible! The lad was resilient, filled with life enough for three men. He could not just simply slip away like this.

He was spared further reflection as Dorcas and then Agnes returned with the requested supplies. Raina glanced up, apparently doing a quick inventory. "I'll need more cloths; his blood will not cease flowing from the wound." After the women left, she at last addressed him. Icily. "How could you let this happen?"

He had been turning that very question over in his mind and had come up without an answer. "What could I have done to prevent it?"

"You never should have left him!" she charged. "As his lord, you are responsible for him. For all of these people." She shook her head, bracing her hands on the edge of the table. "How pitiful to care more for the dead than the living." Her sharp exhalation of breath was like a knife to his heart. "When are you going to stop turning your back on the people who care about you?"

She asked the question with such pain in her voice, and such absence of malice, that it rendered him unable to

speak for a long moment. He stared at her back, willing
her to turn around yet at the same time hoping she would
not. He couldn't bear to see her scorn. "What will you
have me do?"

"Pray, if you can do naught else," she replied curtly,
pouring a bit of the wine over Alaric's wound.

Gunnar frowned. Prayer had never gotten him anywhere in the past, and he didn't see how it could help now.
Why would God listen to him at this late date? Why would
anyone help him, for that matter?

He watched Raina blot the wine with a cloth, taking
charge of a situation that had really been his to manage,
and his heart filled with pride . . . and shame. Here he
stood, at her back, worthless and unsure of what to do
while she adroitly took on his responsibility. He had never
felt so useless, so utterly dependent on another human
being.

And then he realized that perhaps there was something
he could do for Alaric after all. . . .

Raina placed the cloth on the table and let out a deep
sigh, staring up into the rafters. "Gunnar, I apologize. I
didn't mean to snap at you. But you must understand, I'm
frightened. Alaric's wounds are grave, and I simply don't
have the skills—"

She turned around to face him and her voice cut short.

He was gone.

Chapter Sixteen

Raina had several of the men help her move Alaric to a small antechamber located off the hall. She remained all night at his side, keeping vigil over the brazier to make sure the room stayed warm and that she had light enough to watch Alaric's condition. She had changed the wound's dressings several times during the night, had even tried to stitch it closed, but the cut was too long and too deep, and bleeding still. Her main concern had become seeing to Alaric's comfort and keeping the wound clean and bound. She could only pray that she had done well by him.

In the hours between wrappings, her mind drifted to Gunnar. He had not returned at any time during the night, and now that it was morning, she wondered if he had gone for good. She regretted her harsh words to him about Alaric, but perhaps he needed to hear them. His aloofness infuriated her, made her want to poke him, jab him until he finally admitted that he could feel it. No one was without feelings, not even him.

She learned from Agnes that he had not killed Burc after all, despite the fact that, according to the old woman, everyone in the keep felt he had good reason. So it seemed Gunnar was not entirely without mercy. Still, she could not purge from her mind the sight of him beating Burc so violently, so relentlessly. Heaven have mercy, but it was not hard for her to imagine that same rage unleashed on her father. The thought terrified her, but if her father had done what Gunnar vowed he had, she could well understand his hatred.

She felt a hand on her shoulder and lifted tired eyes to see Agnes standing beside her. "Ye've been 'ere all night, girl," she said softly. " 'Tis long past dawn. Go and rest now; I'll watch after 'im."

Raina shook her head, frowning as she looked upon Alaric's wan face. "Nay, I'll be fine. I cannot leave him yet."

Agnes patted her shoulder, then lumbered over to place another log on the fire. The sound of booted footfalls hastily approaching from the corridor rose above the snap of the flames, drawing both women's attention from the boy. Raina felt a surge of emotion when she saw Gunnar's drawn but handsome face appear in the doorway. Behind him stood a white-haired stranger.

Gunnar's heart lurched when his gaze lit on Raina. The disdain with which she had regarded him before he left had all but vanished as he looked upon her now. Now she looked at him with relief, hope, and something more. Her tremulous smile made him long to embrace her, to ease the worry from her brow. But the fear that she might reject him kept his feet firmly planted at the threshold, his hands stiff at his sides.

"Is he . . . am I too late?"

"Nay." She reached up to mop Alaric's forehead with the edge of her sleeve. "He's alive, but I fear not much longer."

The resignation in her voice shook Gunnar, for he'd never heard it there before. At that moment he had the profoundest desire to protect her, to safeguard this precious woman from ever feeling as afraid and defeated as he so often had. He stepped into the room, hoping the reason he'd ridden all night would allay both their fears for Alaric.

"Who is this?" she asked.

"He's a healer," Gunnar replied. "His name is Merrick."

Raina's hopeful expression immediately fixed on the old man as he ambled to Alaric's side and began inspecting the wound. He made a low, contemplative sound in the back of his throat as he lifted the wrapping and peered underneath it.

"I tried everything I could think of," she whispered apologetically, regarding Gunnar with tears shimmering in her eyes. "Nothing seemed to work. His wound is very deep, it won't stop bleeding—"

Merrick grunted in acknowledgment, standing over Alaric as he studied the wound. "It needs to be sealed, burned."

"Burned?" Raina gasped. "What do you mean?"

"To stop the bleeding and bind the skin. You've done a fine job with him, girl. The wound looks clean." Merrick turned to Gunnar. "I will need your blade."

Gunnar nodded and withdrew his dagger, but in the next instant Raina was at his side, grasping his arm and looking pleadingly into his eyes. "Are you sure? What do you know of this healer?"

Gunnar smiled, hoping to reassure her. "Aye, I am sure. 'Tis all right." He was powerless to keep from caressing her cheek. "He knows what to do, lamb. He has done this before." Gunnar's gaze then went to Merrick in warning. "I trust him."

The procedure Merrick prescribed seemed to work, much to Raina's relief. Blessedly, Alaric remained unconscious throughout the ordeal. When the blade hissed against Alaric's skin, Raina fell unconscious for a while as well, but she attributed her swooning more to fatigue than a

weak stomach. Once their assistance was no longer required, Merrick had dispatched both Gunnar and Raina
from the hall so he could finish his work, promising them
that now that Alaric's leg wound was cleaned and sealed
shut, they could expect him to recover in a few days' time.

Raina found herself having to contend with her patient
of the day before, who sat bare-chested on the bed in his
chamber, his arm a bleeding mess. With a wine-soaked
cloth, she wiped away the crusted blood, inspecting the
damage. Most of the stitches remained intact, but some
had been ripped loose—likely during his confrontation
with Burc—and would have to be resewn. Determined not
to meet his intent gaze, which had been fixed on her from
the moment he arrived back at the keep, Raina began the
task of mending and blotting the wound.

"This feels very familiar," he remarked wryly, his voice
startling her so much, she nearly dropped her needle.

"Aye, familiar, save that nothing is the same."

She let the comment hang between them for a long moment and felt him tense in her hands. She thought about
everything that had happened between them in the past day,
from the tender kiss of the morning and its painful denoue-
ment to the damning evidence of the rings marking her
father's guilt. And, perhaps most disturbing of all, seeing
Gunnar in such a stark and frightening new light. "I'm not
the same person I was yesterday," she said at last, knotting a
completed stitch. "Neither are you."

"Ah, my sweet lamb, you may have changed, but I have
not." Raina's hand stilled. His pulse beat strongly beneath
her fingertips, and she recalled his embrace of the day before, how gently he had touched her. How different from
the beast she witnessed last night. "Perhaps until now you
have only been seeing what you've wanted to see," he
suggested. "Last night you saw me for who I really am,
what I have been all along."

"Nay," she argued, "the man who sat in this very spot yesterday morn, who kissed me with such tenderness—"

"Is the same man who took you from your home and has kept you in this place against your will." He tilted her chin up to face him. "The same man who desires you so, he can remember no other woman before you and is certain there will be no woman after."

Raina turned away, desperate to deny what she saw in his dark eyes, unwilling to name it. Yet wanting so badly to believe it.

Gunnar's voice grew mild, but deep with determination. "He is also the man who would kill without a speck of remorse any cur who threatens you with harm."

"Don't," she said. "Do not say you did it for me."

He looked at her intently. "You are the reason I did not slay Burc last eve. Had you not been standing there, I vow I would have been unable to stop myself." He touched her cheek, cradling her face in his palm. "Would that you hadn't seen me like that, but I will not apologize for doing what I did. And if you can look upon me now with only fear . . . or revulsion . . . so be it. To my mind, 'tis a small price to pay to be able to see your face and know that you are all right."

"I will not be all right when you turn that same rage on my father. Have you given a thought to that?" His hand fell away. She watched his eyes darken, watched his expression shutter, but she could not keep the question from spilling from her lips. "Does it matter how I will look upon you if you follow through with your revenge?"

His jaw remained set, firm as granite and uncompromising.

"Nay," she whispered. "What matters to you is your own pain, your own notion of justice."

She might have expected him to explode in anger, but

his resolve didn't show any sign of cracking. "He destroyed everything that ever mattered to me. And as for justice, well, his hands are stained with many lives. Taking his would hardly even the score."

Raina swallowed the lump of regret that suddenly lodged in her throat. "And even now, that's what you want, then, to even the score?"

"An eye for an eye."

"Vengeance is not the only answer." Her voice sounded desperate, even to her own ears, but she didn't care. She *was* desperate. "Gunnar, I can no longer deny that my father must have had a hand in what transpired at Wynbrooke. What happened to you and your family was tragic, inexcusable. Time can't change what occurred, but time can change people. Whoever my father was then, he's not the same person now."

Those dark, unreadable eyes bore into hers, but she held firm, determined to reach him. "Don't you see? If you kill him now, in cold blood, you commit the same crime you accuse him of. You have a choice in this. Be better than you believe him to be. Turn the other cheek, my lord."

"Love thine enemy?"

"Is that such a difficult idea to fathom?" she asked, her voice wavering with hurt. She knew what it was to love her enemy. Heaven help her, it hadn't been hard to do at all. But loving a wounded, bitter man was far different from forgiving a monster his crimes. Neither could it be any small feat to find affection for the kin of that monster, never mind love. Knowing this did little to ease the ache inside her, however.

"Ah, lamb, I don't want to hurt you. It was never my intention to hurt you."

"You haven't. You've been kind and honest when you had every right to despise me. What hurts is seeing you in pain, seeing how it's affected you. I wish I could take back what happened. I'm sorry for everything I said to you last night. I'm sorry I pushed you away. I've been so very confused these past few days. . . ."

He reached out to gather her into his arms as he settled back against the bolster. "More than you can possibly know, my dear lady, I regret that we had to meet under these lamentable circumstances."

Raina closed her eyes, leaning into his warm caress. "I do know," she whispered fervently, "I do."

They remained still, embracing for a precious silent moment. Then Gunnar's breathing deepened, his touch growing light until at last it fell away, leaving her as tenderly as it had come, and Raina opened her eyes to find that he had fallen asleep. She watched him for a time, this tender, confusing man, and when she knew for certain he would not awaken, she whispered that she loved him.

Raina found Merrick in the kitchens, stirring a potion over the hearth. He looked up with a warm smile as she entered, and taking his kind gesture as a welcome, she went to his side. "I've just come from looking in on Alaric," she said. "My apologies for doubting your skill, Merrick; he looks very well. Far better than he would have fared under my care, I fear."

"Bah." The old man wagged his hand at her. "You did well enough. The lad is fortunate to have had you. Not many healers, and particularly not many females, would have been able to stomach such an unpleasant wound."

"Well, I'm grateful to you just the same. . . . I'm certain Gunnar is, too." Raina thought she noticed Merrick's expression tense somewhat at the mention of Gunnar's name but could not be certain, for he abruptly returned his attention to the hearth. "What have you in there?" she inquired.

"Oh, 'tis a bit of rowanberry and herbs which should help bind the skin and ward off putrefaction." Raina peered into the steaming cauldron over Merrick's rounded shoulder. She wrinkled her nose at the thick brownish-yellow foam gathered on the surface of the potion. "Know you aught of herbs, girl?"

"Nay," she answered, moving away from the bitter steam. "My mother did, but she died when I was very young and, alas, I never learned."

"Well, mayhap I can teach you whilst I'm here, eh?" He turned, smiling. "Every good healer needs know something of herbs."

"Oh, I—" Raina started to tell him that in truth she was not a healer, then thought better of it. It was clear to her that Gunnar had not told Merrick precisely who she was or how they had come to be together at the keep. He likely hadn't had the time, or perhaps he didn't feel it necessary. Whatever his reasons, she was inwardly grateful for the omission of that shameful bit of information. If Merrick thought she was simply one of Gunnar's folk, or even his mistress, it suited her well enough. For the moment, it simply felt good to be able to talk to someone without having to acknowledge her predicament. "I'd like that very much," she replied.

"Here," Merrick said, indicating that she take the long-handled wooden spoon he used to stir the potion. "I wager your bones are younger and more spry than mine. Stir this whilst I rest for a bit, eh?" Raina gladly accepted her post at the cauldron while Merrick settled with a sigh and a groan onto a stool behind her. "Tell me, girl, are you the reason for the change I see in him?"

Merrick's question nearly caused her heart to cease beating. Did he know who she was after all? And exactly what change did he refer to? She stirred the potion briskly, attempting to hide her astonishment. "I'm not sure I understand what it is you are asking, Merrick."

There was a long stretch of silence behind her, and

Raina knew the old man was studying her, seeming to wrestle with what he was about to say. "You might be the keep's healer, but I suspect 'tis not the whole of it, eh? I'd wager a guess you're also his lover, but there is something more. . . ."

"I've come to care a great deal for him," she admitted quietly.

"Ahh," Merrick replied with evident satisfaction. "Then it would seem your tender care has benefited more than just young Alaric."

"What do you mean?"

"He has gentled. I saw it in his eyes when he came to Wynbrooke a few days past, and I see it even more now. The boy I knew cared not a whit for anyone but himself, and his hatred."

"The boy? You knew Gunnar as a boy?"

"Aye, I knew him. Before . . . and after—"

"The siege," Raina finished for him.

" 'Twas no siege," he whispered tightly. " 'Twas a slaughter."

The sorrow in the old man's voice made her squeeze her eyes closed. The passage of time had done little to expunge the memory, even for him. "What happened that day, Merrick?" Raina asked, steeling herself for the entire, awful truth. "And please, I need to know everything."

Chapter Seventeen

Raina returned to Gunnar's chamber sometime later, her heart weighing heavy as a stone. Because Merrick knew not who she was, he had spared her no detail about what had taken place at Wynbrooke thirteen years past. She'd listened in mute horror to it all: William Rutledge's death in tournament, the subsequent attack on the Rutledges' home, the bloody aftermath of the siege, and the terrible pain suffered on the boy Gunnar had been.

After hearing all of that, how could she expect Gunnar to turn the other cheek, to forgive? Mother Mary, but if she had endured the same agony, she wasn't certain that she herself would have the strength of character or the charity of spirit to forgive and move on. And as for begging Gunnar to allow her father a chance to explain, what could he possibly say? What could possibly excuse such unwarranted, unconscionable violence?

Even though Merrick's account of her father's treachery pained her, oddly enough, Raina felt grateful, for the truth had also freed her. No more would she live in protection, sheltered from reality. Though she had been born into a lie, she would reclaim her life as her own, starting now.

She opened the chamber door and found Gunnar standing before the window. He regarded her over his shoulder as she entered and closed the door. Despite the gash on his arm, he had somehow managed to don a tunic. "I've nigh slept away the entire morning," he remarked as Raina came to stand behind him.

Gently, she wrapped her arms around him. He tensed, drawing in his breath, then relaxed, reaching up to grasp her arms with his warm, battle-roughened hands. He let out a ragged sigh as she moved her hands down to gather the hem of his tunic. His voice was husky, hesitant. "Ah, lamb . . . Raina, what are you thinking to do?"

She said nothing as she drew the tunic up over his stomach, urging him to lift his arms as she brought it higher. He chuckled, nervously it seemed, but he lifted his arms. She pulled the tunic over his head and tossed it to the floor.

"Raina—"

Ignoring the tension of his voice and body, she smoothed her hands over the surface of his back, fanning them over his shoulders and committing every ridge, every plane, to memory. She leaned in to trace a kiss along the scar that ran nearly the length of him, a tender apology to the boy who had suffered it and willing acceptance of the man who wore it now.

He moaned tightly as she brushed her lips over his skin, tasting him, wanting him. When she nipped his neck, he turned in her embrace and grasped her arms, holding her away from him even though it was clear from his smoky gaze that he wanted to pull her close. "Have you any idea what you are asking for?" he growled.

"Aye," she replied without hesitation, "I know," and she moved back into his embrace.

"Raina, my sweet lamb . . . this won't change anything. It can't—"

She placed her finger against his lips. "You told me once that when we came together it would have naught to do with virtue or vengeance. I bid you, my lord, uphold your vow." She moved closer still, her lips nearly touching his, tempting him to kiss her. "I don't want to talk about tomorrow, or the past. . . . I don't want to talk at all."

With a harsh, heated oath, Gunnar dipped to capture her mouth with his, groaning as Raina opened her lips to him. She let him in, trusting him to teach her, eagerly following his lead. The erotic sensation of his tongue, teasing and tasting her mouth, ignited a flame deep within her. A strange, beckoning heat . . . and she so wanted to burn.

She nearly cried out when his lips left hers, and did when they drifted down her neck and lower, settling on one taut nipple. He crouched before her, one strong hand caressing her back and buttocks, the other kneading her breast as he suckled her to a hardened peak through her gown. She moaned, plunging her fingers into his hair to hold him close, longing to feel his mouth on her skin. As if he sensed her every need, Gunnar lifted the hem of her gown. He dragged it slowly up and hesitated at her hips, his warm breath stirring the down between her legs the moment before his lips pressed shockingly against her. Raina gasped, trembling as he breathed her in, drawing her curls between his lips as he left her to place a tender kiss upon the bare flesh of her hip.

She quaked as a tremor rocked her, spreading a liquid heat to her limbs. Mercy, how she desired him!

She urged him upward, wanting to pleasure him as he was so exquisitely doing to her. He came to his feet, caressing her body every inch of the way and bringing her bliaut up with him. He pulled it over her head and dropped it beside his tunic on the floor. Raina stood before him, naked and unashamed, as his eyes drank her in from head to toe. He made no move to touch her, though his fingers flexed . . . trembled.

"You are so beautiful," he rasped. "So beautiful."

Hesitantly, he met her gaze, as if he yet expected her to reject him. Raina smiled and extended her hand. He grasped it firmly, hauling her against him, the look in his eyes pure exultation. Splaying his hand at her back, he held her close, kissing her and moving his thigh between her legs until his desire surged full and hard between them.

"God help me, Raina, I want you," he murmured against her neck. *"I want this."*

Her knees gave way beneath her as Gunnar swept her into his arms and placed her on the bed. He stood beside her, his heavy-lidded eyes holding her gaze as he loosened the ties of his braies and stepped out of them. Her attention slipped to that magnificent male part of him and her eyes widened. She couldn't help it; she gasped.

Gunnar's rich chuckle brought her back to his face. "I-I'm sorry," she whispered, embarrassed and breathless. " 'Tis just . . . well, I've never—"

"I know," he said, and climbed onto the bed beside her. "Are you afraid?"

"Nay." She looked to him again, finding it impossible to focus on little else. "Well, mayhap a bit . . ."

He smiled tenderly. "Give me your hand."

Raina blinked up at him. She gulped and offered him her hand. He smoothed it down over the hard planes of his chest and abdomen, into the crisp curls between his thighs. She closed her eyes as her fingers touched the silky strength of his erection, felt it warm and smooth against her palm. Her breath caught in her throat. Oh, to be touching him so brazenly!

He curled her fingers around the width of him, then slid his hand up her arm, letting her explore him on her own. His sex pulsed in her grasp, so thick and strong, so alive and wondrous. She squeezed him, stroking her fingers up his length and down, marveling at the sheer and thrilling power of him. When he moaned, she stopped abruptly, drawing in her breath.

"Nay, don't stop," he whispered. "It feels good."

She was glad of that, for it felt very good to her, too. Raina caressed and experimented with him, learning which movements elicited the most pleasurable sounds and which areas were the most sensitive to her touch. She could have gone on exploring his body and its fascinating responses for hours, but Gunnar stopped her, placing his hand gently over hers.

"You seem to have gotten over your trepidation." His grin was a wicked one. "Now 'tis my turn to torture you, lamb."

And what sweet torture it was!

Gunnar kissed nearly every inch of her body, stoking the flames within her to a blazing inferno. His tongue and lips and hands seduced her skillfully, his masterful strokes wringing the most wanton sounds from her lips, and Raina gave in to him with abandon. He pleasured her in ways she had never dared imagine, seeking out her most feminine secrets and claiming them with his fingers and, heaven help her, his tongue. His loving torture left her breathless and slick with desire. He intoxicated her, filling her senses with a wild and provocative promise of something more to come . . . something more wondrous than even this incredible experience. She trembled, pulse quickened, in anticipation of the journey.

Gunnar moved over her then, slipping his hands beneath her back and arching her into his embrace as he kissed her belly, her breasts, her neck, her lips. Dizzy with heightened sensation, Raina knew only that she wanted more. Her hands entwined in the damp, silky hair at his nape, and she hungrily pulled him closer. She felt his hand move between them to cup her woman's mound, squeezing and kneading her until she could scarcely breathe. Sparks exploded behind her closed eyelids when his finger began a delectable swirl about that part of her that ached so keenly for his touch. She shuddered, moving unabashedly against his hand as his seductive rhythm intensified. His kiss deepened, matching the ardor of his tender assault on her body.

The power of the first tremor jolted Raina's eyes wide open. Its brilliant warmth seized her very core, clutched her womb, then spread like a hundred tiny raindrops to her limbs. She closed her eyes, savoring the feeling, welcoming the pleasure. A wave of glistening light washed over her, then another as Gunnar caressed her. She wondered suddenly if her body shimmered outwardly as surely as it did inside. She prayed it did, for she wanted Gunnar to know what incredible joy he had given her. With all her heart, she wanted to do the same for him.

Her eyes fluttered open to find him looking down at her, smiling as if he did feel some measure of her delight. When had he stopped kissing her? Her cheeks flushed with embarrassment to think he had been watching her the entire time. And she could not pray the darkness concealed her shameful indulgence, for the late morning sun blazed full and bright in the room! He did not seem to mind; in fact, he seemed quite pleased, bracing himself above her on one arm and peering down at her.

"That was"—she searched for a word to describe even a fraction of what she felt—"it was . . ."

"Only the beginning," he said, and covered her with his body.

The feel of his weight atop her, his crisp chest hairs tickling her nipples, his belly flattened against hers—and the unmistakable evidence of his desire for her pressed firmly against her thigh—rendered her mad with want.

She had heard a woman's first time lying with a man was often unpleasant, but after what she had just experienced, she knew it for a terrible lie. No amount of pain could diminish the joy she had felt in those precious moments, no amount of fear could keep her from wanting him fully—from wanting him inside her. She slid her hands down his back to his buttocks, pressing him to her, communicating her need.

He groaned, kissing her deeper, and moved his hips until the crown of his sex rested at the mouth of her sheath. He lingered there as he kissed her, tenderly at first, then deeper, moaning as he slid his tip against her wetness. Rocking his hips ever so slightly, he touched her gently yet insistently. She clutched him tighter, urging him to enter her, needing him to claim her.

He broke their kiss, their lips scarcely touching, and whispered, "Are you sure? Because if you want me to stop a moment from now . . ."

Unable to voice her reply, Raina arched her hips to meet him, looking deep into his eyes and hoping he could see that she had never been more sure of anything before in her life. She closed her eyes and pulled him down, kissing him fully, slipping her tongue between his lips. He accepted it hungrily, hooking his arm under her and bringing her off the mattress as he pushed past the resisting maidenhead.

Raina felt the twinge of mild pain and drew in her breath, but Gunnar held her close, stilling inside her as she adjusted to his presence. The discomfort passed a few moments later, giving way to a pleasing warmth and an exquisite fullness that defied description. Her senses filled with him: the sweetness of wine in his kiss, the velvet softness of his skin, the musky warmth of their bodies together. She smoothed her hands over his back and shoulders, gently moving her hips.

Gunnar's muscles tensed beneath her fingertips, and he began to move, very slowly, very gently, rocking against her, filling and withdrawing. He kissed her lips, her chin, her nose, holding her tight to his body, pressing into her until Raina could scarcely discern where she left off and he began. He loved her tenderly, patiently, easing into her even though his body had become like granite. She sensed he wanted more, that he awaited an indication of her readiness to accept the full measure of his passion. She clung to him, wrapping her legs about his waist as she pulled him deeply into her.

He needed no more invitation than that.

Gunnar surged into her, thrusting with force enough to touch her very heart. Raina took him in, urged him to go deeper, wanting to feel him lose control, to know that she was the cause. He swore an oath as she met his thrust with one of her own, and Raina watched him rocking above her, his eyes squeezed closed, the muscles in his neck and shoulders taut and hard as stone. He crashed against her, over and over again, his entire body tensing with the effort.

She wanted to study every nuance of the moment, every emotion that played on his face, but the fire rising inside her demanded her attention. It burned hotter than any flame she had felt before, bathing her in a queer liquid heat that she knew would imminently consume her, body and soul.

Gunnar deepened his strokes, coaxing her toward the flames.

Feeling him tense inside her, Raina's fire exploded into an inferno. She caught her bottom lip between her teeth to bite back the cry of ecstasy that threatened to break free.

"Nay, lamb," he rasped. "Let me hear you. Let me know how I please you."

His gentle coaxing being all she needed, the cry burst forth from her lips as her very soul seemed to shatter in a million shimmering pieces. All the while he took her higher and higher, thrusting into her trembling body until he, too, cried out with his own release. A soothing warmth spread over her as Gunnar collapsed atop her, his weight an odd comfort despite the knowledge of what she had just relinquished.

And it was not her virtue that she sensed she would miss, but her heart.

Without leaving her body, Gunnar rolled to his side, gathering her into his arms. Raina pressed her ear to his chest, listening to his steady heartbeat as he stroked her hair. He said naught, and neither did she, both content in the moment and savoring their precious, if fleeting, oneness.

As Raina's breathing slowed to match his and she drifted to sleep in his arms, she wondered if anyone else had ever known such pleasure.

She truly doubted it.

Chapter Eighteen

Raina woke to feel Gunnar's knuckles softly grazing the slope of her cheek. Blinking her eyes open, she took a moment to adjust, not only to the afternoon sunlight but also to her new perspective on the man smiling down at her. How could she ever have thought him cruel? This beautiful, rugged face, gazing at her so tenderly could never be considered harsh. Those full lips, curved in a sensual smile, could bring only pleasure.

It was with no small amount of disappointment that she noted he had already dressed.

"How do you feel?" he asked gently.

In truth, she had never felt better, nor more alive. Her body seemed to have come into its own, shedding more than the burden of chastity during their lovemaking. Being with Gunnar like this felt good; it felt right. She smiled. "I feel wonderful."

"Are you hungry?"

"Only for you," she said, drawing him toward her for a kiss.

"Ah, have a care, lamb. You'll spoil me." He pecked her on the nose, then pulled her up from the bed. "Come. I've got a basket of food waiting for us in the bailey. Let's leave this place for a while."

Raina nearly sprang from the bed, hurriedly donning her bliaut and following him outside.

A short while later they were deep in the woods on his destrier, nearing the far edge of the pond. Gunnar reined in where a great old willow arced to form a canopy of dripping, silvery leaves. The thick bough stretched out over the embankment, its frondy streamers just barely skimming the surface of the water. Wildflowers and soft forest moss perfumed the light summer breeze. Overhead a robin trilled its song.

"What a beautiful place," Raina mused as Gunnar dismounted, then lifted her to the ground. "It feels like paradise here, so secluded and peaceful. So different from Norworth—"

She bit back the comparison a moment too late. It lingered on her tongue, bitter as bile. How she hated to make mention of that place now, to admit the stain of her relationship to a man capable of such atrocity. But before she could stammer an apology for calling up a reminder of the past, Gunnar was grasping her hand and pulling her into his embrace.

He lowered his mouth to hers and captured her lips in a wild, soulful kiss that chased away her gloom and despair like a balm to a burn. "This is paradise," he murmured against the delicate skin of her throat. "And this . . ."

His mouth drifted lower, his tongue exploring the curve and dip of her bosom, teasing the sensitive crevice between her breasts while his hands roved freely, kneading and caressing her until she nearly swooned in his arms. Too soon he broke away, growling his reluctance. "Now come with me, before I ravish you where you stand. I mean to make the day last."

Dizzy with longing and willing to submit to him wholly, Raina followed when he grasped her hand and led her to the water's edge. He turned abruptly and kissed her again, deeper than he had before, as if he could scarcely keep from claiming her mouth. And the hunger she tasted on his lips was even more evident in his smoldering eyes. He removed her gown, taking the same care one might when unveiling a priceless, holy relic. His own tunic he stripped off and flung to the ground, hose and braies following in like fashion.

Unclothed and fully aroused, he asked, "Does the thought of bathing with me now frighten you as it did the other day?"

Sweet Mary, but he sounded almost hopeful, postured with his arms crossed over his chest and feet spread shoulder-wide like some bold pagan conqueror. There was something quite endearing in such a blatant display of masculine arrogance, and Raina fought hard to keep from giggling. Instead, she smiled coyly, then let her gaze travel the length of him with deliberate, languid cool, pausing midway to admire the sheer magnificence of his naked body. He was grinning like a cat in the cream by the time she met his eyes.

"Do I look frightened, my lord?" she answered at last, full of playful challenge.

He laughed aloud at that, a hearty bark of humor that warmed her to her soul. "Nay, you saucy, wanton wench!" he exclaimed, "I should say you don't! But you might at least pretend and spare a man his pride!"

With that, he scooped her into his arms and carried her into the pond, their mingled laughter reverberating over the surface of the water. Waist-high, he set her down on her feet. Raina felt a keen sting as soon as the water reached the tenderness between her legs, and she sucked in her breath.

Gunnar winced, hugging her close. "I'm sorry, lamb. Does it pain you much?"

She shook her head; already the discomfort was passing.

"Damnation," he muttered, "I had no right—"

"I gave myself to you willingly," she interjected, stopping him before he apologized further for what had been the most heavenly hours of her life. "You had the right because I gave it to you. Because I wanted to."

He exhaled a weighty sigh before his lips met hers. His kiss was tender, achingly sweet, but it tasted of remorse and she wanted to weep. "Ah, Raina," he whispered, "I didn't deserve so precious a gift. You should have been able to share your first time with your husband one day, not me."

That stung worse than any physical damage she might have suffered in loving him. She couldn't bear the thought of being without him now, or the prospect of being intimate with another man. But Gunnar was a warrior, accustomed to battles and fighting, not the sort of man to make designs for a family and a future. Least of all with the daughter of his sworn enemy.

And even if he were, her father's plans for her had been set long ago. For most of her adult life, he had kept her squirreled away at Norworth, guarding her chastity like the king guarded his gold, waiting until he found the right match for her. A match that would bring more lands and wealth to the d'Bussy purse. He had made no secret of his hopes that she would marry a political man, someone with ties to the royal court.

With a shudder Raina recalled the aging earls and lascivious barons her father had entertained at the castle— recalled, too, her father's angry lectures after she had rebuffed their attempts at flirtation, even going so far as to empty a cup of wine on one man's fine silk tunic when he had the temerity to reach under the table and squeeze her thigh.

Suddenly Dorcas's suggestion of a few days before— that she try to persuade Gunnar to keep her—didn't seem quite so preposterous. More than anything she had ever wanted before, she yearned to remain with Gunnar. Forever, out here in paradise where she felt whole. Where she felt a vital part of something positive and true. Where she felt at home.

But she would not beg him nor burden him with her problems. She had only a precious handful of days before Gunnar was to meet with her father, and she planned to cherish every moment. Damming her tears with iron-clad determination, she faced him. "My lord, we agreed not to speak of tomorrows or regrets. Pray, don't disappoint me with talk of them now."

He kissed her palm. "Anything to please you, my lady."

"Very well," she replied with a lightheartedness she truly didn't feel. "Then indulge me in a race. I expect you are a passable swimmer?"

He chuckled. "Passable, aye. My father often joked that I was born with gills."

"Indeed? Well, my lord tadpole, I hope you are a charitable loser. If you had looked closer this morning, you might have noticed that my feet are webbed."

"Mmm, I was meaning to ask you about that," he teased.

Raina pushed him, laughing as she wriggled out of his reach and began to swim away. "The goal is the far side of the pond. Winner names a boon!"

She swam as hard as she could, kicking and pulling long strokes through the water, using her head start to full advantage and making excellent time. The finish well in sight, she glanced behind her. No Gunnar. Where had he gone? Treading water, she spun around, searching for any sign of him. When she looked back to the adjacent shore, a twinge of disappointment—and surprise—shot through her.

Gunnar's head and shoulders broke the surface of the water about ten paces from the shoreline. Fie, he had beaten her! Perhaps he did have gills; he must have swum the entire distance underwater! He turned, standing chest-high in the water and grinning at her.

"Shall I name my boon now or later?" he asked.

He hadn't yet touched the shore, Raina noted with a glimmer of satisfaction. She could still win. She kept swimming, casually now, lest he suspect what she was about. "How did you learn to swim below the surface as you do?" she queried, drifting closer.

"My father taught me. I reckon I was swimming not long after I learned to walk."

Nearly to the place where he stood now, she decided to attempt a distraction. "I should think I'd be afraid to drown with my face so long in the water. How can you hold your breath all that time?"

"Practice," he said with a shrug. "And control."

"Well, I am duly impressed, my lord." He grinned at her praise. Pride was evidently potent bait. Poor tadpole, he was about to bite the hook. "Will you show me again how you do it?" she coaxed.

"As you wish." He began to submerge himself, slowly, all the while his eyes on her.

The instant the top of his head went under, Raina lunged forward, pulling for the shore. Strong arms wrapped around her waist just two strokes later, halting her progress and drawing her backward. She shrieked as Gunnar hoisted her out of the water and draped her over his shoulder.

"You don't play fair, my lady," he charged on a laugh, lightly smacking her bare rump. Up the embankment he tromped with her, then set her down. "Now, since I have won by default, I shall have to think hard on a fitting boon." He gripped her buttocks and pulled her against him, grinning wolfishly as his erection swelled to life between them.

"Not so fast, my lord," she argued, stepping out of his embrace with mock admonition. "You carried me ashore, which means we arrived at the goal together. We both win, therefore we each can claim a boon."

"Hmm," he growled, "not only a bold cheat, but a clever one as well. Have you always been this impertinent?"

"Always."

He chuckled. "I might have suspected as much." Reaching out, he gathered her wet hair into a queue behind her neck, smoothing it back off her face and shoulders so she stood before him naked, her body completely unveiled to his smoldering gaze. "Have you always been this beautiful?" he rasped.

She didn't get the chance to voice her denial. Gunnar's mouth closed over one of her nipples, and she gasped in a ragged breath, all words and thoughts taking flight on silken wings. He knelt before her, suckling her breasts, his lips and tongue so warm on her skin, the peppering of rough growth on his jaw a sweet, savage abrasion.

He moved lower, kissing her belly, and lower still, nipping at the tender skin of her hips. A nudge at the juncture of her thighs and she opened her legs, tentatively, unsure what he wanted of her. But he knew. He overwhelmed her body with his mouth and hands, tasting her and pleasing her in ways she could never have dreamed and even now didn't fully understand. She moaned, feeling his fingers part her, enter her.

"Oh, Gunnar . . ." It came out little more than a strangled whimper. A vow of total surrender. "Oh, yes . . ."

And then she shattered in his hands. All at once her legs turned to liquid, her flesh molten and quivering under his skillful seduction. She wasn't sure if her feet still touched the ground, for inside she was soaring, spiraling high as the heavens on a wave of rapture so exquisite, she nearly wept with the sheer pleasure of it. Wildly, reverently, Gunnar kept stroking her with his tongue. Sucking her. Devouring her.

His name was a murmured plea on her lips as another wave washed over her in glistening ripples of ecstasy. Spent

and dazed, floating back to earth, she became vaguely
aware that he had left her. Where he'd been, the summer
breeze now skated over her, cooling her flushed, perspir-
ing skin.

"Race you back to the other side, my lady?"

Reluctant to let go of her ebbing pleasure, Raina opened
her eyes, trying to make sense of what she was hearing.
Her head still rang with the rush of orgasm, her entire body
slack with passion quelled. Gunnar stood several paces
from her, edging toward the water. Beaming.

"There's a bright red apple in the basket over there.
First one to the other side of the pond claims it."

Raina took a step forward on weak legs. "You wish to
race again? Now?"

"I don't always play fair, either," he said with a wink.
Then he plunged into the water and disappeared below the
surface.

It was all Raina could do just to make it to the other side
of the pond, never mind provide any sort of competition.
Instead she took her time and enjoyed the refreshing coolness of the water, swimming leisurely across the distance.
Gunnar was already reclining on the blanket he had spread
under the willow tree by the time she trudged out of the
water.

Like Adam before the Fall, he seemed blissfully unconcerned with his nakedness, leaning on one elbow as he cut
a slice from the apple with his dagger and popped it in
his mouth. "Two of the sweetest-tasting boons, both in
the course of one day," he remarked. "I am a lucky man,
indeed."

Raina felt herself blush. "You, sirrah, are a scurrilous
knave with a wicked sense of sport."

He chuckled, slicing and offering her a wedge of apple
as she took her seat beside him. "And you are a sore loser,
lamb. Eat your apple."

She munched the piece he gave her and another. When there was nothing left but the core, Gunnar pulled the basket over and rattled off the inventory of items he had purloined from the kitchens: a loaf of dark bread, a wedge of cheese, some strips of smoked venison, and a skin of wine. Hearty fare for a picnic, but Raina suspected they would be working up quite an appetite.

Grazing companionably next to him after Gunnar had broken the bread and served the cheese, Raina wondered how it was possible to feel so comfortable with this man she hardly knew. She knew him intimately, of course. Deep inside she even felt certain their souls were entwined, that perhaps they had been somehow since the dawn of time. But looking at him now she realized just how little she truly knew of him. Of his past.

"You say your father taught you to swim. Was he a good swimmer himself?"

He glanced at her for a long moment, as if assessing the purpose of her query. "Aye," he answered finally, "the best in the shire." His gaze averted, he busied his hands with the dagger, using the tip to dislodge a stone at the perimeter of the blanket. "He was a good teacher as well, physically adept at many things, though he preferred his academic pursuits."

"He was a scholar?"

"A student of life, to hear him tell it," Gunnar said with a distant smile. "But, being the eldest son and heir, his course was decided the day he was born. There would be no time for books and learning. His would be a fighting man's life, a knight beholden to his liege. That didn't stop him from lining his walls with texts and papers, however." He chuckled wistfully. "Nor from filling mine and my mother's heads with stories of the Greeks and their ancient philosophers."

That is, until her father slew that gentle man and put an end to his learning and stories, Raina thought. Guilt made her voice thready. "He must have been a remarkable man."

"They were both remarkable, my parents. Fair-minded, hardworking. Decent people."

"Does it bother you to talk about them . . . with me?"

"Nay," he answered, meeting her gaze again at last. " 'Tis only that I haven't thought of them in so long. Not just . . . thought about them.

"And you, my lady?" he asked after a lengthy pause. "How did you learn to swim? Were you taught, or were you born with these purportedly webbed feet?" He seized one and brought it to his mouth, feigning a toothy assault on her toes.

"I taught myself," she said, laughing as she pulled her foot from his tickling grasp. "I sneaked out of the castle once when I was young, and it was very dark that night. I missed my step and fell into the moat."

He let out an amused exclamation of disgust, chuckling. "Then it serves you right. What were you doing sneaking about in the dark by yourself? Or were you meeting someone?"

"I was running away."

The solemnity of her statement must have surprised him because he cocked his head, scrutinizing her expression. "Why?"

She didn't want to tell him. It cut too close to the bone. She tried to avoid it with the same sort of casual dismissal her father had used so often when faced with uncomfortable topics. " 'Twas nothing, really. A child's foolishness is all."

His intent gaze told her he would not be swayed. "You evidently didn't think so at the time. How old were you?"

"Oh, I don't recall . . . four or five, I would guess."

Five, and it had been the springtime of that year. Not

long before her mother died. Without trying, she could smell burned lavender leaves again, the pungent stink of a healing incense that had often filled her mother's chamber, as it had that day.

Gunnar's voice broke through her thoughts, a gentle whisper. "Raina, sweetheart, why did you run?" He pulled her into his arms, cradling her with the warm length of his body. "You can tell me."

She took a fortifying breath, then let it out, burrowing her forehead in his chest. "Norworth wasn't anything like your home. There were no picnics, no storytelling or swimming lessons. My father was either absent or too busy to trifle with entertaining a lonely child, and my mother scarcely left her chamber most days. . . ."

Without wanting to, Raina could hear her mother weeping brokenly on the other side of a partially open door. She squeezed her eyes shut but could still see that frail body lying in the center of the big bed, her back to the door while a handful of servants tended her. Her mother had hissed in pain as one of the maids dabbed gently at her face with a cloth. Another wrapped her bruised arm in an herb-soaked poultice.

Mama, will you read to me?

At the sound of her voice, the maids had all glanced to where Raina stood in the doorway, clutching her mother's Bible. No one uttered a word. Then a desperate-sounding sob carried across the room.

Get her out of here! I don't want Raina in here!

She trembled at the memory, and Gunnar held her close, caressing her shoulder. His silence, his tenderness, gave her courage. "I suppose I left because I didn't feel that I belonged there. I didn't feel I was wanted."

It sounded worse than silly to her now, admitting to someone who had lost his family to senseless tragedy that she was willing to flee hers simply because of hurt feelings. But it was deeper than that, and for some inexplicable reason, she felt compelled to share the entire ugly truth of it with Gunnar now. "I thought she might be happier if I wasn't around."

"Your mother?"

Raina nodded mutely. "She used to be happy once, long before I remember her. My father said she was the belle of England when they met, but something must have happened to her. Something must have changed her. Perhaps my birth was a disappointment in some way." This last thought she could only whisper, it shamed and hurt her so.

Gunnar's exclamation of disbelief made her look up. "Surely you cannot actually think that." When she could only blink up at him, he chuckled sympathetically. "Raina, I don't know what transpired behind closed doors at Norworth, but I can tell you that your birth was no disappointment to your mother."

She touched his cheek tenderly, moved that he would wish to soothe her after everything her family had cost his. "Thank you for saying so, but you couldn't possibly know—"

"I do know," he said, "because I saw her with you once."

Raina drew out of his embrace, stunned. "When? And where?"

" 'Twas during a feast time at Norworth when I was a lad of perhaps six summers. You were just a squalling babe of less than a year, I reckon."

She could hardly believe it. "You came to Norworth? You remember seeing me with my mother?"

"Aye, though I confess I didn't have much time for infants as a young boy. Beautiful women were quite another story. And your mother was beautiful." He smiled at her appreciatively. "But even she pales beside you now."

Raina let him kiss her, though impatience to hear more

made her break the contact a scant moment later. "You must tell me everything you can recall!"

"I'm afraid there isn't much more to it," he said. "A group of us were taking turns hiding from one another in the gardens after the meal when I heard a woman's voice, sweet and mild, reciting the Psalms."

"My mother." She knew it without asking.

"I crept around a rosebush and found her sitting on a bench in a quiet corner of the garden. You were suckling at her breast, and in her lap was an open Bible. She was reading softly, both of you the picture of bliss. The image burned into my mind. 'Twas the most profound expression of love I had ever seen. I just stood there, listening and watching, until one of my friends spied me and dragged me off to the game again." He paused suddenly. "Why are you crying?"

"So many times after she died I would take that Bible down from the shelf and read it, certain I could hear her voice forming the words. Believing I could feel her arms around me. I thought it was only wishful thinking. A dream."

"Nay, not a dream," he said, smoothing her hair.

Though this new information eased her heart, a new trouble formed in a dark corner of her mind. What sort of nightmare could have turned her mother into the sullen creature she remembered? What kept her prisoner in her chamber for so many years? She felt an explanation forming and tamped it back down. It was too horrible to contemplate.

Gunnar lifted her chin and brushed away a straggling tear. "The sun is nearly setting, and you have yet to name your boon from our race," he reminded her, gently guiding her to less distressing subjects. "What will you claim as your prize, my lady?"

She nearly voiced the answer that rolled so easily to the

tip of her tongue. She wanted his heart, his love. But she could not ask for that. She didn't think she could bear it if he denied her. Instead she said, "You've shared this day with me and given me something precious to cherish about my mother. 'Tis boon enough."

"If you will not name your prize," he teased, "I'll be glad to claim it for myself."

Raina laughed as he began to cover her with his body. Of their own accord her thighs spread for him, and he wedged between them. "Are you trying to frighten me, my lord?"

"You don't look frightened," he joked, returning to their banter of a few hours ago. "Name your boon, wench."

"Very well, then," she relented with mock exasperation. "As my boon, I wish that we could stay here forever."

Laughing, he rolled with her until she was on top of him, her legs between his. "You'd wish never to leave this glade? How would we spend our days? I think I should like to hear this."

He closed his eyes and settled beneath her, waiting expectantly. Bringing her hand up to stroke his hair, Raina studied his handsome features, from the faint creases at the corners of his eyes and the strong ridge of his brow to the trace of shadow on his chiseled jaw. So unmistakably a man, yet he looked so innocent at times. She longed to cradle him in her arms, to soothe his worries and share his triumphs . . . always.

And because she loved him dearly, without regret, she opened her heart.

"We would spend our days like this one, no interruptions, no troubles. Out here, where everything is fresh and green, and no one could find us. We'd have each other and want for naught."

"A pleasant enough idea, but what would we eat?" he

asked. "And where would we live? Surely, even as bliss-fully happy as we'd start off, you—and your belly—would be cursing my hide come winter."

"You fill my appetite, and your arms are warm. I vow I'd need no other comforts." She scowled and tugged his ear. "This is my wish. You are supposed to be listening, my lord."

"Well met, my lady, so I am . . . and with great interest." His lips twitched into a rakish smirk. "Now, tell me of our nights."

"Hmm," Raina mused, envisioning endless evenings in Gunnar's arms. "Our nights would be wondrous, magical. You would love me thoroughly, ensnaring my heart and soul with your wicked, sweet torture, and I would devote myself to discovering a new way of pleasing you each and every night . . . something to make you so dizzy with want for me that you'd never leave my side for even a moment."

He pulled her hand to his lips and kissed her palm. "With nights so filled with passion, doubtless there are children in this dream as well?"

"Oh, aye," she whispered bravely. "Strong, handsome sons who would grow to be fine men like their father."

Gunnar grunted. "I'd like a girl. Pert, like you, with your same impish nose and a smile to charm her father into doing whatever her heart desires." A furrow rankled his brow suddenly, and he scowled up at her. "Nay, better that she favor her father's surly looks, elsewise I would be forced to spend my elder years chasing off hordes of be-dazzled swains."

Raina giggled, picturing an aged Gunnar purposely scar-ing the wits out of unsuspecting would-be suitors. "Her fa-ther would be the only man in her eyes," she whispered, "at least for a time." She smoothed his brow, letting her fingers then wade through his hair. "But one day she will meet someone who will storm her heart with such tenderness, she will want naught but to spend every waking moment in his arms."

He paused before asking, "And what if no man met with her father's approval?"

"Then her father's heart would surely be broken, for a love as strong and true as that seeks no permission. It knows only that it must be." She held her breath through the silence that followed, fully aware that they could as easily be speaking of themselves.

"Ah, lamb," he said at last. He kissed her hand and pressed it to his heart. "Wishing can be dangerous business. And dreaming only makes reality harder to accept."

Raina slid off him, and he rose up onto his elbow and gazed down at her. "We can't hold on to wishes or dreams, but we can hold on to each other. Hold on to me now." The look in his eyes deepened, and he pressed her to the blanket. She clutched him to her, holding him tight as he loved her in the only way he dared.

Chapter Nineteen

Alaric woke that next day, and in the eve, the keep feasted on roasted wild boar. The lad being yet too weak to rise, Gunnar and Cedric carried him out to the hall so he could partake of the festivities he had been so instrumental in making happen. They placed him in Gunnar's chair at the lord's table, beside Raina, who beamed to see him up and around.

It seemed to her that an oppressive cloud had somehow been lifted, not only from her life but from Gunnar's as well, and indeed from the entire keep. With Burc's antagonistic presence gone and Alaric well on the way to recovery, the castlefolk became animated, going about their usual tasks with a lighter step and ready smiles. She turned to Gunnar, who sat on a faldstool to her right, and found him smiling, too.

Her heart swelled as she drank in the reborn hall.

Torches lit every corner of the modest room, illuminating it and everyone inside with a warm, golden glow. A spit had been raised over the central hearth where the boar had been roasting all day, filling the keep with its mouthwatering aroma. Agnes and the other three women carried out an astonishing array of breads and root vegetables, along with a seemingly endless supply of wine and ale.

As honorary lord of the keep, Alaric was served first, his trencher dwarfed by the huge shank of boar presented him by Wesley, who had been commissioned cook for the eve. The lad's eyes nearly popped from their sockets as he stared at his meal.

"I'll be glad to take a bite of you now!" he declared. Then, to the delight of everyone gathered, he hefted the leg to his mouth and tore off a large chunk.

After everyone had eaten more than their fill, the boar's head was given a place of prominence beside Alaric, who stared at it with the morbid curiosity of a lad of his years.

"What a dreadful-looking beast," Raina said, cringing to be so close to its evil, sightless sneer. "Its eyes seem to follow me."

Alaric grinned at her. "Like as not, it's never seen a prettier face," he replied, and blushed wildly.

"I'll thank you—and your ugly boar—to keep your eyes to yourselves," Gunnar warned with a smile, leaning across Raina. "Is it not enough I forfeit my chair to your tender arse? Must I now compete with you for my woman as well?"

His woman.

Raina's heart tripped and she fought the urge to lovingly place her hand on his head, which hovered so near her breasts. Did he consider her his woman? She didn't dare contemplate what that might mean, simply basked in the warmth of possibilities.

She was not able to linger there long, for Wesley jumped onto a table near the center of the hall and clapped his hands for attention.

"My lords and ladies." He bowed with all the courtly air of a royal troubadour. "In honor of our young Lord Alaric, who has so graciously gifted us with a meal we are likely to be tasting for many a day"—he clutched his stomach and belched loudly, earning guffaws and a rousing flurry of pounding cups— "I would like to bestow on him a song."

Gunnar groaned beside Raina. "The only thing worse than Wesley's singing is his rhymes," he told her with reluctant mirth. "But don't tell him so; I'm afraid he fancies himself something of a bard."

Raina watched with delighted expectation as Wesley squared his shoulders, then cleared his throat.

> *This boar we did eat was a mean one,*
> *Its bite clear as bad as its breath.*
> *The lad may be lame, but he's brave just the same,*
> *For its flesh might as yet mean his death!*

Wesley clutched his gut and doubled over, leaning forward precariously close to falling off the table. A wave of laughter and applause circled the room before he righted himself with a spirited hop and turned to face Gunnar and Raina.

> *Now, Lord Gunnar, he scares these poor beasties,*
> *They see him and flee him right quick.*
> *And wenches, they swoon when they spy him,*
> *For his blade's nigh as big as his—*

"More wine!" Gunnar blurted, vaulting to his feet. "Another flagon of wine!"

Raina looked at him with fascination as he resumed his seat. He was blushing! She laughed out loud, hiding her giggles behind her hand as the page rushed to fill Gunnar's tankard. He gulped a large mouthful as Wesley leapt off the table and the hall erupted into loud cheers and jests about their lord's virility.

"I couldn't be entirely sure without making the comparison myself," she whispered, "but I suspect Wesley may be right in his assessment."

Gunnar looked at her slack-jawed and in obvious shock,

then downed the rest of his wine. "Have a care, my lady, elsewise you may find yourself whisked out of this gathering to do just that."

She nearly called him on the challenge, but the raucous sounds of makeshift music drew her attention back to the hall. Odette was atop a table, hoisting her skirts and baring her sturdy ankles as she danced to the rhythm of banging cups and clapping hands. Wesley, Cedric, and a couple other men hastily pushed all but Odette's table to the far walls, creating an open area in the center of the hall. Rupert, the young page, hopped onto the table and grasped Odette's hands, dancing with her. Someone else took Dorcas by the arm and swung her in a wide arc to the center of the hall.

Raina found the revelry contagious and joined the clapping, tapping her bare foot under the table. She knew Gunnar watched her, but she didn't feel inhibited in the least. Things like this never happened at Norworth. Meals were ever stuffy affairs, even when jongleurs came from distant places to entertain. Her father had always discouraged dancing and celebration, except when he was entertaining noblemen or other dignitaries. But Raina was not going to think about that right now. Tonight and for the next three nights she had remaining with Gunnar, she was going to enjoy herself.

So when Cedric appeared at the lord's table a moment later, requesting to dance with her, she took his hand and followed him out to the circle of revelers.

Gunnar watched Raina spin about the floor on Cedric's arm, laughing gaily, her unbound hair floating behind her like a veil of silk. Her bliaut was in tatters, its pale green color all but lost amid the stains and dirt that soiled it. To anyone else at that moment, she might have looked like an unfortunate waif with her bare, dirty feet and torn, flopping sleeve, but to him she was radiant. A faerie princess, and he stood enchanted.

"Why did you not tell me you had d'Bussy's daughter?"

Merrick's question drew Gunnar's attention sharply to the old man. God's wounds, he hadn't even noticed him approach. All he had noticed, and all he could focus on still, was the woman lighting up his hall . . . and his heart.

"Your men have told me of your plan to bargain her for her father. Do you really think that is a wise wager?"

Gunnar thought about the day he'd struck that bargain. It seemed a lifetime ago. " 'Twas the only choice I had at the time."

"And now?"

Gunnar scowled, pensively tracing the rim of his cup with his thumb. "I'm not certain."

"It seems to my mind that you've wagered something you're now unwilling to give up, eh? Mayhap 'tis time to let the past go, lad."

"I can't, you know that. I made a promise. I staked my damned life on it!"

"And what of her?" Merrick nodded in Raina's direction. "You mean to tell me you've made no promises to her?"

Gunnar thought about the day before in the glade, when she told him of her dream for them, her innocent wish for a peaceable life together. "She's asked for none; I've promised her naught."

Merrick pursed his lips and let out a long sigh. "Think you that a promise is binding only if you voice it?" He shook his head gravely. "Sometimes the promises we don't make are the most important ones to keep."

Raina's laughter drew Gunnar's attention like a physical caress, leaving him shaking with want to take her in his arms and demand that she tell him what to do, that she wring the promise from him that he so wanted to make.

She glanced his way, and their eyes met across the room. Her laughter melted into a warm, innocent smile, and he knew she'd never ask him to break his vow, no matter how it pained her.

She trusted him to do right.

That realization hit him like an iron-fisted blow to the gut. He broke her gaze, unable to bear the idea that he might disappoint her. That she might hate him.

And in just four days' time.

"Think on it, lad," Merrick advised soberly. Then he rose and walked away.

As Wesley gathered Raina's hands in his and spun her round in the center of the crowd, Gunnar took the opportunity to quit the hall without her notice. He had to get out of the stifling confinements of the keep, had to get away from it all.

Away from Raina.

Away from himself.

He nearly bolted down the stairs to the muddy bailey, heedless of the rain that beat down upon his shoulders. The heavy downpour did little to muffle Merrick's words, which echoed in his ears as he mounted his destrier.

Sometimes the promises we don't make are the most important ones to keep.

Damnation! Why had he allowed himself to feel anything for the woman? It wasn't as if he was some beardless youth, sick with lust for his first lover. And God help him, but it was more than lust he felt for Raina. Much more.

How had he let it happen? How was it he had managed to keep control all these years only to lose it to a strong-willed, tenderhearted lamb? How had he let her get inside of him?

Saints' blood, but how would he ever let her go?

Gunnar jabbed his heels into the mount's sides, urging it into a thunderous gallop. The rain stung his face as he sped through it, drenching his hair and tunic. He charged into the darkness, not knowing where he was going, nor caring. He crashed through bracken and thundered over hills, past landscapes made ghostly and black by the storm.

He was lost now and did not care, racing blindly in the dark toward nothing, toward a future of nothing . . . a future alone. His mount was tiring beneath him, huffing and slick from the rain and sweat, its muscles tight with strain, but Gunnar pressed the destrier on, needing the speed, needing to hear the pounding of its hooves. Anything to drown out the sound of his heart being torn asunder in his chest.

The storm raged on outside him as well, great claps of thunder booming overhead and shaking the earth. And then a large bolt of lightning zigzagged out from the heavens, so pure and white and strong it might have been thrown from God's own hand. It arrowed down in blinding fury and struck a large oak that stood in the path less than a furlong away. The ancient tree roared, cracking and groaning under the force of the splintering blow. Orange flames and white-hot sparks shot out from the massive trunk as it split in two, exploding into the cool, dark night.

Gunnar's mount shrieked and in that next instant it reared, tossing him from the saddle.

He crashed to the ground. His vision went black as he struck the hard earth. All the air in his lungs left on a wheeze. Stunned, he lay there on his back, unable to move, unable to draw breath, blinking up at the sky and gasping futilely like a fish washed ashore. Rain spattered his face. Smoke from the smoldering, hissing oak drifted on the wind, stinging his eyes while his head swam with a flood of hazy images and sounds.

Raina's face floated before him, so innocent and lovely. She smiled down at him tenderly and he murmured her name, or at least he thought he did. He felt it resonate in his every fiber and bone, the melody of her name both an agony and balm. He thought she might reach out to him, prayed she would, but her sweet expression became pained, her gaze distant and shimmering with unshed tears.

How pitiful to care more for the dead than the living.

Nay! He wanted to yell it, scream that it was not true, prove it to her, but she was fading, drifting away from him, her features growing pale and paler still, until she was no more than a whisper of gray smoke swirling off into the darkness.

Gunnar squeezed his eyes shut, swallowing past a lump of regret that had formed in his throat. Never in his life had he felt so empty and completely alone. More than alone . . . he felt lonely. So scared and tired and in need of comforting.

Whether it was the wind or the rain or a trick of his rattled mind, he knew not, but beside his ear he heard the soothing hush of his mother's voice, whispering that he would be all right, that she loved him.

Remember your father's courage . . . his honor . . . make me proud.

The plea that haunted his dreams for so long, the words that urged him on, beckoned him to fight, to avenge his parents' deaths now suddenly seemed so different. Gentle, speaking not of vengeance and death but of something else entirely. Life. Love.

Jesu, could he have been wrong all this time?

What courage did it take to slay a feeble old man? What honor was there in stealing his daughter? None, certainly, and he doubted his parents would take any measure of pride in what their son had become, nor in the meaningless ruin he had made of his life.

Some part of him knew it would take far greater courage to face his enemy with peace in his heart, to hear him out, accept his apology, and forgive. He knew, too, that as long as he held Raina against her will, captive in his home and in his heart, honor would never be his to claim. But did he have the strength to do what he now knew to be right?

God help him, he wasn't certain.

All his life he had fought his feelings, denied his fears, beaten his weaknesses. For thirteen years courage and honor had meant vengeance. Now, when he was so close to having it, it seemed the definition had changed. Like his mother's plea, courage and honor no longer meant what he'd believed all along that they had. He had found them both in a proud woman with a gentle heart and a loving spirit. His beautiful Raina, his beloved.

As Gunnar picked himself up from the ground and mounted his horse, his mind was on neither courage nor honor. All that filled his thoughts as he rode back to the keep—what soothed his soul—was a desperate longing to be in Raina's arms, safe and sound, sheltered from the storm and the terrible reality that they would soon be parted.

Chapter Twenty

Lightning cracked across the sky, and the loud roll of thunder echoed in the bailey, shaking the tower keep and setting Raina's nerves further on edge. Twice this hour she had peeked through the crack between the shutters, hoping to spy Gunnar riding within the safety of the curtain wall. Twice she had been disappointed. Anger turned to worry that he was out in the midst of the storm. Why had he gone? And where?

Raina sat on the bed, knees drawn to her chest, waiting and watching the night candle burn to a smoldering stub. It had been several hours since the keep had been abed and still no sign of him. What if he was hurt? Or, dear God, what if he'd decided to confront her father this very night?

She had already settled it in her mind that she would accompany Gunnar to the meeting, prepared to defend him against her father in any way she could. Determined to make peace. Neither man would inflict harm on the other with her present—that much she knew. That much she trusted. But should the matter come to a choice between returning to Norworth and remaining with Gunnar, Raina was prepared to bid her father farewell forever.

Panicked that he might have decided to leave for Norworth without telling her, Raina was just about to don Gunnar's mantle and ride out after him when she heard the gate grind open. In the space of a heartbeat she was at the window, fumbling to unfasten the shutters. Her fingers trembled with anticipation, but at last she freed the bindings. She flung the shutters wide open and peered out anxiously. Cold rain slanted in through the window. Below, in the bailey, a dark knight leapt from his mount. Her heart slammed against her ribs.

"Gunnar!" She lifted her hand and laughed with near-hysterical joy at his safe return. He hesitated, looking up to where she stood in the window, but his expression was concealed by the driving rain and the dark of a moonless night. He threw the reins to an approaching guard and bolted into the castle.

Raina ran from the chamber to the stairwell, hearing his spurs clink on the steps as he took them two at a time. Relief and something so much stronger flooded her senses in the moments it took for him to reach the top. Her breath caught in her throat at the sight of him, a wet and haggard warrior, his hair plastered in slick, raven spikes to his face. His tunic, soaked and dripping, clung to him like his own skin. His grin was lopsided and completely unrepentant.

She threw her arms around him. "I was worried."

Her intended scold had somehow been reduced to a whisper. The words scarcely left her lips before he caught her behind the knees and scooped her into his arms, carrying her to his chamber with a look of passionate determination in his blazing dark eyes. He kicked the door shut with his foot. Depositing her on the mattress, he stripped off his baldric and scabbard, then pulled his wet tunic over his head, throwing it to the floor.

Raina felt compelled to fill the silence. " 'Tis been several hours since you left, and the storm . . ." Her voice drifted to nothingness as Gunnar climbed onto the bed. "Have you nothing to say?"

"Aye," he growled. "Your worries were wasted."

He crawled toward her on the bed like a sleek, wet panther stalking his prey, the muscles in his arms and shoulders bunching and flexing with each move he made. He looked unearthly, animalistic, and Raina willingly surrendered to his power. She drew in her breath when his arm snaked out and seized her ankle, pulling her down onto her back. In one fluid movement he was upon her, his chest pressing against hers, further soaking the thin fabric of her bliaut. He pressed into her, melding their bodies together as he buried his face in the crook of her neck.

"What have you done to me?" He swore an oath as she ran her fingers down the length of his back, pressing her hips into his.

The feel of him, so hard with need, so filled with want for her, was intoxicating and gave Raina courage to explore his body. Her fingers slipped beneath the waist of his braies to feel the soft skin of his hips. He groaned when she moved to the front, splaying her fingers in the crisp hair she found there and moving the back of her hand against the thick heat of his desire.

Sensing his anticipation, she moved to grasp him firmly in her palm, smiling as he hissed a sharp breath. Velvety steel surged tighter as she stroked him, slowly at first, then quickened her caress in response to his body's fevered reaction. A deep growl rumbled in his chest. "My God, woman, you'll unman me in my braies."

"Good," she purred. " 'Tis only fair that I make you lose control of your body as you so like to do to me."

He rose on his elbows and looked her in the eyes. "Turnabout is fair play, lamb, and I'm finding that I rather like losing control."

He swallowed her laughter with a kiss. She reached down, unfastening the ties at his waist and shoving the linen trousers down his hips, freeing him from the confines of his clothing. She curled her hand around his pulsing heat again, delighting in its palpable surge of silken power. She brushed the moist tip with her finger, tracing a wet ring around the crown of his manhood. His breath was ragged beside her ear as she continued to tease him, rejoicing in the moans and sighs she elicited with so simple a gesture.

She stroked the length of him, tentatively at first, then more boldly when his hips began to move with the motion. Impossible as it seemed, he grew larger in her grasp, filling her hand so that she could scarcely close her fingers around him. She had only a moment to marvel at the idea before his hand found hers and stilled it, bringing her fingers to his mouth. He kissed her hand and placed it against his chest. His heart thundered beneath her palm, nearly as fevered as his breathing.

He kissed her wildly, moving over her and spreading her thighs with his knee. The urgent weight of his erection nestled between her legs, then pressed forward, gliding easily into her. He groaned as he buried himself deep within her, filling her exquisitely as he sheathed himself to the hilt. Raina's hips arched against him, coaxing him deeper, wanting him fully. Her hands gripped his shoulders, pulling him closer, holding him tighter as he surged into her, his strokes at once hungry and fierce.

He took her savagely, with a driven quest to impale her very soul, to brand her as his own. His need for her unnerved him. His want to possess her consumed him. He thrust into her, harder and deeper, as if to crawl inside of her, wanting her to feel the breadth of his wanting, the power of his desire for her. With a final surge, Gunnar dove to the crest of her womb, rejoicing in her whimper of release. Slowly, with a control that surprised him, he withdrew nearly to leave her, then slid back in, his strokes long and deep, bringing her to the pinnacle of yet another wave of ecstasy.

She cried out, the most delicious sound to his ears, and her hips came up to meet his bold strokes. Gathering her trembling shoulders to him, he pressed deeper, his own desire claiming his senses and his control.

She held fast to him, meeting his strokes and pressing heated kisses to his neck, beneath his ear, her breath hot and panting against his skin. Each thrust went deeper, made him harder, drove him closer and closer to climax, until with a final surge and a strangled cry, he exploded inside her, his seed coming fast and wild, spilling into the searing heat of her womb.

Some reckless part of him hoped it would take, indeed, secretly hoped that he had already gotten her with his child. It was a fool's wish to be sure, and worse, a selfish desire to know that no matter what happened when he met her father, he would always be a part of her and she of him. But she deserved better than his bastard. She deserved far better than he could ever hope to give her.

Still, that didn't stop him from thinking about spending the rest of his life at her side. Since she'd shared her innocent wish for a future together, Gunnar had been entertaining similar notions. Agonizing over the prospect of having to contend with her father in a few days. Imagining himself wed to Raina, picturing her resplendent and heavy with his babes.

Each moment he spent with her made the dreams seem more real. Made the hopes seem more possible. Every time he kissed her, he thought about what could be.

Dangerous business, dreaming. Was that not his warning to her just yesterday? He had to put an end to it before he started making promises he wasn't sure he could keep.

As if he needed further torture, Raina nestled deep into his embrace and kissed him below the ear. "I love you," she said, and an agonizing silence began to stretch between them. When he didn't respond, she said it again.

He moved off her, rolling onto his back to stare sightlessly at the rafters. His exhaled breath was deep, rasping as he weighed what he was about to say. Beside him, Raina shrank away, her body tight with mounting apprehension.

"I cannot keep you here any longer," he said at last, amazed that he was able to form the words. "I'm sending you home, back to Norworth. You'll leave in the morn."

"Tomorrow? Why?"

He moved to the edge of the bed, sensing her confused, stricken gaze fixed on him. "Because it's time," he answered gruffly. "Long past time, I reckon. We both knew this day was coming, Raina, sooner or later."

"Aye, later!" The pain and shock in her voice stabbed him, sharp as any blade. "We still have four days left together—"

He forced himself to face her. "Four days and then what, lamb? I've taken too much from you already, and soon I will be faced with the very real possibility of taking something else away from you—what remains of your family."

"You mean more to me now than anything . . . or anyone else!"

"Ah, Raina. Don't fool yourself into thinking you no longer care for your father now that his past sins have been exposed. You said yourself he has never treated you unkindly, that the man you know is not the same person who wronged me. 'Tis a far easier thing to deny your love for him now, lying beside me in my bed, than it will be should you have to look upon him dead or damaged by my hand."

Even in the dark he could see her face register distress at the idea. "Then you still intend to carry out your plan for vengeance, after everything—"

"I still plan to meet him, aye. Not even what we have shared these past few days can change my intent on that score. But I vow to you, the first blow will not be mine. Beyond that, I cannot warrant a thing."

"But if you don't have me to bargain with, he has no reason to come," she pointed out. His Raina, rational even when her heart was breaking.

"Tell him I've sent you home as a gesture of good faith. If he has acquired any amount of honor since the time I knew him, he will meet me, with or without my using you as bait. And if he is half the man you once thought him to be, he would want you there no more than I."

"Gunnar, I want to be with you. You need me! What if something should happen? If I'm there, my father will be more receptive to you, more willing to discuss peaceful settlement—"

"My decision is made, Raina. I don't want you there."

She paused before asking, "Because you're afraid you won't be able to slay him in my presence, as happened with Burc?"

"Ah, lamb, I had hoped you might know me better than that."

"I'm not certain what I know anymore. I thought there was something between us. I thought things were different now. I thought things had changed. . . ."

When he heard her voice break, he reached out to touch her cheek—then abruptly pulled his hand back. Comforting her now would be a greater sin than sending her away hurt. He could not give her false hope of a future together.

Not when he wasn't certain if he would ever see her again.

Though his own thoughts about vengeance and the confrontation with d'Bussy were now conflicted, in light of his having taken Raina hostage, Gunnar could not be sure the baron would arrive willing to talk rationally. And while he had no intention of striking the first blow, he could not guess at the baron's designs for the meeting. Already d'Bussy could be laying a trap or plotting an ambush.

The thought of dying had never scared Gunnar before, and in truth, it didn't now. What made his stomach churn was the thought of Raina being there to see it. Killing was an ugly thing to witness even in the best of circumstances, and not something he could bear to suffer on a woman as gentle and good as she. And knowing his fierce lamb, he could not be sure that she would stay out of harm's way should the situation turn combative.

If she knew how strongly he felt about her, if she knew how much he wanted her in his life now and forever, it would only make her more determined to be with him when he met her father. And that was a risk he was simply unwilling to take.

He rose and strode to the door on weak legs. Before quitting the chamber, he said, "I'm sorry I've hurt you, Raina. But this is for the best. You'll have to trust me."

Morning came too soon, and Raina woke alone in Gunnar's bed. She slowly donned her bliaut and a pair of leather shoes Agnes had brought her; she even took the time to braid her hair, hoping and praying that in his absence, Gunnar had not intended to send her home without bidding her farewell.

Home.

Strange, but Norworth no longer meant home to her. The thought of returning to that place and the lies it housed made her tremble with dread. And now the inevitable had come early. Had she really thought this moment would never arrive? Had she really expected that she'd never have to say good-bye to Gunnar?

How bold she'd been these past few days, inviting him into her arms—into her body—proclaiming that there be no talk of the past or regrets, talking instead of dreams and wishes and forever. How brave of her to say that in loving him she knew what she was asking for, that she was prepared for the consequences. How naive she was to think she could go on unchanged after knowing the pleasures of his body entwined with hers.

She realized now that she had actually convinced herself she could deny her past, forget it even existed. But being with Gunnar had made her believe many things.

Even that he loved her.

She clung to that faith as she blotted away her tears, trying to convince herself that the ache in her heart would not be a lasting one. He had promised her nothing, gave her no firm hope that he would come for her once his conflict with her father was resolved. Still, she prayed he would.

In her mind she envisioned a scenario where Gunnar and her father met and talked out their differences, where the two of them rode back to Norworth in peace if not friendship, and where she and Gunnar were reunited, never to part again. Gunnar had warned her about dreaming and wishing, but her foolish heart refused to listen . . . even now.

From the corridor, what seemed a world away, came the sound of approaching footsteps. "Beggin' pardon, milady," Agnes said softly. "They're ready for ye outside."

Reluctantly summoning every ounce of courage she had, Raina stepped out of the chamber. She hadn't even left Gunnar's keep and already she missed him. Already she mourned losing him. Damp cold from a steel-gray sky bit into her skin as she descended the stairs leading from the keep to the bailey. She held her chin high, though her heart was heavy, her steps leaden.

Across the bailey Cedric and Wesley had already mounted, the latter holding the reins of Alaric's chestnut palfrey for her. She stood there, frozen at the bottom of the stairs, unable to take the first step away from the keep.

Mother Mary, but all she wanted to do was run back inside and lock herself in forever. Agnes nudged her from behind with a gentle pat to the shoulder. "Go on now, milady," she whispered, and flashed her a genuinely warm smile.

Weakly, Raina began the long trek toward the horses, stepping past each face she had come to know and love: Rupert, the shy young page, smiled at her; Odette and Dorcas both murmured well wishes for her safe journey and a good life; all the men who had spun her around the hall last eve sent her off with kind words.

Next she passed Merrick, who opened his arms to embrace her. Raina crushed against him, breathing in the scent of herbs that clung to his clothes and his beard. "He won't betray your trust in him," he whispered beside her ear. "Even if he can't say the words, he loves you, eh?" She backed out of his embrace, Merrick winked. "Remember what I told you, eh? *Trust.*"

Raina nodded numbly and moved toward her mount. Her gaze fell to Alaric, who stood between two men, his arms draped over their shoulders for support. His leg had to pain him terribly, yet he had come to see her off. A sob tore free from her throat, and she slipped her hands beneath his mantle, fiercely hugging his bony torso. "I will miss you very much, Alaric."

She felt his arms come down around her as he embraced her, balancing his weight on one foot. "The keep will not be the same without you, milady. Neither will Lord Gunnar . . . nor I."

She released him, stepping back and rubbing her hands over her arms. She felt so cold, so empty. A light rain had begun moments before, but it wasn't until now that she'd felt the chill. Alaric unfastened his mantle and draped it over her shoulders.

"Nay," she said. "You don't have another."

He shook his head, holding up his hand to quell her protests. "I insist."

Raina threw her arms about her friend's neck, holding him tight. "Then I will take it, but only if you allow me to return it to you very soon."

He nodded as she stepped away from him and fastened the mantle about her neck. She turned to her mount and slipped her foot into the stirrup. Alaric beamed up at her. "The horse is yours to keep for good," he said with a grin. "Milord has given me another . . . a handsome white destrier. A man's mount," he announced proudly.

Nigel's destrier, Raina surmised, and felt her heart lighten to see Alaric's joy. She could picture him atop a white charger, a chivalric knight in shining armor. He would make a fine soldier and, one day, a fine husband.

Reluctantly, she settled into the saddle, looking over the bailey one last time. So much had happened in the short time she had been here; she had become a part of these people's lives, and they a part of hers. She vowed never to forget a moment, no matter how far away her life took her. No matter how many years passed.

"Milady," Wesley said, reining his destrier about, "are you ready?"

Nay, she thought desperately, she would never be ready. A gust of wind buffeted her, as if to push her from the bailey. It seized her mantle, thrashing it about her ankles furiously.

Perhaps it was a trick of the wind that drew her attention, making her look up to the wall walk . . . *where he stood.* A stoic figure in black, his dark hair whipping about his face and shoulders. His jaw was set, his eyes hard as he watched her from above.

When she spied him there, Raina froze, her eyes refusing to blink, refusing to turn away from his image. In that instant she memorized him where he stood, an impassive warrior, a gentle man. She loved Gunnar with her entire being, would have surrendered her life to him as surely as she had already surrendered her soul.

If he wanted her.

"Milady." Wesley's voice was soft behind her. "We must be on our way."

Raina nodded her acknowledgment, her eyes still fixed on the man she loved. She longed to leap off her mount and run to him, to enfold herself in his embrace, never to leave his side. She closed her eyes against the pain in her heart. Then, with great effort, she lifted her hand to bid him good-bye.

He did not see, for he had already turned to walk away.

Gunnar stepped away from the wall walk, fighting the urge to go after Raina or to call her back, knowing he had done right, even if being without her felt wrong as wrong could be. He had taken the coward's way out in avoiding her—last night and this morning—but in truth he wasn't sure he would have had the strength to stand before her and tell her good-bye. Just watching her cross the bailey and ride through his gate was difficult enough.

He thought he would feel better about his decision once she had gone, but found his heart ached keener with every lurching beat. Only a handful of moments since her departure and already he missed her. Saints' blood, but how would he ever live a lifetime without her?

Standing on the parapet, the wind biting his face and snapping his mantle around his legs, he made a solemn vow that they would be together again—whatever the cost.

Chapter Twenty-one

Norworth rose straight and foreboding against the bright midday sky as Raina and her two escorts cleared the forest surrounding the expansive motte and bustling village at its base. The two days of travel had passed more quickly than she might have expected, due mostly to Wesley's unflagging efforts to keep her spirits up with jests and songs.

Now that they had reached their destination, however, nothing could brighten her mood. Wesley likely sensed her dread, for he reined in beside her and placed his hand gently on her arm. "You're home, milady, safe and sound."

Raina nodded absently, staring out at the castle that had been her haven for all her life. Strange how its grand towers and imposing facade no longer bespoke home. Her heart found home in the ramshackle ruins of a northern countryside keep, with a renegade knight on a black charger.

She turned to Wesley and Cedric, nearly ready to plead that they wheel about and take her back with them. But in the distance, the trumpeter's blast sounded from the castle wall, announcing their arrival as if to tell her for certain it was too late to turn back.

"Lord Gunnar asked me to give you this once I'd seen you home, milady." Wesley withdrew a small square of folded fabric from under his mantle. A thin leather cord was tied around the package, securing it on all four sides. "He said to tell you to keep them safe for him."

Raina accepted the tiny gift with bittersweet gratitude, eager to see what it contained yet determined to share it with no one. Whatever Gunnar gave her, she would cherish forever.

"Go on now," Cedric said, interrupting Raina's quick embrace of Wesley. "Yer father is sure to be waitin' fer ye."

Raina nodded sullenly and urged her mount into the clearing. She turned, lifting her hand to bid the two kind men farewell, watching as they melted back into the forest, desperately clinging to everything she was leaving. Only when she could see them no more did she turn her head toward Norworth.

The wall walk teemed with activity as guards flocked to the parapets to hail her approach. One voice rose above the rest, and Raina looked up to spy her father, shoving his way to the fore of the crowd gathered on the tower.

"Raina!" he cried, bracing himself between two merlons and peering over the edge of the wall. "Oh, praise God, my Raina!"

Her broken heart gave a small leap to see her father's face, to hear his voice . . . despite everything she had learned about him. Despite all he had done, he was all she had. And she needed his comfort now more than ever.

"Papa!" she called, and urged her mount to a gallop as he dashed away from the wall toward the keep.

Within moments she passed under the shade of the gate and crossed the drawbridge that led to the inner bailey. Her father, looking haggard and worn, appeared at the keep's arched entryway. His thinning hair was a wreath of wild tangles around his head, his clothes rumpled and soiled worse than her own. He skidded more than ran down the wide stone stairs, then raced heavy-footed into the courtyard as she brought her mount to a halt. Raina nearly threw herself into his waiting arms.

Her father's tears flowed as freely as hers, soaking her

shoulder as he buried his face in her neck and wept like a babe. Raina held him tight, shushing his wracking sobs with reassurances that she was truly there and unharmed.

As he clung to her, murmuring incoherently into her shoulder, Raina noted with an odd sense of detachment that he hadn't bathed in recent days and, perhaps more disturbing, that he smelled heavily of wine. If he were any other man, the notion might not have troubled her, but he was her father, a man who never imbibed. She suddenly felt terribly guilty to think what losing her had driven him to . . . when all the while she was contenting herself in the arms of the enemy.

Heaven help her, but she had to tell him. Had to tell him everything. Pulling her father away from her, she smoothed his brow, caressed his gray and grizzled cheek. "Papa, there is so much you must know."

His head bobbed absently, his expression bland, unfocused. "Aye, of course, of course."

The crowd who greeted her arrival from the tower had now gathered in the bailey, surrounding Raina and her father in a ring of excited demands to hear all the details of her time with her craven captor and how she managed to escape. Raina answered none of their questions, eyeing her father's disoriented countenance with grave alarm.

"Papa, please," she whispered, "what I need to say must be said in private."

At her fervent plea her father snapped to attention. Placing his arm about her shoulders protectively, he ushered her through the excited throng, waving them off as they converged on the keep. "Away!" he bellowed. "Can you not see my daughter is tired? Away, away! I would have time with her alone!"

He led her into the keep and past the great hall to his solar. She followed him, pausing in the center of the room as he turned to close the door behind them. She could scarcely believe what his haven had become in the time she had been gone.

A tray of half-eaten food sat rotting in the corner beside a spilled flagon of wine. It seemed that nearly every cup in the keep had found its way into this room, some of them sitting in a carefully placed row on his window ledge, others scattered haphazardly wherever they had fallen. A chill passed through her as she turned to face her father, who stood now a mere shadow of the man she had left here just one week ago. She wrapped her arms about herself, knowing that she might never again find comfort in his embrace.

"You are cold," he announced, and dropped to his knees before the hearth. He gasped suddenly, then reached in and retrieved a scarred and blackened object. He clutched it to his chest as if he meant to conceal it, then turned guiltily to face her. "I did not mean to burn it," he whispered fiercely, shaking his head like a repentant child. "Truly, I did not!"

Raina moved closer, peering at what he held, and she nearly wept. He had burned her mother's Bible.

His jaw quivering, he held it out to her like he might hold a tiny bird in need of mending. Soot covered the front of his tunic and smudged his chin where the book had rested against him. "I'm sorry, Margareth," he murmured, blinking up at Raina. "I'm so sorry."

The Bible tumbled out of his shaking hands and broke open as it fell to the floor. Its beautiful illuminated pages, which had given Raina so much joy as a child—and which meant so much more to her now—were no more than indiscernible spatters of color amid a sea of black, the edges eaten away by fire. This last piece of her mother, gone.

"I have destroyed everything," her father mumbled from where he sat by the hearth, clutching his temples. He shook his head woefully. "Can you ever forgive me?"

Raina kneeled beside him, taking his dirty and wrinkled hand into her grasp. "Papa, what has happened here? What has happened to you?"

"Nothing, child," he whispered finally. "Nothing of any consequence, now that you are home."

He moved to embrace her but Raina pulled away, gripping his shoulders. "You must stop shielding me from the truth," she said. "Look at me, please, and see me as I am. I'm no longer a child in need of your protection."

He frowned, then rose to his feet. He righted a toppled wine flagon and looked at her meaningfully. "I never meant to return to my old ways, but the thought of losing you—" His voice choked off and he drew in a shaky breath. "I'm a weak man, my daughter. I could not bear it alone."

Raina felt guilty tears prick her eyes. "I'm sorry you were worried about me. I'm so sorry for what you've been through this past week."

He chuckled bitterly, shaking his head. "You shame me by apologizing for what I brought upon you, Raina. It breaks my heart to think what you must have suffered—" A sob wracked his hunched shoulders.

Raina thought about her time away from Norworth and what it now meant to her. "I did not suffer, Papa. Gunnar is a good man; he was very kind to me."

The baron slowly raised his head. He turned to face her, his brows knit together in dawning comprehension. "He, *Gunnar*, treated you kindly. . . ."

"Aye," she replied gently, trusting him to see the truth.

He seemed to deliberate on the idea for a long time, then asked simply, "Did he . . . tell you about me? I imagine you have heard terrible things."

"Yes, Papa, I have heard terrible things. I know what happened between you and the Rutledges, but I would have you tell me why." When he would not face her, she prompted, "Papa, what's done is done. You can't change it, and you can't hide from it any longer. I am your daughter and I love you. I deserve to know the truth."

He smiled wistfully and brought his hand up to touch her cheek. "You were the only part of her that I could ever hold, the only part of her that ever loved me."

Something unsettling began to coil in Raina's stomach at the reference to her mother. "How does my mother relate to what happened between you and the Rutledges? What has she to do with it?"

"She has everything to do with it . . . and nothing at all." His voice faded to a whisper. "Would that she had loved me, even a little bit, I might have been content."

Raina squeezed her eyes shut to hear the admission of this, another falsehood. Her father had always told her that his marriage was a love match worthy of the bards. Was anything she believed based in truth?

"I have lied to you about a great many things because I was ashamed, daughter. Only now am I learning the true meaning of the word." He paced away from her as if he could not say what needed saying if he had to meet her eyes.

"Contrary to what I've told you, your mother wed me through no choice of her own. She was betrothed to another when first I saw her. Lovely Margareth . . . the most beautiful creature I had ever lain eyes on. I decided at that very moment she would be mine. She loved a knight in her father's court, but he had no lands, no promise of a future, no designs on fame or fortune. To my benefit, her sire was a shrewd man with an appreciation for ambition. What I lacked in wealth, I compensated for in drive and aspiration. He granted me her hand, and we were wed in the weeks that followed.

"Our marriage was the beginning of my decline. She was so noble, carrying out her every duty with grace. To anyone looking at our life together, we were the picture of marital harmony. No one but the two of us knew the farce we lived.

We hardly spoke except on matters of the household. Word arrived some years later that the knight she loved was killed in battle. While she wept, I rejoiced, hoping that with his death I might at last have her for myself."

Raina's heart broke for her mother's loss, but she reached out to comfort her father. She had never realized how weak a person he was. "Oh, Papa, how it must have pained you to live with those feelings."

"Do not weep for me," he said brusquely. "You've not heard the worst of it. After this man's death, I believe she no longer wished to live. She withdrew from everything she seemed to enjoy. Her smiles, which were infrequent at best, ceased altogether, as did her weeping. She was a shell of the woman who so captivated me. But her beauty remained, and other men sought her favor."

He looked to Raina and heaved a woeful sigh. "When she became pregnant with you, I saw the promise of what could be. The idea of a babe brought joy to her life . . . and mine. But our happiness was not meant to last. Curse me, but I would not let it; I didn't trust it to be real. When you were born, I saw in you every swain who'd dared to look upon her in our years together, and jealous suspicion consumed me. I could not shake my doubt, and so I . . . punished her for it."

Raina squeezed her eyes shut as the weight of his confession sunk in. Here it was, the answer to the riddle of her mother's despair, the explanation of her self-imposed solitude. Now it all made sense: the endless days her mother spent locked in her chamber, the constant burning of herbs, the maids and their foul-smelling poultices. All the times her mother shut her out, drove her away. It wasn't that she didn't love Raina. She didn't want her daughter exposed to what she had suffered. "How could you beat her?" Raina asked numbly.

"I wanted to hurt her as the thought of her lying with another hurt me. I knew it was wrong but I couldn't control myself. She swore her innocence, but in every man who looked at her I saw a lover. No one could have convinced me differently at the time, though many tried."

"And the Rutledges?"

"I insisted your mother accompany me to a tourney at Wixley. Soon after we arrived she spied her cousin and left the loges to speak with her. When next I saw her she was standing beside William Rutledge. Her slipper had become soiled, and he had stopped to clean it off on the edge of his mantle. She bestowed on him a smile I would have gladly slain a dozen men to see—just once—directed at me." His chuckle was brittle and filled with resentment. "No matter what I did for her, I met with indifference, and this simple deed performed by a relative stranger elicited her favor."

He paused, a pained expression on his face. "I was insane with rage. Rutledge and I went on to compete in the tourney, he unaware of my murderous intentions. When the opportunity came to stay my hand or deliver a fatal blow, I chose the latter. Your mother was horrified at my actions, and she knew my motivation. She paid me back in kind when she took her own life that eve."

Now the argument Raina had overheard as a child came back to her in shocking, horrific clarity: her parents' early arrival from the tournament, the accusations, the shouting . . .

" 'Twas as if I had something to prove to her, as if to tell her that while I could not make her love me, she was still in my control. She proved me wrong, but she left me with a motherless child and a void in my heart that ached to be filled. I turned to the other person who had lost because of me—Rutledge's widow. I wasn't surprised when she denied me, but anger took command of my reason and I seized Wynbrooke, intending to bend her to my will. She would not yield, so I broke her like I could never break your mother. She lost her life, and her son was there to witness my crimes against her. . . ."

"Gunnar," Raina whispered, feeling a tear slide down her cheek.

"My knights reported him dead, felled by a blade." He grew very quiet, reflective. "Looking at the carnage in my wake, I could not believe what I had done. I was appalled. When I returned to Norworth I vowed to change. I swore I'd be a better man—for you. All I wanted was to be worthy of your affection."

"Denying your past and burying lies beneath more lies was no way to live, Papa. I can't tell you that I would have understood then—I don't, even now—but I would have loved you for telling me the truth. You never gave me the chance."

"Oh, Raina! What can I do to make this right?"

"You can meet with Gunnar tomorrow," she said frankly. "You can tell him what you have just told me, and you can ask for his forgiveness."

Her father frowned. "Is that why he sent you to me, to have you plead with me to meet him?"

She heard the suspicion and mistrust in his voice and felt a twinge of sympathy. Here was a man who had lived his life in constant fear of discovery, never certain where his enemies lurked nor when they would surface. Now he seemed uncertain even of her motives. "He sent me home to show you that he was willing to listen. He said if you had honor, you would be at Wynbrooke tomorrow whether or not he held me hostage. He trusts you to do what is right . . . and so do I."

Raina left him standing there in the center of his solar and mounted the stairs leading to her chamber. She requested a bath be brought up and fresh clothing laid out, then waited until the maids left before she retrieved the small gift from Gunnar. Settling into the warm, rose-scented water, she held the packet in her palm, untying the leather cord and then carefully peeling away the linen wrapping.

Her breath caught—love and joy and sorrow twining together—as she beheld Gunnar's precious gift. The twin ruby rings glistened in a shaft of light pouring in from the window, potent reminders of all she had shared with him. All she had lost.

Keep them safe for him, Wesley had said. But what did it mean? Was it Gunnar's way of saying good-bye forever, or a pledge that he intended to return to her one day?

She could not bear to think she might never see him again. Nor could she bear to place the smaller ring on her finger, not until she knew Gunnar would wear its mate. She refused to surrender that hope, damming the tears that threatened to fall. She would not give in to despair, and she would never give up on Gunnar.

Threading both rings as a pendant onto the leather cord, she then fastened it behind her neck. The cool gold bands settled between her breasts, close to her heart, where she vowed they would remain until she saw Gunnar again. Even if it meant a lifetime.

Chapter Twenty-two

News of Raina's unexpected arrival at Norworth could not have reached Nigel at a more inconvenient time. He had only just plucked a young village girl from her work in the fields and had her pinned beneath him in the brush when the herald's call of approaching riders had sounded. Discerning from the tone that the visitors were friend rather than foe, he smiled down at the sobbing maiden.

"Shh," he hissed, pressing his finger to her lips. Then he jerked her tunic down from the neckline.

A jolt of lust shot through him as he gazed upon her small, budding breasts. This one was perhaps the youngest of the girls he had recently sampled. Nigel drew in his breath. He could scarcely wait to taste her.

From behind him someone cleared his throat.

"Mayhap you'd be interested to hear that Lady Raina has returned." His tender prey forgotten for the moment, Nigel rose to his knees and looked over his shoulder to where Evard stood, scowling reproachfully. "She arrived a short while ago," the knight advised.

"Alone?"

"Two of Rutledge's men escorted her to the edge of the woods—"

"I want to see them," Nigel demanded, rising off the girl and coming to stand.

"They've gone," Evard replied, then added rather sourly,

"Lady Raina appears in good health, if the question plagues you."

Nigel smirked, mumbling the requisite praise for her well-being. The peasant girl clutched her torn bodice together at her chest and, choking on her sobs, scrambled to her feet. "Stay," Nigel ordered her. "I've not yet told you to go."

Evard swore an oath. "Have you not had your fill of virgins for a time, man? Must you plant your bastards in all their bellies?"

Nigel chuckled, casting a sidelong glance at the girl. "Like father, like son, I reckon." He looked back to the grim-faced knight. "Go back to the keep now, Evard; I was just about to give this fertile-looking field here a proper plowing. I'll be along shortly." He turned his attention to the trembling young girl as the knight stalked off. "Come now, sweeting, do cooperate with your lord, hmm?"

Moments later Nigel emerged from out of the thicket, wiping the sheen of sweat from his brow. He belted his sword back on, then vaulted onto the baron's own mount, which he had taken for himself after losing his to Rutledge the week before. Kicking the beast into a full gallop, Nigel thundered into Norworth's bailey. A shout to an approaching squire garnered him the knowledge that Raina had retired to her chamber.

Nigel bounded up the circular stairwell and rapped on her closed door. He did not bother to wait for her reply before entering.

Standing beside a tub of milky bathwater, Raina whirled to face him, clearly startled. She flushed, hastily smoothing down the skirts of a red samite bliaut. Her pale, delicate feet were bare, her hair unbound and curling about her in damp spirals that reached nearly to her hips. He cursed his timing; it seemed if he had been but a moment sooner, he might have caught her before she had donned her gown.

Soon enough, he thought. Soon enough he would be free to gaze upon her all he wanted. Smiling, Nigel crossed the room to catch her in his arms.

"Raina, thank the saints you're home!" He inhaled deeply of her cleanness, holding her tight despite her stiff response. "I was tending to some business in the village when I heard you'd returned." He smiled with private humor. "I came as quickly as I could."

She shrank out of his embrace, wrapping her arms about herself. Her brow furrowed into a troubled frown. "Nigel, what has happened here? My father—"

"Is not well," he finished for her, pacing to the open window to look down upon the bailey. "The baron can scarce command a thought of late, much less a keep. Rest assured, however, I've made every effort to acclimate myself to the role of castellan in his stead." He glanced over his shoulder to Raina and saw that her frown had not diminished. Thoughtfully, and with the warmest expression he could affect, he added, " 'Twas no small task to concentrate on affairs of business when my heart ached only for your safe return."

It earned him a weak smile. "Thank you for looking after things."

Nigel scowled, perplexed at her sullenness and his apparent failure to comfort her. He turned from the window to face her, and his eye was drawn to the bed.

There, draped over the edge, were the tattered remains of Raina's gown. Beside it lay a man's mantle. Nigel moved to the bed, his dander rising the closer he got. Raina's bliaut was torn and stained, the skirt frayed and black about the hem; one sleeve had been rent at the shoulder. Gritting his teeth, Nigel reached out to touch the faded silk, letting his hand graze the bodice. His gaze slid to the mantle, and he took the edge between his fingers.

Strange, he thought, that a hostage be offered the warmth of her captor's cloak. "I understand he released you."

"Aye," she answered. "He no longer seeks vengeance. He did not wish to use me against my father, so he sent me home, as a gesture of good faith—"

"Good faith?" Nigel let the fabric fall with deliberate disdain, regarding her over his shoulder. She looked at him with the innocent, trustful gaze of a child. What naïveté. He chuckled lightly. "Good faith, indeed." He paced to the window, where he leaned on his hip, crossing his arms over his chest. "How many kingdoms have been lost to a rogue's pledge of good faith?"

"He is no rogue," Raina averred, "and his word is honorable. I trust him."

Nigel scoffed. "By the Rood, Raina! Why, to hear you speak, one would think—" His blood froze, curdled with the sour realization suddenly dawning on him. Jaw clenched, he turned his head slowly, knowing his face must surely reflect his disgust but unable to mask it. "Have you developed *feelings* for him?"

Raina glanced away, unable or unwilling to hold his gaze. "So much happened while I was with him," she whispered vaguely. "Nigel, I don't expect you to understand—"

"Did you share his bed?"

The calmness of Nigel's voice surprised even him, for inside he was a torrent of anger, physically trembling with it and ready to explode. Her silence in response to his question proved intolerable.

"Answer me!" He shoved off the window ledge and crossed the floor to where she stood. He clutched her arms in his fists. "Tell me, damn you! Did you let him touch you? *Did you spread your legs for him?*"

"Nigel, please." She twisted and tried to pry his fingers from her arms. "You are hurting me!"

Nigel felt himself harden as her struggles increased.

Her virginity, which had never been his to claim, had been stolen from him. She had held him off for years, and now this. Painful as her betrayal might be, some tortured part of him wanted—nay, needed—to hear the words. "How long did it take him to seduce you, Raina? A day?" He grimaced, nearly shaking her. *"Mere hours?"*

He sensed her fear and released her at once, knowing he must tread carefully. He still needed her, needed her trust. While it had taken only a bottle to control the baron, Nigel knew that Raina would not bend quite as neatly to his will. She never had.

A part of him had actually hoped she might never return; it would have made his plans for taking over the baron's reign that much easier. But here she stood, whole and hale. And now the deadly meeting Nigel had been counting on to eliminate one—if not both—of the obstacles standing between him and Norworth's barony was likely never to occur. He was back where he started. If he had a prayer of claiming Norworth, he would have to dispose of the baron himself and wed his only legitimate heir.

Convincing Raina of his affection had been difficult before, but now, in light of her evident feelings for Rutledge, it would be impossible as long as the brigand lived. There could be no doubt that Rutledge had used Raina; any man would in the same situation. He was likely boasting of the ease with which he'd claimed d'Bussy's faithless daughter, doubtless plotting to raid at the first opportunity. The rogue may have plundered Raina's body, but Nigel refused to surrender anything else to him.

And if she bore the bastard's whelp, he would drown the brat before it had a chance to take its first breath.

"You will tell me everything, Raina. Where to find him, how many men he has . . . his weaknesses. I shall lead the entire garrison if I must to ferret him out—"

"Nay!" Raina clutched his arm and looked pleadingly

into his eyes. "There will be no more violence! Please," she whispered, "I have asked my father to meet with Gunnar on the morrow . . . to discuss peace."

Gunnar.

Hearing the rogue's name on her lips was like a blade to Nigel's gut, so distracting he nearly didn't grasp the rest of what she said. The words filtered in slowly, burning through the haze of his rage. She had asked for a meeting between him and her father. To discuss peace. Nigel lifted a contemplative brow. "I see. And did the baron agree to this?"

"He agreed to nothing, but I am hopeful he will."

Absently, Nigel nodded. Perhaps there was some good in this recent complication after all. With Raina safe at home, Rutledge no longer held any bargaining strength. And if the baron was clever, he would indeed meet with Rutledge on the morrow, under the guise of peace. Then, when the opportunity arose, Nigel and his army would pounce. Rutledge would no longer be a threat, and as soon as possible afterward, the baron would suffer a terrible, fatal accident. Norworth, and Raina, would at last be his.

"Well, then," Nigel replied, "I pray the baron sees the wisdom in your gentle request, my lady." With a sober nod of his head, Nigel walked past Raina and out the door to begin planning.

That eve, Norworth's great hall buzzed with excited conversation and good cheer. Before the start of the meal, everyone in the keep had filed past the lord's table to bid Raina welcome and to express their relief for her safe return. She sat beside her father on the dais, feeling out of place and awkward, like a guest rather than lady of the keep.

Nigel had said nothing to her since their conversation in her chamber, and she was glad to be free of his censure.

She knew he was upset, doubtless thought her a fool for allowing herself to feel for Gunnar, but how could she explain? How could anyone understand what had transpired between them in the short time they were together?

She ate her meal in silence, occasionally braving a glance to her left, where her father sat. He had said nothing to her either, and she sensed his pending response to her request weighed heavily on his mind. He reached out and drained his chalice for the second time in the past hour. From his place on the baron's left, Nigel beckoned a page to the dais. He indicated the baron's tankard with a slight nod of his head, and the young boy lifted his flagon to refill the cup with spiced wine.

Raina placed her hand over the top of her father's cup. "Nay, no more wine. Please bring us some honeyed mead instead." The page hesitated, looking to Nigel for confirmation. When Raina repeated the request more firmly, the lad nodded and hastened away to carry it out.

She was still wondering what Nigel was about when the chair beside her scraped against the floor and her father rose to his feet. He cleared his throat above the din of conversation and eating. From the corner of her eye, she saw Nigel lean forward expectantly as the hall settled into attentive silence, all eyes trained on the dais.

"By the grace of God, my daughter has come home to us," the baron announced. A cheer went up, followed by another, then a round of thunderous applause. To Raina's alarm, someone yelled for Gunnar's death. Her father raised his hand for silence. "I thank God, but I must also give thanks to her captor." Several men exchanged confused glances while others fell into wary silence. "If not for his mercy, she would not be here now. That is why I have decided to meet with Rutledge on the morrow, alone as he requested, to discuss peaceful settlement of our differences."

Raina exhaled the breath she had been holding and came

to her feet beside her father. She kissed his cheek. "Thank you," she whispered.

"I for one don't trust him," Nigel announced belligerently. He spoke to the men seated in the hall rather than lifting his gaze to the baron. "I say we meet him as planned . . . with our army. Only then can we be assured of future peace."

Assenting shouts traveled the hall.

"Nay," the baron countered, his voice commanding attention. "I'll not deceive him. My daughter promises me that he is trustworthy. Her word is enough for me." He turned back to his people. "And that should be enough for all of you."

Nigel's voice cut through the amity as everyone resumed their seats. "What if peace on his terms comes at the price of Norworth lands or moneys? How much should we be willing to forfeit for this rogue's promise of peace?"

"My daughter's safety and happiness is worth more to me than any holding. I trust you do not mean to dispute her value."

"Nay, my lord," Nigel acquiesced in a tight whisper, "of course not. But what about me? If you surrender to this miscreant, where does that leave me?"

"It leaves you where you've always been. A knight in Norworth's command."

"But think you I am not due some consideration of mine own?"

"I have seen to your comforts as best I could." Raina could not see her father's face, but the restrained anger in his voice was unmistakable. "You should be grateful for what you've enjoyed through my benevolence."

"Indeed," Nigel muttered through gritted teeth. "And so I am, my lord. Grateful for your every charity." His smile was thin, as was his subsequent chuckle. "I have served you well all my life, and never have I asked for aught in return. No lands, no coin. Nothing. *Not even the benefit of your name.*"

The whispered words had scarcely left Nigel's mouth before the baron's hand shot out to strike him, splitting his lip with the impact. Raina gasped. It seemed as if the weight of a thousand stones lodged in her chest at that moment. Denial, fueled by a dawning realization so profoundly abhorrent, rose like bile in her throat.

All at once the memories of Nigel's years of romantic pursuit flooded her mind, turning her stomach so that she nearly retched where she sat. She heard the murmur of bewilderment traversing the hall, vaguely aware that no one, save those on the dais, knew what had spurred her father's violent reaction.

Nigel stood up so sharply that his chair toppled behind him. His gaze flicked to Raina's and held it for the briefest moment. Tears glistened like ice crystals in his eyes; then they vanished, along with any trace of emotion, as he turned his attention back to her father. With an empty-sounding chuckle, Nigel brought his finger to the corner of his mouth and wiped away the pearl of blood that beaded there.

"Nigel—" the baron began, reaching out to him, but Nigel had already leapt from the dais to stalk out of the hall.

Too stunned to speak, Raina could only stare at her father in mute shock. His outstretched hand hung suspended before him for a long moment, then fell limply to his side. His features drooped into a pitiful frown. Slowly, he turned to face her. He said nothing . . . but there was no need. The truth was written plainly in his eyes.

Eyes that, for the first time, she noticed were the same shade of blue as Nigel's.

Chapter Twenty-three

Nigel left the castle in a rage, cursing himself for losing his head in the hall. Now surely Raina knew that he and she shared the same sire. No matter, he decided, for kin or nay, he intended to wed—*and bed*—Raina, then claim Norworth for his own. Of course, there was no question that the baron would never allow their union to take place.

And there seemed but one solution to that problem.

Needing time and space to think on the best means to that end, Nigel headed for the next village and the tavern where in the past he had found comfort in a drink and the pallet of a warm wench. Having sampled most of the tender young village girls the past week, he had since become tired of their wailing and screaming. Tonight, he wanted a woman. He really wanted Raina, but he would have to wait to take her.

He entered the dank outbuilding with purpose, his senses immediately assailed by the stench of sour ale and woodsmoke. His favorite whore, ensconced on the lap of a large, grizzled knight, glanced Nigel's way as he closed the door behind him. She smiled over the man's shoulder, indicating her room in the back of the establishment with a quick glance in that direction. Nigel nodded once in acknowledgment, taking an overflowing mug of ale from the tray of a passing maid. She squawked but he paid her no mind, tipping the cup to his lips and letting the warm drink spill down his chin and onto his tunic.

As he passed the table, he snagged the arm of the whore, pulling her from the other man's lap. "Save some for the next man, will you, friend?"

The knight rose, kicking the bench away from him, his hand flying to his sword. He glared at Nigel, his bruised and swollen eyes narrowed to puffy slits in his large head. "I know ye," the man said.

"Aye, well, I'm known by many people," Nigel replied boldly, assessing the knight's shabby appearance with a flick of his eyes. His nose was distended and skewed to one side, clearly broken. The scab on his lip indicated a recent altercation, and from the looks of him, he had not come out on top. "I've never seen you before, and I've no wish to know you now." Nigel made to leave with his whore, but the knight seized his arm.

"I can tell ye where the d'Bussy wench is." He flashed a greedy, nearly toothless smile. "For a price, that is."

Nigel jerked his arm from the man's grasp with a sneer. "You'll not make much of a living selling old news, man. I already know where she is." The knight scowled, taking his seat on the bench and muttering into his cup of ale. Nigel watched him, noting that perhaps there was something familiar about him . . . mayhap he had seen him before. "How is it you came upon this tardy bit of information?"

The knight swilled the rest of his ale, then plopped the empty cup on the table. He peered at Nigel, holding his palm open and pointing to it, indicating payment up front. Nigel dismissed the whore with a slap to her behind and sat on the bench opposite the knight. He took out his purse, setting it on the table in front of him. The clink of coins put a nasty glimmer in the knight's red-rimmed eyes.

"I was there when he took 'er," he said.

"Rutledge?"

The knight nodded. "Served the whoreson for a time as a free lance. Me name's Burc." He extended his hand to Nigel, who let it hang there unmet. With an indignant sniff, the knight finally let it fall to his side. "We 'ad a disagreement, ye might say, and parted ways."

Nigel could see the evidence of that disagreement in every bruise and gash on the man's face. His interest piqued, he snapped his fingers at a serving wench to refill the mercenary's cup. "So, I take it, then, your blade is again for hire?"

"I go where it suits me, aye." Burc took a long draught. "I could lead ye to 'is keep if ye plan to reclaim the woman."

Nigel laughed. "There's no need, man. He released her, can you credit that? She arrived just this afternoon, with two of his men as escorts, no less."

"Why?"

"I have been asking myself that very question. She says he now wants to meet the baron to discuss peaceable settlement on the morrow."

Nigel could scarce contain his rage over the prospect. He could not let a truce occur. If he hoped to secure Norworth and its holdings for his own, he needed Raina's hand, and to obtain that, he had to eliminate the baron. Rutledge's death would only sweeten the victory.

"Mayhap there is a way we can both obtain satisfaction," Nigel said after some careful thought. "How would you like a chance to settle the score with Rutledge . . . permanently?"

The mercenary didn't miss a beat in answering. "The bastard's 'ead and a purse as well? Why, 'ow can I resist?"

"Indeed," Nigel concurred, tipping his cup in a grave toast.

A couple of hours later, Nigel threw a coin on the table for his ale and left the tavern, fairly gloating over the ease with which his plan was taking shape. He had no misconceptions that a man of Burc's caliber could be trusted to keep the truth of their meeting a secret, no matter how much he was paid for the crime. But then, Nigel had no intention whatsoever of paying the greedy sot even so much as a farthing. Nay, Burc's reward when he came to collect would be the cold steel of Nigel's sword biting into his fat throat.

The deed would be done, no coin would be lost, and none would be the wiser. Nigel chuckled aloud at the deftness of his wit—and the prospect of his boon come tomorrow eve.

Now all he had to do was convince the old baron to put aside his contempt for Nigel's unfortunate birth, if only for a day, and allow him to ride along to the clandestine meeting with Rutledge, where he might guard his side as any allegiant son would want to do.

Baron d'Bussy and Nigel set out for Wynbrooke early that following morning. It had taken only a couple flagons of wine and a healthy dose of guilt to convince the old man to allow his bastard son this one honor. Nigel now rode at his father's side, watching a vein tick in the side of his ruddy neck and anticipating the moment it would cease . . . for good.

He smiled, nearly giddy with the idea that he would be the one to do the deed.

Beside him, slouching in his saddle, the baron let out a lengthy sigh. "My bones are growing weary of riding," he murmured, his speech slowed from too much wine with his morning meal. "How much farther do you reckon we have yet to go, my son?"

Nigel ignored the endearment, shutting out the stab of guilt he felt at hearing the acknowledgment voiced at last. The old man said it only because he was drunk and had forgotten himself for a moment. It was too late, anyway, Nigel reasoned. It meant nothing. Norworth needed a new lord, someone stronger than this feebleminded, sloven drunkard. Norworth needed him; it was his birthright. Time he set about claiming it.

"Not much farther," Nigel replied evenly, scanning the thicket of woods ahead of them and deciding it looked secluded enough for his task. "It won't be long now."

Gunnar approached Wynbrooke soon after dawn, conflicting emotions buffeting him with every step his destrier took nearer the keep. During the ride south to his familial lands, he had nearly come to terms with the idea of letting d'Bussy live.

He doubted he would ever forgive, and certainly never would he understand, but he no longer needed to stain his hands with the baron's blood to move on, to live his life in peace. Something inside him had gentled, had softened the old feelings of hatred and hurt, had made him take joy in living and gave him hope for tomorrow.

That something was Raina.

She was inside him. Inside him and around him, in everything he did and felt and thought. She was his life. Loving her as he so fully did, he could never bring her pain, could never make her suffer the loss of family that he had. And if he could have her in his life, he knew he would feel that loss no more.

Letting the warmth of that notion embrace him, Gunnar urged his mount forward and up the hill to the castle to await the baron's arrival. He was halfway there when something whisked past his head and landed on the ground behind him with a solid thwack. Stunned, he pulled the reins and cast a quick glance over his shoulder. "What the devil—"

He spurred his destrier, scarcely having time to register the meaning of the attack before a second arrow flew, this time closer to its mark. The bolt whizzed down from the tower and grazed his right arm with searing pain.

"D'Bussy," Gunnar cursed, charging up the rest of the incline, sword drawn, prepared to kill or be killed.

A clatter from above him on the roof echoed in the bailey as he leapt from his horse. Damning himself for being fool enough to trust a proven deceiver like the baron, Gunnar dashed up the stairwell that spiraled through the heart of the keep toward the portal opening of the tower roof. He smashed the wooden plank open with his forearm, nearly daring the assailant to fire on him as he hoisted himself up.

All that greeted him was quiet: a momentary, eerie pall that belied an attack waiting to happen.

Gunnar pivoted, weapon raised as he made a quick assessment of the rooftop, noting the abandoned open wine flask and the quiver of arrows spilled in the corner near the wall. Bow and archer were nowhere in sight. A breeze kicked up, nearly masking the soft click that came from behind a large barrel, likely once filled with oil and left there from the day of siege.

Gunnar took one step forward, and his attacker sprang from his hiding place, armed with a loaded crossbow and a murderous gleam in his eyes. Gunnar experienced but an instant of surprise, and then anger burned to the fore.

"I should have killed you when I had the chance, Burc."

The mercenary chuckled, lowering his head and squinting over the bow. "Doubtless ye wish ye 'ad now. Drop yer blade."

Gunnar took a step forward, his eyes trained on Burc's. "So, my old enemy has taken to paying other men to do his misdeeds, has he? What did he promise you in return for my head? A nice plot of land? A handful of coins? I do hope you got your payment in advance, because you won't be collecting any time soon."

Burc shifted, readjusting his aim. Sweat beaded on his brow. "I said, lay down yer arms."

"Nay," Gunnar replied coolly, "I don't think I will. Your striking me on the motte had little to do with skill or aim, more likely beginner's luck. 'Tis obvious from your handling of that weapon that you've never so much as held one before."

Burc scowled. "Another step and I'll skewer yer carcass where ye stand."

"You're drunk and you have one bolt. Take your best shot. For I promise you, you'll be dead before you make it to the rest of your supply."

Burc's gaze slid to the side as if to gauge his chances of reaching the cache of spilled arrows. The instant his attention flicked away, Gunnar surged forward, knocking the crossbow up with the flat of his blade. Burc discharged his weapon. The arrow soared up past their heads to arc, then disappear, over the battlement wall.

With a growl Gunnar hooked his foot around Burc's ankle and shoved him. Burc took two stumbling steps backward and dropped the crossbow. Armed with his sword, Gunnar charged, striking with a heavy downward swing. Burc rolled to his side, narrowly avoiding the cleaving blow. In the next instant he rolled back. Gunnar's weapon snapped out of his grasp.

Burc's hand reached out, clutching and groping, nearly seizing Gunnar's ankle. Gunnar kicked him away, stretching to reach the crossbow. His hand closed around the shaft just as Burc's hand closed around his leg. Burc gave a hard tug.

Irate and cursing, Gunnar rose up, twisted around, and punched Burc square in the face. He cried out; his grip relaxed immediately. Gunnar scrambled to pick up an arrow from the dozen scattered on the floor, threw it into the weapon, set the bowstring, and leapt on top of Burc.

He straddled him, pinning the knight's arms at his sides,

the crossbow loaded and poised at his forehead. Burc didn't move, scarcely breathed, though his eyes blazed with animosity. "Bastard should have asked for a demonstration of your skills before he enlisted you to kill me," Gunnar taunted.

"Aye, well, 'e didn't much care 'ow I did it," Burc sneered, "only that ye were good and dead by day's end."

Gunnar's innards coiled with rage. He had been betrayed. A fool. Ten times a fool, he had trusted a scoundrel and walked right into a trap. But the thing that burned worst of all was that he had *hoped* for a peaceful meeting. Curse his pitiful hide, but he hoped for it even now.

He wanted answers. Damnation, he would demand an explanation. He would drag Burc with him to testify to Raina of her father's continued deceit, and depending on her reaction, Gunnar would either take her with him or say good-bye to her forever. One way or another, his conflict with d'Bussy was at an end.

"Get up," he said, and began to ease off Burc, gripping the crossbow in his left hand as he made to rise. All at once he felt Burc's body tense beneath him, felt his legs draw up. In the next instant, Burc's feet were in Gunnar's gut, and with a heaving grunt, he shoved him off.

Gunnar flew backward, crashing against the wall. The crossbow went skittering across the rough stone of the rooftop, beyond his grasp. Cold, steel arrow tips bit into his back and jabbed his arms where he landed, and his vision spun from the impact.

"Now ye die," Burc seethed as he scrambled to his feet and drew his sword. Arms spread wide, he barreled forward, teeth bared, snarling savagely.

Instinctively, Gunnar's hand went to his scabbard . . . and clutched naught but air. The realization sobered him instantly, his vision clearing as he reached behind him and grasped the slim shaft of an arrow.

Burc lunged at him, sword raised over his head.

With a sharp flick of his wrist, Gunnar let the bolt fly.

Burc froze. His jaw went slack. A look of sheer surprise washed over him, and his arms fell limp at his sides. His wince turned to a befuddled frown. The sword dropped from his hand, clattering at his feet. With trembling fingers, he touched the slick bolt protruding from a growing scarlet stain at his chest. "Jesu," he gasped, a look of stunned disbelief on his face, "I am dead!"

"Aye," Gunnar observed blandly, rising up and scrutinizing the wound with a casual glance, "in a few hours. But first you will make the trip back to Norworth with me."

Chapter Twenty-four

Raina kept herself busy in the kitchens most of the day in an attempt to keep her mind off the meeting between Gunnar and her father. She had found it hard to concentrate on even the most mundane task, her fingers trembling with anticipation and her heart nearly leaping out of her chest at the slightest noise. When one of the castle hounds barked, she spilled an entire bowl of trimmed green beans and was still on the floor picking them up when the trumpeter's blast sounded, announcing the arrival of her father's riding party.

She vaulted to her feet and threw her handful of beans into the bowl. "They've returned!" she cried, nearly breathless with excitement as she dashed over and embraced Eda, the cook, who had patiently endured her assistance all day. "Oh, Eda, they have returned!"

"Thank the saints," the woman replied with a smile. "Mayhap now I can get some work done."

Raina laughed, spinning on her heel, then lifted her skirts and dashed out of the kitchens and through the great hall. "They've returned at last!" she announced gleefully to the group of knights conversing around one of the trestle tables.

The chains supporting the drawbridge ground noisily in the bailey, echoing down the winding corridor as the great wooden gate was lowered over the moat surrounding Norworth Castle. A hopeful image of Gunnar and her father riding side by side eagerly leapt into Raina's mind. The urgent clatter of horses' hooves sounded atop the drawbridge, quickening her pace—too quick, for she nearly lost her footing on the narrow stairs leading from the keep to the bailey.

She was laughing as she ran across the grassy courtyard, giddy with joy at the prospect of being united with Gunnar once again. Castlefolk, drawn from their work at the announcement of their lord's arrival, watched Raina with open curiosity, but she didn't care what they thought. A crowd had gathered near the gate, and she waded through them, trying to move toward the front.

Nigel was the first to thunder through the arched gate of the barbican. He was shouting something, reining in his mount, but Raina was only vaguely aware of him or his voice. She listened instead for two more horses on the drawbridge.

The crowd behind her began to disperse, as did a few to her sides, but it was the people in front of her that Raina wished would move. Standing on her toes, she bobbed to look between their heads and over them, straining to catch a glimpse of her father and Gunnar. Surely they would not be far behind. Moments passed. Where were they? Commotion grew to a din behind her.

Then the drawbridge began to creak back up into a secured position.

"Nay!"

Raina's voice rose above the crowd. The men turning the drawbridge winch ceased and looked down at her from their posts, their faces solemn . . . damning.

Suddenly, Nigel's shouts became horrifically clear: *Ambush! Rutledge betrayed us! Our lord is dead!*

"Nay," Raina whispered, shaking her head. It could not be true! "There must be some mistake!"

But the drawbridge chains groaned again, and the great wooden barrier closed with a heavy boom. The bailey came alive with activity as the castle was secured. Peasants scurried around her, driving chickens and sheep into their pens and clearing the courtyard.

Raina stood dazed and numb before the iron-banded panels that now separated her forever from Gunnar. *He could not have betrayed her!*

Grief and anger collided within her, and she railed at the drawbridge, throwing her fists against the solid wood as if the physical pain would somehow crush the deeper anguish. A tortured cry keened on the wind, ringing in her ears, before she realized it was her own pitiful voice. Feeling a hand come to rest on her shoulder, she turned to find Nigel, his cropped hair sweat-soaked, his jaw tense and smeared with blood.

"Oh, Nigel, nay! Pray, tell me this is not true!" she pleaded. "What happened? Where is my father?"

"Dead," Nigel said simply, "killed by Rutledge's traitorous hand."

"Nay." Raina mouthed the denial, taking in the visible signs of struggle on Nigel's person: The cut on his lip from the night before had been split open anew; a bruise shadowed his jaw. Stains from grass and dirt marred his russet-colored tunic; a swatch of fabric had been torn from the hem.

"By the grace of God alone," Nigel continued, "I was fortunate enough to get away."

"I do not believe it." Nigel glanced up and met her gaze, his own chilling as winter itself. "I *cannot* believe it," she asserted with quiet resolve. "Gunnar would never do something like this. *I trust him—*"

A haunted look swept past Nigel's eyes; then he frowned. "Your naive trust in a rogue has proven the death of your father, Raina. For the sake of us all, perhaps now I should be the one to decide whom we should or should not trust."

Too stricken to respond, Raina numbly allowed Nigel to wrap his arm about her shoulders and escort her through the crowd of morose onlookers, toward the keep. All the while she weathered the sting of his accusation, fighting desperately to hold back her tears. Dear heaven above, had her trust in Gunnar been misplaced? She clutched the leather cord at her neck, drawing strength from the fact that he'd given her his rings and assuring herself that he would not have so cruelly betrayed her.

When they reached her chamber and Nigel closed the door behind them, Raina asked, "What really happened this morn?"

His attention snapped to her, narrowed on her. "My lady?"

"Gunnar would not have simply attacked without provocation. You must tell me precisely what transpired at the meeting."

"We never made it as far as the meeting. *Gunnar,*" he sneered, "laid in wait for us along the road. *Gunnar* ambushed us and murdered your father in cold blood. Now you tell me, what more do you need to know?"

"Why?" she whispered, refusing to cower under Nigel's rising anger. "It doesn't make sense. . . ."

Instead of raging at her, Nigel chuckled. " 'Twas just as I suspected. He used you. All he ever wanted was your father's lands and your father's power—"

"That's not true! He never wanted any of those things."

"Aye, he did, and evidently, badly enough to kill for them. It seems the only thing he did not want was you."

Though she had succeeded in holding back her doubt thus far, Nigel's assertion struck her to the quick. A sob tore from her breast, and a flood of tears spilled down her cheeks. She could not summon strength enough to deny what he'd said, could scarcely keep her legs from crumbling beneath her.

Nigel looked at her with feigned pity, then pulled her into his embrace, shushing her and stroking her hair. His voice was a pained whisper beside her ear. "It sickens me to recall the besmirching remarks the bastard made on your honor. 'Twas bad enough my suspicions proved correct, but for your father to have heard the details of your shame voiced by the blackguard himself . . ." He let out a woeful sigh. "Would that they had not been the last words he heard before he took his final breath."

Raina could take no more. "Enough!" she cried. "Please, enough!" She thrust him away from her, her ears ringing with the awful notion, her heart feeling as if it were being rent from her bosom.

Her body racked with sorrow, she threw herself onto her bed and buried her face in a bolster. She heard Nigel step to the window and draw the shutters closed, blotting out the sounds of activity in the bailey and plunging the room into darkness.

"Beleaguer yourself no more with thoughts of him. I rather doubt he will ever darken our threshold again." With that, his footsteps retreated and he left the chamber, closing the door behind him and sealing Raina inside with her grief.

Sweat-soaked, bloodied, and fatigued, Gunnar arrived at Norworth's massive gate as the sun began to dip below the horizon. Burc rode tethered behind him, draped over his mount and very near death. At their approach to the gate, a guard on the barbican called for them to halt and state their business.

"My name is Rutledge; I've come to speak with the baron," he replied.

The guard stared down at him for a long moment before beckoning another to his side with a wave of his hand. The two conversed urgently before the second disappeared from the ledge and the gatekeeper addressed him once more. "State your business," he repeated, leveling his crossbow at Gunnar.

"I would speak to your lord as to why he hired this man to murder me."

Nigel appeared on the parapet, peering over the edge. "What the devil—" he gasped, his face blanching. Regaining his composure, he barked, "What do you want, Rutledge?"

"I want an explanation as to why this assassin was sent in the baron's place to a meeting meant to be peaceful. I demand an audience with d'Bussy—"

"An audience with the baron?" Nigel chuckled, shooting amused looks at the men gathered around him. "Come now, Rutledge, that would be difficult, considering the baron's current physical state."

Gunnar frowned, wondering if d'Bussy was ill or if some other ailment had detained him from the meeting. It did not matter. He would stand before the man and demand answers even if he was on his deathbed. "Admit me entry, damn you. Surely one man is little threat against the baron and all of his guards."

"And I am to trust you come alone?" Nigel called. "Truly, you must think me the veriest fool to believe your pledge of peace once again."

Something was amiss. If Gunnar could not tell from Nigel's smug expression and his cryptic responses, he would have seen it in the puzzled, expectant looks of the guards. Nigel was conspiring with someone, and it seemed quite possible from the wicked gleam in his eye that Nigel, rather than the baron, might have called for Gunnar's death. Now more than ever, he needed to see d'Bussy in person, and Raina, too, for the unsettling feeling in his gut told him she was in peril as well. "I don't know what you've done, Nigel, but I swear to you, I will uncover your treachery and you will pay. Damn it, open this gate!"

Nigel considered the request for a long moment, then acceded with a curt jerk of his head. The drawbridge lowered and Gunnar led Burc's mount across the great expanse of wood planks, warily eyeing the score of guards as they glared down at him from the crenellated wall walk. Murder lurked in their faces, a look Gunnar had worn often enough to recognize on sight. Yet none of them made an untoward move. As Gunnar neared the portcullis, one man spat into the moat.

"Murdering whoreson," someone grumbled from atop the wall.

Murder? It would appear he was accused of such, yet he was the intended victim. He was the one who should be hurling angry accusations. *Unless something had befallen the baron.* No sooner had the thought flickered through his mind than the portcullis grated open and the gate swung wide, revealing a glowering Nigel flanked by at least a score of armed men.

"I cannot decide whether you are the bravest man I've met," Nigel said, his smile fading, "or the stupidest."

"Move aside," Gunnar ordered, "lest I deem myself your judge and executioner."

Nigel laughed aloud. "*My* judge and executioner? What did you think to do, Rutledge, simply march in here by yourself and claim what you've been trying to steal from the first?"

"I warrant you are the one with the avaricious goals." Gunnar nudged his mount farther into the bailey and drew the reins of Burc's destrier until it came up beside him. "I suspect this man can testify to the baron as to the depths of your perfidy."

"There is precious little of import to the baron at the moment," Nigel said, scarcely able to contain his mirth.

Gunnar's gut clenched. "Bloody hell! What have you done—"

"Nay, not I, Rutledge," Nigel interjected. *"You.* 'Tis what you have done that concerns us all." He snapped his fingers and nigh a score of guards closed ranks on Gunnar. "Take him away."

"Bastard!" Gunnar leapt from his mount and drew his sword. Instantly, Nigel jumped back into the crowd of soldiers.

"Seize him!" he shrieked, but more than a dozen blades were already poised at Gunnar's throat.

The guards stripped him of his weapons, two men stretching his arms taut while Gunnar struggled futilely to break free. Four other guards pulled Burc from his mount and deposited him on the ground at Gunnar's feet.

Once both of them were subdued, Nigel smoothed back his hair and tugged the hem of his tunic back into place. He came within spitting distance of Gunnar's face and whispered, "It will give me great pleasure to slowly—and very agonizingly—finish what this incompetent lout was sent to do."

A sickening dread flickered in Gunnar's gut as Nigel turned his attention to Burc and crouched down beside him.

"P-please . . . have . . . m-mercy," the knight sputtered.

"Oh, I will, Burc." Nigel nodded grimly and reached out to wipe a bloody smudge from the man's cheek. The day's last rays of sunlight glinted on the slim blade of the dagger Nigel then withdrew from beneath his mantle. With a quick movement, he slid the blade between the knight's ribs and jerked it upward. Burc's eyes widened; his breath caught in his throat, erupting in a faint gurgle.

"You'll tell no tales today," Nigel whispered, resheathing his knife as he came to his feet. He announced blandly, "This man is dead."

"Nay!" Gunnar shouted, bucking against the guards who

held him. "Damn your black soul, you murdered him! You murdered d'Bussy as well, didn't you!"

"Take the prisoner belowstairs to await me," Nigel ordered coolly, then waved his hand over his shoulder in Burc's direction. "And dispose of this carcass, before it rots."

Chapter Twenty-five

Raina spent the remainder of the day and the whole of the night in her chamber, unable to bear the idea of facing a castle full of people who, as Nigel had informed her, likely blamed her for their lord's demise. She refused to leave the sanctum of her room even when she heard the hall belowstairs being prepared for the first meal. Grief and guilt left her empty, but without an appetite for food or any other comfort, save the quiet of her chamber.

She sat on her window ledge, staring out at the fast approach of dawn and welcoming the end to the darkest day of her life. Yet through her pain, despite her anguish, she prayed for the chance to see Gunnar again.

She had not removed his rings. The feel of those precious gifts, nestled between her breasts and close to her heart, infused her with strength, with hope. Grief plagued her and doubts assailed her, but her faith in Gunnar remained. She could not have been wrong to trust him. Not after all they had become to each other. He loved her; she felt it in her very soul, believed it with all her heart. She needed to believe it, now more than ever.

A sharp rap on her door sounded, jolting her back to bleak reality a moment before Nigel entered her chamber. He was dressed in fine cream-colored silks, newly fashioned it seemed, and more befitting a high lord than one of his foot soldiers. His flaxen hair gleamed nearly as bright as his eyes, his sparse little beard neatly trimmed and waxed into a grim point at his chin. If Raina felt as though she had died yesterday, it seemed Nigel had been reborn, cast in the role of baron and unabashedly delighting in it.

"I am told you will not be breaking fast in the hall," he said with an imperious scowl.

He smelled of heavy perfume and wine as he swaggered toward her perch at the window. Something in his expression made the hair on the back of her neck prickle to attention.

Her brother.

How long had he known of their true relationship? And why had he kept it from her? If it was evidence of duplicity she sought, it seemed she need not look any farther than Norworth's own walls. Deceit abounded in this keep, and all her life she had been unaware of it. So naive! No more, she vowed.

She pivoted on the wide ledge, placing her feet on the solid oak of her chamber floor. "Nigel, I want to see my father."

"Impossible," he rejected softly, coming to stand beside her and gazing out over the bailey.

"I must see him with my own eyes."

He turned his head to face her, his expression stony. "I said nay, Raina. Trust me, you'll not want to look upon him in death."

"But what if he is alive? You left him alone out there. How can you be certain he is dead?"

"I am certain," he said with impatience. "He is dead."

"Then if you are right, at the very least he deserves a proper burial, here at home. I want you to send a search party out to locate him—"

"They will never find him."

His clipped reply was so resolute, so cold, Raina nearly shivered. "Then you must lead them. Please, Nigel, I beg you. Do this one thing for me . . . for our father."

"Our father," he whispered quietly. His bravado dimmed markedly with the simple forming of those two words. He scoffed. "What did he ever do for me besides push me away, forsake me, and deny me what was rightfully mine?"

The bitterness in his voice made Raina ache inside. She had never been denied any of her father's affection. But she had been denied the truth. "How long have you known, Nigel?"

He pursed his lips and let out a heavy sigh. He attempted a chuckle, but it was a terrible, humorless sound. "I suppose from the moment the slut who bore me first realized she could wound me with the knowledge."

"If you knew all this time, why did you keep it from me?"

"He made me vow, told me he'd as soon slit my throat as have you hear he had lain with a filthy peasant whore."

"So, my fa—" Raina squeezed her eyes closed against the pain of this further betrayal by her father. "Then he knew as well that you were his son?"

"He did. He knew it, and he hated me for it. Many times I wondered why he did not do away with me. Of course, letting me live—in his very keep—was much slower torture. Every day I saw the breadth of what I was denied, and every day I hated him more and more." He looked at her suddenly, his eyes filled with some emotion she did not understand. His voice was soft, regretful. "I wanted to hate you, too. God's truth, I tried, but you were always kind to me, called me your friend." He reached out and caressed her cheek, then let his knuckles gently graze the length of her arm. "Before I could help myself, I was falling in love with you."

At first she doubted she had heard him correctly— hoped she hadn't. But he was looking at her so strangely now, so covetously, that she had to swallow her revulsion. "Nay." She backed away from him, feeling her skin crawl where he had touched her. "Nay, I don't want to hear this."

"I know it must come as quite a shock to you. But I hope, with time, you will come to love me as well . . . *as my wife.*"

She sucked in her breath, aghast. "You can't be serious," she cried, feeling her insides twist and coil in budding panic. The bed suddenly came up against the backs of her thighs. "We cannot marry, Nigel; the Church would never allow it. For pity's sake, we are kin!"

He shrugged and came toward her. "Aye, but now the only two people who know that unfortunate fact are right here, in this room. I have no cause to bring attention to our mingled bloodlines—"

"I certainly do!" She sidled away along the length of the bed, refusing to turn her back on him.

He advanced slowly, his chuckle low and wicked. "But you won't."

"You cannot force me into marriage, Nigel. I will never stand for it!"

"Oh, I think you will," he replied with a confident smile. "In fact, you will stand before a priest in the morn—"

"Nay!"

"—and you will pledge to love, honor, and obey me *unto death* . . . or I will deliver up your precious lover's head as a wedding gift."

Raina froze, her heart nearly ceasing to beat. *Gunnar.* "Do you know where he is? Oh, God, Nigel! What have you done to him?" She raced forward, clutched his sleeve. "Please, I beg you, tell me—"

"Ah, that's more like it, my love." He grinned smugly. "I do know where he is, and as for what I've done to him, well now, that remains to be seen."

"You must take me to him!"

"Mayhap, after we are wed." He smoothed her hair back from her face. "Mayhap not even then. You must trust me; I know you are capable because you trusted him. Perhaps if I take you to my bed you will be more inclined to do so, hmm? Was that not all it took for you to turn traitor to your father with him?"

"I am no traitor," she averred hotly. "And neither is Gunnar. So far as I have seen, the only person skilled in treachery is y—"

"Have a care with that sharp tongue, my lovely," he chided, placing his finger against her lips. "Best you learn now to keep my mood pleasant, for I can just as easily lock you up in the bowels of this keep as I did . . ."

He did not have to complete the thought. The truth was there and he knew it as well as Raina did. Gunnar was at Norworth. Raina tried to keep the relief from showing on her face, but inside her entire body sang with joy. She wanted to laugh, to cry, to scream her relief. Gunnar was there, and she knew in her heart that he was alive.

And she would find him.

"I will be watching you closely," Nigel warned, "and I expect you to dine at my side—quietly, and cooperatively— this eve when I announce our decision to marry." She started to protest, but he hushed her with a lift of his brows. "If you won't do it for me, do it for Rutledge. He's in quite a state, and I don't know how much more of my temper the poor wretch can take."

Raina endured the evening meal at Nigel's side on the dais, quietly accepting the castlefolks' condolences and weathering the traveling whispers of blame and doubt. Nigel did not even trifle with affecting a pretense of grief, instead enlisting a troupe of jongleurs to entertain and breaking out cask after cask of wine. It did not seem to bother him in the slightest that only he took any measure of enjoyment in the inappropriate gaiety of the meal.

Neither did it appear to faze him to hear the gasps and

stunned reactions of the folk when he stood on the lord's
table and made his announcement that he intended to
marry Raina in the morn.

Raina, alternately torn between weeping and screaming,
found it difficult to keep her emotions concealed. Bewildered hesitant congratulations were offered up by the men
and the women of the keep, no one daring to question either the timing or the basis of the union. As Nigel told
them, Norworth needed a lord and he was only too hon-
ored that Raina had asked him to serve them in that ca-
pacity at her side, as her husband.

Only after Nigel had gone off to lead a dance did Raina
allow her composure to slip, praying that Gunnar was all
right. She nearly jumped out of her skin when someone
placed a tender hand on her shoulder.

"Oh! Evard," she said on a deep exhalation. "You
startled me."

The guard's wizened face was etched with concern. "Is
aught troubling you, my lady? I mean, aside from all that
has . . . occurred of late."

"Nay," she lied as brightly as she could, her gaze on
Nigel, who was busy toying with the laces on one of the
female entertainers' bodice. "I am—*I will be*—fine, thank
you."

He did not look convinced, leaning in to speak softly.
" 'Tis not my place to say, and my apologies if I offend
you, my lady, but your choice in husband leaves many of
us to wonder if you are not making a hasty decision due to
your grief over the loss of your father—and the surrounding
circumstances."

She looked at the old guard's face and knew she could
be honest with him. "Whatever Nigel has told everyone,"
she said in a hushed whisper, "I know that Gunnar had
naught to do with what occurred yesterday. Further, I'm

certain that if I could see my father, I would have proof of Nigel's duplicity."

Evard smiled an understanding, sympathetic smile. "I can assemble a search party, my lady," he offered.

Hope began to flicker in Raina's bosom; she was not alone in this after all. Still, the odds of locating her father—whatever had befallen him—were slim. "Wynbrooke lies many hours to the north of here, and though I know my father did not make it as far as that before he was . . ." She could not speak it. "I cannot tell you for certain what path they took, but—"

"We will find him," Evard assured her. "I'll not return until we do."

She squeezed his hand gratefully, thanking him for his loyalty and whispering a prayer for his success as he stepped off the dais and motioned for a group of men to follow him out of the hall.

A few hours later Nigel had at last tired of celebrating and, grasping Raina's elbow, entreated her to follow him abovestairs to her chamber. He stopped at the door and faced her, blocking her path within. "I could not help but notice my hall was missing a handful of men at the close of sup—Evard, John, and Delwyn, to name a few. I do hope you aren't brewing up a scheme in hopes of putting off our pending nuptials."

"I sent them out to find my father. As your interests seemed elsewise occupied, I took it upon myself to have him brought home."

He smiled thinly. "Ah, Raina. Ever the devoted daughter. I can only hope you'll make as true a wife."

"I will," she answered evenly, "though not yours."

"Stubborn unto the end, I see. Well, it makes precious little difference now. Prepare yourself, my love, for in the morning you and I will be wed, and come tomorrow eve"—he grinned wolfishly and opened the door to let her pass—"I will be planting my heirs deep and frequently within your belly."

"Over my dead body," she declared as she stepped inside.

Behind her, Nigel's answering chuckle was a maniacal titter. "Nay," he returned, "as it would seem, 'twill be over your father's dead body." He grasped the iron latch of the door. "Pleasant dreams, sister dear," he hissed as he pulled it closed.

The entire keep was abed and the hour was late when Raina stole out of her chamber in search of Gunnar. Armed with a small dagger and carrying a tallow candle to light the way, she crept down the narrow, spiraling staircase that led to the keep's oubliette, the place of forgetting.

Greenish-brown moss grew thick on the walls, attesting to the prison's lack of recent use, and the steep stairs were slick with moisture. The air grew colder and more fetid the lower she climbed into the abyss.

At last she reached the door to the prison chamber, its iron-banded panels black with age and damp to the touch. She listened a moment for signs of life beyond that door and heard nothing. Steeling herself for the worst, she grasped the cold metal lock bar and lifted it up, then pushed against the heavy oak panel. The leather hinges groaned as the door yawned into the blackness.

A rush of damp, cold air assaulted her senses, carrying with it the stench of mold and decay. The light from her candle did little to illuminate the room, which might have been a blessing. If the walls of the stairwell made her cringe, the walls of the prison were positively revolting. Her stomach lurched violently and bile rose in her throat as she peered about the room. Reeking mold and mildew stained the walls and formed a slippery paste on the stone floor.

She pivoted with her candle, hoping to find a greater

source of light when a slash of blackness caught her atten
tion on the wall to her right. Praying it was a torch, she
braved a step into the darkness. Groping the slimy stone
wall, she inched her way toward the sconce and touched
the flame of her candle to the torch wadding.

Flames leapt to a blazing orange, blinding her as the
room filled with shadow and smoke. Wiping her bleary
eyes as they slowly adjusted to the light, she turned away
from the wall, and a strangled gasp caught in her throat.

There, in the corner, bound by iron cuffs at both his
wrists and ankles, was Gunnar. He was slumped against
the wall, sitting, for the length of chain at his arms would
not permit him to lie down. His head was lolled forward
on his chest, his tunic stained with dried blood and dirt
He was not moving—mayhap not even breathing, she
realized in terror.

"Oh, Gunnar!" She went to his side, her knees collapsing
beneath her as she crumpled to the floor before him. Her
hands hovered over his head and shoulders, as though she
was too fearful to touch him and find him cold. "What has
he done to you! Are you all right? Please, wake up!"

He roused at last, responding to her voice with a rusty
groan, and Raina embraced him as tenderly as she could,
plunging her fingers into his tangled, matted hair and
pressing kisses to his brow. It seemed to be a terrible strain
for him simply to raise his head, and when he did, Raina's
stomach clenched in a tight knot. His face was beaten and
bloodied, his lower lip split and crusted over with dried
blood. His right eye was swollen shut; a large bruise blos-
somed high on his cheek.

"Oh, Gunnar, I'm so sorry!" she cried, brushing the hair
from his eyes. "If I had known . . ."

He grunted something inaudible, the heavy iron chains
rattling and clinking against the stone wall as he tried to

move. "I—" He coughed violently, doubling over and hissing with the pain of it. "I . . . didn't kill—"

"Shh, my love, don't try to talk," Raina soothed, claiming one moment to caress his face and hair, relishing the feel of him, so grateful that she'd found him. She hated to release him, but time was too fleeting if she was to free him from his imprisonment. She withdrew her dagger and began to work on his manacles. "Hush now, I'm going to help you out of here."

But he would not be silent. His voice was strained and wheezing from what must have been several broken ribs. "I didn't kill him, Raina. No matter what Nigel might have told you, I didn't do it. I would've died before I'd hurt you like that."

"I know." She met his gaze with the same intensity she saw in his eyes. "I never doubted you for a moment."

"Ah, lamb, the way we parted—it was wrong. It killed me to send you away like I did. I only wanted to know that you'd be safe."

"I should have been with you—"

"Nay," he said gently. "And you shouldn't be with me now. 'Tis too dangerous. What if Nigel should find you here?"

"I don't care. I wasn't sure I'd ever see you again. I'm not about to leave you now. Not ever. I'm going to get you out of here or die trying." She dug the point of her dagger into the cuff at his right wrist, twisting it about in an effort to free it, but the blade tip was too large.

"Damnation, woman, it's no use! You cannot risk it!"

"What I cannot risk is losing you again. Besides, Nigel won't harm me as long as he can use me."

"Raina, don't be foolish. My life means nothing, but I can't bear the thought of you meeting with harm." She kept working on his bindings with complete determination. "You are a stubborn wench," he said on a strangled laugh.

"You're just now realizing that?" Raina smiled, though inside she was quaking, knowing her attempts to break his bindings were hopeless. After several more fruitless tries, Gunnar grasped her hand in his.

He shook his head slowly, acknowledging their defeat. Then he glanced down to their entwined fingers. "You're not wearing my ring. Did Wesley—"

"Aye, he gave it to me. I have both of them here, close to my heart." She reached up and unfastened the cord that held those precious mementos. "Keep them safe, you said."

"I trusted you to know my meaning—that I would come back for you if I could."

She laughed, a bittersweet mingling of joy and relief. "I hoped that was your meaning. But I couldn't bear to wear mine until I knew yours rested on your finger as well. Now, give me your hand, my lord."

Raina slid the weighty band onto his finger, and he echoed the gesture, placing his mother's ring on the fourth finger of her left hand. "Ah, lamb," Gunnar rasped against her cheek. "I love you. I love you so very much. I was a fool to ever let you go."

"Well, then, see that you never do it again," Raina scolded gently, and pressed her lips to his.

Their kiss was tender and too long in coming, their embrace fierce—both of them knowing that this could be their last moment together, yet determined that it be just a very dark beginning to a future bright with promise.

It was then they heard a low, growling chuckle coming from the darkened stairwell.

Chapter Twenty-six

"How very touching."

Raina glanced over her shoulder to see Nigel lurking in the shadows at the base of the stairs, leaning one shoulder against the arched stone wall. His right hand rested casually on the hilt of his sword. "I warned you I'd be watching you, my sweet. Now what did you think to accomplish by coming down here in the wee hours of the eve? A daring midnight rescue, perhaps?"

"I just wanted to see him again." She looked back to Gunnar, her eyes trained on his as she discreetly slid the dagger toward him, "to say good-bye." Gathering her courage, she came to her feet, facing Nigel.

"Truly?" he drawled. "It didn't sound like good-bye to me." He pushed off the wall to move toward her in a wavering swagger. "You surprise me, Rutledge." He flicked a glance past Raina's shoulder as Gunnar struggled—and failed—to come to his feet. "I would have expected to find you dead by now." He chuckled. "Or rather, hoped."

"What kind of monster are you?" Raina charged, putting herself between Nigel and Gunnar. "How could you do this?"

"I'm not yet done, love. In fact, I've come to finish it now. Kindly move away from him, will you?"

"Nay," she replied. "You will leave him be, Nigel. You've nearly killed him already."

"An oversight I intend to rectify. Step aside." When she would not budge, he sneered over her shoulder at Gunnar. "Such a willful wench, is she not?" He glowered at her. "That, my love, is one trait I'll not brook in a wife."

"Wife?" Gunnar's voice behind her was choked, disbelieving.

"Did she not tell you?" Nigel clucked at Raina, wagging his finger. "Oh, shame, lady, leading this poor wretch on. Aye, Rutledge, Raina and I are to be married in the morn."

"I would sooner die—" she averred, but Nigel's hand snaked out sharply, seizing her by the hair. He wound his fist in the unbound tresses and yanked her savagely to his side. Her attempts to keep from crying out failed her as a pained whimper escaped her lips.

The chains that bound Gunnar to the wall jangled as he struggled against them. "You whoreson coward! I'll kill you!"

"I would very much like to see how you'll manage that," Nigel taunted, stepping forward and bringing Raina on her knees to within inches of Gunnar's grasp.

Slumped over and coughing, looking as if it took all of his strength just to remain upright, Gunnar met her gaze. His eyes were so filled with emotion, moist with pain and something so much deeper, Raina's heart wanted to break. She brought her hand up, reaching out to him, needing to touch him for what she silently vowed would not be the last time.

Nigel jerked her back with a vicious snarl. "She's mine now." He twisted his fist in her hair so that she had no choice but to look up at him. "Mine to do with what I will." Shamed, Raina felt a tear roll down her cheek.

"Unhand her, damn you! Let her be or I'll—"

"Or you'll what?" Nigel prodded. "What if I should take her right here, toss her skirts up and swive her, right on the floor at your feet?" As if to demonstrate, he leaned forward, shoving Raina's head down and flattening the side of her face against the cold, damp stone. "Tell me, Rutledge, whatever will you do?"

"Step closer, you miserable whoreson, and I'll show you." Though Raina could not see him, Gunnar's rage was evident in the lethal calm that permeated his threat.

"Tsk, tsk," Nigel admonished from his safe distance, "so impatient to feel my blade at your throat." Chuckling and seemingly unconcerned, he placed his foot at Raina's back, then, releasing his grip on her hair, shoved her down to the floor.

Raina sensed Gunnar reaching out as if to break her fall, heard the snap and jangle of his chains as they drew taut and jerked him back. She scrambled away from Nigel, gripping the wall to steady herself as she came to her feet, trembling, her cheek stinging from the scrape of the floor.

"You damnable coward," Gunnar cursed, "why don't you fight me? Your quarrel is with me now, not her!"

"So it is," Nigel hissed, casting Raina a sidelong, meaningful glare as he drew his sword. "And 'tis past time I put an end to it."

"Nigel, please, nay!" In her peripheral vision, Raina saw Gunnar crouch to retrieve the dagger from beneath his boot. Nigel saw it soon enough as well.

"What's this? You mean to fend me off with that puny weapon?" He took a jab with his broadsword, but Gunnar stood and deflected it with the length of chain at his arm. "Look how much bigger my blade is, Rutledge. You don't stand a chance."

Nigel lunged, cleaving the air with a violent swing of his sword. Gunnar only narrowly escaped its path, pressing his back flat against the wall.

As Nigel stepped closer and made to take another swipe, Raina flew at his back, scarcely registering Gunnar's plea for her to stay as she wrapped her arms around Nigel's neck and tried to pull him down. He stumbled, arching his back and prying at her arms with his free hand. She clung to him, desperate and snarling with rage. Nigel twisted in her grasp, finally shaking her off and thrusting her away from him as if she were no more than a slight irritation. She landed hard on her rump and felt the cold steel of Nigel's blade at her cheek.

"I should hate to scar that pretty face, my darling," he warned. He spun around and stalked back to Gunnar. "You're upsetting my bride, Rutledge. Why don't you yield now and let me finish this quickly?"

"I'm eager to finish it as well," Gunnar growled, and beckoned Nigel forward with a curl of his hand.

Behind Nigel, Raina scooted quietly away, determined to help Gunnar and inching toward the only weapon she could think of—the torch blazing on the far wall of the cell.

Nigel drew back his sword and swung at Gunnar. He ducked, then came up quickly, sticking Nigel in the side with the dagger. Nigel sucked in his breath and took a step backward, his feet scuffing on the stone floor. With a roar he charged forward again, raising his weapon high over his head with both hands.

Raina struggled to free the torch from the sconce, her fingers trembling, heart racing.

Behind her she heard a heavy clink as Nigel's sword came down on Gunnar, heard the mingled grunts of both men . . . then Nigel's wicked laughter.

"What a pity," Nigel taunted. "Your poor little blade is broken and alas, our fun is ended."

Raina pulled the torch down and turned to see Nigel, his blade pressed at Gunnar's chest. The dagger she had given him lay in two pieces on the floor.

"Which would you rather I cut out first, Rutledge, your heart or your ball—"

He didn't get a chance to finish. Summoning all of her strength, Raina ran up behind him and cracked the torch atop his head. He stumbled, dazed. He spun around and came toward her with murder in his eyes. "You should not have done that," he snarled.

Raina screamed, raising the torch high and hitting him again, this time in the forehead. Reaching for her, cursing her, Nigel started to lose his footing, stumbling backward into Gunnar's chest.

"Bitch!" he screamed, and made to come at her again. Dear lord, he was going to kill her. . . .

In the space of one terrified heartbeat, Gunnar wound the length of chain at his arm around Nigel's neck and gave it a hard yank, efficiently snapping his neck. Nigel's limp body slid down the front of Gunnar's legs and pooled lifelessly at his feet.

"Gunnar!" Raina threw the torch to the stone floor and dashed into his open arms. She kissed his lips, his face, his hands, hugging him fiercely and so very glad to feel his embrace. "Thank God," she whispered. "Oh, thank God it's over!"

He slumped against her for support, and she realized just how battered and weak he actually was. "Here, let me get you out of those bindings," she said, and, reluctant to leave his arms even for a moment, bent down to retrieve a ring of keys from Nigel's baldric.

She freed the last iron cuff and was helping Gunnar to the top of the prison stairwell when Evard and his men thundered down the corridor toward her. "My lady!" he exclaimed. "What the devil—"

" 'Tis all right, Evard," she said. "Everything is all right now." At Evard's gesture, one of the men came around the other side of Gunnar and lended his shoulder for support. "Did you find my father?" she asked numbly.

"Aye, my lady, we did. He had managed to crawl out

from the woods where he was attacked and into the path, but . . . I'm sorry, he was already gone when we found him."

She nodded solemnly and made to move past, her concerns centered wholly on Gunnar now.

"Lady Raina," Evard continued, "you were right about Nigel's treachery." He held out a swatch of russet silk. "This was clutched in your father's fist."

Raina glanced at it disinterestedly, having no need to inspect it closely to know for certain the fabric would match that of Nigel's torn tunic of the day before.

"I will see to it that the blackguard pays—"

Raina shook her head. " 'Tis over, Evard," she advised him quietly. "Nigel is no longer our concern. You'll find him belowstairs. All that matters now is Gunnar's health; help me get him out of this place."

Epilogue

England, 1154

It was a time of new beginnings, not only for England and her new French king, Henry II, but also for the monarch's newly sworn vassal, Baron Gunnar of Rutledge Castle, and his beloved bride. The couple had put their pasts well behind them, eagerly embracing the peace and order that arrived following the death of the old king and his lawless ways.

As Norworth had been one of many castles constructed during Stephen's reign and without permission, it—along with hundreds of others—was pulled down at the onset of King Henry's rule. Neither Raina nor Gunnar felt a pinch of regret to see the castle fall. Their home was a smaller keep, a modest holding high in the north country and, Gunnar thought with pride as he urged his mount up the keep's sloping motte, one soon to be rebuilt with funds granted by Henry himself.

He could hardly wait to give Raina the news.

Passing through the open gate, he heard her voice in his heart before the sound reached his ears in the bailey. The melody she sang was sweet, melancholy, drifting from the open window of the lord's chamber to fill the air with innocence and love of life. He had never heard her sing, and now, having missed her for nearly a sennight, Gunnar's heart tripped at the most beautiful sound he had ever heard.

Heedless of decorum or the need for appearances, Gunnar threw his reins to Alaric and leapt from his mount in one move before dashing for the keep like a beardless youth sick with love. Raina's voice embraced him as he took the stairs two at a time, his spurs clinking loudly with each footfall.

When he reached the top, he realized with no small amount of disappointment that the sweet music had ceased. Agnes scurried from his chamber, smiling at him broadly. "Welcome, milord," she said. "Yer lady wife awaits ye in yer chamber."

Gunnar scratched his head, venturing a puzzled look over his shoulder as the old woman made her way down the corridor, trying unsuccessfully to muffle her giggles in the fabric of her wimple.

The door to the lord's chamber was open, and Gunnar could hear the soft sounds of trickling water coming from within. He stood in the doorway, taking in the glorious sight of Raina in her bath. She smiled at him warmly. With the setting sun framed in the window and illuminating her hair, she looked radiant, ethereal. The fiery ruby ring on her left hand—the one that matched his own—winked at him from across the chamber as if to assure him that he had at last come home.

"I missed you, husband," Raina cooed, her loving expression warming him to his soul.

"And I, you, wife. I have news from our king, but first I should like you to continue with your song, my lady love." Gunnar entered the chamber, closing the door behind him. He wanted no interruptions this evening.

Raina blushed and caught her lip between her teeth. "Nay, you'll laugh," she said, making a small, self-conscious splash in the water.

"I vow I'll not laugh." Gunnar grabbed a faldstool and brought it behind her, seating himself and lifting her unbound hair, spreading it over the back of the tub. "Please, continue."

Retrieving the brush Agnes had left, he began to comb Raina's thick, silky tresses, letting his fingers wade through the luxurious weight of it. Raina settled into the tub, tipping her head back and closing her eyes while he attended her. She sighed contentedly, then began to hum.

The tune was mysterious but vaguely familiar. As Raina softly whispered the words, Gunnar felt certain he had heard it before, a long time ago. He wanted so much to kiss the upturned face of his angel wife, the lamb who had so easily captured his wolf's heart. But he let her sing, inwardly rejoicing that she was his as he was hers.

And there would be plenty of time for kissing now that he was home.

"Are you not the least bit curious what it is I am singing, my husband?"

"Mmm?" He looked up from his work to find Raina staring up at him. He smiled indulgently. "What is it you sing, my wife?"

" 'Tis a lullaby. Agnes taught it to me."

"Ah." He kissed her forehead and returned his attention to the dark, silky waves of her hair. "Sing it again; I rather like it."

"I fear you shall grow quite tired of it in time."

Gunnar smiled. "Do you mean to tell me 'tis the only tune you know?"

"Nay," she said with a soft laugh, "but 'twill be one you'll hear oft enough, for I shall be singing it to our babe come summer."

Gunnar's hand stilled as her words sank into his brain. Raina's eyes were smiling brightly up at him as he met her gaze. His puzzled expression must have been enough for her to know his thoughts, for she nodded her head excitedly and began to laugh.

"You mean—" he began, but his heart soared into his throat and cut the rest of his question off.

Raina nodded again, turning in the tub to face him. This time her smile was tremulous. "Does it . . . please you, my lord?"

Gunnar shook his head in bewilderment; then, spying her crestfallen, worried look, he blurted, "Does it *please* me?"

He threw the brush into the water and scooped Raina up out of the tub with a triumphant shout. She clung to him, wrapping her arms about his neck, her rich laughter tickling his ear and warming his already burgeoning heart.

"She wants to know does it please me!" he yelled, spinning her around before setting her softly on the bed. He placed a tender kiss to her lips. "My lamb, *my love,* let me show you just how much."

If you loved the passion and adventure of
LORD OF VENGEANCE,
turn the page for a sneak preview
of Tina St. John's exciting new historical romance,

Lady of Valor

Coming in late Spring 2000

Prologue

The dead man lay there, motionless and sprawled on the dirt floor of the tent where he had crumpled moments before. The bleeding wound at his side spread out like spilled wine, staining his Crusader surcoat and the ground beneath him a deep crimson-black. Left arm outstretched, his fingers were curled into the hard-packed earth mere inches from the boot of an English soldier.

Cabal—Blackheart, as he was better known—stood in the dim illumination of a sputtering candle that had been upset during the struggle and considered that clawing, desperate hand with sober reflection, like a man awakened from the depths of a black and heavy dream.

Outside the tent, darkness had settled over the desert, cooling the vast sea of scorching sand but doing little to calm the bloodlust of the Crusaders camped there. The bonfire the regiment had lit hours before would burn long into the night, as would the men's drunken voices, raised in celebration of the day's small victory.

God's army had taken a village, and with it scores of Muslim lives. Never mind that the numbers included women and children; they were all soulless heathens according to the Church. As such, they had been afforded less regard in their slaughter than would the lowliest vermin. But the dead were the fortunate ones. They were spared the horrors suffered by those left living as prisoners of the Cross.

Cabal ran a hand over his grimy, bearded face and blew out a weary sigh as he stared down at the dead man. Damnation. How had things come to this? What manner of unfeeling beasts had they become in His name?

Clumsy footsteps scuffed in the sand outside the tent before the flap was thrown open and a laughing soldier shuffled inside, bleary-eyed and stinking of too much wine.

"Sir Garrett, ye selfish bastard! Do ye mean to keep the chit all to yerself?" The mercenary drew in a choking gasp, stumbling back on his heels. "God's wounds, what happened—"

When the soldier made to advance, Cabal held him off with a dismissive flick of his hand. Crouching beside their fallen commander, he reached out for a jeweled dagger that lay next to him, slick with its owner's blood. "I came upon the struggle too late," he explained. "There was no saving him."

"She killed him! The damned Saracen whore killed him!"

"She was no whore, Rannulf, only a child." Cabal could scarcely contain the edge of disgust in his voice. "No more than ten summers if she was a day."

Rannulf sputtered. "Child or nay, she will suffer—"

Cabal rose abruptly and faced Rannulf, his head inclined forward under the cramped slope of the tent's ceiling. "The girl is gone," he said, meeting the soldier's wild-eyed gaze.

Rannulf frowned, then looked past Cabal to the severed length of rope that had been tied about the child's neck as a leash when Garrett had plucked her from the crowd of screaming villagers that afternoon, intent on keeping her for his own base amusement. Rannulf's expression was suspicious, questioning.

Cabal answered frankly. "I set her free."

"Set her free? So she can stab another man in the back?"

Coolly, without response, Cabal turned the ornamented blade over in his hand and cleaned it on the edge of his surcoat. His palm now bore the scarlet outline of the dagger's carved handle, but he made no attempt to wipe the stain away, remaining deliberately contemplative in the face of Rannulf's incredulous scrutiny.

"What's wrong with you, Blackheart? I've seen you level whole cities on Garrett's orders without mercy! You of all people should want vengeance for his murder—the man was your best friend!"

There was little point now, Cabal reasoned, in arguing over what he might have felt for Garrett of Fallonmour. It certainly wasn't friendship. And he needed no reminders of all he had done at his commander's direction. His soul would bear those scars until damnation finally claimed it.

"This war has made animals of us all," Cabal said at last, pointing the killing end of Sir Garrett's blade at Rannulf to drive home his meaning. "I will hear of no man seeking the girl out, nor any other Muslim peasant, in retaliation for this . . . inevitability."

As the word formed on his tongue, Cabal's eye was drawn to Garrett once more, to the slack expression of the man who just that morning had been boasting of his home in England, regaling those who would listen about his plans to expand his keep and his designs on the King's court. Garrett of Fallonmour spoke often and at great length of his holdings, describing with a steward's eye for detail the worth of every building, beast, and field in his control.

And Cabal had listened, at first for no other reason than that Garrett's bragging drowned out the echoes of the dead and dying by day, and at night kept the eerie silence of a sleeping desert filled. But soon enough, Cabal began to feel the prickling awareness of awakened greed, and a burning resentment for all that he could never have.

Garrett had been quick to discern Cabal's interest and make use of it on the field, where he employed Cabal as his personal guard. In exchange for promises of a position at Fallonmour, Garrett had commanded Cabal's unquestioning obedience. Mayhap, he told him, there might even be a tract of land for his own one day, if he proved loyal on campaign.

And Cabal had proven loyal. He rode into battle at Garrett's side and had saved his life more than once. He killed on command and destroyed without mercy. He was swift and efficient, and if anyone doubted the fitness of his *nom de guerre*, they need only look to the trail of blood and cinders left in Blackheart's wake for proof. For two years, Cabal had functioned without conscience, for the sake of a handful of promises.

Those promises, empty as Cabal suspected they were, had now been swallowed up by the desert sand, along with Garrett's miserable life. Not on the battlefield, where he had cheated death with Cabal's assistance, but here, in the relative safety of his own tent. And Cabal had done nothing but watch, stoically, as everything he had worked for drowned in a pool of blood at his feet.

The irony of the situation gripped Cabal fully, and he swore a vivid oath. Then he began to chuckle—a deep, uncontrollable rumble of laughter, completely devoid of humor. When he looked to Rannulf, the mercenary was gaping at him as if he'd lost his mind; in truth, mayhap he had.

"Clean up this mess," he ordered Rannulf. "And see to a means of disposing of the body. I won't leave it to the infidels for their sport. No man deserves that brand of treatment . . . not even him."

Leaving the soldier to stare, bewildered, after him, Cabal

stepped out of the stifling pall of the tent and into the deep desert night. The gathering around the bonfire had grown since he had first left the camp. Victory shouts echoed into the darkness and the fire blazed higher than it had before dusk. From the supply tent at the west end of camp came a soldier carrying a full tankard of wine. He walked on unsteady legs down the dirt path that stretched out between the tents, making his way back to the celebration.

"You there." Cabal's hail brought the young man-at-arms to an abrupt halt before him. "What's going on out here?"

"S-sir?"

Cabal gestured to the boisterous crowd. "Tell those idiots to douse the flames before they lead Saladin's assassins straight into the camp to cut our throats."

The soldier stared at him, swallowing hard, as if the shock of being addressed directly by the one known as Blackheart had robbed him of his voice. Though not an unusual reaction, particularly among the younger knights and mercenaries, tonight it strained Cabal's patience.

"What are you gaping at, man? Tell them to put out the fire and get their drunken arses to their tents! We march for Asouf in the morn."

"B-beg pardon, sir, but . . . have you not heard? The war is over. King Richard signed a treaty with Saladin this very morn; the messenger came and went just moments ago to spread the word." Awkwardly, the soldier offered his tankard to him in a trembling gesture of goodwill. "The first ships sail for England in a few weeks. Soon we'll all be home!"

Home.

Cabal had never known the meaning of the word. He stared unseeing into the flames of the distant bonfire, hating Garrett in death more than he had hated him in life.

He cursed the man for turning him into the beast he'd become and damned himself for allowing it. And for what? Now that the war was ended and Garrett was dead, it had all been for naught.

But as he took the cup and drained it, Cabal began to taste the promise of a better life; he began to see his destiny. And what he envisioned was not the France of his birth, nor the Norman estate where he had spent a hellish youth. What he saw waiting for him was a lordless English demesne . . . called Fallonmour.

Chapter One

England.   Midsummer, 1193

The day dawned in much the same way as the hundreds that had come before it, but this time Lady Emmalyn of Fallonmour felt an odd quickening in her veins—a queer sense of hopeful anticipation that roused her before the sun's first rays lit her chamber. Something was in the air; she could feel it.

Would today be the day?

Excited to find out, she washed and dressed quickly, then quit her chamber and descended the stairwell that spiraled through the heart of the castle. She moved hastily and on light feet, knowing she would have only this short while to claim for her own. Before long, the entire keep would wake and her daily duties as castellan would begin anew.

Seeking Emmalyn out as well would be the visiting seneschal, sent to Fallonmour three days ago by Hugh, her brother by marriage, and, since Garrett's departure three years past, her overlord. Hugh's dour old servant had informed her last eve of his intent to go down to the village at first light for the weighing of the newly sheared wool and an assessment of the fields' bounty due his liege.

Emmalyn fully intended to cooperate with the accounting, as she always had in the past, but she disliked the man's tactics and particularly his harsh treatment of her folk. She would accompany him to the fields, she had told him firmly, and they would go when she was ready. At present, she had other, more pressing priorities to attend to outside the keep.

Fallonmour awaited a new arrival.

Emmalyn crossed the bailey, anxious with anticipation by the time she reached the stables. The head groom, a large, graying bear of a man, was already at work, tools in hand. He greeted Emmalyn with a wide smile when she entered the outbuilding.

"How does she fare this morn, Thomas?"

"Well, milady. Only a matter of a day or two now, I reckon."

Emmalyn looked into her mare's soft brown eyes and smiled. "Did you hear that, Minnie? You're going to be a mother soon." The bay blinked her black lashes and nuzzled Emmalyn's outstretched palm. Then she nipped her. Gently, but enough to make Emmalyn yelp in surprise.

" 'Tis all right; I'm fine," she assured Thomas when he dropped his tools and hastened to her side.

He bent to retrieve something from a bucket on the floor, then gently cleared his throat. He was holding an apple and a small knife in his hand. Sheepishly, he held them out to her. "Apologies, milady, but I fear I've spoiled her of late. She looks fer a treat every morn now—gets downright surly if denied it overlong. I beg pardon, milady, if ye be displeased."

"You have a kind, giving heart, Thomas. You needn't ever apologize for that. Besides," she relented with a soft laugh, "it seems I am as much to blame as you for Minnie's poor behavior. While you have been spoiling her with apples in the mornings, I have been doing the same after supper each afternoon. 'Tis a wonder she hasn't tired of them by now."

Emmalyn had scarcely sliced off the first crisp wedge

when the mare nudged forward and stole it from her fingers. While Minerva munched contentedly, Emmalyn stroked the rough silk of the horse's large head and neck. "I reckon she is due some special treatment, is she not? After all, 'tis not every day Fallonmour hosts a royal birth."

She could hardly contain her pride: Minerva's foal was sired by Queen Eleanor's finest stallion. The breeding was a gift from Her Majesty, during the dowager queen's last visit to Fallonmour, and something Emmalyn prized dearly. At her side, Thomas beamed his assent, then picked up his tools and returned to his tasks with the other horses.

"Milady!"

From the bailey came a bark of alarm. The mare started, tossing her head and whinnying, eyes wide. The shout startled Emmalyn as well, who whirled toward the heavy pounding of running feet as they neared the stables. One of her fostering pages skidded to a halt in the doorway, breathless.

"Milady, come quickly!"

"What is it, Jason?" she scolded. "You frightened poor Minerva nigh to death—"

"Arlo sent me, milady! You must come at once—he's in the south field! Hurry!"

At the mention of the seneschal's name, Emmalyn bristled. It did not surprise her that Hugh's man would waste no time in defying her instructions, but what troubled her more was the urgency in Jason's voice. Doubtless Arlo had threatened the boy with some form of bodily harm if he did not carry out the order to fetch her at once. Or perhaps the seneschal had taken it upon himself to terrorize the villeins in the name of commerce. "I've had about enough of Arlo and his bullying ways. Where is he now, Jason? The south field, you say?"

The page shook his head fiercely. "Nay, milady, 'tis not

Arlo in the south field, but a rider! He approaches Fallon-mour as we speak!"

"A rider?"

"A knight, milady, wearing the white cross of a Crusader!"

Instantly, Emmalyn felt her confidence falter. She drew in a deep, strengthening breath and made sure her voice remained steady, even if it was little more than a whisper. "A Crusader? Are you certain?"

"Aye! Riding a great black steed and heading for the castle! Milady, think you 'tis Lord Garrett, returned at last?"

Garrett.

Could it be? After three years without a word from him, had he now come home? News of King Richard's returning army had been circulating for many months now, and Emmalyn had been expecting to see Garrett ride through Fallonmour's gates, preparing herself for the eventuality of her husband's homecoming and how it would impact life as she had come to know it in his absence. But she wasn't prepared. She knew that now, feeling her stomach tighten and twist with every passing moment. She struggled to appear calm. "Tell Arlo to assemble the folk in the hall, Jason. I'll be along in a moment."

Emmalyn turned back to Minerva's soulful gaze and idly stroked the mare's neck. Already her hands were shaking. Mercy, but she had to collect her thoughts. Collect her nerve. Perhaps the war had changed her husband. Gentled him. Perhaps things between them would be different now.

She was different. No longer the child he married, but a woman of twenty summers. She had managed Fallon-mour and its holdings during the more than three years he had been away, acting as castellan and negotiating with tradesmen, even fending off a raid on the village last autumn. So why should the thought of facing one man—her husband—still terrify her so?

Beside her, Thomas's voice was a low, soothing drawl. "Courage, milady. Ye'll be fine."

Emmalyn nodded, but her smile was weak. She straightened her shoulders and marched out of the stable and across the bailey toward the keep. Castlefolk tending their work glanced at her as she passed them, clearly aware of the approaching Crusader and watching for her reaction to the news. But Emmalyn kept her chin high, her gait purposeful.

To mask some of her own internal disquiet, as she neared the keep she called out orders to a knot of people standing idle in the bailey. "Nell, shoo those chickens back into the roost. Alfred, see to it that straw and fresh water are brought to the stables. And Jane, find Cook. Tell him to warm the venison and lamprey from last eve and use the fresh beans I brought in from the garden yesterday. Bring bread, too, but not the dark—fetch the lightest loaf you can find. Make sure there is wine on the dais, but it mustn't have any grit, so strain it twice before you decant it."

Emmalyn did not slow her pace until she had ducked under the cool shade of the pentice, an arched gateway that led from the bailey to the keep. She stood there a moment, thankful to be away from watchful eyes while she summoned a steady breath.

Dieu, but how quickly Garrett's expectations came back to her, even after all this time. All the demands he placed on her, from the way he wanted his meals prepared to the way he required Emmalyn to dress in his presence. She'd had three years to make her life her own, to come out of the shadow Garrett had cast on her. Three years of freedom, yet she felt her hard-won confidence slipping away even before he darkened Fallonmour's threshold.

Could it be so easy to fall back into that life now? Could

he control her that effortlessly? Nay! She could not allow anyone to do that to her again. Not now. Not ever.

Knowing Garrett would expect her to greet him dressed in her finest gown, her disobedient hair braided and modestly covered, Emmalyn mounted the keep stairwell, taking a small amount of rebellious pleasure in her current state of drab attire.

She'd had no use for richly toned silks or embroidered slippers in recent days, favoring instead the russet wool tunic she wore now and her practical leather boots. There was no bejeweled girdle circling her hips, only a utilitarian belt adorned with nothing more than a sheathed dagger and ring of jangling keys. She usually plaited her blond hair, simply to keep it out of her way while she worked, but in her haste to dress this morning she had left it unbound. Its weighty mass tumbled over her shoulders and down her back in a tangle of unruly curls that was sure to set Garrett's teeth on edge.

But she willed herself not to let the thought of his displeasure sway her as she passed her chamber door and climbed the rest of the way up to the tower roof. Two of Fallonmour's knights stood at the farthest parapet, shielding their eyes from the rising sun as they looked to the far hill.

" 'Tis been too long since I last saw Lord Garrett," said one man to the other. "I vow he looks bigger now, does he not?"

"Aye, and hale, too. See how bold he sits in the saddle!"

Emmalyn came up beside them nearly without their notice. She peered over the ledge at the approaching knight and dread coiled in her belly. The men were right; he did look larger than even she had recalled.

Gone was the rounded slope of Garrett's shoulders; now they looked nearly the width of his steed's broad back. The long red surcoat he wore was faded and torn, a tattered rag that did little to conceal the muscular bulk of the man it clothed. Indeed, from where she stood, Emmalyn could see the power in his thighs, the proud set of his spine as he guided his horse at an easy gait over the plain. There was an air of calm about him now, a self-assurance and regal bearing that even this distance could not disguise.

Though she fought it, curiosity began to stir in Emmalyn's mind, a subtle interest that made her study him more closely.

The black destrier she had given Garrett as a wedding gift—a beast he could never tame and had always despised for its willfullness—now cantered cooperatively beneath him, completely mastered. Horse and rider made an admittedly impressive picture, a striking image of the homecoming hero, but something was not quite right. With a mingling of wonder and suspicion, Emmalyn watched the firm but respectful way he handled the stallion, the way he made no move to dominate it, yet retained absolute control.

And then she knew.

" 'Tis not him," she said with quiet, utter certainty.

"Milady?"

Emmalyn turned away from the wall-walk to head back for the keep, but stopped when she heard the guard's puzzled question. "He rides my lord's mount," she confirmed, "but that man is not my husband."

PRINCESS

by Gaelen Foley

Darius Santiago is the king's most trusted man, a master spy and assassin. He is handsome, charming, and ruthless, and he has one weakness—the stunning Princess Serafina. Serafina has worshiped Darius from afar her whole life, knowing that deep in the reaches of her soul, she belongs to him. Unable to suppress their desire any longer, they are swept into a daring dance of passion until a deadly enemy threatens to destroy their love.

Published by Fawcett Books.
Available at bookstores everywhere.

HIGHLAND BRIDE

by Janet Bieber

As proud as any of the Highland barons, the new chieftain of the MacKendricks is the equal of friend and foe alike—with one exception. She is a woman. Flame-haired and glorious, Madlin mourns the father and brothers who died by the sword of the clan Fraser. She will retaliate and bring peace the way brave warriors have done for centuries—by kidnapping and wedding the enemy.

Sir Ewan, knight of Scotland, is the unforgiving pawn in Madlin's daring plot to forge a clan alliance. But as Madlin faces her new husband, she fears it is she who is at his mercy, for now Ewan lays siege to her body and soul.

Published by Fawcett Books.
Available at bookstores everywhere.

MIDNIGHT ON JULIA STREET

by Ciji Ware

The sultry allure of New Orleans comes to dazzling life in this enthralling tale of romance and mystery that sweeps from the modern heart of the Big Easy back to the shimmering city of a century past. Reporter Corlis McCullough's search for the truth drives her to chase a story involving historical preservationist King Duvallon, an adversary from her college years. After a decade, he still manages to incite her fury—and worse: a growing attraction as strong and unstoppable as the tides along the Delta.

Published by Fawcett Books.
Available in bookstores everywhere.